The Art of Faking It

Sumaiya Ahmed

ISBN: 9781072775966

The Art of Faking It

Sumaiya Ahmed

To John, I love you forever.

"It's one of those things people say. 'You can't move on until you let go of the past.' Letting go is the easy part, it's the moving on that's painful. So sometimes we fight it, trying to keep things the same. Things can't stay the same though. At some point you just have to let it go. Move on. Because no matter how painful it is, it's the only way we grow." — *Grey's Anatomy*, Meredith Grey

TRIGGER WARNING

mentions of abuse and self-harm
depression

CHAPTER ONE

"YOU NERVOUS?"

Sabrina looked over at Veda, who was sitting on a beanbag, flipping through a tattered copy of *A Little Princess*. It was the following Tuesday and Sabrina was getting ready for her date with Daniel. They'd been talking since Friday night, when he messaged her on Instagram, after Sabah had told him about her *totally hot, totally smart cousin*—which is what they called each other, to people who, basically, were white, since it was just easier to explain. They had hit it off almost instantaneously, talking through the night into Saturday morning, even though Sabrina had to be up at five A.M., because she started work at seven, and the Sainsbury's she worked at was in Great Portland Street, which was about forty odd minutes away. They scheduled in a FaceTime call Saturday night, after he got back from an engagement party and it was, well, nice.

"Not particularly," she responded, turning back to face the mirror, as she swept her brush lightly across her cheeks, dusting blusher on to bring some colour to her face.

Other than the fiery red lipstick she planned on wearing. Sleek's All Fired Up liquid lipstick was one of her top three favourite reds. "It's just a date. I've been on plenty of those."

"No, you haven't."

"Shut up."

"You're *so* nervous," Veda laughed.

"I am *so* not!"

"Ok, if you say so."

"I do," Sabrina deadpanned, turning back round to look at Veda. "I'm not nervous. I'm actually kind of excited. It's been a while."

She was also feeling kind of guilty. It felt like she was cheating on Musa. But she was doing her best to brush those feelings aside. It wouldn't help any, to be thinking of him on this date with an extremely attractive, extremely talented guy who, by the looks of his page, was an artist. She let out a slow, whistling exhale, and put The Body Shop blusher brush down, part of a sixteenth birthday gift from her cousin, Nafisa. Ever since her cousin had gotten married a few years ago, she'd felt a distance in their relationship. She supposed marriage came with change, but it wasn't like she'd ever been particularly close with Nafisa anyway. Sabrina's relationship with Layla, a friend of five years since they'd been paired together in first year Psychology class in sixth form, had changed somewhat since she'd gotten married a little more than three years ago—they rarely talked, but when they did, everything was fine and it was as if no time had passed at all since they last spoke, often spanning a few months.

Carefully lining her lips with a brown lip liner from

Barry M, Sabrina again thought over her choice of outfit. She was wearing the same skirt she'd worn when she met Soran, the first guy she'd slept with after Musa, a black and white dogtooth skirt with a paper bag waist from Primark, paired with a black ribbed V-neck top, showing just a hint of her cleavage. Under her clothes, she wore a new black silk and lace bra and thong, with sheer black stockings, bought from Agent Provocateur last Wednesday. Most of her lingerie came from Ann Summers, and only Agent Provocateur when she wanted to spoil herself.

She leaned back, briefly staring at herself, thinking she did a pretty damn good job with her makeup. Sabrina slowly applied the red lipstick, mouth parted. She hadn't really heard of the diner Daniel was taking her to, *The Shack* based in Central London, with a modern American theme. The pictures of the food she'd found on TripAdvisor and Instagram looked appealing, as well as aesthetically pleasing. The diner did, too.

"Are you taking a jacket?" Veda asked.

"Yeah, my leather one," Sabrina replied, twisting the lid back into the lipstick tube.

"The All Saints one or the Missguided one?"

"Missguided. And I'm thinking of wearing the black Chelsea boots?"

"Sounds good. You're gonna be tiny next to him."

Sabrina grinned, "He's a whole fucking foot and two inches taller than me."

"You're just a midget."

"Leave me alone, you *rude* ass doo-doo head."

"Remind me again, how old are you?"

"Younger than you."

3

"Clearly," Veda snorted, dropping Sabrina's book onto the floor.

"Why are you putting my book on the floor? Put it back on the shelf, man."

"You're becoming more and more like your mother every day."

There was a beat of silence.

Sabrina gasped loudly, turning round fully to face Veda, as she slid *A Little Princess* back into one of the shelves Sabrina had, taking up an entire wall, weighed down by various other books.

"*Take that back*," Sabrina hissed.

"No."

"You're a bitch."

"Is it really?"

"I'm telling your mum."

"Go ahead," Veda smirked. "She won't give a shit."

"Bite me."

"Tell Daniel to do that."

"I shall," Sabrina said, after she'd spritzed her face with her nearly finished bottle of the All Nighter setting spray. "How do I look?"

"Like you're going to eat him alive."

"Kita?"

Veda laughed. "You look fucking sexy, man. Fifty quid says he's going to get a boner when he sees you."

"I'm not betting on that," Sabrina rolled her eyes. "I know he will."

"Your humbleness never ceases to amaze me."

"Thank you."

Sabah had texted a little earlier, during her break,

wishing good luck for the date and to update her on how it went. Sabrina hadn't bothered with a reply, thinking she would message back after the date had ended—and it was now nearing eight P.M., and Daniel would be waiting to pick her up outside Upton Park station, since she hadn't wanted to give him her address, in approximately twenty minutes. But it was fine, since it only took six minutes to walk there.

After putting on a pair of giant gold hoop earrings, Sabrina tidied the clutter on her dressing table; putting the makeup products back in their rightful places, save for her powder and lipstick. Those, she'd be taking with her. She kept her brushes and beauty blender out, thinking she'd give them a wash the next day.

"When are you meeting your friends?"

"Um," Veda furrowed her eyebrows. "Not sure. Probably half nine. Why?"

"Emne zikayram," Sabrina responded. She took her jacket off the back of her bedroom door. Her phone was in her hand, a small black bag with a gold chain over her shoulder. "Let me know when you're with them."

"Acha."

"Great," she smiled, looking over her shoulder at Veda, as they descended the stairs, leading into the hallway where the other three bedrooms and bathroom were.

Her phone vibrated with a text.

Daniel at 19:37: *I'm about ten minutes away from the station. I'll see you soon. Hope you're dressed nice ;)*

A smirk graced Sabrina's lips. She quickly typed out a response.

Sabrina at 19:39: *are you worth dressing nice for*

though . . .

Daniel at 19:43: *Ouch. And here I thought you liked me*

Sabrina at 19:44: *who lied to you? and stop texting. focus on ur driving. thanks x*

Daniel at 19:45: *Aw, are you worried about me? :)*

Sabrina at 19:45: *no. why would i be?*

"Is that Daniel?" Veda asked, as they stood at the bottom of the stairs, Sabrina's gaze locked to her phone.

"Hmm?" she hummed, distracted. "What?"

"*Interesting*," Veda laughed.

"What is?"

"Nothing," Veda said, though the widening smile on her face implied otherwise. "It's just . . ."

"*What?*"

"You're into him."

Sabrina gaped, speechless. "I haven't even *met* the guy."

"You will be, in a few minutes."

"Not the point at all."

"Oh, but it is. You're so into him."

"No, I'm really not."

"Mhm, if you say so," Veda's smile was still intact.

Sabrina rolled her eyes, choosing not to respond, as she slipped her ankle-length boots on. It was no point arguing with Veda when she made her mind up about something. Her teasing was relentless.

"Share your location with me, by the way," Veda was saying, as Sabrina grasped the cool, gold door handle. "So I know where you are at all times. I mean, he's still a stranger. So."

"Sure, yeah, I'll do it now, babe," Sabrina replied, pausing in the doorway. She went onto Find Friends, iMessage, WhatsApp and Snapchat to do so. "I'm sharing it on four different things, ok."

"Good."

The Shack was lit up with geometric ceiling pendants, making the diner bright in the darkened night outside. Its floors and counter tops were a light brown marble, walls covered in mahogany panelling and lined with black and white pictures of the London skyline, along with New York and Seattle. The seating consisted of light grey booths and tables, and a tall counter with a long row of bar stools, more than half of them occupied, matching the rest of the décor. On the far right were two doors, labelled **STAFF ONLY**, and a little further down from those doors, behind a wall almost shielding it from view and away from all the booths, were another two doors, leading into the bathrooms. There were only two, one for men and one for women, and they were just as pretty as the rest of the diner. Between the two doors was a potted yucca elephantipe. While the décor of *The Shack* was all modern, the food they served and the way the booths were all in the centre and against one wall, with the counter on the opposite wall, kind of reminded Sabrina of *Pop's*, from *Riverdale*.

It was a little after ten P.M., and Sabrina and Daniel each had milkshakes in front of them, having finished their meal about half an hour ago. The reviews she'd read were right, and the pictures she'd seen *definitely* didn't do the

7

place any justice. It was like a little piece of heaven—and the price of the food they'd ordered didn't make Sabrina wince in Broke Student; thankfully it cost much less than what she made in an hour. Their total was less than twenty pounds, to her relief, including the strawberry milkshake she'd ordered, and the chocolate one he was sipping on, eyes locked on her face.

"Can't get enough of my face?" she asked him, red lips tilting up into a small smirk.

He grinned. "Is it that obvious?"

"Little bit," Sabrina raised her eyebrows. "*Some* would say it's a little creepy."

"Do you think so?" He was smirking back at her, and it took all her willpower to not grab his face in her hands right then and kiss the fuck out of him.

"Personally, I'm totally fine with you admiring my beauty."

"Someone's a little vain."

"Just telling it how it is, b."

Daniel laughed, the low sound making Sabrina clench her thighs together. "I like your honesty."

"I think there's a whole lot more that you'll like."

"*Oh?*"

She rested her chin on her hand, meeting his crystalline blue eyes. "Come with me to the bathroom?"

His eyes glinted with a look Sabrina couldn't decipher, tongue darting out to lick his lower lip. She wanted his tongue on other parts of her body.

Sabrina breathed out slowly when he nodded.

They stood up, heading towards the bathroom quickly, hand-in-hand. Sabrina ignored the loud thumping of her heart, the excitement rushing through her veins.

Pushing open the door to the women's bathroom, they slipped inside. Daniel locked the door. Sabrina faced him, eyes trailing over his face, the tanned skin of his neck, the broad shoulders and muscles, accentuated by the pale grey top he wore, paired with black jeans and black Timberlands. He was a male Adonis, looked every inch like a god.

Sabrina inhaled. She took off the bag from her shoulder, dropping it onto the bathroom counter.

Daniel took a slow, measured step towards her, and she tilted her face up, looking into his eyes. He grabbed her face in his hands, gently, and leaned down to kiss her. Her eyes fluttered shut and she lifted her arms, looping them around his neck, kissing him back instantly, with no hesitation. His lips were softer than she could've imagined and he tasted like chocolate. Daniel's hands swept through the golden strands of her hair, down to her back. She moaned quietly.

That was enough for him to lift her up into his arms. Sabrina gasped a little against his mouth, and he took that as an invitation to sweep his tongue into her mouth. Placing her down gently onto the counter, Daniel stood between her legs, holding Sabrina close against his body.

He pulled back slowly, kissing along her jaw line, slowly pressing open mouthed kisses against her neck. "You absolutely sure you want to do this?" His words were murmured against her neck, biting down gently on the skin.

Sabrina ran her fingers through his silky hair, "yes. One hundred per cent."

Daniel kissed her on the mouth again. Paused.

Moved back. Gazed at her intensely. "Tell me, at any point, if you want to stop, ok? If you feel uncomfortable or anything at all, tell me." He kissed her again.

"Safe word's *bubblegum*," Sabrina said against his mouth.

He smiled.

A little more than an hour later, Sabrina and Daniel were seated in a little bar in Notting Hill, laughing. The bar had dark wooden flooring, deep brown leather booths and matching bar stools, the wall behind the counter they were sitting on entirely shelved with bottles of alcohol, from wine to rum to vodka to whiskey. Soft music played overheard. They were both tipsy, blackberry juice mixed with rum coursing through Sabrina's bloodstream, while Daniel was drinking whiskey neat. A slow smile graced his face as he looked at her.

"So, tell me," Sabrina was saying, taking a long sip of her drink. "How does a teacher afford a Porsche?" she pointed at him, then her eyes widened. "Wait, oh my god, don't tell me. You're a fucking undercover mafia boss aren't you?"

Daniel laughed, "no, god, no. My family is, uh, rich, I guess. And I make a lot of money from selling my paintings. They're actually featured in that new gallery that just opened up four months ago, in Shoreditch."

"Ah," she nodded solemnly. "Your family's part of the bourgeoisie, huh? The elite one percent of the, um, population."

"Yes, basically."

"So why are you a teacher then? Shouldn't you be, like, I don't know, CEO of a major multibillion pound company?"

Daniel laughed again, lifting the glass to his mouth. He took a long sip. "No, my father is still CEO. He will be, for a long time. My older brother, Caleb, is COO of the company, whereas my sister and I decided to step out of that mould and chase our own dreams. Neither of us were particularly interested in running the company. So my brother took the reigns—he'd been groomed to take control of it, anyway. He wants to. It's his. Completely will be. After my dad decides to hand it over to him." Daniel paused. "Or dies, I guess."

"You say that as if you're waiting for your dad to die." Sabrina was amused.

"Jesus, *god*, no," Daniel let out a laugh. He put his hand on her thigh, beneath the skirt revealing an inch of the lace on her stocking clad leg. The warmth of his hand seared through her skin, and she caught her breath, meeting his eyes. "No way," he continued saying. "I don't want that at all. Fuck, if I could somehow stop my parents dying at any point in their life, I would. My dad is one of my best friends."

"That's nice. That's really nice," Sabrina murmured, then frowned. "*Jesus* . . . you know what I never got about Christianity? Jesus. Like, how can he be the son of god and god in human form? It doesn't make sense. How can he be his *own* son? And what's the Holy Spirit? It's so confusing. Because you see, in Islam, Jesus is just a messenger. The second to last one, I mean. After him is Muhammad."

Daniel smiled wryly, "I don't know. Uh, yeah, I was never really one for religion. My family aren't religious at all. The only time we ever go to church are during weddings or funerals."

Two stools away from Daniel sat a man, a mop of dirty blonde hair and dark eyes. He was fair skinned, a tattoo sleeve on one arm, a cross necklace hanging over the black t-shirt he wore. "You Muslim?" he asked Sabrina, nursing a glass of brown liquid. It sloshed around as he brought it to his mouth.

She looked at him, over Daniel's shoulder. His arm curled around her waist, as he turned his body slightly, glancing at the man.

Sabrina laughed a little, "no. I mean, I was. I'm not now."

Daniel looked at her. "What do you mean?"

"I was born into a Muslim family. But I left Islam a while back."

"Why?" the man asked.

Looking back over at him, Sabrina hesitated a little. "Uh well . . ." she bit her lip, not wanting to give him, if he was an Islamophobe, any more reason to hate on the religion she'd been brought up to follow. "I guess there were just aspects of the religion I didn't really agree with. It just felt like rules and regulations to me, some of it was just so . . . *restricting* and I felt stifled. Don't get me wrong, it is still a beautiful religion, and like if I were to believe in any religion at all, if I didn't disagree with the religious ideologies as a whole, I would choose Islam. But I just don't like religion in and of itself." She paused. She'd offered up too much information. "There were just some minor parts of Islam that I didn't want to adhere to, and I found myself questioning it more and more every day. So I just . . ." she shrugged. "Left it."

"I see," the man responded. "Thank you."

"Um, you're welcome," she laughed. She looked back at Daniel and smiled.

He was watching her, a curious look on his face. "You're smart."

"I like to think so. I mean, I didn't get Firsts in all my essays for nothing, three years straight. Not that I know what my results are for the last two essays I did. But—"

Daniel cut Sabrina off with a kiss, laughing.

"That's not what I meant. But I'm glad to know you're achieving Firsts," he murmured against her lips. He moved back, smiling at her.

"Mmm, it is pretty amazing." Sabrina smiled tipsily. "Kiss me again."

He complied with her request, laughing as they kissed. She tasted his laugh in her mouth, threading her fingers through his hair.

Her bag vibrated on the bar top, buzzing against the slightly scratched up wood with a few dents scraped in.

"It's pretty late, I should take you home," Daniel said.

"We both drank alcohol. You can't drive and—" Sabrina kissed him. "I *really* want to go down on you right now."

His car was parked in the parking lot of the bar, a sleek black Porsche amidst other fancy, ridiculously expensive cars.

"My place isn't too far from here," he winked, still smiling, and stood up.

Sabrina got to her feet, fingers grasping the bar top for support—the stool she had been sitting on was slightly high, and her feet didn't even touch the ground. She swung her bag over her shoulder, watching as Daniel left a twenty pound note beside their glasses, waving a quick *bye* to the bartender when he bid them adieu.

They stumbled out of the bar, laughing and kissing.

Around them, the usually bustling street was silent, save for a few cars cruising down the road, headlights a bright beam in the black. The streetlamps standing on the pavements did a good job in lighting up the night, as the couple walked towards a line of three black cabs waiting just down the road. A group of four women were laughing, chattering loudly, as they pulled open one of the cab's doors, the fluorescent light shining down on their hair. One of the women had been wearing a sash labelled *BRIDE*, whilst the other four women's sashes read *TEAM BRIDE*.

"We'll get a cab to make it quicker, even though it's just a few minutes' walk," Daniel said quietly, as they paused in the street, his arms encircling her waist. She smiled prettily up at him.

They got into one of the cabs, and Daniel gave his address to the driver, his gaze never once leaving Sabrina's face. Her hand was on his thigh, creeping closer to the bulge in his jeans. His fingers tipped her chin up, as he brushed his lips across hers. Sabrina hadn't planned on going round to his, but she wanted to feel his hands and mouth on her again, and she wanted his dick in her again. It had hurt a little, but not in a painful way—it was more like an uncomfortable stretching as she'd taken in his length, because *fuck*, he was just as big as Soran had been, maybe an inch longer, and thicker. And she really shouldn't be comparing, shit. Not that she *was*. It was just—he was so *big* and she hadn't expected that, at all.

Sabrina hadn't sucked him off when they'd been in the bathroom and it was all she could think about right now, and she really wanted to. She wanted to see the look on his face, make him gasp, and realise that she was the best he'd ever had. Because she sure as fuck *would* be.

It was close to one A.M. when they got to his house, and she didn't even notice Daniel quickly paying the driver, as they tumbled outside. Her legs were wrapped tightly around his waist again, as he walked into the driveway of his home.

He unlocked and opened the front door, the bright light of the foyer making Sabrina blink rapidly. She glanced around a little, noting the grand staircase leading up to the landing. There were two floors from what she could see. Daniel kissed her neck, kicking the door shut, returning her attention back to him instead of the fucking mansion he lived in, with marble floors and a goddamn grand staircase.

Barely noticing him moving, mouth pressing a soft kiss to her forehead, Sabrina gently bit down on his neck, soothing it with a little lick, humming in appreciation.

Doors slid shut in front of her, making her eyes widen in shock. She pulled back, staring at Daniel.

"You have a fucking lift in your house?"

He looked at her, a hint of a smirk on his face. "I have more than just a lift, babe."

SUMAIYA AHMED

CHAPTER TWO

THE NEXT THREE days went by quickly, what with Sabrina spending the entirety of Wednesday with Daniel, after he had called in sick at eight A.M., and then turned to face her, a wide grin on his face, asking how she liked her eggs cooked for breakfast, as well as Thursday and Friday evening spent in his company, after they both got off from work. *Sunny side up*, she'd told him, a little dazed from the realisation she'd woken up in his bed and there was an en-suite, with four cream hued steps leading into it. And, she was mystified to see, there was a sliding stained glass window looking into the bathroom—that was currently open—with a large, claw foot bathtub a few feet in front of it.

Pushed up against the wall below the window was a silver crushed velvet chaise lounge. There was an archway to the right of his bed, leading into a walk-in wardrobe/dressing room. If she had any questions about just how wealthy Daniel was, they all disappeared the moment she'd walked down the stairs, hands trailing along the banister, admiring the massive chandelier seven feet above her head in the foyer. His house, with four bedrooms including his, plus an annexe with its own private entrance, was the kind she'd spent years dreaming about one day buying.

His kitchen was even more beautiful, with light wooden flooring, a white marble breakfast counter and tiling beneath the white cabinets and counter top, a white glass dining table with black leather chairs looking into the garden, through floor to ceiling French double doors. She had sat one of the chairs at the breakfast counter, watching him as he made their breakfast, an hour and a half after they'd woken up, he called in sick, and they had delicious morning sex. Her muscles were aching and she could barely walk, much to his amusement and satisfaction. From his smile, she suspected his apology for making her thighs, abdomen and arms ache weren't sincere. Not that she minded. But her vagina was sore. Her jaw ached. The sex they'd had had *clearly* been an entire body workout. But she wasn't complaining.

Daniel had made them a full English breakfast and coffee, and then they spent the whole day just hanging out indoors after going to pick up his car from the parking lot of the bar he'd left it at the previous night, watching *Buffy the Vampire Slayer* and then ordering in pizza. He'd driven her home the next morning at six A.M., promising to take her to his favourite restaurant that evening.

Which he did.

On Friday, they went bowling and had sushi.

It was now Saturday, just gone eleven, and she was in Westfield Stratford with her cousin's daughters', Amanee and Hifsah. They were waiting for Tasnia outside H&M, so they could finally watch *End Game*, and Sabrina had called in sick at work, claiming she was coming down with a serious case of flu. She glanced at her phone again, it was ten past eleven, and the movie started at half past—but it probably wouldn't, because of all the adverts and trailers beforehand. But the girls still wanted to get to the cinema earlier, since all the seats were booked out and it would be packed.

"Why is she taking so long?" Amanee complained, a scowl on her face.

"She said she's walking up the stairs now," Sabrina replied, typing out a reply to Elle, a friend she'd made in Japan and went to the same university as Veda, who was asking if she was free for dinner on Wednesday night, just the two of them, because it had been a while since they hung out, and did she want to go to that Thai place they went to last time, with the really nice calamari and noodles.

"Oh!—" Hifsah said, making Sabrina look up. "She's here."

Tasnia, Amanee and Hifsah's cousin, walked through the doors into the mall, a smile gracing her face. She reached over and hugged both Hifsah and Amanee.

"Fucking finally," Sabrina muttered. "*You* took your sweet ass time," she said pleasantly to Tasnia, returning the hug.

"Sorry, it was the train," Tasnia shrugged apologetically.

"Acha, we have no time for chit chat. Let's go," Sabrina commanded, leading the way through the throngs of people. It was always bloody packed with crowds on a Saturday, and she hated coming to Stratford.

The four of them quickly went up the escalators and walked into Vue, having to walk up the escalators there since they weren't working, making Sabrina grit her teeth in annoyance. She felt a flicker of anger simmer in the pit of her stomach, shooting through her veins like liquid fire, bubbling beneath the surface. It felt almost like she was going cross-eyed, looking at the steps as she slowly walked up them, adjusting the bag on her shoulder. They'd bought Subway sandwiches and nine cookies from Sainsbury's to munch on whilst in the cinema, not wanting to pay a ridiculous fiver for the snacks there. Tasnia had bought popcorn from the pound shop in her area that morning, with a bottle of water for herself and Sabrina.

Sabrina showed the cinema attendant the booking confirmation on her phone, and when he nodded at them, saying "screen ten is just straight ahead and to the right", they glided through, eyeing the movie posters hanging on the walls. Once they got to the theatre room, they were the only ones there. But then again, they *were* fifteen minutes early.

Amanee opened up her sandwich, claiming she was starving and took a huge bite. They were also catching the end of another movie, which Tasnia said was *Little*. Sabrina stretched her legs out onto the seat in front of her, knowing she wouldn't have the luxury to do that once people started filing in, filling up the room. Behind their row were the VIP seats, which were the ones they usually sat on, despite never actually picking those particular seats. They'd never gotten caught.

"Do you have tissues with you?" Tasnia asked.

"Uh, no, why?" Sabrina replied, arching an eyebrow at her niece.

"Because my friend said it's really sad and apparently we'll definitely need tissues. Amanee, you're *definitely* going to cry."

Sabrina cracked a grin, "you should've seen her when we watched *Kabhi Khushi Kabhie Gham*. She was bawling her eyes out, more than I was, which is saying something because I'm such a baby. My mum was just there, staring at us like *what the fuck* and laughing."

"Oh, my god," Tasnia's eyes widened. "We should have a day where we just watch Bollywood movies. It'll be so fun."

"Sure," Sabrina said.

"Which ones though?" Amanee asked.

"You haven't really seen any of them, so we'll start with the classics, like *Main Hoon Na*, which is the best one *ever*. I cry every time I watch it," Sabrina said.

"By the sounds of it, you cry at every movie you watch," Hifsah interrupted, laughing.

"Shut up," Sabrina rolled her eyes, smiling. "As I was saying, before I was so rudely interrupted—" at this, she gave a pointed look to Hifsah, who smiled sweetly. "There's also *Dilwale Dulhania Le Jayenge* and *Kuch Kuch Hota Hai*, but I didn't really like that one much. *Om Shanti Om* is pretty good, too, oh my god and Deepika is in it. She's so beautiful."

"Who is she?" Amanee asked.

"How do you *not* know who Deepika Padukone is?" Tasnia stared, dubious.

"Only the most gorgeous woman to ever grace this earth," Sabrina replied, sighing. "She's in *Cocktail* too, which is actually my favourite movie. Musa told me about it. I watched it after we—" she stopped, catching herself. She felt a hollow pang in her chest, the kind that was always there whenever she thought of him, and, sadly, that was almost all of the time. (Except the past three nights: she was way too distracted to think of anything, besides how glorious Daniel looked naked and how hot he was, skin gleaming with sweat, a hand around her throat as he— ok, *no*, the point was, she hadn't thought of Musa, not on Tuesday night and all through Wednesday when she was with Daniel. But—she *did* on Thursday, until that evening when they went to that restaurant he was talking about, *Bella's Kitchen*, a cute little Italian place nestled in the quiet town of Meadowbrook, which was an hour's drive from London, and then she thought of Musa on Friday, 'til Daniel picked her up outside the school she worked at, a charming smile on his face, and he beat her in bowling— *but*, she told him, pouting, *it wasn't her fault because it was her first time*.) But, still, she was remembering Musa telling her about *Cocktail* and how it felt, holding his hand, with him laughing at her, surprised, when she said she couldn't speak or understand Hindi, and now, her cheeks burned hot with an aching sadness as she looked away from the girls, staring at the screen as the credits rolled for *Little*.

"We should learn to speak Hindi," Amanee said, breaking the brief silence that had fallen over them.

"Yeah . . ." Sabrina murmured. "Oh, and there's

that movie on Netflix you'll love, guys. It's about a girl who's gay, and the issues surrounding it. It's an Indian movie; it made me cry so much. I watched it when I was at Fulkumari khala's house the other day, and bored out of my fucking head." The other day was actually a little over a month ago.

"What is it called?" Hifsah asked.

"Um, *Ek Ladki Ko Dekha Toh Aisa Laga*. It's amazing. We'll have another girls day or something soon, and watch it, yeah?"

"Ok," Amanee smiled. None of them said anything about Musa, knowing it was a sensitive topic for their aunt, even after all this time. "I can do mehndi on you, too."

"Ooh, yes, and we can have, like, a bunch of desserts," Tasnia piped up, looking excited.

Just then, people began coming into the screening room, and the smell of buttered popcorn reached Sabrina's nose. It made her mouth water, and she told Tasnia to pass her the bag of popcorn she'd bought. It crinkled as she opened it, and she reached her hand in, grabbing a handful, before passing it to Hifsah.

Pretty soon, some time between the lights switching off and the screen widening a little bit, coming a few inches forward, the adverts and trailers coming to an end, the room filled up and there weren't any empty seats left. All that could be heard, in the silence of the copyright warning, was the crunching of popcorn and nachos. Sabrina began to unwrap her Subway sandwich, biting her lower lip when the paper scrunched loudly. A guy two rows in front of her looked back. She froze, before resuming taking out her sandwich.

The opening credits started as soon as she took her first bite.

Iron Man was dead.

Sabrina was quietly sobbing, doing her best to wipe away the tears as they rolled down her face. Morgan was sitting outside with Happy, and he had just told her that he would get her all the cheeseburgers she wanted. Around the screening room, there were quiet sniffles, watching as the scene moved on. Sabrina had cried during the movie more times than she could count on one hand alone, and it didn't seem like the tears would end just yet. Iron Man's death was heartbreaking, ripping open a hole inside of her as she watched everyone dealing with his demise. And oh, god—no, Captain America was *old* now and giving his shield to Falcon. It only made her cry harder, knowing he'd finally lived his life with the person he loved, the way he couldn't before.

She felt sad, wishing she could have that with Musa and knowing it would never happen because he'd made his choice and it didn't include having her in his life. The final credits rolled, the clanging of Tony Stark building his armour from the first movie bringing tears to Sabrina's eyes. After a few more minutes of quietly sitting, the room slowly emptying out, Hifsah broke the silence between the four of them.

"So are we leaving now, or just sitting here forever? Because we *do* have to go to sasa's house."

Tasnia let a small laugh, "Yeah, we'll go now."

They all stood up and walked down the stairs, out into the hallway, where a few people were lingering; lost in conversation about the masterpiece they'd just seen. It was one of those movies, Sabrina knew, that was going to stay with her. She sighed, following Amanee as she headed into the bathroom. She—Sabrina, that was—needed to wash her hands and fix (and reapply) her lipstick, because she was pretty she sure it was smudged now. The fluorescent lighting in the bathroom was harsh, making her squint slightly, after having been in a dark room for three hours and a bit, as she, Amanee, Tasnia and Hifsah wandered over to the sinks, to wash their hands. Sabrina looked into the mirror—her lipstick *was* smudged.

She got out Sleek's Old Hollywood liquid lipstick, vigilantly reapplying it, leaning forward to take a better look at herself. Behind her, Tasnia and Hifsah were discussing their plans afterward, having dried their hands on paper towels. Amanee got out a red lipstick bullet, putting it on her lips slowly. They were both dressed in all black, and looked more like sisters than Hifsah and Amanee did, that day.

"Ok, let's go," Sabrina said, once she'd wiped away the smudged red stain beneath her lip.

As the girls exited the cinema, walking out of the shopping centre, Sabrina had mapped her cousin's address, disdainfully realising that he lived just in the exact same area as her. Thankfully, he didn't know what her door number or road name was. In the time it took them to walk to the bus stop, Sabrina's phone vibrated with an incoming call from her mother.

She answered it warily, "asalaamu'alaykum,

25

amma."

"Tui khoy ekhon?"

"We're just waiting for the bus now," Sabrina replied, looking up as a bus came towards their stop. It wasn't the one they needed.

"Acha, zaldi ays, khaani dhaani shobta ready."

"Ok."

Ruksana hung up, leaving Sabrina to sigh. It didn't matter that the food was ready. She didn't care. She didn't *want* to go to Rashid's house, but her mum was forcing her, plus she had to take the girls too. Sultana, however, was at work and Adam had gone to Cornwall for the weekend with Miriam, Leanne and his girlfriend, Rose. A few minutes later, the bus came, and another thirty minutes later, Sabrina was walking to her cousin's house, dread building up inside her.

"You live near here, right?" Amanee asked Sabrina, looking back at her. Amanee and Hifsah were walking in front Tasnia and Sabrina.

"Yeah," she replied. "Two roads away from him."

"Oh, wow, that's so close," Tasnia said, kicking away a stone.

"I fucking know," Sabrina groaned. "Don't tell him. I don't want him suddenly popping round."

"Let's hope your mum hasn't said anything, then," Amanee sniggered.

Sabrina glared at the back of her head, wrapped in a chiffon black hijab. "Knowing her, she already has."

They arrived outside Rashid's house.

Sabrina sighed.

Hifsah rang the doorbell. His wife, Alina, opened

the door, smiling at them.

The moment Sabrina stepped inside, she felt a pulse of red-hot burn inside her, rolling through her system like a tidal wave. She swallowed, trying to calm down. Rebecca, Fahmida's three year old daughter, came running down the stairs. The sight of her, in a light blue dress, with little sequins on the skirt, hair tied up in two pigtails, *almost* softened Sabrina's anger. Almost. But it was the kind of anger that bubbled and simmered and boiled beneath all the smiles, waiting to spew over and it was the kind of anger that Sabrina had let build up inside in her, and she was close to letting it spill and splash everything in its blood red fury, staining everything red and raw and angry and furious.

"How was the movie?" Alina asked them, as they took their shoes off.

Sabrina didn't respond.

"It was good," Tasnia said. "Amazing."

"We cried," Amanee added.

"I didn't," Hifsah pointed out, making her sister roll her eyes.

Alina laughed, "Why don't you girls put your coats and bags away, then come down to eat."

It wasn't a question, but they agreed anyway.

When Sabrina was in year seven, there was an assembly on anti-bullying, given by Mr. Bailey, the head of year. This was before Lakeview Community School got a new head teacher, who changed the entire school system and introduced Houses, like they were in Harry Potter or something. It was the eleventh of November, 2009, Sabrina remembered that—a Wednesday, and she had Maths first period. She was sitting in the second row, beside one of the girls in her form class, playing with the loose thread in her cardigan, the school logo emblazoned on the left breast pocket. Something Mr. Bailey said caused her to glance up at him, the light dancing across the rectangular glasses he wore, wooden ladders behind him—because they had their assembly in the sports hall.

"You shouldn't suffer in silence," he had said, and it made Sabrina feel something weird in the pit of her stomach, eyebrows furrowing together as she thought over his words. She knew it was about bullying, but her mind was replaying the . . . encounter that she had faced the previous week. And every week before that, for the past *two* years. She barely heard the bell ring, but slowly rose to her feet when her form class got called to exit the sports hall, heading to their first lesson. Sabrina hated Maths, she wasn't any good at it, and she sat by herself, right at the front, because she didn't like anyone and they were all too loud, too boisterous—the kind of people that got into trouble almost every day, got in school suspension every other week. Well, except for Yvonne, a cute Filipina girl Sabrina was friends with. She was the only one Sabrina could stand. But she sat at the back, too, with the rest of the girls.

Mr. Bailey's words circled through Sabrina's mind the rest of the day. She didn't notice when, as she was leaving the English block third period, Mina and Felicity teased her about liking Ryan (she didn't.) She didn't flinch when Kelly tugged on her bra strap, making it snap against Sabrina's back, asking why she even wore a bra when she didn't have boobs (she did, but they were just hidden beneath the black kameez her mother made her wear—until she got to year nine, and decided she would start wearing polo shirts and tight fitted trousers, alternating with skinny jeans, even though nobody was allowed to wear jeans in school.) She didn't even care when, in fifth period P.E., her team yelled at her for accidentally kicking the ball into their own goal (she *told* them not to pass the ball to her, to completely keep it away from her—it wasn't *her* fault nobody listened.)

By the end of the school day, at three P.M., when it had begun to rain, big fat water droplets falling and splashing onto Sabrina's hijab as she walked home, she was thinking about *telling* someone. Maybe it was finally time to do that. But—but what if nobody believed her? The thought raced through her mind, like a taunt, the kind Felicity and Mina used to belittle her, making her feel inferior, and she sucked in a deep breath, closing her eyes briefly as a large droplet fell onto her forehead, sliding down her face like an ice cold teardrop. Thunder rumbled overhead, the pavement quickly turning dark as silver strings began shooting from the clouds, turning the world around her slick with water, hammering against the parked cars. She had an umbrella in her bag, a black one her father had bought her, but she didn't bother taking it out.

The students milled around her, walking in groups or in pairs, laughing and talking, popped out their umbrellas, pressing down onto a button that made the umbrella fire out and open wide, covering them from the rain, almost like a stunned bird just beginning to take flight. She didn't notice the cold seeping into her skin, or the lace untying from her combat boots until she nearly tripped, barely hearing the laughter behind her. Sabrina squatted, moving so she was half on the grounds of the church she was walking past, to tie up her laces. She didn't meet anyone's eyes as she resumed walking, her arms swinging by her sides as she sped up, trying to get away from the people she went to school with as soon as possible. She hated them, and she had four more years until she left.

There was a feeling of unease swimming inside her, a kind of fear that made her bite down on her lip as she knocked on her front door. She didn't have a key. Her mother opened the door.

Later that night, Sabrina, with her heart in her throat, hands shaking, texted Veda, saying she had something important to tell her. Veda replied straight away asking what it was, and then taking in a deep breath, Sabrina typed out the message she had never been able to say to anyone ever since it first began. She hesitated before pressing send, shaking.

Veda at 20:23: *u rlly need 2 tell someone—an adult. Dts disgusting, omg. Ew I cnt believe that hpnd, it's horrible. Are u ok?*

Sabrina at 20:25: *I kno :/ but idk who 2 tell, im scared. Wot if no one belvs me?*

Veda at 20:26: *They hav 2, no one can make that shit up. Tell ur brother, he'll do something abt it*

Sabrina at 20:27: *I'll tell Nafisa afa, shes his sister. Omg im so scrd*

Veda at 20:28: *Don't b, ur gna b fine dw. Let me*

no wot happens

She took in another deep breath, fingers shaking. She made a few typos and cursed, before erasing the message and starting again. She read over it five times before sending it.

Sabrina at 20:36: *afa, I hav smthng 2 tell u. um, ur brother, abbas has been touching me in places he shuldnt, since I was 9. I nvr told anyone bcoz I ddnt think anyone wuld belv me, but 2day there was an assembly n mr bailey said we shuldnt suffer in silence n I kno its wrong so I wanted 2 tell u, bcoz I want it 2 stop n he nearly raped me last week but rumena bhabi was coming upstairs so he stopped. He told me not 2 tell anyone bcoz he wuld get in 2 trouble n told me 2 promise I wuldnt tell*

Nafisa called her a few minutes later. "Are you ok?"

"Yeah," Sabrina replied, voice shaky. Her heart was pounding against her ribcage and her mouth was dry. "I'm fine." She always said that. Whenever someone asked her how she was, Sabrina would always say *I'm fine.*

"You know I believe you, don't you?" Nafisa asked, voice soft.

"Yeah, I do."

"Ok, good. I called him and yelled at him. I'm out right now so I can't come over. But I told him to stay away from you. Does your mum know? Or your dad?"

"No, and I don't want them to. I don't want there to be another family feud, like there is with boro khala." The fight with Bipasha was between Fulkumari khala's husband and Sabrina's dad, and maybe Nafisa's dad as well. The sisters still spoke, but secretly, not letting their husbands know. Sabrina didn't know why, eight years later, the feud was still going strong and she didn't know all the details about how it begun either. All she knew was that her dad completely forbade her, her mum and her siblings, from visiting their aunt or speaking to her.

"I don't think that's going to happen, but ultimately, it is up to you. But I think we should tell Fahmida or—"

"No, I don't want anyone else to know," Sabrina interrupted, panicked.

"Alright, ok, we won't tell anyone else then. And I've told him to completely stay away from you. If he is ever near you again, tell me, or go somewhere else where you're not alone, ok?"

"Ok."

Now, back in Rashid's house, it was nearing seven P.M. and Sabrina, Amanee and Tasnia were called downstairs because it was time to go to Amina khala's house. Hifsah had left a little earlier with her parents, along with Sabrina's mother, khala and Tasnia's mum. The room they'd been sitting in was small and empty, space only for a single bed and a small desk and wardrobe, or a nursery. Jumping off the windowsill, Sabrina exhaled slowly, and threw on her hijab, irritation flickering through her like a lit flame.

She walked down the stairs, followed by Amanee and Tasnia, manoeuvring past Rebecca and her brothers, Ali and Ibrahim. They were standing at the bottom of the stairs, waiting for Fahmida.

"Are you leaving?" Ali asked Sabrina. He was ten.

"Yep," Sabrina replied, unable to muster any warmth in her voice. "I'll see you . . . on Eid, I guess."

"Yeah, see you then. Bye," he said.

Rebecca waved as the three girls walked out of the house.

Amanee and Tasnia waved back, Sabrina smiled slightly.

"Who's driving us back?" Sabrina asked, glancing around.

"Uh, I don't kn—" Tasnia trailed off, spotting her uncle Abbas on the road opposite them, beside a lime green car.

What the fuck, Sabrina raised her eyebrows, jaw tightening as Tasnia walked to the car. "I'm not getting into his fucking car," she told Amanee.

"Are you going to get the bus?"

"Maybe."

"I'll see if I can come with you. Let me go tell him," Amanee said.

Sabrina walked with her towards the car, getting her phone out of her bag. She had six unread messages, two of which were from Daniel. It eased the violence rising inside of her, but not completely.

"I'm gonna get the bus—" Amanee started to say, before Tasnia cut her off.

"No, you're not, I don't care. I'm not going alone. Get in here now," Tasnia commanded.

Sabrina sighed, shifting on her feet.

Sabrina at 18:53: *are you free to come over later?*

Abbas' voice made Sabrina look up, her eyes spitting fire. Oh, if looks could kill. "Sabrina, you not getting in?"

She scoffed, "I'd rather not get into a car with you,

33

to be honest."

Silence.

Then, "Ok. Bye, bye."

Sabrina rolled her eyes, when the engine revved and he peeled off.

Her phone vibrated with a new message.

Daniel at 18:55: *I'll be there around 9ish, is that alright?*

Sabrina at 18:55: *that's perfect. i've just sent u my address, i'll see you then. x*

Four minutes later, Sabrina shut her front door, yanking her hijab off her head. "Veda, you home?" she shouted.

"Yeah, in my room," came the reply.

Sabrina kicked off her Converses and jogged upstairs, the soft carpeting muffling her footfalls. She paused in the doorway of Naveda's room, watching as the girl zipped up her lace black dress.

"Going somewhere special?"

"It's Chloe's birthday," Veda explained. "So we're going out to a club and then crashing at Jen's."

"Ok, cool. Is Sabah coming home tonight or still staying at Jake's?"

"Staying with him."

"Great," Sabrina beamed. "I told Daniel to come over later."

"*Did* you now?"

At Veda's widening smirk, Sabrina rolled her eyes, stifling a smile. "Yes," she retorted. "I did. Because he's hot and I want sex. *And,*" she added as an afterthought. "He's surprisingly not bad company. We get on."

"I'm sure you do," Veda said in an amused tone of voice.

"You're so annoying," Sabrina huffed, crossing her arms over her chest. Her bag fell to the crook of her arm.

"And yet, you still love me," Veda commented, as she slid her feet into a pair of sky high stilettos.

"Do I? Do I *really*?"

"Shut up, we both know you do."

"If you say so."

"I do say so."

"Hmm," Sabrina hummed, smirking a little as Veda grabbed her clutch bag and walked to where Sabrina stood, leaning against the doorframe. Shoving her back a little, Veda shut her bedroom door, making Sabrina roll her eyes. "You could've just told me to move."

"That's no fun. And remember to use protection," Veda smiled over her shoulder, as she descended the stairs.

"Fuck off. Go get laid tonight."

Veda didn't respond, but her laughter reached Sabrina's ears as she opened the door to the attic. She climbed the stairs, hand gliding across the white glossed banister. She wanted to have a shower before Daniel got here.

CHAPTER THREE

SABRINA HAD MADE chicken pakora, defrosted and heated up some samosas her mother had given her three weeks ago in preparation for Ramadan, pilau, chicken bhuna and dhayl, as well as sabzi bhaji, for dinner. It was this that made Daniel's eyes widen, when she led him into the open plan dining room (which also connected to the kitchen) slash living room, the dishes laid out on the table. He'd let out a shocked laugh, saying he hadn't expected this at all, and Sabrina had smiled demurely, saying she hadn't felt like ordering out and needed something to focus on in the time it took for him to get to here. Daniel had looked at her, smiling, lifting a hand to cup her cheek and then leaned down to kiss her slowly.

They were now sitting opposite each other, having demolished the pakoras and samosas, and Daniel watched her dig into her food, a curious look on his face. Noticing his stare, she glanced up.

"What?"

"Eating with your hand is a cultural thing, right?"

She nodded. "Yep, and a Sunnah—it's what the Prophet did, too. Plus," Sabrina shrugged. "Food tastes better when you eat it with your hand, than with knives and forks. I actually kind of struggle using cutlery when I'm at restaurants and I order chicken or steak or something, since I'm so used to eating with my hands."

"But you're not Muslim?"

"No, I'm not. But some of the stuff, it's ingrained me, so I stick with it. I even recite some surahs when I'm scared shitless," she laughed.

"Ah, gotcha. What are surahs?" Daniel asked.

"A surah is a chapter in the Qurān."

"Oh, right, that makes sense then. Especially if it's something you've grown up with. And," Daniel smiled, putting down his knife and fork. "I think I'll try using my hand."

Sabrina felt herself smiling as she watched him slowly, almost cautiously; mix the chicken with the rice. He was adorable. A warm feeling glowed inside her, and she let a shuddering breath, dropping her gaze back to her plate of food. She mixed the dhayl in with the chicken bhuna and rice, taking a small bite.

"This is really good," Daniel said after a while. "You're an amazing cook."

"I know," Sabrina smirked. "My mum taught me well." And then, "you don't find it too spicy, do you?"

"Uh, it is a little, but nothing I can't handle."

"Good, I was worried it would be too much for you. I'm used to eating spicy food, I tend to add more but—"

she stopped, seeing his grin. "What? Why are you smiling at me like that?"

"No reason," he continued smiling, the kind of smile that lit up his entire face, eyes crinkling at the corners. She could've sworn his eyes looked even bluer, like a cloudless sky reflecting in the waters in Seville on a bright summer's day, kind of like sapphires catching the sun, almost like a mix between azure and turquoise blue. It stirred something inside her, and she frowned a little, continuing to silently eat. She shoved it back, squashing away any semblance of feeling. It wasn't time. This wasn't it. "When did you learn to cook?"

"Um," she said. "I learnt how to make stuff like pasta and lasagne when I was fifteen, and curries and bhajis when I was, I think, sixteen or seventeen, I can't quite remember. Before that, I'd usually help mum out with the peeling and chopping of things. And stirring."

"That's pretty good," Daniel said, taking a big bite. "God, this is fucking amazing. Can you cook for me every day?" He laughed, the summit of his pearly teeth glinting beneath the bright lights. Sabrina started smiling, slowly shaking her head. She took a small bite of the chicken.

"Thank you, and sure, as long as I get something in return."

"Oh, you *will*," Daniel said, smiling now. Smiling, smiling, smiling.

She felt something flutter in her stomach. *For god's sake, Daniel.*

"You cook, right?"

"No, I just starve myself when I'm at home," Daniel replied, amused.

"Ok, smartass."

He laughed. "Yeah, I've learnt how to make quite a few dishes. I always cooked with my grandmother whenever I stayed over."

"Tell me you use herbs and seasoning. *Please*."

"I do, don't worry," Daniel's eyes twinkled at her. She crossed her legs beneath her, a mouthful of rice and chicken in her mouth.

"No matter what I make," Sabrina said. "I have to. Like with everything. I make pasta the Bengali way; chuck in a bit more than a spoonful of curry powder and whatnot. It adds flavour, you know? White people food is just so," she wrinkled her nose. "*Bland*. No offence."

Daniel smirked at her. She blushed a little, cursing inwardly. "None taken, love."

"Try the vegetable bhaji," Sabrina told him. "It's my second time making it. So . . . I hope it came out ok."

"I'm sure it did," Daniel said, as he put some on his plate carefully with his left hand. "Here, bring your plate closer."

The ease with which the two of them had settled into each other almost unsettled Sabrina, making her feel slightly conflicted about how she was supposed to feel. It had been a week of constant talking, which included the night they'd fallen asleep in the same bed, a day they'd spent together, attention undivided by any kind of distractions, totally plugged off from the world, and evenings in each other's company, talking about their days at work and their colleagues and what they were looking forward to in the weekend. Sabrina felt her shoulders tense up a little, as she listened to Daniel talk about his day, *ooh*ing and *ahh*ing in all the right places, unable to keep from smiling when she looked at him. Each time she was with him, it was like coming up for air after drowning for so long.

She didn't know how she was supposed to feel about this, or him. Because the last time she'd been in a no-strings-attached type of situation, it was months before she met Musa and she couldn't stand the guy, at all. Sabrina wasn't even sure why she slept with him. The guy she was in a friends-with-benefits kind of thing with, that is. Not that they were even friends. More like acquaintances, if that. Maybe it was just for the experience. Maybe to just be able to say she had sex.

Now, as she watched Daniel clear up their plates from the table and head into the kitchen after they finished eating, she wondered whether she should broach the subject of *rules* with him. Having rules, particularly when it came to certain types of situations—especially ones that meant not falling head over heels for the guy you were fucking, were essential and it was a way to safeguard her already trampled heart. No, she thought to herself as she took the frying pan she'd made the sabzi bhaji into the kitchen and placed it on the stove. Best not to do that, not just yet. He was washing the plates, the sleeves of his pale blue button down shirt rolled up to his elbows. The sight of that made Sabrina falter, staring at him, lips parted.

Her phone buzzing against the black countertop, next to the cooker, drew her attention away from him. She released a breath and tucked her hair behind her ear, grabbing hold of her phone.

"Everything ok, babe?" Daniel asked, glancing at

her over his shoulder.

Sabrina blinked at him, startled by his choice of endearment. "Uh," she responded. "Yeah." Looking at the message from Sultana, she leaned against the edge of the bench. "It's just my sister."

Tana ♥∞ at 22:52: *I heard that bastard was there today. U ok?*

Sabrina at 22:53: *yeah, sweetie, i'm ok. he was gonna drive me, tas and amanee home lol but i told that dickhead i didn't wanna get into a car with him. he was like 'ok bye bye' like a little bitch.*

Tana ♥∞ at 22:55: *LOOOOL what a dickhead, who does he think he is? Hope he dies slowly and painfully. Why don't you reopen the case?*

Sabrina at 22:56: *i would, but then they'd ask all these questions about why i closed it originally etc etc and its just gonna be too much. the system is skewed to hate people like me. & obvs mum and dad are gna go ballistic if i mention wanting to go to the police about it again.*

Tana ♥∞ at 22:57: *You were 12, surely they'd understand it was because of the fam. And you were a victim. Allāh, our family disgusts me so much :/*

"Sabrina," Daniel said, voice soft. She looked up at him. "Are you ok, babe?"

"Y-yeah, I just . . ." she paused, her words tying a knot in her throat, wrangled together, as she sucked in a deep breath, trying to get air into her lungs. Everything suddenly seemed too small, like the walls were caving in on her, and she moved, her phone slipping out of her hand. Daniel caught it before it hit the ground, his hand gripped around the pop socket, raising his eyebrows as he placed it face down on the counter. It buzzed with another message, which they both ignored.

Sabrina took in another breath, feeling his arms around her waist. He'd moved a little bit closer, holding her in his arms. Her face was pressed against his shirt, the white button squashed against her cheek as she slowly lifted her arms, to wrap them around him, hands against his shoulder blades. She reached his chest, too short for him to tuck her head beneath his chin, but it was ok—because she was listening to his heartbeat, and it was soothing the roaring inside her head, the pounding of her heart, the shaking of her hands, the gasping for air.

"You're ok, love," he murmured soothingly, rubbing circles on her back. "You're ok. I'm here, I've got you. It's ok. You're ok."

His words made tears prick her eyes and she inhaled sharply, his scent flooding her system. It was one thing to be comforted on the verge of a breakdown, but for that comfort to be from someone she barely knew, it made her feel embarrassed, ashamed even, and her face heated up.

"I—" she started to say, swallowing, tilting her face back to look up at him. "I'm sorry."

"You have nothing to apologise for," Daniel said, confused.

She bit her lip, "right. Yeah. Sorry."

He smiled at her, a thumb tracing her lower lip. "Do you want to talk about it?"

Sabrina paused, thinking. And then she was talking quietly, looking at his face, gauging his reaction, telling him everything. "My cousin sexually abused me as a child, for two years, from age nine to eleven. I didn't tell anyone except Sabah's sister, Naveda, and his sister, Nafisa about it until a year later, when I was in year eight and kind of broke down to the Child Protection Officer at school about it. She notified the Social Services, who got in touch with the police—a few months later, they came to school and I got taken out of class. It was during a PSHE lesson and we were watching *UP*." She took in a slow, deep breath, her eyes searching his face. He looked back at her, his hands still on her back.

"I told them what happened, even though they knew, they just wanted me to tell them my story. That, I think, was in November, which is funny because it was November the previous year when I told his sister and she yelled at him and shit. Anyways, um, so that afternoon, when the feds and Social Services were at my school, they decided we'd tell my parents. So they took me home. I think it was, like, two o'clock or something. My dad came home a few minutes after. My brother was at work and my little sister was at school. The police told them about what he, Abbas, did to me and my dad, like, looked at me and was like *is that true*? And I just—" Sabrina swallowed, hard. "Started crying and ran into my room. But I could hear everything they were saying, because we lived in a flat at that time, and it was all one level. So I was just listening to the police explaining everything to my parents, and my mum was just asking all these questions about what would happen to him and shit, which I mean, ok, I kind of get, because he's her nephew. Her sister Amina's son, but still, it sucked. It was as if I didn't matter at all, you know?"

Daniel let out a sharp exhale, closing his eyes briefly. When he opened them again, fury shone in them, shadows lingering behind the crystal blues.

Sabrina continued talking. "That night, after the feds left, telling me they'd be in touch and I'd probably have to go to the police station to record a statement about what had happened and they'd contact him too, my uncle came over. He's my mum's other sister's husband, Fulkumari khala's husband, I mean. He came over. And my dad told him everything, even though the police told my parents to, like, not say anything to anyone." She laughed, sharp and bitter.

"So anyways, my uncle basically told me to not go ahead with the case and people would talk, they would say shit and it would affect my chances of getting married, I would get blamed—it would ruin the family's reputation and honour, and what would people say about me and my family if it got out into the public. He said all of that, and then I went to bed, crying again and thanking god my little sister was oblivious to what was happening. The next day, my brother found out everything and my mum took me to Amina khala's house because, obviously, she had to tell them what was happening and they needed to discuss the course of action to take. Which, by the way," Sabrina sighed, resigned. "Was to tell me to close the case, obviously, because they needed to protect their honour, since that's the most important thing. And today he was there, at my cousin's house, obviously, since Rashid is his brother. But he had the nerve to ask me if I was going to get into his ugly green car, which why the fuck would I, you know? And I guess it kind of just made me so angry seeing him, and seeing my mum be all normal and shit, not giving a damn."

Her words, finally spoken, made her feel a little lighter, because now she let him see the vulnerability behind the cool girl act and it probably wouldn't hurt so much if he decided to leave now. And it felt good to speak those words out loud. Because she hadn't done that in so long, and it she felt like she was dying today.

"I'm sorry you had to go through that." His voice was carefully controlled, a tone she couldn't pick up rumbling beneath it. "It's awful and—" Daniel sighed, pinching the bridge of his nose. "God, I wish I could take away the pain you feel."

Whatever reply Sabrina had been expecting, it wasn't that.

"That's not your responsibility."

"Maybe not," Daniel agreed. "But you didn't deserve that and it wasn't your fault. Your family is despicable for acting that way."

"Believe me, I know."

"If I ever see that son of a bitch, I'm going to fucking make him wish he was dead."

Sabrina stared at him. "What?"

"Your parents should have done something to protect you. You're their daughter for god's sake." Daniel sighed. "Are you ok?"

"I am," Sabrina said, lightly brushing her fingers across his jaw, his beard tickling her fingertips. "I'm ok."

Daniel shifted on his feet, and Sabrina moved with him, adjusting their stance so her back was against the counter, one of his hands on the middle of her back and the other hand a little lower. She thought back to when she told Musa, late at night, when they were on the phone, a few days into their relationship. He'd been furious.

"You deserve so much goodness," Daniel murmured quietly. "You know that?"

She didn't think she did, not at all. But she said, "Yes."

"Sabrina, you're so strong, you survived the worst thing that happened to you and are making something of yourself." He was looking at her in a way that made her blush, and she looked away. "I'm being serious, love. You're *amazing*. I admire your strength and your courage. You took that pain and used it to build yourself up, and you're going to be a counselling psychologist? You're using what you went through to help other people to deal with their pain, to help them come out of their hole. That's remarkable. That's strength."

"Shut up," Sabrina mumbled, cheeks flushing pink.

He laughed. "It's true. You have to know that. And thank you for trusting me enough to tell me. It means a lot."

"Well, I had a mini attack in front of you."

"Still. You didn't have to, but you did."

She shrugged, tiptoeing, burying her face in the space where his neck met his shoulder. She breathed in, swallowing his scent. "You smell nice."

"Do I?" His voice was amused.

"Mmm," Sabrina hummed. "It's yummy."

"You know what *else* is yummy?"

She moved, looking at him, lifting an eyebrow. "Me?"

A smirk glossed his mouth. "Yes."

They were quiet for a moment. Finally, Sabrina said, "We should have some dessert."

Daniel looked at her and she looked back at him, her gaze drifting to his mouth.

"Kiss me," she said softly.

So he did. Softly, at first. Just a light brush of his mouth on hers. Sabrina tiptoed, wrapping her arms around his shoulders. She bit his lower lip gently and he groaned, opening his mouth a little, lifting her up into his arms. She giggled into his mouth, felt him smile. It was nice, kissing him like this, being comfortable with someone straight away. Sabrina hadn't felt like this in a long time, the calmness swooping through her, and it was refreshing and new and, surprisingly, not that hard. It was a welcomed distraction from the chaos of her life. A momentary relief, in a world that was a mess, because sometimes all you needed was just a few minutes. A few minutes to be free from the sad, dark, harsh truth of reality, a few minutes to distract you from a world that was determined to break you. Because when it felt like your life was falling apart, having just one person who could take you away from it all was worth everything.

CHAPTER FOUR

THE NEXT DAY, following the end of her shift, several hours after Daniel had dropped her off that morning at six fifty A.M., Sabrina was walking out of Sainsbury's. She was meeting Sabah at *Fairly Odd Pizzas*, a place that was their de facto clubhouse, where they'd religiously been going to since finding it accidentally after going to see *Happy Death Day*, starving and craving pizza with a cheese stuffed crust. The place they found, opposite a *Nando's* and *Costa*, nestled in between a Chinese restaurant called *The Dancing Cat* and a dessert place named *Sugar and Chocolate*, served delicious pizza on wax paper, laid over a plastic plate, patterned with red and white checks, silverware neatly placed on tissue, and had a gelato bar and some of the best coffee Sabrina ever had. They'd been going there once a month, ever since, always on a Sunday, when they both finished work at three P.M., just a fifteen minute walk from each of their job locations, from two different directions.

Sabrina was wearing the black tank top she'd had on under her uniform, dressed in high waisted black cigarette trousers and black brogues, fishnet socks covering her feet. Her leather jacket, the one from All Saints this time, shielded her arms and shoulders from the slightly chilly breeze, despite the warmth from the shining sun. She looked at her phone, typing out a reply to Sabah, letting her know she was thirteen minutes away now and couldn't wait to see her.

Sabah split her time with staying at her boyfriend's place, at work or at home with Veda and Sabrina, when the latter two girls were taking breaks from studying or not at work. It had been easier for her to tell her parents she was moving out, because when she *was* (kind of) living with them (her parents, that is), she spent weeks on end at Jake's. At that point, her parents had just given up trying to convince her otherwise. With Veda, it had been more of a shock.

Just as she crossed the road, her phone rang, and she winced, flicking the button to turn the ringer off, silencing *Happier* by Ed Sheeran, a song that always made her think of Musa. Sabrina had spent almost every night for a year listening to that on repeat, along with *Three Empty Words* and *Honest* by Shawn Mendes, sobbing, unable to stop once she'd started. Her tears, surprisingly, never seemed to run out, despite crying a few times a day, and every night for a year. And then finally being able to stop, if only for a while. Before the tears started again, for another few months. She took in a slow breath, inhaling deeply, remembering that this time last year, her and Musa had been talking: they'd tried to be friends again. But then he left. And it broke her all over again. Sabrina looked down at her ringing phone. Daniel was calling.

She answered. "Hey, Daniel."

"Hi, beautiful," a smile in his voice. "How was work?"

"Long and tiring. A little busy. We had an audit today and had to sort out the entire shop before the lady got there, and believe me—trying to take out all the expired products, from every single aisle, in one hour, was not an easy feat."

His laugh was almost orgasmic. Sabrina felt herself smiling as she walked, sidestepping a group of tourists. She rolled her eyes. "I can imagine," Daniel said. "What are you doing now?"

"Meeting Sabah at *Fairly Odd Pizzas*."

"Wait." He paused. "*Fairy Odd Pizzas* as in *Fairly OddParents*, the cartoon?"

"Yep." Sabrina's smile widened, tucking her hair behind her ear. She missed her helix piercing. "Exactly like that. Shit, I used to love that show."

"Me too, love. It was one of my favourites. Along with *Tweenies*."

"Oh my god, Tweenies was *the* one! I loved watching *Come Outside* and *Clifford the Big Red Dog*. It made me want a giant red dog of my own for ages."

"Lizzie wanted to paint our dog red when she was eight," Daniel laughed. "But our parents found out and put a stop to that plan. To say she was disappointed would be an understatement."

"Tell me you're joking." Sabrina was laughing,

turning left down a familiar street. It held more memories than just walking past it to get to the pizza place. There was a hotel at the end of that street, one she'd stayed in with Musa. Her gut twisted as she walked, letting out a shuddering breath.

"I *wish* I was. Poor Hedwig was terrified."

"Your dog's name was Hedwig?"

"Yep."

"See, now I'm upset. Hedwig's death was the one that ripped into my soul."

"Let me make it up to you by taking you out tomorrow night."

"That was smooth," Sabrina chuckled. Her phone buzzed with a message from Sabah. "But yes, ok."

"Excellent. I'll text you details tonight. Have fun with Sabah. Tell her I say hi."

"Will do," she murmured in reply. "Remind me to take you to this place. It's heaven."

"I'll take your word for it, babe." She could hear the smile in his voice.

Her pulse jumped and she swallowed. "Bye."

"Ciao, bella." The line clicked dead.

A few minutes later, Sabrina sauntered into *Fairly Odd Pizzas*, spotting Sabah at the table they had claimed for themselves. She walked over, after waving a quick hello to the guys, pulling out the wooden chair, a smile on her face. "Did you miss me?"

"No," Sabah replied, a hint of a smirk on her face. "But I *do* wonder who gave you all those lovebites."

"I'd say your dad, but that's gross and he's my cousin."

51

"You're nasty."

"You love it," Sabrina winked.

Sabah merely rolled her eyes in response, looking down at her cracked phone screen. "What pizza do you want to get this time?"

The two of them had tried every single thing on the menu over the past year, not getting sick of any of the items. A few feet away from them, one of the guys, Ashton, was rolling dough on the wooden board. His brother, Grayson, was taking out a freshly made pizza from the oven, with the sticker labelled HOT stuck on the metal bar above it, half faded. Over their heads, music played, Here Comes the Sun by The Beatles. Sabrina rolled her eyes.

"Half pepperoni, half veggie supreme? Extra cheese?" Sabrina suggested.

"*Always* extra cheese." Sabah laughed. "Garlic bread for starters?"

"Obviously. I want apple juice, too."

Flashing a quick smile, Sabah slid out of her chair, phone in hand, and walked over to the counter. She quickly spoke to the guys making their food, and Sabrina took her time to glance around the familiar restaurant. They'd been coming there so often, they were on first name basis with the owners, almost close enough to consider them maybe friends, and often got free food, despite refusing to *not* pay. It was like Sabrina's home away from home away from home, one of her sources of comfort in the absence of Musa, a place she found after him, because this was how she saw things now: Before Musa, With Musa and After Musa.

The familiarity of *Fairly Odd Pizzas* wrapped her

up in its warmth, the scent of freshly baked pizzas, garlic bread, chilli cheese bites and the large slices behind the glass counter making her stomach rumble loudly. Both she and Sabah always got a whole pizza for themselves, foregoing the slices that weren't enough for them—because there was never enough for how many the two of them wanted, except when they first stumbled into the place, looking around, thinking *it's quite cute in here* and browsed the menu, each choosing a pepperoni slice first. It had been like taking a bite of Eden, and then they ordered an entire pizza, hands greasy with oil, mouth shiny as they bit into the cheesy bread with tomato sauce and pepperoni and peppers and sweetcorn. First, it became a weekly ritual to come there and that's when they got to properly know the brothers, Ashton and Grayson, Roberto (their stepfather whose family it belonged to) and Katherine (their mother.) When, in Sabrina and Veda's second year of uni, they decided to move out and Sabah joined them, they changed it to a monthly thing, deciding to save money and not consume as many calories.

But it was, by far, the best pizza Sabrina had had, and she'd had a lot of pizza from a lot of different places in all the years she'd been alive. She had taken home to her parents a box of the veggie supreme pizza a few times, smiling at their reactions once they'd bit into it, asking her where she'd got the pizza from *because it was delicious and the base was perfect*. Ruksana hated thin pizzas, complaining that it just didn't taste right. It was something she, and Sabah and Veda's dad, had moaned about on Sabrina's sixteenth birthday, when they ordered pizza that was too thin, too crispy, the crust too hard.

Sabah came back just then, getting into her seat opposite Sabrina, furrowing her eyebrows at a message— no doubt from her boyfriend. He was the only other person she really talked to, or spent time with, other than her family.

"Everything good?" Sabrina queried, smiling in thanks at Grayson when he brought over her glass of apple juice, ice floating in it. He slid over Sabah's water to her. She didn't look up.

"Um, yeah. Just some family issues with him. But tell me," she tore her gaze away from her phone. "How's it going with Daniel?"

"Pretty great, actually. He's nice. I told him about what I went through, you know? Last night, when he came over."

"Yeah, Veda told me he did, when I spoke to her. What did he say?"

"That he'd kill Abbas if he ever saw that son of a bitch."

"He should get in line, then." Sabah's eyes narrowed. "I wanna slit that motherfucker's throat."

"Please don't. I don't want you going to prison for homicide."

"It's ok; Veda will get me out of it. And Elle. And hey, you're supposed to be helping me bury a body, remember? You know how to get away with murder."

Sabrina laughed. "Just because I watch the show doesn't mean I know how to do it in practice, sweetie. *But* anyway—back to Daniel, he says hi."

"Marry him."

"What the fuck? No."

"Why not? Your babies would be adorable."

"I don't want to marry anyone."

They paused as Grayson got over a plate with four garlic bread slices on it, his phone to his ear, speaking to his mother. Sabrina smiled at him again and he winked at her, walking back behind the counter. He went through a swinging door, after telling Ashton to keep make the pizza a little spicier for the girls. Ashton rolled his eyes, saying he knew. Sabah laughed at that, before turning her attention back to Sabrina, a serious look on her face.

"You're just saying that because of Musa. The right guy will come along and make you see your worth and how much better you deserve than that cheating asshole. I never liked him."

"Yes, you did."

"At the start," Sabah sighed, folding the garlic bread in half and taking a giant bite. She chewed for a while, slowly. And then said, "Yes. I did. And then he made you cry. So I started hating him. And he's rude."

"Just like you."

"He's pretty and rude, like me."

"You're both so alike, it's kind of scary." Sabrina swallowed the bite of garlic bread in her mouth, and grabbed the second.

"Your two favourite people are basically the same—I don't think that's a coincidence. Are you sure you're not secretly in love with me or something?"

"That's classified information."

"Sabrina, suck my left toe."

"I'd rather not, darling. Your feet are ugly. Just like your face."

"Have you even looked in the mirror recently?"

"*Hey*!" Sabrina frowned. "I thought you said my new hair made me glo up."

"I lied."

"Bruv, I hate you."

"Liar, liar, pants on fire." The grin on Sabah's face made Sabrina roll her eyes. "Anyways, back to Daniel. You should marry him. Make sure to tell your parents you're marrying a white guy when I'm there though, so I can record their reaction."

"A) I'm not marrying him," Sabrina argued. "And B) Adam's girlfriend is white anyway."

"He's been with her for years. When is he planning on telling your parents?"

"Fuck knows. He knows they're going to flip out. But he's just delaying the inevitable. Miriam and Leanne love her. She's Muslim. He should just rip the Band Aid off."

"When did Rose become Muslim anyway?"

"Um, I think when she was twelve? I'm not entirely sure."

"You know what you could do?" Sabah leaned forward, grinning. Sabrina raised her eyebrows, taking a slow sip of her juice. "Tell your parents Daniel converted to Islam. Even if he hasn't. He can pretend. I mean, he'll technically have to, anyway. Just like we're pretending to be good, devout Muslamics."

Sabrina snorted, covering her mouth. Her shoulders shook as she laughed. "Oh, god."

"Is that what you said when Daniel hammered you?"

"Amongst other things."

"*Juicy*," Sabah smirked. "Give me details."

"*No*. Never. But he stayed last night and dropped me off at work today. He's an angel, I swear. I almost had a fucking breakdown in front of him last night, before spilling my guts."

"You broke the rules. The guy is only meant to see your breakdowns at date number seven."

"Well, technically, that was date number five. And you're not supposed to have sex on the first date either, right? Guess I'm just a born rule breaker."

"You saucy little minx."

Both girls stared at each other, then burst out laughing.

"Where did I even get that from?" Sabrina wondered out loud. "I don't know why I just randomly started saying it."

"And now you have me saying it."

"Oops."

There was a moment of quiet, and in that quiet, Sabrina's thoughts flowed to Daniel and the previous night, the ghost of a smile flitting across her face. They'd ended up having sex in the kitchen, on the wide countertop beside the cooker, her legs wrapped around his waist, similar to how they'd first done it in the bathroom of *The Shack*. Afterwards, she'd cleaned up the counter, laughing with him as he sang along to the songs he'd put on shuffle on Spotify, busting terrible dance moves and grabbing her hand. Sabrina told him she couldn't dance to save her life, warning him she'd probably end up stepping on his feet, but he only smiled in response and so, they waltzed around the kitchen and sang off key. Well, Sabrina did, anyway. She couldn't sing either.

Later, they were sitting on the black leather sofa with a built in electric recliner, and a charging cable, discussing their childhood accidents, the ones that left behind scars. Sabrina was sitting cross legged, facing Daniel, her back against the armrest. Sabrina had a faint, kite shaped one on her left ankle from falling onto a daa, which she explained to him was basically a boti knife, but people from Chittagong and Sylhet commonly called it a daa, when she was four years old.

"I shut a door on my thumb when I was six," she told him, recalling the memory and she cried until her mother had wrapped a plaster around it to stop the bleeding and held her, watching *Dora the Explorer* with her.

Daniel's childhood was a little wilder, climbing trees and exploring the woods a few miles from his uncle's house in America, where he spent a few summers. He'd been riding his bike one hot summer, sweat gleaming on his forehead, going uphill to look at the sunset, his siblings in tow. Somehow, he'd fallen, maybe going too fast, the wheels going over a sharp rock, he couldn't remember. But he fell off his bike and twisted his ankle, landed awkwardly and scraped his elbow and temple.

"That happened to me once," Sabrina said. "Not falling off a bike, I mean. I don't know how to ride a bike—"

"*What?*"

"Shut up. I just never learned. Anyway, I was running, I can't remember why, with some of my cousin's kids on my dad's side of the family and I tripped and, like, scraped my temple and knees. It was all bleeding so much, and I was scared shitless, because I knew mum would have a go at me for falling."

"Shit," Daniel laughed. "How hard did you fall?"

"Really hard. I was limping for ages. It was both knees as well." Sabrina shook her head. "The amount of times I've fallen because of me running is crazy. Totally put me off it for a while."

He sniggered. "You're just *weak*."

"I am *so* not."

"In the time that I've known you, how many water bottles did you ask me to open?"

"Leave me alone, they were just *really* difficult to open, ok. My hand hurt."

"Sure, sure," Daniel was smiling. "Whatever you say, babe."

"You're an ass."

Daniel raised his eyebrow and lunged at her, his hands going to her waist. She shrieked, laughing, when he tickled her. "Say that again."

"Oh my god, *stop*, you're torturing me!" Sabrina cackled. Her laughter was loud and she bucked her hips, back arching over the sofa's armrest as he continued tickling her, laughter tumbling out of his mouth.

"How is it torture when you're laughing?"

She shrieked again, batting her hands on his shoulders, twisting a little. He grinned at her, running a hand under the oversized t-shirt she wore, stroking her breast. Daniel adjusted their positions so that her head was resting against the armrest, and she was looking into his eyes. Sabrina stared at him, a smile still on her face. And

59

then, with his other hand, he tickled her again, causing peals of laughter to escape her.

"Say you're sorry," Daniel said in her ear, laughing. "God, you're so *cute*. I love your laugh."

"Daniel," Sabrina giggled. "Shit, oh my god, I'm sorry. I'm *sorry*," she yielded, a snort escaping her as she laughed. A blush stained her cheeks. She gasped when he stopped, his fingers splaying out over her stomach. They gazed at each other, both grinning. He looked at her mouth and leaned forward, resting his forehead against hers.

"You're beautiful," he murmured softly.

"I *know*, right."

He cracked up, lifting his head. "God, and here I was, trying to be romantic and you just—" he stopped, laughing. Beneath him, Sabrina's smile widened, dimples deepening, cheeks starting to hurt. Her thighs were a little achy from their earlier endeavours, but it was a sweet, welcomed ache.

"My bad." She sat up a little when he moved back. "Aren't you glad you listened to me and brought a change of clothes?"

"Admit it, you like sleeping with me."

"I thought that was obvious, no?"

"No," Daniel rolled his eyes. "I mean *sleeping* as in *just* sleeping."

"*Pfft*." Sabrina scoffed. "Whatever gave you that idea?"

The smirk on his face made butterflies beat their wings in her stomach and she swallowed, lifting her hands to fix her messy hair. She used the hair tie around her wrist to pull her hair into a low ponytail. As the minutes wore on, the two of them switched the TV on, Daniel convincing her to continue watching *Game of Thrones* from where she left off in season three, and Sabrina placed an order for dessert.

She ordered a double chocolate cookie dough for herself with extra slices of strawberries, and Daniel got a large slice of carrot cake, with two scoops of gelato. They were curled up together, his arm around her, her head on his shoulder, as Daenerys got her dragons back. Truthfully, Sabrina was a little bit confused about what was happening, but then again, she hadn't watched it in about five months, after stopping halfway through the season. Daniel's beard rubbed against the top of her head, and Sabrina moved a little, pressing her lips to the pulse in his neck. She kissed him lightly, and then turned her attention back to the screen, wrapping an arm around his stomach. She felt him glance at her briefly, and when she looked at him, he was smiling.

"How much longer 'til my cake gets here?" he asked.

"Um, the driver's on his way now." Sabrina checked UberEats. "One minute. He's just coming down the road now."

"Thank god." Daniel's mutter was quiet, making Sabrina chuckle. "*What*? I want cake."

"You should ice my cake," Sabrina said casually, eyes on the TV.

Daniel looked at her. "Are you on the pill?"

Her lips tilted up into a small smile. She *was* on the pill; she had been since the start of the New Year, since her period was starting to become irregular again, and when she did get them—the pain was excruciating. Sometimes, being a girl was not fun.

"I am," Sabrina replied.

Just then, the doorbell rang. Daniel rose to his feet and stretched, his t-shirt lifting and revealing a strip of his smooth, ivory skin. Sabrina slapped his ass as he took a step away from the sofa, and he paused, looking back at her. She smiled innocently. A small grin tugged on his lips. As he went to open the door, Sabrina checked her phone and saw a message from Sabah, asking if they were on for the next day, their meet up at the pizza place they'd claimed as their own, a tradition that had been going on for a little over a year now. She replied *yes, definitely, I'll see you tomorrow*, as Daniel came back into the room, a white paper bag in his hand, the receipt stapled to it fluttering as he walked over to her.

He put the bag down on the coffee table, sitting down next to her. Sabrina shifted, leaning over to get their dessert out of the bag. Daniel's carrot cake was in a large plastic container, and she placed it in front of him, getting out two plastic cups of gelato, vanilla and pistachio, cool against her fingers. Her cookie dough was in a big paper box, a plastic cup of vanilla gelato with it. Inside the bag, there were also tissues and plastic knives, forks and spoons. She passed him the plastic cutlery, setting down the tissue in front of them, and moved the paper bag onto the carpet, beside the back leg of the coffee table.

"It's really good," Daniel said, taking a bite of the cake. He scooped up some of the pistachio gelato with his spoon, and put it in his mouth. Sabrina looked at him, cookie dough and a strawberry in her mouth. "Here, open up."

Doing as she was told, once she'd swallowed her food, Sabrina opened her mouth, watching as Daniel put a forkful of cake into her mouth. She chewed, slowly, looking at him. He then motioned for her to try the pistachio gelato, which she did, after a moment of hesitation.

"I've never had pistachio flavoured ice cream before."

"Nice, right?"

Nodding, Sabrina loaded a big piece of her cookie dough onto her spoon, carefully putting it into Daniel's container of cake. "Try it."

Now, Sabrina sat in front of Sabah in *Fairly Odd Pizzas*, a smile dancing on the edge of her lips, waiting for their pizza to be done, so she could eat. There were a lot of calories she'd need to burn off later that evening, and her thighs were protesting at the thought, but she wanted to maintain her flat stomach, the faint abs she'd gotten after intense workout sessions every day. Sabrina had never been fat, but she'd always wanted a flat stomach. It took cutting out a lot of food, a strict diet and exercise regime, a while After Musa, to get to that stage. Though now, she did go back to eating some junk, she made sure to burn more calories than she ate, not resting until she knew she had, or was too exhausted.

A burst of laughter to her left made her glance over at the group she'd seen a few times before in the restaurant, always in those same seats, three guys and a girl, sitting close to the counter, an aura of ease surrounding them. The girl had a large slice of pizza in her hand, her midnight black hair tied in a fishtail braid, resting over a shoulder, a white, fur trimmed bubble jacket over the back of her chair. Sabrina thought it looked like a big marshmallow, but in a cute way. She watched them as they talked, only able to see the faces of the girl and two of the dark haired guys, since the blonde was sitting with his back to her. One of the guys, with a military buzz cut, stubble shadowing his jaw, a diamond glinting in his ear, dark eyes, caught her watching them, and flashed a smile at her, lifting a glass in acknowledgement. She flushed, mustering up a small smile in return, and turned her attention back to her companion. Sabah was on her phone, tapping away at her screen. Sensing eyes on her, she looked up. The two of them often got mistaken for being sisters when out, and on one memorable occasion, when Sabrina got her nose and helix pierced, they'd both been dressed in black crop tops and, where Sabah wore black jeans, Sabrina had worn faux leather black trousers (that she'd now donated to charity.) A man, short, wide, had glasses, saw them and grinned, "*Twins!*" He'd exclaimed. "*I have sisters.*" Sabrina and Sabah had promptly burst into laughter, linking arms as they continued walking into the tattoo parlour.

Another time, when in Paris, and passerby's eyes kept flicking from Sabrina's chest to Sabah's legs, a man had cat-called them from his bike, shouting compliments, calling them *pretty sisters* at a red light.

The song changed from *Here Comes the Sun* to *Yellow Submarine*, and Sabrina stifled a sigh. Grayson came over with a smile, a large flat pan, with a half pepperoni half veggie supreme pizza on top, in his hands. He gently placed it onto the table.

"Want anything else?"

"No, thanks, Grayson," Sabrina smiled, breathing in the wafting pizza smell. "We're good for now. But how are you? What's been happening in the last month?"

He laughed. "Well, I proposed to Juniper. Our wedding's going to be next year, summer. Ashton," he nodded toward his brother, who was standing next to the table where the other customers sat, talking. "Is graduating in July, so we're all pretty excited about that, too, especially mum. Speaking of, when's your graduation?"

"Holy shit, that's amazing. I'm so happy for you. Congratulations!" Sabrina beamed, jumping up to give him a hug. He laughed. "And, my graduation is July tenth." Grayson took a step back after she released him and sat back down, nodding, and held up a finger.

"Shit, let me get your plates."

Sabah bit back a laugh, watching as he went round behind the counter, and grabbed two white plastic plates and wax paper, placing them neatly over the top. He set them down in front of Sabrina and Sabah.

"So, you ready?" Grayson asked her, as she took a slice of pizza from the pan, and Sabah did the same. Her mouth watered at the smell, oil stain left behind on the empty triangle where it had been. Sabrina lifted the large pepperoni slice, one hand on the crust, the other holding it up as she bit into it.

Swallowing before she replied, Sabrina nodded. "God, yeah," she licked her lips. "Fuck, Grayson, this is amazing. And yeah, I'm more than ready. I can't wait to be done. Even though," she added. "I'm going to be studying again in September. But still."

"Yeah, I get you. The relief after handing in all the

final submissions is unlike anything else. And hey, you get a long summer, so there's that."

"Mhm, yeah, that's true. Elle and I are going away in August, so I'm looking forward to that."

"Oh, yeah? Where you going?"

"Um, so we've planned to hit up Indonesia first, and then go to Malaysia, Thailand, Singapore, the Philippines, Korea and Cambodia. I'm literally counting down the days."

Grayson let out a low whistle. "How long for?"

"Five weeks."

"That's going to be hectic. But fun. You've got to recommend some places there for me. Juniper and I are still deciding where to go for our honeymoon."

"For sure," Sabrina smiled at him. She took another big bite.

"Great. It's on the house today. And," he said, when she started to speak. "No arguing. Think of it as an early birthday gift."

"My birthday's not 'til the end of May," she pointed out.

"Hence it being early."

"Grayson, no—"

"La, la, la, la, la, I can't hear you," Grayson said, walking away.

She burst out laughing. "*Real* mature, Gray."

The girl with the fishtail braid looked over at her, and Sabrina held her gaze for a moment before glancing away. Sabah was finished with her first slice, and popped the small bite of the crust into her mouth.

"How long are you gonna be at Jake's?" Sabrina

asked her, dropping the pizza onto the checked wax paper, a few crumbs from the crust dotted around it. She picked up her glass, taking a sip of the apple juice.

"Not sure, I might come back tomorrow. I've run out of clothes. Plus, Ramadan starts soon, so mum's gonna want me to go round." Sabah replied.

"Ah yeah, same. Are you going to fast?"

"Nope. You?"

"I'm not too sure. Might keep a few, I like the spirituality and meaning behind Ramadan."

"Yeah, it's nice. I'm just thinking about Eid, to be honest."

"Ah shit," Sabrina laughed. "I don't have anything to wear for Eid."

"I swear you have five new dresses?"

"Yeah, but three of them are more wedding party type dresses and the other two, I've worn once already. The pink one was to Tawhid's cinipaan and the black one to Aisha's cinipaan, which basically means that I can't wear them for Eid."

"Aisha is Tasnia's older sister, right?"

"Yep. How do you keep forgetting them all?"

"Because," Sabah said, picking up a sweetcorn that had fallen off her pizza. "You have way too many people in your family."

"Well, I can't help the fact all my aunts are ancient and married with kids who are married with kids of their own, one being married herself," Sabrina sighed.

"Our side of the family is so much less complicated."

"*Is* it though?" Arching an eyebrow, Sabrina

grabbed a second slice. "Most of the cousins, who are your aunts and uncles, are basically married to each other. It kinda makes it a little bit more complicated, when trying to explain how I'm related to both the bride and groom, or the kid can call me daadi *and* nani, since both her parents are . . . *god*, I don't even know. Their parents are cousins, so that makes them cousins, too, right? It's so confusing."

"I just can't believe you're a *grandma*," Sabah snorted, cackling.

"Shut up."

"Ok, nani."

"Dhurr bedisha goror bedisha."

Sabah spluttered with laughter, putting her pizza down. "You fully sound like your mum."

Narrowing her eyes, Sabrina bit into her pizza. "That's rude."

"It's just the truth."

"You know what else is the truth?"

"What?"

"You being ugly."

"You're just jealous."

"Er, no. Ugly peanut head."

"*Hey*, leave my peanut head alone."

"No."

"I take offence to you insulting my head," Sabah sniffed.

"And I," Sabrina smirked. "Do not give a shit."

"I'm telling your mother."

"Be my guest."

"I bet you won't have that attitude when I tell her you're fucking a white guy."

"You do realise I could tell your parents the same thing, right?"

"Well, yeah," Sabah laughed, folding up her pizza and putting it in her mouth. She chewed and swallowed it before speaking. "But my mum won't freak out as much as yours will. Your mum will probably faint and puke and cry and curse you into the next millennium."

"Always so dramatic."

"That's probably where *you* get it from."

"Rude."

"Look who's talking," Sabah quipped, rolling her eyes.

Sabrina didn't respond, instead demolishing the slice of pizza in her hand that left her fingers greasy with oil, the wax paper a little darkened with oil stains. As she ate, her gaze wandered over to the group of four, as one of the dark-haired guys stood up, looking at his phone. It was the one who'd smiled at her. He leaned over, hugging his friends, and held his arms out for Ashton, who had just come back from behind the swinging door. Ashton, rolling his eyes, a small smile on his face, moved forward and hugged the guy back. He laughed. The girl yelled something in Japanese at him, grinning.

He shot her the finger in reply, and headed towards the door, his eyes meeting Sabrina's. He smiled at her slightly before leaving.

The song changed again.

"C'mon, play something *other* than the fucking Beatles," the blonde guy said loudly. Sabrina bit back a laugh.

Ashton said something in response, voice quiet.

69

Sabah's phone buzzed on the table, an audible hum in the quiet of the restaurant, without any songs playing, what with Ashton and the blonde were arguing over the music to play. Sabrina looked at Sabah, as she picked up her phone, answering the call. *It's Jake*, she mouthed.

Sabrina and Sabah left *Fairly Odd Pizzas*, after they both threw down a tenner onto the top of the glass counter, dashing out the door before Grayson or Ashton could make them take the money back, yelling a quick bye over their shoulders. Outside, the glare of the sun was a little brighter, beaming down on them, candyfloss clouds floating along the sky, as if it was their stage and they were the stars. They walked down the street, not talking, but it was comfortable, the kind of quiet that let Sabrina know she wasn't alone, and it wasn't empty, the kind of quiet that told her she didn't need to try grasping at words to fill the silence. It was just a pause, a moment that could be broken, without it being the end.

Around her, the world continued moving, cars driving down the roads, people bustling past them, immersed in their own lives, in pairs, in groups or alone, laughter and conversations flowing all around, and in that moment, Sabrina thought it seemed like a perfect paradox to how she felt every day. *Alone.* She was alone and lonely and broken, and had to put on a mask, to show everyone that she was doing fine now, that she wasn't just as much of a mess as she was in those days, weeks, months following her break up with Musa. And it was so exhausting. Because she'd been ok last night, with Daniel, and she was kept busy at work this morning, so she didn't have time to slow down and stop and think about how she was *feeling*.

Because the truth was, she just wanted to stop feeling. She wanted to *stop*.

She swallowed, trying to fight back the feelings climbing inside her, like monsters coming out to play once the sun set, when darkness spread its magic across the city and the stars blinked to life, floating like gemstones in the sky. Beside her, Sabah had her phone in her hands, messaging Jake, oblivious to Sabrina's inner turmoil. She hated this: it could be a normal day, where she was surrounded by love from her family and friends, like today, cracking jokes with her day ones, and still—*still* she'd feel like she was dying inside, wishing she could share this was Musa. Wishing it would hurt less, wishing she could just *stop* loving him, so maybe she could finally breathe, without feeling as if she was choking on his absence, as if she was sinking beneath an ocean of salt water.

It had been so long since they ended, and after everything, Sabrina was still living in the memories of what used to be, hoping against hope for what will never be, because he'd walked away and left her behind, and she was scrambling, trying to piece back together the shattered pieces of her heart, of what they had. But no matter how hard she tried, it would never fit back together.

A sob rose to her throat, and she breathed in deeply through her nose, knowing that if she opened her mouth, she would start crying. She blinked furiously, thanking the god she didn't believe in for wearing waterproof mascara today and not the YSL Babydoll mascara that was her favourite. Sabrina just wanted to not think about him all the time, to not break every time his name was mentioned. To forget how he broke her beyond repair, ruined her for all other men, and even though she'd slept with two since him, and was still fucking one of them, it was still him, *always him*, that she wanted to spend the rest of her life with.

He'd ended things with her days before she started university, and she'd spent those first few days in bed, a ghost or a shell or just a girl who'd gotten her heart broken, unable to sleep because she was no longer listening to the sound of his voice, because they always talked on the phone or were on FaceTime before they went to bed, or unable to eat because she stopped caring about herself. Because what was the point. He didn't want her anymore. He didn't want her anymore. And she'd completely given up.

The only reason she'd gone to uni on the first of October was because Adam made her, and because she knew Musa wanted a partner who had ambitions, who had a goal and she wanted to be that for him. Back then, she thought all they needed was some time. *Just some time apart and then we'll be okay and we'll get back together.* But that time turned into three months, and then six months, and then a year. And then one year and six months.

It took a long time to accept that they were, well and truly, over, and even then, Sabrina held a small fire of hope in the darkest, quietest part of her soul, somewhere nobody could get to, because it was for him, just for him. Because he had always been the person who made her smile when she was exhausted, the first person she wanted to share everything with, whether it was good or bad, and she wanted to hear about his day, eighteen thousand variations of it, every day, forever, because he was her forever, even if she wasn't his. And realising this *hurt*, so much, and she was still trying to adjust, still trying to learn how to walk past certain places and smell a particular perfume or listen to a song without thinking of him, without remembering him.

"Are you going straight home?" Sabah asked once they got to the train station and through the barriers.

Sabrina blinked, looking around, clearing her throat to hide the sad creeping up inside her. "Uh, yeah, I am."

"You good, man?"

"Yeah, of course." She forced a smile onto her face. "I'm fine."

"Sure?"

"Obviously. Why wouldn't I be? Everything's great."

"Duh, of course," there was a smirk on Sabah's face, amusement glimmering in her eyes. "You have a hot guy in your life that looks like a cross between Captain America and Thor." That was true. Daniel did kind of look like that, except he was much prettier, strikingly handsome in a way that it sometimes hurt to look at him, in a way that Sabrina sometimes couldn't believe he wanted *her*.

"Everything you just said, plus he's intelligent and passionate about art and loves his family immensely," Sabrina agreed, as they walked towards the stairs leading to the underground. She felt a throb in her left temple, and sighed, knowing she was on the verge of getting a headache, and tears behind her eyes, waiting until she was alone to spill over.

"Not to mention," Sabah added. "He's fiercely protective."

"How do you know that?"

"Didn't he say he wanted to kill your paedophilic cousin?"

"Um," she said. "Yes."

Musa had said the same thing when he found out, and so had Soran. But it didn't mean it would ever happen or anyone ever would. It was just something someone said, not making the words have any meaning.

"There you go then. Anyways, text me when you're home, ok?"

"Ok, you too. Eat something healthy for dinner."

"Yes, *mother*."

"Amar gu kha."

"Yuck, no. You eat your own shit."

Sabrina let out a laugh that sounded, in her ears, like she was trying hard not to cry. "I'll see you when I see you. Love you."

"Love you too," Sabah said, turning left and jogging down the stairs, leading to the Northern line trains. Sabrina stood, for a moment, in the middle between the two staircases, staring at the space where Sabah had been. She was hoping Veda would be home when she got there, to help distract her from her own mind. She had faced her pain head on, every hour of every passing day, and now she was so tired, so exhausted, of feeling the same thing, and just wanted to *not* feel, for once. It was getting tedious, repetitive, boring, and so, as she walked down the stairs slowly, hearing a train coming to a stop at the platform,

Sabrina told herself that today, tonight, would be the last she cried over him.

CHAPTER FIVE

ON THE FOURTH day of Ramadan, Sabrina was sitting across from Veda and Elle, a mug held between her palms, her fingers clasped around it. The warmth from the coffee heated up her cold hands, and as she lifted it to take a slow sip, that same warmth slid down her throat. The girls, (well, Elle actually), had decided on going somewhere new for brunch today, a place in Meadowbrook called *The Pancake Palace*. It was different from their usual picks, attested by the fluorescent lights and the worn leather booths, the sticky table tops with scratches tainting the wooden surface. But despite this, the stack of pancakes they were each served, complete with fresh fruit, picked up that day from the market that was brought in just as they walked through the open door, and whipped cream, a dollop of Nutella and powdered sugar, and bacon for Veda and Elle, was good. It was pretty damn good.

Meadowbrook was Elle's hometown, and she'd

moved to London three years ago to study at UCL, a choice her parents were immensely proud of. They did, however, make it a point to call her every few days, check in on how their youngest daughter was doing and if she needed any money to get her by. It was no myth that life in London was expensive.

"See?" She was now saying to both Veda and Sabrina. "I told you. It's *life changing* here. The food here is a religious experience, seriously."

"It is amazing," Veda agreed, putting a forkful of pancake and banana into her mouth.

"Aren't you glad you came here, now?" Elle laughed.

"Well," Sabrina said. "It's not my first time in Meadowbrook. But yeah, definitely. This is the food of angels."

"Wait, what?" Veda looked at her, questioning. "When did you come to Meadowbrook?"

"With Daniel," she shrugged.

"And you never mentioned this because?" Elle raised an eyebrow.

"Uh," Sabrina cut up a strawberry and bit into it, the juice running down her chin. She wiped it away quickly. "I didn't think it was that big a deal?"

"*Dude*," Elle shook her head. "It's my hometown. Of *course* it's a big deal."

"Sorry," Sabrina replied.

"Where did you go, when you came here?"

"Wait, how does he know about Meadowbrook? A lot of people don't." Veda sipped her coffee.

"Um," Sabrina said. "We went to *Bella's Kitchen*

and," turning her attention to Veda, she continued. "Bella is an old family friend of his. His mother knew her from when they were in school or something."

"Makes sense," Elle nodded. "Bella is from a rich family."

"So why'd she settle in Meadowbrook?" Veda asked.

"Why do a lot of rich, white folk settle in quiet places?" Sabrina replied.

"Touché."

"She's a lovely woman," Elle said. "She catered my older sister's wedding. Her food is to die for."

"Apparently," Veda said wryly. "*Everyone* here can cook."

"No wonder there are so many restaurants," Sabrina laughed. "And yeah, I met her. She is so sweet. It's cute how it's a family run business. Daniel said his parents have a house here, that they rent out."

"Mm," Elle nodded, wiping up some syrup and whipped cream with her last bite of pancake. "I'm not surprised. A lot of people do."

"So what's happening with Daniel anyway?" Veda asked, smoothing down her perfect hair, neatly parted in the middle.

Sabrina paused, the coffee mug clasped in her hands, which wasn't resting on the table or at her lips, kind of hovering in the middle. "Nothing, really," she shrugged. "He took me to watch *Aladdin* last Monday—"

"The musical?" Veda interrupted.

"Yes," Sabrina said slowly. "The musical. And then we had sushi, which was nice. Um, and then we kind of

talked the rest of the week, since he had work and marking
to do, for his students. And I was busy with my placement
and had overtime. But on Friday, we went white water
rafting and had fish and chips for dinner. He drove me
home. I gave him a blowjob in the car. We had sex, after
he'd pulled over into this, like, empty road."

"Wait, wait, wait," Elle smirked. "*You* went white
water rafting?"

"Yep," Sabrina responded. She finally brought the
coffee to her lips, and sipped.

"And fucked him in the car?" Veda raised an
eyebrow.

"Yep."

"I see," Veda said, her expression changing into one
of amusement. Sabrina sighed.

On the drive home, after the blowjob she'd given
him at a red light that they were stuck at for half an hour
and after the quick, fumbling sex in an empty road, halfway
down the winding streets leading back into London,
Sabrina and Daniel talked about musicals. *Aladdin* was the
first one she'd watched, she told him, watching him as he
drove. He looked at her, surprised.

"Really?" Daniel asked.

"*Really*," she confirmed.

"Well," Daniel said, a slow smile appearing on his
face. "I'm *honoured* to have taken your musical virginity."

Sabrina had burst out laughing in reply, shaking her
head. Her hair fell in waves and loose curls around her
shoulders, glossy and sleek, looking like liquid gold in the
dark of the car, the red glow from the taillight of the car in
front of them beaming through. Daniel slowed to a stop at

the red light, just coming out of Central London. "You're so annoying," she said, smiling.

"Don't act like you don't love it."

"Love is a very strong word."

"And yet," Daniel said, his hand on her knee, palm up. She threaded her fingers through his, watching his hand close around hers. "You do."

"You're delusional."

"And you're just in denial."

She rolled her eyes, fighting the blush threatening to colour her cheeks pink. "I think," she said, changing the subject. "I might want to watch *Wicked* next." The lights changed from red to amber and then to green, the car ahead of them moving forward. Daniel started driving again, squeezing her hand gently, before moving it to the gear shift.

"Yeah?" he was smiling, eyes focused on the road. "We can go for your birthday. May twenty-seventh, right?"

"Um, yeah." Sabrina felt confused. What—he was suggesting they spend her birthday together? The two of them. Together. Sabrina breathed in sharply, thinking that maybe she should tell him that this, what they were doing, was casual—she had no expectations for it, there was no commitment, they weren't together and he didn't *need* to spend her birthday with her. Because they weren't in a relationship. But she found herself staying silent, and then he spoke again.

"Great. I'll book the tickets and make a dinner reservation. Do you want to go on the day or before it? I mean," here, he looked over at her. A car's headlights, driving towards their direction on the opposite lane, shone through their windshield, dancing across his face. His eyes looked brighter. Her breath caught in her throat as she stared at him, cheeks heating up. She swallowed, annoyed at her body's reaction to him. "Do you have plans with your family or your friends?"

"Um," Sabrina said again. She wanted to kick herself. God, why was she acting like such an *idiot* right now. "Yes," she finally said. "I always spend the actual day with family and friends, but since it's Ramadan, I will be spending my birthday evening with my family, and the following day with friends."

"Ok, cool. That's fine. We'll do something the day before. I'll do it tonight when I get ho—"

"You don't have to," she interrupted, looking at his side profile. His jaw line was sharp, his beard shadowing it, soft and thick against her hands when she cupped his face, kissing him. She shook those images away, memories of a few hours ago, a week ago, bouncing around in her head. "That's fine. Daniel. We can just—"

"No," Daniel shook his head. "We're watching *Wicked* and then going out for dinner. And then *maybe* I'll give you some birthday orgasms."

Sabrina felt a smile curve her lips up, dimples winking at Daniel when he glanced at her, smirking. "What do you mean maybe?" eyebrow arching, she crossed her arms over her chest, shifting on the leather upholstery. "You damn well better."

"So demanding." He turned left, after exiting a roundabout.

"You say that as if you never—"

"Shh."

"Don't tell me what to do," Sabrina narrowed her eyes at him, jutting her chin up. Daniel looked at her for a quick second, cheeks lifting as he smiled, before turning his attention back to the road ahead of him.

"Why not? You love it when I tell you what to do."

"That's *only* in bed, babe."

He laughed softly. "You know," Daniel said after a while, speeding up a little bit as he drove. "I was thinking—"

"Oh dear," Sabrina replied, biting back a laugh when Daniel threw a half withering, half amused look at her. His lips twitched slightly, as if he was trying not to smile.

"*As* I was saying—"

"Mm, go on," she said, giggling. He glared at her. She just beamed at him. He sighed, shaking his head, muttering something about her being *insufferable and lucky you're so damn cute.*

"Interrupt me again and I'll—"

"You'll what?"

Daniel sighed, then laughed. They entered a tunnel and Daniel rolled the windows up. "I'll punish you."

"How are you going to do that, daddy?" Sabrina batted her eyelashes at him, biting down on her lower lip. She was trying not to laugh.

"You'll see when we get to yours."

"Who said I was going to invite you in?"

"Oh, you *will*." Daniel's voice was low, an underlying current of an unspoken promise lingering. Sabrina just continued to look at him, imagining the scenarios of what could happen, of what would probably happen, when he parked his car in her driveway, though neither she, nor Veda or Sabah had cars, and opened the front door.

A little more than an hour later, Daniel rolled up outside her house, turning the engine off and turned to look at her. They stared at each other silently for a few minutes; the only sound was their breathing, and the distant police siren from a few streets down, the sound of a dog barking in the house across from Sabrina's. Without words, Sabrina looked away first and opened the car door, stepping out into the warm night. All the lights were off in her house. Sabah was at work and Veda was out with a few friends, prepping for her exam on something to do with criminal justice.

She unlocked the front door, Daniel's hand on the small of her back, anticipation a fire in her belly, smouldering through her, lightning quick. They walked inside and she switched the light on, swathing the hallway in brightness and she blinked. He shut the door behind him and then pushed her against it, his hands cupping her face, tilting her head up as he leaned down; pressing his mouth against hers in a kiss that made her knees weak and fireworks explode in her mind. She clutched his shoulders, fingers gripping onto his leather jacket. They kissed for what seemed like forever, his hand running down her face, skimming the side of her breast and waist and then up her back, strands of her hair around his fingers.

"Let's go upstairs," Sabrina breathed against his mouth. They did.

Presently, Sabrina let out a shaky breath and took another long sip of the coffee, leaving just dregs in the mug. She swallowed, pulling herself out of the memory of last Friday night. Across from her, Elle was talking about Sabrina's feelings (*which she didn't have*, she'd groaned in reply, exasperated) for Daniel.

"I'm not entirely sure I *believe* you," Veda said, tracing the rim of her mug with a perfectly manicured finger. "There's no way you're not into him, given all the time you spend together. And you talk. Constantly."

"I'm really not into him though," Sabrina argued. "I should know. I'm aware of my feelings, or lack thereof. Yeah, we talk and spend time together. But really, all it is sex. That's it. Nothing romantic about it, at all, ok, so can we please, for the love of god, just drop it?"

Veda and Elle exchanged glances, both smiling in a way that said they knew she was lying (which she wasn't) and it creeped Sabrina out, since their widening grins resembled the Cheshire Cat. Their smiles were accompanied with teasing comments making Sabrina roll her eyes as she glanced around *The Pancake Palace* which, despite its name, served things other than just pancakes, taking in the white-washed interior and the glass counter that had all sorts of pies behind it, where a man with black hair streaked with silver sat, thumbing through a book.

The other customers in the restaurant was a girl, tall, jet black hair, large brown eyes, honey brown skin, a few tables away from where Sabrina was sitting, nursing a steaming cup and a plate of pancakes and a blueberry muffin, and four teenage boys, discussing an upcoming football game against another school in the area. They were loud, laughing, and annoyed Sabrina. She audibly sighed, and turned her attention back to her friends, who were done talking about her feelings (which she didn't have, for god's sake) about Daniel and were now talking about places to go for Sabrina's birthday.

"Maybe *Mango Tree*?" Sabrina piped up, tucking her hair behind her ear, fingers brushing against the silver hoop. "It looks really nice there."

"Yeah, we can do, hon. It's your day anyway. You decide where we go," Elle smiled. "And I was thinking, maybe we go to a spa as well?"

"God, yes, please," Sabrina laughed. "I need that."

"The mind-blowing sex with Daniel not enough to alleviate your stress?" Veda quirked an eyebrow. Sabrina narrowed her eyes and opened her mouth to respond, when her phone, beside her on the booth, vibrated with a message from Daniel. She looked at the notification and chose not to respond.

"*First* of all," she began, in reply to Veda. "I am not stressed. And second of all, I just want to get pampered, so shut up."

"Mhm," Veda replied, smiling. "Methinks the lady's desire for a young man named Daniel is—"

"My only desire for him is *sexual*, *not* emotional," Sabrina said loudly. The group of boys glanced over at her, their words coming to a halt. She flushed, and then lowered her voice. Elle was laughing and not bothering to hide it. "You're both so *infuriating*, oh my god."

"Your reaction is what's making us continue," Elle said after she managed to stop laughing. "Although," she added. "We *do* think you fancy him."

"That's just because you're both dumb," Sabrina grumbled.

"Hmm," Veda chuckled. "We should get going. I want to get some more revision done today. We have an exam in a week." Meaning her and Elle. Well, Sabrina did too, actually.

The three of them, after they piled their plates up, leaving the cutlery on top of the last plate, mugs pushed together in the middle of the table, stood up and went over to the counter. Elle was smiling at the man, and handed over a twenty and a ten pound note, hushing Sabrina and Veda when they protested against her paying; saying that the following week, one of them could pay for her, followed by an eye roll. Soon after, they walked out, beneath the gold awning of *The Pancake Palace*, and Sabrina found herself glancing around as she linked arms with Elle. The wide pavements were lined with various shops and restaurants, and a pub that was dimly lit, making Sabrina think back to the one in Notting Hill, before she went back to Daniel's for the first time.

A few yards away was *Bella's Kitchen*, beneath a red awning, the glass doors and windows were wide, showing the interior of the restaurant that made you feel as if you'd been magically transported to the very heart of Venice. Meadowbrook was undergoing a new development on the other side of the town, where brand new houses with stone steps leading up the front door and marble floors and high ceilings were being built, seducing the townsfolk into considering making a purchase. Sabrina spied an advert for Veronica Hale, housing and interior designer, on a bus bench, her arms crossed over her chest, dark hair shining, lips curved into a subtle smile, eyes serious.

"Hey, Sailor," Elle suddenly yelled, startling

Sabrina. She looked at the girl Elle had called out to, having just come out of a bookstore, a paper bag swinging between her fingers. The girl glanced up, looking at Elle, a wide smile crossing her face.

"Oh my god, Elle, hi!" She shouted, running across the road, when the cars had slowed down. "How are you?" The two of them hugged. Sabrina and Veda looked at each other.

"I'm good, honey. How are you? And—*oh*," Elle stopped, then introduced Sailor. "Sweetie, these are my friends. Naveda, I go to uni with, and Sabrina is her cousin. Guys, this is Sailor, she's my parents' neighbour."

Sabrina smiled politely, muttering a soft *hello*, as they continued talking. ". . . and I'm just super *excited*, because Grayson's amazing, and we knew it wouldn't take long 'til he proposed, you know? You're coming to the wedding, right?" A brief pause. "I mean, it's in summer, next year, I mean, but oh my god, it's going to come *so* quick."

"Wait," Sabrina said, staring. "Grayson? Are you talking about Grayson Prescott?"

"Um," Sailor blinked. "Yeah. You know him?"

"Yeah, I do. He's a really great guy. I go to *Fairly Odd Pizzas*, like, all the time. I had no idea Juniper was your sister. It's a small world."

"Shit, *yeah*," Sailor laughed, the wind ruffling her hair. "It really is. I take it you've met her then?"

"Once," Sabrina nodded.

"Ok," Veda sighed. "Now that we've established the world is a tiny place, and also one that is dying, can we leave now? *Please*? I just," she said, looking at Sailor.

"Need to get cracking on with revising. I've kinda put it off to the last minute, and it's in a week, so I really need to revise today."

"Law, right? God, good *luck* with that. I would just *die* if I studied Law; I find it such a drag." Sailor wrinkled her nose, letting out a laugh. Sabrina smiled slightly.

Elle gave her a quick hug, and they said their goodbyes, promising to catch up soon, and then she led the way to where she'd parked her car. Sabrina slid into the passenger seat this time, putting her seatbelt on. It was one thirty P.M. when Elle drove out of the main street, driving past large, detached houses with sprawling front yards. "There's Bella's house," she said, as they went past a house painted a light blue. She pointed things out as they went ("the woods are that way, I used to play there all the time as a kid" or "there's a ballet studio just down that road, if you go straight and then turn right, past the little corner shop" and "my granddad lives on the end of that street"), and Sabrina sat back, listening, watching, asking occasional questions—there was an empty studio along one of the roads, opposite a library and an Indian restaurant, which used to be owned by this couple, years ago, Elle explained. It was another dance studio, unlike the other one she'd talked about which was for ballet only.

Sabrina had turned the radio on, listening to Mariah Carey's *We Belong Together*, making her sigh and roll her eyes. The last time she'd heard that was the previous July, when she'd gone out for a meal with Musa, his treat.

In the back seat, Veda was on the phone.

". . . I'm not sure what you want me to say, Jess. Look, why don't—" a pause as she listened and then she

88

sighed, tucking her hair behind her ear. "Seriously, it's not right dragging me into this. You guys have to sort out whatever issues you have, with *each other*. I'm not getting involved."

Sabrina glanced at her, shifting in the seat. Veda looked at her, rolling her eyes, listening to whatever Jess was saying on the other end.

"Yeah, I get that," she said after a moment. "But maybe she has her reasons, you know? Either way, talk to her about it. I'm not picking a side. It's childish."

As Veda continued talking, Sabrina let her hand hang out of the open window, feeling the breeze against her hand. The wind swept through her hair and she heaved out a sigh, shoulders sinking beneath the white peasant blouse she'd picked out after hours of browsing through *Forever 21*'s website. The rest of the ride back to London was silent, save for the music on the radio, and it let Sabrina get lost in her thoughts. She'd started her period late last night, after breaking her fast at sunset with her family, coming home just before ten P.M., when Adam had driven her home, Miriam and Leanne accompanying them.

Sabrina's experience with religion, with Islam, was flighty. Even before Musa, she'd begun to question it, hating all the rules demanded of her, what was the *point* of covering up, when people would still look, because monsters were monsters, regardless of what you wore. She found herself feeling like a fraud whenever she prayed her salah, going through the motions because she would be condemned to hellfire otherwise. It made Sabrina wonder, how god could call himself the most merciful, when he had written hell to be the final place for the people he created, knowing the choices they would make. How could god, Sabrina thought, be known as the most loving yet punish every act of love because they didn't fall under marriage or heterosexuality? It was cruel, creating humanity, giving them a heart to love and a soul that had known another, loved another, long before swimming their way past every constellation and galaxy, to a womb where they grew, nurtured by a mother who would—or should—tear the world apart to protect her child. It was brutal to create a person, knowing they could never act on their love for someone that was the same sex as them, unless they wanted to be damned to an eternity in hell.

It was these questions that she could never find an answer to that pushed her away from a religion, one that she still respected, despite almost every part of it saying she would go to hell for breaking all the rules, for going against it and leaving its folds—but was god not the most merciful? Was god not the most forgiving? That was what made her, after talking to Musa for the first time during one particular shift at work, when he decided to help her reduce the prices of the items that were expiring on the day, start to read into it again, thinking maybe it wasn't so bad, maybe religion was more than just its rules and regulations.

After a few weeks, she started to believe again and she told Musa this one night (or morning, depending on how you looked at it), when they were on FaceTime at two A.M., and he was eating Krispy Kreme doughnuts. He had smiled in reply, an excited look flickering over his face, saying "I'm proud of you, baby" and "good, it's good that you're coming back to the deen, I want to see you in heaven", and she'd laughed and said "I want us to go into heaven together, hand in hand".

And she did. God, she wanted that.

She wanted the two of them to have an infinite number of forevers, a lifetime together, to spend every day looking into his eyes and hearing his laugh, because she had forgotten the sound of it. She couldn't remember his laugh or his voice anymore, and it hurt, because it had been her favourite sound, listening to him talk—it soothed her to sleep. She wanted to just hold his hand and sit next to him, in silence, listening to the sound of her heart beating, feeling every breath, the wind caressing her skin, sweeping through her hair, tilting her face up to the sun, the love of her life beside her. She wanted to see his face when she told him she was pregnant, the happiness in his eyes so bright, it almost blinded her. She wanted him and her, always.

But sometimes when you wanted something so bad, you end up losing sight of it. You clutch onto it so hard, not wanting to let it go even though it was already slipping out of your fingers, even knowing it won't happen, but praying or hoping with everything inside of you, that it would. Maybe one day. It ended up becoming the only thing in your line of sight, because you were trying so hard to keep it close, tugging and tugging, when everyone around you was telling you to just . . . *let go*. Because you needed to realise that still holding on, after all this time, was just destroying you from the inside, stealing every bit of happiness that you could've had, if you just gave it a chance.

The next evening at Adam's house, Sabrina was sitting on the sofa, waiting for the pizza to arrive, with Sultana, Miriam and Leanne watching *Beauty and the Beast*, as her parents argued in the kitchen. Their voices were loud, not nearly drowned out enough by the increased volume of Lumiére and Cogsworth singing when Belle sat down to eat. She wasn't paying attention to the movie, despite it being one of her favourites, and her brother was sitting beside her, his head tipped back, an impassive look splayed out over his face, staring up at the ceiling.

When he was little, their parents hadn't fought nearly as much as they did after Sabrina came along, and suddenly, overnight, it was like everything was an issue. The rice was too soft, or the food wasn't what Mohammed wanted, or the handle of the saucepan had gotten burnt, or Ruksana wanted more money than just a twenty pound note to go shopping, or the croissants expired in two days *so why did you buy them?*, or . . . the list went on, and it drove Sabrina insane. So she was glad when she moved out, but she felt a little guilty leaving her sister behind to live with the mess that was their parents' relationship.

Sabrina had, on more than one occasion, asked her mother why they didn't just divorce and the response was always the same: they were married, they had responsibilities and despite everything that happened, they love each other, and people would talk. It never changed, over the years, and Sabrina began to resent them, just a little, for making her and her siblings witness the fights, the toxicity of their relationship, the constant screaming and the hits. But—that hadn't happened in a while or in a few years, and she was grateful, thankful to not have to see her mother bleeding, trying to compose herself and wipe away the tears and cover up the bruises.

It made her wonder what her future held, if she would constantly have her parents' relationship to look at in comparison, whether that was all that lay ahead of her. It seemed like, no matter how hard she tried to drown out the noise, it only got louder, and each time, when it seemed like maybe things had improved or maybe they were ok, *bam*. It went right back to the beginning and the screaming started back up again, doors slammed, plates were thrown, the food staining the walls and hitting the floor. Once, when she was in year seven and Adam was staying late at the library and Sultana was at mosque, her parents were fighting. Or rather, her dad was shouting at her mum, voice booming around the tiny flat they'd lived in all those years ago.

She'd been in her room, talking to her friend Jason, a super smart, super cute boy two years above her (they first became friends on Facebook and then met during at lunch in school, after Sabrina had slipped out a lie to her 'friends' at the time), on MSN, when the yelling first started. She'd paused, hands poised over the keyboard, cocking her head, listening, waiting, breathing quietly. Her heart was pounding in her chest.

And then she heard it.

The sound of a hard enough hit to make her mother fall: the dark hand of her father, palm-up, leaving behind a blood-rushing-to-the-surface, bruising, mark that told the tale of an angry man and a soft woman, her snowy white skin tainted with ownership, curving the soft shell of her body into obedience as he kicked her in the stomach, the ribs, and Sabrina tore out of her room, heart in mouth, pulse racing. She stopped in the doorway, seeing her mother cowering. Anger and fear blurred her vision.

"Tumi kita khoray?" she said, words strangling in her throat. Her mother's eyes lifted to meet hers, red rimmed.

"Go," her mum said. "Sabrina, go back to your room."

Her father looked at her, anger twisting his face into something Sabrina recognised, as much as she didn't want to. It was always the face she saw in her childhood, looking at her mother, mouth foaming with angry words and furious tones and rage, rage, rage. Her heart thudded, fear pulsing through her.

"Amma." Sabrina's voice was shaky.

"Go," Ruksana said again.

So she did, looking back over her shoulder as she walked the short distance back to her room. Her father began to raise his voice again and her mother rose back to her feet, fingers grasping onto the wall for support.

In her room, Sabrina had broken down into tears, once she'd shut the door behind her, hand over her mouth. She told Jason what happened and asked him to distract her. He'd sent over some music for her to listen to. And she did, with tears streaming down her cheeks.

Another time, when Sabrina was seventeen and her sister was at school, revising, and Adam had taken his daughters to the local farm to see the alpacas, she could hear her parents yelling in the kitchen. This time, it was about a disagreement to do with the family and money. She walked out of her room, standing on the landing, looking down. Hearing her dad's voice getting louder and louder made her swallow and run a hand over her hair. She jogged down the stairs, almost tripping, but she righted herself quickly, grabbing the banister. She walked into the kitchen quickly, just as her father raised his hand.

One minute, she was standing outside the kitchen.

The next, she was standing in front of her mother, her hand grabbing her father's wrist.

There was a beat, a moment, when everything was silent, and all they could hear was the bass from outside, the car parked on the road, right out front of their house. She dropped her hand from her dad's wrist, mouth dry, heart hammering against her chest as if it were about to jump out, and her mum's fingers were soft against her shoulder blade, a gentle touch.

Mohammed lifted his hand again, swearing at her, about to smack Sabrina. Just then, her mother grabbed her and pushed her, so she was standing with her back against the sink and Ruksana was in front, shielding her daughter's body. "Don't touch me," Sabrina spat. "Amareh soyo na," she repeated it in Bengali, voice low, angry, even.

"Ya Allāh," her mother murmured, quietly. "Surah Fatihah for ekhon, zaldi."

"Shuworor—ami shaytan ni beh? *Ami shaytan ni?*" her dad shouted, taking another step forward.

"Oh, *fuck off,*" Sabrina yelled.

But now, in the living room, with the Ramadan Kareem banner hanging over the faux fireplace with fairy lights strung around it and a little white table that had two Ramadan advent calendars, a few books about the stories of the Prophets, duās, and respecting parents, for the girls, and colouring pencils and candles decorating it, to the right of the fireplace, with two white iron wrought chairs in front of it, a fluffy pastel pink cushion on the seat, Sabrina was sitting, staring blankly at the TV screen, beside her brother, behind her sister and nieces. They were sitting on the carpet, cross-legged. Miriam and Leanne were sitting close together, their backs against their dad's legs.

The film wore on, with Belle's father getting locked up and Belle seeing it in the mirror. Sabrina's gut twisted and she blinked back tears. They heard a crash from the kitchen. Adam bolted upright, gently moving his legs away from where his girls were leaning against them. Sabrina stood up and they looked at each other.

He moved toward the slightly ajar living room door, looking at Sultana, who was watching them. "Tana, take them to my room," he ordered, voice even. "Finish watching the movie there."

She nodded, and ushered Miriam and Leanne to stand up. Together, they all walked out of the living room and walked down the hallway. They stood in the centre of the passageway for a moment, to go in two different directions, and once out there, the screaming got louder and they could hear Ruksana crying. Over the noise, Sultana was talking.

"Ok, girls, we're watching *Beauty and the Beast* upstairs. The last one to get to your dad's room is a rotten egg."

Miriam and Leanne looked a little worried, and as Miriam opened her mouth to speak, no doubt about her grandfather yelling in the kitchen, something about Sabrina and Adam and Sultana's nana, Adam told his daughters to go upstairs. So then they did, running.

Sultana followed, after casting a look at Sabrina, who looked back at her for a brief second. Adam walked into the kitchen, Sabrina close behind him. She found herself reaching out for his hand, needing that semblance of comfort for what they were about to see, what they were about to walk into.

To the outside world, Sabrina's family seemed perfect. A son with a great job, earning enough money to buy himself a house in Central London but choosing to stay close to his parents, and two daughters aiming to go down the doctorate path, one to do with mental health and one to do with surgery. People looked at them in public, seeing a family, all together, whole and happy, when they were anything but. That was the thing appearances: you could put on this mask and be anything or anyone you wanted to be, let people see what they wanted to. As long as nobody looked too close, and nobody ever did, they couldn't see the cracks in the foundations, or the concealer covering up the puffy eyes from spending all night crying or the purple bruise from an abusive husband.

When the pizza arrived forty five minutes later, everyone was scattered around Adam's house, doing their own thing. Sultana was still with the girls, now watching *Moana*, whilst Adam was in the kitchen with their mum, and their father was in the living room, watching something on ATN Bangla. Sabrina was in one of the spare rooms, browsing

Instagram. After intervening between the volcanic fight between her parents, her father had slouched off into the living room, muttering about his wife and her family, and her mother took in deep breaths, covering her eyes as a tear slid down her red cheek. Adam had taken control then, making sure she was sitting down and he'd made her a cup of tea, getting out those puff pastry biscuits they all loved, and sat with her. Sabrina had stood by the fridge, not knowing what to say, swallowing back the lump in her throat, as years' worth of memories played through her mind, like snapshots of a movie.

She pushed away the feelings mounting inside her, mindlessly scrolling down her feed. She paused as she came across Daniel's recent upload: a picture of him in a white t-shirt, faded blue jeans, in a bar that looked a little familiar, with two men on either side of him. The three of them were sporting wide grins, and the one on Daniel's left had his arm slung over his shoulders. She stared at it for a few minutes, realising it was the one the two of them had gone to on their first date. Almost hesitantly, she double tapped it, seeing it had gotten over one hundred likes already, with more than twenty comments.

After staring at the photo for a while longer, she switched to Netflix, thinking that maybe a movie would help to drown out her thoughts. Just as she was about to start watching *Dead to Me*, her brother called for her, Sultana and his daughters to come downstairs, "food's here". She paused, her thumb hovering over her phone screen, where the pause sign was looking up at her. To go downstairs meant facing the awkwardness that would settle over them, a blanket of silence so loud, it would be deafening. It was the kind of quiet that made it obvious something wasn't right, that everything was falling apart, and nothing could be done to stop the cracks from widening and splitting, tearing apart at the roots.

She lazily stood up and lifted her arms over her head, stretching, a yawn escaping her mouth. Her brother called her name again. Sabrina sighed, then grabbed her phone, and walked to the door, turning the cold metal handle in her hand. The door grazed against the light brown carpet, the sounds of her nieces talking floating up to her, the smell of pizza and BBQ wings making her mouth water.

"Coming," she shouted back. She stopped outside the bedroom, looking toward the stairs, and then shook her head, breathing out slowly. Not wanting to go down just yet, Sabrina slid into the bathroom, flicking the light switch. She stood in front of the sink, staring into her reflection. The girl looking back at her had sad eyes, bloodshot with the lack of sleep, so familiar. Sabrina knew those eyes; she'd seen them every day when she looked into the mirror since she was nine years old, until one summer, when she changed and was happier, lighter, for the first time she could remember. And then autumn came and the leaves began to fall, shades of brown and red and oranges dancing as they fell to their deaths. With the seasons changing and the leaves falling, Sabrina's happiness died, too.

CHAPTER SIX

WHEN ADAM FOUND out about what Abbas had done to Sabrina, he stormed over to their aunt's house, fist rapping against the front door furiously. His eyes were dark and angry, fury rolling off of him in waves, the cold winter air sharp and brittle against his skin, until the door opened and warmth enveloped him. His mother, Sabrina and Sultana had rushed out, following him, though Sabrina, unlike their mother, didn't want to stop him from what he was about to do. She wanted to see her older brother beat her abuser bloody, she wanted to see the blood spraying the walls and staining the linoleum flooring, she wanted to see the fear in that monster's eyes as he realised what he did had consequences, even if it wasn't jail time.

They were all in the kitchen. Abbas was standing by the sink when Adam rushed at him, fist flying into the face that haunted Sabrina's nightmares: the face of a man who ripped away the innocence of her childhood, shaped her behaviours in ways she didn't understand until more than five years of therapy told her that the way she was acting out was an attempt to gain back the choice of who she let touch her body, to get back the control and the rights that were taken from her at nine and at ten and at eleven. The hit wasn't expected, and Abbas had stumbled, knocking back against the windowsill. There was no hesitation before Adam kept pummelling him, fist flying over and over and over again into that face.

Abbas had lifted his hands to try and push Adam away, but Adam only swore, lifting his cousin up by the collars of his shirt, slamming his head against the window pane. Adam yelled, words that Sabrina couldn't remember, as she stood by the kitchen table, watching. Her aunt had come into the kitchen, hearing the commotion, and was yelling at Adam to stop hitting her son. Ruksana was telling him to stop. Rumena, Abbas' sister in law and bhabi, were watching, eyes wide. Sultana had her hand in Sabrina's, silent, taking in the unfolding scene, where her older brother knocked a predator to the ground. The top of his boot slammed against Abbas' stomach and then at his face, against his cheekbone. Adam kept kicking him, still yelling, ignoring the pleas to stop from behind him from the women who chose to protect the man that hurt his sister. It was almost ironic. How they were telling Adam to stop hurting the person who never once stopped abusing a child, even though *he knew it was wrong*—because of course he did. He had told Sabrina not to tell anyone.

Abbas spat out blood and, then, managed to get in a hit, throwing a punch at Adam's thigh. Adam laughed in response and kicked him in the hand, stepping on his wrist, hearing a snap. A shout of pain. More yelling. More hits, all from Adam. He was seeing bright, burning red, fury clouding his eyes as he bent down, shouting right into the face now contorted in pain and smacked against the ground, shrugging off the hands that tried to get him off the now terrified, bleeding man. Abbas then got another kick to the abdomen, the chest, and he was coughing up splotches of blood as he tried to curl his body away, trying to shield himself from the coming blows.

Everything, in that moment, was black and white, except the blood that was splattered against the floor and the walls and staining the net curtains, like a murder scene. Amina was screaming at Adam to stop, having failed at getting him to get off her son. Ruksana was telling him to stop, that god would punish Abbas for his actions. Sabrina was emotionless as she stood there, staring, watching the blood stain everything red. Her brother was furious, and feeling the rage and anger pulsing through him, all of it rushing to the surface and covering his sight in a veil of scarlet. His knuckles were slick with blood; it stained his hands, his clothes.

Adam was breathing heavily, shoulders rising and falling rapidly, chest heaving as he stared down at the monster whose blood he wanted to taste, see the life fade from that bastard's eyes.

"*You son of a bitch*," Adam had snarled, venom coating every word.

BOOM.

A kick to Abbas' stomach. The bastard coughed blood.

CRUNCH.

Adam's fist connected with Abbas' face. He was unconscious at this point, blood pooling across the floor.

CAPOW.

Adam continued throwing hit after hit, seeing his baby sister's frightened face, hearing his parents' going off on her for getting the police involved.

Blood continued spilling out of Abbas as Adam kept kicking, punching. Just then, Nafisa had come home from university. Shock made her freeze in the kitchen doorway. Adam wanted to taste and see and feel the life draining out of the piece of shit that had hurt his sister. Anger wasn't enough to describe how he felt.

SLAM.

Amina had collapsed, air scarce and thin and out of reach. Her head smacked against the ground.

WHIZ.

Rumena kneeled beside her mother in law, as Adam finally stopped hitting the person he wanted to kill.

SCHLAP.

"C'mon," Adam said to Sabrina and Sultana, walking away from the bleeding, broken body lying on the floor. "Let's get out of here. You want to go to the cinema?"

Sabrina nodded in reply. So then the three of them left, letting everyone else deal with the aftermath.

It was golden hour. The sunlight seeped in through the window, the sky varying shades of lilac and peach and pink against the backdrop of lavender and violet, wisps of clouds floating as if pulled by strings commanding their every move. Sabrina was sat on one of the sofas beside Sultana and Tasnia. Across from Tasnia were Amanee and Hifsah, Rebecca, Ali and Ibrahim. On the left of Sultana, sitting on the stools that were put there for this evening, were Reajul and Fahim, two out of three of Abbas' sons.

Sabrina was facing the window, the gleam of the setting sun, as it sunk into the horizon, bounced off of the window panes and journeyed into her eyes. She squinted slightly, and dropped her gaze to her plate of kisuri, sanna and salad, along with two samosas and two vegetable spring rolls, foregoing the pilau that everyone else in the room was having. Just then, Tasnia's older brother, Rafi, came into the room, a white plate, with blue floral patterns on the edges, in his hands. He glanced around the room and took a seat on the armrest beside Sultana. Just then, the athaan rang out from Sultana's phone, and they heard Rumena tell them it was time to eat, their day of fasting had come to an end.

Everyone, almost simultaneously, recited the duā to break their fast and take that first bite of food. Sabrina watched, silent, as they had their dates and then drank water, deeply.

"How are you lot finding ruza?" Rafi asked after a while, around a mouthful of samosa. He swallowed, then glanced at Sabrina. She shrugged in reply.

"It's fine. I'm not exactly fasting at the moment. But it was fine when I did keep, like, two." Her voice was flat, emotionless as she spoke. "What about you?"

"Yeah," Rafi nodded. "Same. I mean its fine."

"I don't even feel it, to be honest," Sultana said.

"I'm just tired most of the time, instead of hungry."

"That's because of the lack of food and water," Sabrina said.

"I'm aware," her sister rolled her eyes, putting a small spoonful of pilau in her mouth. "God, it really makes you think. About the people suffering from poverty around the world, I mean. Like, look at us. We get to have sehri and iftar, but they're lucky if they can even have one meal on a normal day."

"That's the point of Ramadan," Reajul said. "Ain't it?"

"Well, yeah, we all *know* that," Amanee sighed. "It's just sad. That's what she's saying, dumbass. We're so lucky and privileged. And we still complain."

"First world problems," Sabrina muttered, taking a giant bite of the kisuri. Too much kisuri and not enough salad in that spoonful. She pulled a face.

"How come you're not having fulaw?" Rafi asked her.

Every Ramadan, Rumena bhabi hosted an iftar party-slash-gathering, and the guest list was exclusive to her husband's siblings and their spouses and children, plus Sabrina and her family since they lived just down the road. This year, though, Adam had taken his daughters to spend iftar with Rose, Irina and Daisy. It was a cute setup in the four bedroom house Irina and Daisy lived in, right on the edge of London, more on the Essex side. Sabrina had been there a few times for dinner, appreciating that the woman who raised the love of her brother's life wanted to get to know the sisters of the man her daughter was enamoured with. All three women—Irina, Rose and Daisy—shared the same features, looked as if they'd simply been copied and pasted into the world: auburn ringlets, green eyes, a smattering of freckles, tall and willowy figures.

The relationship Rose had with her mother was one that Sabrina envied, wishing she could have an easy relationship with the woman who birthed her. While Sabrina loved her mother, she didn't often like her, and it made her gut twist and her heart clench painfully when she thought that. But it was true. Ruksana was a woman that put the family's reputation and honour before the mental wellbeing of her children, always using the words 'what will people say' whenever one of them dared to venture out of the mould they'd been placed in, whenever they expressed an opinion or made a mistake or didn't want to go a social event or wanted to get some goddamn justice. Because it was always about what people would say. Her parents were traditional, bringing over the norms and values of their Bangladeshi culture with their migration across the seas and lands they crossed when they chose to make London their home.

They'd left behind their family and friends, the memories of their childhood, but dragged with them every aspect of a culture that had its fingers wrapped around the throat of every brown girl, claiming their voice and freedom the moment they slipped into existence. It made Sabrina bite down on her tongue hard enough to taste blood, the metallic tang bitter in her mouth, as the words she wanted to scream rose up, up, up in her throat, strangling her. Her birthright was enduring a lifetime of affliction in silence, in acceptance; because that was the way her mother had done it, and her mother before her, and her mother before her, and her mother before her.

But Sabrina didn't want to.

She would choose not to.

The moment her parents had slammed shut the door to her chances of seeing Abbas locked up, of seeing him pay for his crimes, she vowed to be better than that, to be different, to make her own choices and live her life however the fuck she wanted. Consequences and reputation be damned.

So as Sabrina continued to silently shovel food into her mouth, thinking it didn't taste like her mum's cooking, she wanted so badly, more than anything, to be in the haven of her bedroom, with its slanting ceiling and surrounded by her books and too many candles. Around her, everyone was chatting about school and end of year tests and exams, groaning about the unfairness of the education system and everything in between.

". . . And these private school kids have an unfair advantage, because they have the money. Everything's neatly laid out for them, everything is open to them, because of the connections they make from the ridiculously expensive schools they go to and the connections their parents have." Tasnia signed. "Like, take Eaton for example. A private boys school and if you go there, you're set for life. Every opportunity is handed to you. You just have to drop that name and you get what you want. It's like an exclusive club."

"Didn't Mr Arnold go to Eaton?" Hifsah asked. "With the previous Prime Minister. That David guy."

"Yeah," Amanee replied. "He did."

"I want my kids to go to private school," Sultana

said. "It would be amazing for them to have that opportunity, for them to get an amazing education with the very best teachers."

"It's a pile of *shit*, all of that," Tasnia said. "We still get good education even if we're not paying fifty thousand pounds a per year to attend a school."

"It's not always about the education," Amanee said. "It's the network that's important. They're what gets you somewhere in life."

"But," Sultana countered. "So does your brain and your work ethic. If you try hard enough, you'll get to where all those rich, upper class, private school kids are. It's worth so much more when you achieve something on your own merits."

"We have to work twice as hard to get there, to even get a shred of what they have."

"Tasnia, yeah, that's true. It's harder for us in this world as a minority, and Muslim at that, but the world is changing. People are changing. Our generation *is* the change. If you want to get to the top, you work for it. You can't be letting money or people stop you from achieving that. If you want to become a fucking business owner, then *work* hard to *get* that bread. There's no point," Sultana said fiercely. "Sitting on your arse and complaining about how the system and the world is unfair. If you want it to be different, then you have to do something about it and do what you can to pass your exams. Everyone says GCSEs aren't important but they are, because they're the first stepping stones into the world. After that, it's your A Levels that determine what uni you end up going to. And then it's all on you. You do good, you meet people, you work hard, you make a difference in this world. But don't do nothing and then complain that the world is out to get you or treats you unfairly."

"That," Rafi said, scraping his spoon across the plate, as he finished off his food. "Was so *profound*."

"You should be a motivational speaker," Hifsah said.

"Fuck that," Sultana replied. "I'm going to be a doctor. I'm going to save lives."

"You're gonna be a doctor too, right?" Amanee said to Sabrina, who was staring blankly at her plate, now empty of the sanna. She slowly lifted her spoon of salad to her mouth, when Amanee sighed loudly, saying "oh my god, she's not even listening," and proceeded to throw a spring roll at her.

Sabrina blinked when it bounced off her cheek and fell onto her lap. She looked at it then looked up at Amanee, who was stifling her laugh. A silence had fallen in the living room, everyone waiting to see her reaction. "You did *not*," Sabrina said. "Just do that."

"Oh, but I did." Amanee was grinning.

"Uh oh," Sultana sniggered. "You're so dead." Her words were directed at Amanee who shrugged, then flinched, startled, when a samosa bounced off her head, landing on her plate.

"It is *on*!" Sabrina announced, when Amanee looked at her. In reply, Amanee chucked a handful of pilau at Sabrina, half of it sprinkling onto the floor and on Tasnia, who said *what the fuck*, annoyed.

"*Food fight*," Reajul yelled, dumping the food on his plate over his brother's head. Ali laughed loudly, ducking when Ibrahim tossed a samosa at him. It hit the wall behind him and fell to the floor.

That was all it took for the rest of them to get into motion, rising from the seats on the sofas or stools or armrests, dashing whatever available food there was left on their plates and hurling it at one another. Sabrina let the kisuri on her plate trickle over Amanee's head, cackling with laughter as it slid down her forehead and the bridge of her nose and then hit the wooden flooring beneath her feet. Amanee gasped.

Before Sabrina could grasp what was happening—or stop it—half of the pilau that had Amanee had left on her plate was overturned on her head, the rice raining over her hijab and falling around her like rain. She shook her head, and lifted her hand, brushing the rice away from the top of her hijab.

Around her, everyone currently in the living room continued pelting food at each other and, when they ran out of that, the cushions that had been arranged prettily on the sofas. Sultana squealed, running toward the door leading into the garden when Hifsah chucked water on her face from the entirely full glass that had been left, abandoned, on the table.

"Oh, *fuck*," Sultana said, dripping wet, bits of pilau still on her shoulder. Sabrina brushed it off, smirking. She lifted a hand over her face when Rafi dashed a cushion at her.

"Aw, no," Reajul suddenly said. "I didn't get to have my samosa."

"There's one there," Amanee said, pointing to the one on the floor, beside the coffee table. Tasnia snorted with laughter, and soon, everyone else joined in, guffawing loudly at their terrible food fight with not nearly enough food to throw and the mess they created in the living room, because *shit*, the oil from the pilau would stain the sofa and rug. But in that moment, as the eight of them basked in that moment of fun, free from any expectations or burdens or memories flickering like a shredded flag on a broken down sailboat, bobbing along the murky depths of a vast ocean, Sabrina thought that *this was nice. This* was one of those rare moments when she didn't mind so much about having to come to Amina khala's house.

But of course, like everything else, this came to an end, when a few minutes later, the living room door opened and Rumena bhabi came into the room. She looked around, horror and disgust evident on her face, before beginning to raise her voice, yelling at each of them. Sabrina tuned out of the lecture and motioned for Sultana to follow her as they ducked out of the room, leaving Rumena's daughters and their cousins to deal with the repercussions of the food fight, hijabs stained with oil spots from the pilau and samosas being thrown at them, feeling filthy with the residue of oil glossed fingertips.

The two of them quickly rushed out the front door, surging past Rashid as he came out of the kitchen, and held hands, laughter echoing in the twilight sky, hues of pink chasing the dark blue, a faint glimmer of stars gleaming in the slight darkness once the sun had sunk into the horizon. The short distance between Amina's house and Sabrina's parents' house was less than two minutes and as Sultana unlocked it and they stepped inside, Sabrina breathed in the familiar scent of the house she'd lived in for four years.

"Ok, so," Sultana said. "I'm going to use the upstairs bathroom—"

"Uh, no, the fuck? You're not."

"Yes, actually, I am. I live here, you don't."

"Which means I should get to use the bigger bathroom—"

"I don't *think* so."

"Why the fuck *not*? I'm basically a guest."

"It's just a fucking bathroom. The downstairs one is nice, anyway. You used to always be in there, remember?"

"If it is *just* a bathroom," Sabrina ignored her sister's last point. "Then let me use the one upstairs."

"No," Sultana said cheerfully and ran up the stairs in record speed, leaving Sabrina to fume in the hallway downstairs, arms crossed over her chest.

Muttering under her breath, she turned the light on for the downstairs bathroom (or was it technically a shower room, since there was no bathtub in it? Just a humungous shower stall, two sinks, a freezer—because two others weren't enough—and a toilet with a deep blue, ocean themed toilet seat that also had shells decorated on it. Not actual shells, obviously), and washed her hands. The house her parents had bought, after years of living in a tiny flat about two streets away, had five bedrooms, two bathrooms, a dining room, a kitchen and a pretty big garden that her mother used to grow her khodus, tomatoes and various other vegetables, plus chillies.

Several minutes later, Sabrina had grabbed a few clothes that she'd left behind the last time she stayed round, and hung them over the heater. She stepped into the running shower, and closed her eyes after adjusting the temperature of the water, letting it wash away the day's dirt and grime. The heat around her enveloped her in its warmth, a steamy hug wrapping around the gold of her skin, dancing along with each movement of her hand as she shampooed and conditioned her hair with a cherry blossom and strawberry scented shampoo. Each movement was slow and careful, almost methodical, as she cleansed herself.

I want to go *home*, she thought, watching the shampoo duds slide down her forearm. This place, her parents' house, even during the four years she'd lived there, had never felt like home.

CHAPTER SEVEN

THE SUN HUNG high up in the sky, sheathing the city in a sweltering heat with little to no breeze on Monday afternoon. It was luminous as it beamed down, casting its rays through the open window of the staff room. There, Sabrina was fanning herself with a folded up scrap paper, instructions on last week's homework for the year four students printed on it. She had a glass of apple juice in front of her, ice cubes filling the top. Beside her, flipping through a worn copy of *My Sister's Keeper*, was Josephine. A gorgeous TA with a smile that was all wishes on stars and soft like angel feathers, and the only person from work that Sabrina allowed on her social media.

They were sitting on a grey couch that was pushed up against the wall, beneath a small window that looked into the mini garden the school had, complete with a pond with a frog and some fishes. Despite the open windows, there was no breeze coming through, and the fan in the corner barely did its job to cool them down. There were several other teachers in the staff room, as well as the counsellor that Sabrina shadowed, who was also her mentor, and the school librarian.

This school was one that Sabrina had attended, halfway through year one and all of year two, until the start of year three, before her family had moved to east London, where they'd lived ever since. All the teachers from back then had left and the school had changed immensely, from what little Sabrina could remember. And it was just a few minutes' walk from Musa's house. Which was a total coincidence.

When she'd first contacted Place2Be, the organisation that trained counsellors and had various courses in order to be one, she'd listed the schools closest to her. It just happened that this particular school was one of them, and one she'd attended all those years ago. And it just happened that they'd put her through to this one.

She hadn't realised, at the time, how close it was to Musa, until she'd walked past the road behind his apartment block, spying the building and the familiar peach hued balconies. Sabrina had never been inside, of course. Musa lived with his mum and older brother. It was once that she'd seen the place, when they'd been driving back from a movie and dinner and he had to run up to grab his charger since his phone was dying. So he had parked outside the block, and she'd stayed in the car, waiting.

"I can't believe how hot it is," Josephine ("call me Jo, *please*") McAllister was saying. It pulled Sabrina out of the reverie into which she had drifted.

"Hm?"

"The weather," Jo raised an eyebrow. "It's very hot."

"It *is*? *Really*?" Sabrina gasped. "I had *no* idea."

"Ok, no need for all the sarcasm. What's with you?"

"Nothing. I'm just so fucking exhausted. The heat turns my brain to mush."

"I thought your brain was mush already." Jo's voice was amused. Sabrina could *hear* the smile in it.

Her eyes were closed as she responded. "Your comment is not appreciated."

"I'd pretend like I cared, but then I'd be lying."

"As if you don't do that already."

"Coming from you, Miss Devout Muslim?"

A pause. Sabrina opened her eyes, and turned her head to look at Jo. "I've never claimed to be a devout Muslim," she snorted. "God. Can you imagine?"

"Not really."

"Gee, thanks."

"Did you want me to lie?"

"Not really."

"*Well*, then."

"Shut up."

"Make me."

"Is that your attempt at flirting? Because if so, it really needs some work."

"Shut up."

"I'm just *saying*."

"You're annoying."

"Mmm, I've been told."

"I'm not exactly surprised."

"*That's* a bit rude."

Sabrina hid the smile threatening to appear on her lips, weightless as a crescent moon, every inch of it concealed with the dark of the night. She was everything her mother had told her not to be, using her feminine charm and sexuality to hush away the demons prowling the streets of her mind. While her sister was the bright allure of the sun, incandescent in her shine, with bronzed skin, apple-red cheeks, dimples that never failed to make anyone give in to her requests and brown eyes that lit up with the kind of innocence Sabrina so desperately wished she had, Sabrina could have stolen the part of the night sky and stashed it away in the pockets of her soul. Buried beneath the pale, glinting sea glass of loss and unrequited love.

She lifted the glass of juice Jo had poured for her once they stumbled into the staff room together, talking about the *Swan Lake* play the kids from year one were going to participate in, sometime around mid-July, before school let out for summer. The drink was cold and welcomed as it slipped down her throat, cooling her for just a second. The ice cubes knocked against her teeth and she took one into her mouth, feeling the ice against the flat of her tongue.

In the moments that passed, she sat silently as her colleagues conversed and ate, discussing their days and their weekends. Kelly—the school counsellor—met her eyes from her spot at the circular table, a mug of coffee in one hand. No matter the weather, Kelly *always* drank coffee. It was her drug. Sabrina flashed a quick smile at her in acknowledgement before looking back over at Jo, who was immersed in the pages of a book that Sabrina had read the first time when she was ten years old and then came back to it three years later. It always made her cry and the movie had made her sob.

When her workday ended at three P.M., Sabrina was surprised to come home and find Sabah in the dining room, drinking tea and dipping a cake rusk biscuit into it. She had sent Sabah a text the day after they'd met up, asking if she'd wanted to go see *Aladdin* with her when it came out in cinemas, even though it looked like it would be really shit and do no justice to the animated version, but hadn't received a reply.

"What are you doing here?"

Sabah lifted an eyebrow and bit the biscuit. She chewed for a bit, taking her time. "I live here, don't I?"

"Well, yeah. But I didn't think you'd be coming back today. You didn't say anything."

"I'm not back. And I don't need to run everything by you."

"Didn't say you did." There was an undercurrent of tension simmering between the two girls, one that Sabrina thought had passed a year ago. "So you're going to his again?"

"Yes. I just came back to pick some more clothes. We're going on a date."

"Oh? That's cute. Where to?"

"Just some place," Sabah replied, waving her hand in a dismissive motion.

Sabrina recognised this: the cool tone she was using, the guarded expression on her face, the carefully chosen information she was willing to part with. It was familiar in a way Sabrina wished it wasn't.

A small sigh escaped her mouth, strands of her hair

fluttering with the breath. She shifted in the doorway to the kitchen, her bag still on her shoulder. "Right," she said slowly. "What's going on?"

"What do you mean?"

"You're being weird."

Because she was watching Sabah's face, she noticed the tick in her jaw, the narrowed eyes, the slight flaring of her nostrils and the deep inhale, and then slow, almost cold smile that lifted her lips up. It was all so familiar. This distance.

"I'm not."

"You kind of are," Sabrina argued. "What's wrong? Did something—?"

Sabah's laugh cut Sabrina off. "No. I'm going upstairs to have a shower, since you seem to want to know my every move. Jake's coming to pick me up around half six, and I'll be out way before then."

Her words lingered in the room long after she'd gone upstairs to have a shower and Sabrina stayed behind, washing the mug and clearing away the crumbs that had scattered over the table. She'd closed the box, tying an elastic band over the flap and put it in one of the cupboards, out of sight. The sunlight dazzled through the double doors leading into the garden, dancing on the surface of the countertops, dust floating around like specks of glitter.

The heat made her hair stick to the nape of her neck, damp sweat pooling under her bra as she stood in the middle of the kitchen. She'd left her bag on one of the chairs around the dining table. As she stood there, memories she'd shoved away were trying to resurface, rattling against the cage she'd locked them in, trying to escape through. She clenched her jaw, nails digging into the soft flesh of her palms, leaving behind crescent moon indents.

"*No*," she said out loud. She didn't know who she was saying it to, but Sabrina didn't care. Whoever was listening should be listening. No. She wasn't going to remember the time she'd crossed the line she never should have. So, no. No. She wasn't going to let those memories come out to the front of her mind. No.

At six forty five, Sabah had left with Jake. Sabrina ended up answering the door when he rang, blinking at the large white man in front of her in confusion, trying to figure out who he was and what he wanted. He'd simply stared at her blankly, before a spark of recognition lit his glacier green eyes, brown eyebrows slashing down, before his mouth curled into an amused grin. She stood there, tilting her head a little to the right, her eyes roving over his face, trailing down his body, taking in the broad shoulders, the t-shirt that looked like it would burst around his biceps, the black joggers covering his legs and the Adidas trainers, thinking *Jesus fucking Christ, he's a tree.* He opened his mouth then, a familiar voice reaching Sabrina's ears.

"You not gonna let me in, Sabrina?" His voice was flat, despite the amused smile that had flitted across his face.

"*Jake?*"

"Who else would it be?"

"Um," Sabrina said. Jake looked back at her, raising

an eyebrow. She flushed and opened the door wider, letting him into the house. He walked in, glancing around and then sauntered into the living room. Sabrina paused, standing still, inhaling sharply as she wondered what the fuck. She hadn't expected to see him, because Sabah was supposed to be done by now, and god, she'd need to *talk* to him.

The memories she'd buried from a year ago rattled in her mind. She swallowed and stood at the doorway. Jake was sitting on the sofa, looking at his phone. The air was tense, awkward. Sabrina looked at him long enough for him to notice.

"Do you want water or juice?" she ended up asking.

"No."

"Ok."

The next three minutes crept by painfully slow before Sabah came downstairs. She'd paused a little on the steps, seeing Sabrina standing at the doorway, arms crossed over her chest. Sabrina turned a little, feeling eyes burning into her back.

"Sabah," she said loudly. "Jake's here."

"I figured," Sabah replied, a flicker of irritation crossing her face. She walked into the living room, shoulder barging Sabrina's as she entered. Behind her, Sabrina tensed, a muscle ticking in her jaw, a flash of anger coiling in the pit of her stomach. She bit it down, watching as Sabah leaned down and kissed Jake, smiling at him. "Let's go."

Now, Sabrina had just gotten off the Hammersmith and City line train, her phone in her hand, earphones blaring *Rewrite the Stars* by Zac Efron and Zendaya. As Zac softly crooned about the girl being his destiny, rewriting the stars and saying that she was his, Sabrina tapped her Oyster on the reader, her golden hair swaying behind her as she speed walked past the crowd of people going in two different directions. They were either coming into the station or exiting, their lives intersecting in this one station, making brief eye contact with strangers they would never see again.

She exited the station, the breeze sending strands of her hair flying around her face. Daniel was there, a bouquet of two dozen red roses and baby's breath clutched in his hands. Almost automatically, a smile appeared as she walked towards him, keeping her eyes on his face. As he stood there, the glints of sunlight reflecting behind his head cast a sparkling halo around his blonde hair, making him look like an avenging angel, dressed all in black. When he looked at her, it was as if he had shattered stars in his eyes, coming to life as his pupils dilated, taking her in.

"Hi, beautiful." His voice rippled through her like an explosion of fireworks, a bright kaleidoscope of colours. Sabrina felt her cheeks flooding with pink, a flush blooming in her chest, a butterfly with its wings spanning out and taking flight, rising from her neck to her face. She smiled wider, dimples winking as she launched herself on him.

Daniel staggered at the unexpected contact, before laughing and adjusting the flowers, thankfully not crushed, in his hand, using the other to press against the small of Sabrina's back, as her legs were wrapped around his waist and her arms were looped around his shoulders. She breathed in his smell, closing her eyes in bliss. "I missed you," she mumbled.

Though she couldn't see, the smile on Daniel's face widened, a small laugh escaping his lips. He spun her around and she giggled, and then blushed—because *god*, she giggled, and Sabrina does *not*—has not—*ever* giggled.

But anyway, after Daniel was done spinning her around and then peppering her face with kisses, a huge grin on his face, he'd put her down so she was standing in front of him, tilting her face up. She was looking at him, noticing for the first time, the faint scar running along his left cheekbone, a pale silvery-white line only visible in certain lights. A frown etched itself onto her features, but she just as she opened her mouth to ask him about it, Daniel leaned down to kiss her.

"Let's go," he murmured against her lips and she smiled in response, drops of sunshine twirling through the air, glimmering on the strands of his gold spun hair.

Their fingers were interlinked as they walked past a *Starbucks* and a *Costa* on the same road, the pavements clear of any dirty stains or rubbish, expensive cars gliding down the road. The houses and buildings towering around them made Sabrina take in a breath, feeling almost out of place in the borough of the one percent. But Daniel's hand holding hers made her feel welcome, an unspoken encouragement making her breathe a little easier.

Four minutes later, Daniel had unlocked his front door and they'd stepped inside. Like the first time she'd entered his house, Sabrina looked around in awe, taking in the gleaming marble floors and the landings of the floors above, everything bright and pretty and definitely costing more than she will ever make in a year, even when she becomes a goddamn psychologist.

"You can leave your stuff in my room," Daniel told her, running a hand through his hair. "And these, obviously, are for you."

She took the flowers he held out from his hands, smiling. "Thank you."

He smiled in response, making her cheeks flush. Shaking away the feelings making her knees stutter and her face feel warmer, Sabrina heard her heels clicking against the floor as she walked to the lift and pressed the button for it to slide open. She felt Daniel come up behind her and press a soft kiss to the sensitive part on her neck, right where her pulse jumped and sped up.

Feeling her breath catch a little in her throat, Sabrina closed her eyes, a small moan leaving her mouth. "*Daniel*," she mumbled.

His hands snaked around her waist, pulling her against his body. "We," he said, teeth nipping against her skin. "Have a lot of time to make up for."

"Mm," Sabrina breathed out. The elevator doors were already open. "Can it wait 'til after we've eaten?" Against her neck, Daniel's lips curved up into a smile.

"Of course, baby. I was thinking, we make pasta?"

"Yes please," Sabrina responded, reluctantly pulling out of his arms and stepping into the lift. She smiled at him, ignoring the way his eyes flicked down her body, the skyfall blue of his eyes darkening with lust glazing them.

Sabrina was wearing a black satin, cowl-neck camisole with fitted black trousers and a gorgeous pair of black Jimmy Choo heels that had been a gift from Adam for her twentieth birthday. The doors slid shut and Sabrina exhaled, staring at her reflection in the mirrored walls. She looked good, despite being completely makeup free and the small, angry red spot on her nose. It made her look like Rudolph. Fuck's sake.

Sabrina had just finished dicing up seven garlic cloves, the knife a blur in her hand. She put the tiny, chopped up pieces on the edge of the knife and let them fall into the pan, where the onions and ginger had turned a gorgeous golden brown. The aroma of the garlic mixed in with the ginger and onion, as Daniel stirred it together, was sweet and lingered in the air. It clung to Sabrina as she put the chopping board and knife beside the sink and grabbed the bowl where the chicken was, cut into small, bite-sized pieces.

She moved the bowl so it was under the tap and ran the cold water, making sure each piece was carefully washed and cleaned. As she washed the chicken pieces, Daniel put the lid back over the pan, and came to stand beside Sabrina, his hand resting on the curve of her bum. She looked up at him, a smile on her face, the night sky in her eyes.

"I have never," Daniel said. "Made pasta with curry powder."

Sabrina laughed. "It's just a little bit, to add some more flavour."

"You just want it to be spicy, don't you?"

"Hmm," she hummed, letting out a laugh. "Maybe a little. But it won't be spicy, babe. Don't worry. Your ass will be fine."

"Yours won't," Daniel replied darkly. Sabrina glanced up at him, raising her eyebrows, smiling, and then tilted the bowl, so the water tipped out of it and ran down the drain.

"Is that a—"

"Threat? No. It's a promise." His lips brushed the shell of her ear, teeth nipping on her earlobe. Sabrina sucked in a breath, a wet heat pooling between her thighs.

"You're mean," she just about whispered.

Daniel's laugh was everything as he lifted the lid and quickly stirred the onions and garlic. Sabrina opened the little jar with mixed curry powder (extra hot) in it, and tapped some out onto a tablespoon. She watched as it dropped into the pot, arm wrapped around Daniel's waist as he mixed it in.

"We'll add the chicken in a few minutes," Sabrina said. "Then the sauce."

"Which one do you want to use?" Daniel asked.

"The alfredo one?"

He looked at her and grinned. "Are you telling me or asking?"

"Fuck you," Sabrina signed. "I'm telling you. I tend to just chuck in whichever sauce I have at the time. It always tastes good."

"I'm sure it does, baby."

"You're annoying."

"And yet," Daniel said, taking the bowl of chicken from her hands and putting the pieces into the pan, slowly, with the tablespoon she'd used to put the curry powder in. "You're so into me."

"I'm just . . ." Sabrina huffed out a laugh.

"Not *that* into you."

"Are you trying to convince yourself or me?"

"Go screw yourself."

"I'd rather screw you."

"And I'd rather women have the right to choose what they do with their own bodies, but hey, we don't all get what we want."

"Nobody ever said America wasn't a messed up country."

"They call themselves the land of the free," Sabrina snorted. "When it was built on genocide, bloodshed and on the backs of slaves. I mean, god, how could Kay Ivey even fucking *think* about signing off on that bill, let alone actually doing it? It's fucked up. Like, what happened to the separation of church and state?"

"It's about the power," Daniel said. "And the unborn baby being something that doesn't exactly exist, so they can pretend to care about it. Unlike the thousands of children in the system, who are abandoned and neglected. That government likes to assert their power over minorities and women, as a way to stay in control."

"The only reason they're even in control is because they were voted in," Sabrina rolled her eyes. "People vote them in. Old white people voted them in, because people our age don't. They say they will online and shout about it on socials, but when it comes to actually doing it, they're all *oh my vote won't count anyway because it's just one vote.* And then when shit hits the fan, they all fucking cry. Social justice warriors, man."

Daniel sniggered a little at her imitation and then sighed, "I know, babe."

"Speaking of voting—" Sabrina looked at him. "Did you vote Leave or Remain?"

He raised his eyebrows. "Remain, obviously."

"Which means you're not a Tory, right?"

"Fuck no, I'm not a fucking Tory. Absolutely not." After a moment, he added, "Although my father and grandfather are."

"Really?" Sabrina stirred the chicken, swapping the wooden spatula for a silver one.

"Yep. And Mum supports Jeremy Corbyn all the way. She grew up in Clapton."

"Wait, your mum grew up in Hackney?"

"Yeah," Daniel laughed. "It's a classic tale of rags to riches."

"How did she get into the money?"

"Writing. Mum's an author."

"God, that is *amazing*. What else are you keeping from me?"

"You'll just have to wait and find out," Daniel smirked. Sabrina narrowed her eyes.

"I'm gonna dash a brick at your head."

"You should give me head instead."

"You really are a writer's son," Sabrina laughed. "Look at you, rhyming words."

"Suck my dick," Daniel muttered.

Sabrina laughed in response, tiptoeing to kiss him on the cheek. He turned his face and leaned down a little, brushing his lips against hers, teasingly. She smiled, parting her lips a little, deepening the kiss. His hard body pressed against the soft, tender curves of Sabrina's body, claiming her as his own, with every brush of their lips, every lick of his tongue against hers. This was more than just a kiss. It was a promise of something more.

Her hands slid beneath the hem of his shirt, feeling the planes of his washboard abs, a thrilling heat jolting through her. A small moan escaped her mouth as they continued kissing; his hands in her hair, strands of sunlight around his knuckles like the straws Rumplestiltskin had turned to gold. It was the kind of kiss that left one panting, taking in sharp gulps of air, fingertips pressed against lips, thinking *did that just happen.*

Lust burned like incense, fire beneath Sabrina's skin, as they finally parted. Daniel rested his forehead against hers, his breath warm on her face. He smelt like all her fantasies and the dangerous seas she had never allowed herself to be swept up in.

When she finally stepped out of his arms, Daniel kissed her on the temple, his lips lingering, before he opened one of the glossy white cabinets and took out the Dolmio Alfredo sauce. His shirt rode up, revealing a sliver of that gloriously tanned back, making Sabrina bite her lip. She let out a shaky breath, tearing her eyes away when Daniel turned around. He twisted the lid open, with Sabrina staring at him, one hand lowering the heat and the other over her steady heart. Daniel looked at her questioningly when he noticed her gaze locked on his face.

"You ok, Sabrina?" the tone of his voice was gentle, different from its earlier teasing tenor, and it made her close her eyes, a cerise pink splotch bursting to life on her cheeks. She swallowed back the thought in her head and willed the blushing to cease, because Sabrina Ahsan *did not* blush. And for god's sake, Daniel Henry Fitzgerald would not be the reason she started blushing. No way. Definitely not.

"Mhm," she said noncommittally.

Daniel looked as if he didn't believe her. "Are you sure, my love?"

Oh sweet baby Jesus. Sabrina released a small breath and nodded. "Pour the sauce in." She didn't make eye contact with him as he overturned the Dolmio jar, letting the creamy white sauce slip into the pan, covering the chicken. She kept her attention on mixing everything together, until the sauce covered everything in the pan, increasing the heat a little. She felt Daniel behind her, kissing the top of her head gently.

Just as he was about to say something, his phone rang.

It was lighting up with an image of his mother and **MUM** beneath it on the screen. Daniel left her, his hand brushing her waist as he walked around to the breakfast counter. He looked at his phone for a few seconds before answering. He took his phone out into the garden patio after sliding the door open, saying "hi, Mum", a smile in his voice.

Sabrina took that time to quickly take in a few deep breaths, thinking that she absolutely did not *like* Daniel. Not in *that* way, anyway. Because liking him meant she was starting to move on from Musa, which wasn't true since she still felt her heart clench painfully whenever she thought of him, tears stealing her breath. She looked over into the garden where Daniel was sitting, on a pale grey hanging swing decorated with a few cushions. He looked beautiful in the glow of the setting sun. She was looking at

Daniel, thinking that this man was a thing of fiction, of fairytales and Greek tragedies. He was good looking in a way that hurt, all sharp cheekbones and an aristocratic nose, piercing blue eyes, the first thing anyone noticed when looking at him, and that light golden hair, the colour of sunshine and starlight. It looked as if it were spun from silk, all perfect and with the kind of face that should've been plastered all over billboards and magazines. As in he had the flawless, faultless genetics that made him look like some kind of god or a prince or like a man who had everything. Or if he didn't, could take it all.

And she could swear, every time he looked at her, it was as if his eyes slit her soul open a little more, pouring a little bit of his light inside. She let out a loud sigh that sounded like the world was crushing her and then picked up the saucepan with the pasta in, taking it over to the sink. She dipped the pasta into a silver strainer and then gave it a quick rinse with cold water. In the next few minutes, Sabrina transferred the pasta from the strainer into the pot with the chicken and Alfredo sauce in, mixing it all together slowly. The scent of the pasta made her mouth water. After letting it heat simmer with heat for another few minutes, Sabrina turned off the burner, watching as the blue flames died.

She reached up to the cabinets on the left, taking out two plates and wineglasses. There were two wine bottles on the marble countertop on the other side of the cooker, one red and one white, and she looked at them, unable to decide which was better to have. "Ugh," Sabrina groaned, and then put a generous helping of the pasta on both plates. She glanced over to the garden again, noticing that Daniel was still on the phone to his mother. His laughter reached her ears and her stomach somersaulted. "Chill the fuck out," Sabrina whispered to herself, opening one of the drawers and taking out two forks.

After rinsing them, she placed them onto the plates and took them both with her out into the garden. Straight away, a smile graced her face when she looked at Daniel, the glow of the sun bright and yellow behind Daniel, a half circle above his head. She gently put the plates down on the black table a few feet away from the swing Daniel was in, and dragged it over to him. He was watching her, smiling, and then nodded to whatever his mum was saying, a gentle "I can imagine it must be hard for them" falling out of his mouth and into the air around them, dissipating with the sinking sun.

"Do you want red or white wine?" Sabrina asked him softly, when he pulled her down onto his lap. Her fingers pushed back the strands of his hair that had fallen into his eyes and she ran her hand along the sharp lines of his cheekbone and jaw, feeling the prickle of his beard tickling her palm.

White, he mouthed in reply and then listened to something his mum said. "Her name is Sabrina," he said. Sabrina raised her eyebrows in silent question. Daniel smiled apologetically. "Um, she's my—we're, uh . . ." he paused, gaze locked on her face. "We're taking it slow," Daniel ended up saying.

Sabrina felt herself tense a little and looked away from Daniel.

The sky was a shade of apricots and pinks and yellows, a glimmer of the sun's rays reflecting in it now.

"I'm not sure, mum," Daniel was talking quietly. "Mum, really—"

When Sabrina looked at him, he sighed, then said, "babe, mum wants to meet you. She wants you to come round for dinner on Friday."

"What?" she blinked.

"Dinner? Friday night? With my family?"

"Um," Sabrina swallowed. Thinking. Thinking. Thinking. Was this a good idea? Was it a good idea to continue this now? God. Dinner with his family. But she knew where she stood *and* it would be a free meal, so there was that and Daniel—well, it wasn't like he could just tell his mother that the two of them were just fucking. Because that's all this was. Nothing more than that. And she'd get free food out of it, if she decided to go. But there was a seed of doubt in the pit of her stomach as she opened her mouth to say no, she was busy, she had plans. Anything. "Sure." The signal from her brain to her mouth of the word she *should've* said was fried. Fuck.

But the smile on Daniel's face made her feel like she'd just answered all his wishes. Her answering smile was hesitant, the ghost of her earlier one, not quite as bright. But it didn't matter. Because Daniel was telling his mum that she would be coming round for dinner on Friday and *yeah, she loves chicken, she likes wine, she's gorgeous*.

Oh god. What had she agreed to?

CHAPTER EIGHT

SABRINA WAS WAITING to buy the most perfect pair of heels she'd ever seen for her birthday. When she got to the counter, humming along to the song playing, she realised she knew the girl behind it.

"Hiya," the girl said, a large smile on her face. Her face was makeup free and she was so gorgeous, it was unfair.

"Hey," Sabrina replied, unable to keep the smile off her face. "You're—"

"I've seen you before, right?" Kira, her nametag read, asked, as she rung up Sabrina's dress and shoes. She put them into two separate, large, glossy peach coloured bags, with *Mabel's Designs* emblazoned across the front in gold cursive. Sabrina inserted her debit card into the reader and then entered her pin when prompted, nodding in response to Kira's question.

"Yeah, in *Fairly Odd Pizzas*." She took her card out

and slid it into her purse. "I mean I've seen you there a lot, with three guys?"

"Ah, yeah," Kira nodded, her smile only widening. It was so bright and cheerful; Sabrina wondered how anyone could be *that* happy. Or perhaps it was just a pretence she put up. "And you're always with that girl. Your sister?"

"Nope." Sabrina took the receipt from Kira's hand, quickly looking over it. She dropped it into the bag with her gorgeous new shoes in. "She's my cousin."

"Oh wow, you guys look alike." Kira's laugh sounded how Sabrina thought sunshine would sound, all of that light brimming with her peals of laughter.

"If you think Sabah and I look alike, you should see my sister."

"You should bring her by to the restaurant so I can," Kira suggested. "I'm there basically every day."

"Hmm, I might do. And really? I mean, it is just a fifteen or twenty minute walk from here, isn't it?"

"Yep and yep. Ashton is my best friend. Well," Kira pushed away her fringe, tucking it behind her ear. "*One* of my best friends, anyway. The other three guys you see me sitting with are my other best friends. Ezra, Wade and Carver."

"That's cute," Sabrina said after a moment. "Having a close-knit group of friends you can trust with your life are important." Why did she just *say* that? God, she was *such* an idiot.

"Totally!" Kira nodded in agreement, leaning forward, resting her chin on her hands. "You so get me. Like, I've known the guys since we were in year seven, you know? We were all in the same classes for, like, everything. And then we went to the same college, and because we all did Psychology for AS, we were in the same class then, too. Until second year, anyway. Because, like," she blew out a breath, her hair flying up like a feather from a fallen angel's wing. "Me, Ashton and Wade ended up dropping it for second year and Carver and Ezra got put into two different classes. And then of course, we, me, Ezra and Ashton, that is, all picked different unis and our timetables clashed during the day so we couldn't hang out so much, even though our unis were all a few minutes' walk or train ride from each other. Crazy, right? Anyway, we always hang out at *Fairly Odd Pizzas*."

"What about Carver and Wade?"

"Oh, they didn't go to uni. Carver did a Digital Marketing apprenticeship after college and he's working for some magazine now. Wade . . . well, he's kinda just floating around, at the moment, from job to job. He doesn't know what he wants to do. But," Kira shrugged. "He'll figure it out. We're all still young. What about you anyway?"

"Um, I'm graduating this year and I work part time at Sainsbury's."

"Yeah? That's amazing. What subject?"

"Psychology. You?"

"Oh, I did English Literature. I graduate this year, too."

"I loved English Lit," Sabrina laughed. "God, I miss studying it and analysing texts. I think I was the only person in my entire school that actually enjoyed writing essays for English."

"Shit, me too. Even now, I still love it. I mean, it is a lot harder, but it gives me such a rush, you know?"

"*Exactly.* Anyways, uh, I best be going now. I have an exam tomorrow, which I haven't even revised for."

Kira laughed, "I would be freaking out if I were you. How are you *not* freaking out? But good luck, I'm sure you'll do amazing. Next time I see you, let me know how it went, ok?"

"Will do. Thanks so much. Have a great day."

". . . and I'm not entirely sure what to do, because now I want to say that I can't go. But that's going to make a terrible impression on his family, right? I mean, Jesus, his dad's a fucking Tory. And they're white. Shit. He's white."

"You're just realising this now?" Veda lifted an eyebrow, glancing up from her textbook. "After all this time?"

"Ugh, shut up, Naveda. That's not the point."

"Then what is?"

"I don't want to meet his parents."

"Why did you say yes then?"

"Because . . ." Sabrina was stumped. "Free food?" she said weakly.

"And you can't get free food elsewhere? You hate white people food."

"*Daniel's* a good cook."

"I'm sure he is," Veda responded drily. "Meeting his family *is* a huge step though. You know that, don't you?"

"Well, yeah. But it's not like there are any expectations. We're not together."

"Does *he* know that?"

"Of course he does," Sabrina rolled her eyes. "Friends with benefits is a thing."

"I'm well aware of such a notion."

"Do you want a medal?"

"Not particularly, no. But I do need to keep revising. And so do you. So get back to it." Veda's words were punctuated with a glare; making Sabrina sigh and roll her eyes, then rise to her feet. She looked at herself in the mirror as she was heading out of Veda's room. Her hair hung down her back in thick, golden blondey-brown curls. Her skin had gotten a little more tanned because of the sun—a rarity in England, but for the past two summers, it had been vibrant and bright and thirty seven degrees at the hottest.

After walking out of Veda's room and closing the door to the stairs leading up into Sabrina's room, she jogged up the steps, thinking about the day ahead. Her exam was at ten A.M. and then she was meeting Sultana at two. Her sister wanted to visit *The Shack* after Sabrina had talked about it enthusiastically, dreamily, contentedly, thinking about Daniel and the way he looked at her and the way he laughed at her jokes and the way he felt pressed against her, inside her, his hands, his mouth.

Sabrina sighed as she opened her HP laptop, the one she'd bought for uni purposes and the second one her father had purchased for her. While opening up her university's Moodle page, Sabrina grabbed one of her textbooks on the desk and flipped it open to the section about Kitty

Genovese and the bystander effect. She skimmed through it, reading the question at the bottom, before signing into her university's email account and Moodle, where she then brought up the lecture slides on psychopath behaviours and negative emotional stimuli. She groaned loudly.

The next four hours passed agonisingly slow as she made notes on brightly coloured flashcards, highlighted them and then summarised them, and then summarised them again. She made spider diagrams and looked up past exam papers. She read JF Dovidio's, SE Gaertner's, K Kawakami's and G Hodson's journal article on interpersonal biases and interracial distrust. Sabrina, though she didn't revise until the last minute, enjoyed reading journals and making notes about them, comparing them with others within the similar category. It helped her with her own dissertation and it was why she got a First in every single essay she'd completed since her first year.

Her grade for it came as a bit of a surprise, since she'd never actually been amazing at Psychology whilst studying at sixth form. She'd averaged Cs and Bs at most, so when she got an unconditional offer to study it at Middlesex University, she'd been surprised, and then elated, when, in her first year, she got an eighty-seven percent for her first ever essay.

In the April of her first year, Sabrina had gotten a job at WHSmith, in Euston Station, right beside the M&S where she'd worked the summer before, where she met Musa. She had seen him around during her breaks, her heart pounding, palms sweating and knees stuttering like silver spoons, because she didn't know whether to approach him or walk past him like she didn't see him. In the end, he made the choice for her, although they'd been just barely friends: he saw her and turned around, walking back into the shop.

She hadn't expected anything different, but it didn't mean it hurt any less. But whatever. That was then and this was now. The September before she began her second year, Sabrina left WHSmith and started working at Sainsbury's, where she'd been ever since. She wanted to leave after six months, but decided not to. It would look good on her CV to have a steady job for more than just a few months, even if she bloody hated it.

A little while later, after Sabrina had turned her laptop off, having decided that she'd done enough revision for the day and deactivated Facebook, she went downstairs, with her phone in her hand. She pushed open the door to the landing, at the bottom of the stairs and saw Veda coming out of the bathroom.

"Done revising?" Veda smirked.

Sabrina closed the door. "I'm going to die if I continue."

"You have tomorrow and Thursday and then you're done for the summer. You've got this. Stop being so melodramatic."

"I hate studying. It's so exhausting."

"Think of it this way—you'll be helping people in the end. And you're going to a great uni for your doctorate, so it's fine. Just keep your goals in mind."

"I guess so." Sabrina huffed out a breath and pulled her hair into a low ponytail, running her fingers through the strands. "I mean, you're right. I know you are. I've always just—" here, she wrinkled her nose, then sighed again.

"Hated studying and revising. It's just . . . a socially mandated path that has been dictated for us even before we were born. As if that's all there is to life. We study for years and then work for the rest of our lives and then die."

"That," Veda said, walking toward Sabrina and then leaning against the wall, arms folded over her chest. "Is so fucking depressing."

"Mm. But true."

"I just hope it's all worth it in the end, you know?" her voice was soft as she looked at Sabrina, who stood beside her, head pressed against the canvas of Ayatul Kursi. The canvas had been a gift from her mother, one that she cherished, so she hung it up on the wall of the hallway. Even if she wasn't Muslim anymore, she still believed in the protection the duā provided.

"God, me too. It's going to be a waste of so much money, and going into debt for no reason, if it doesn't work out the way we want."

The girls were silent for a minute, thinking about their future.

While Sabrina had gone through dreaming of being in different career paths (i.e. interior decorator, magazine editor, human rights lawyer, social worker, counsellor, counselling psychologist), Veda had her mind set on being a barrister from a young age. Out of everyone, she deserved to have all her dreams fulfilled—she worked hard to get to where she was now. Sabrina couldn't imagine her as anything else.

Their silence was broken by Sabrina's phone vibrating. She looked at her screen.

"Is that your lover?"

"Um, yeah."

"Do you *luuurve* him?"

"No. Are you dumb or are you stupid?"

"Neither. I think you should be asking yourself that, though."

"We all know I'm kinda dumb, man."

"Just kinda?" Veda arched an eyebrow, a smirk glossing her mouth.

Sabrina narrowed her eyes. "I hate you."

"Ah, no. No you don't."

"I really, really do."

"You're just stupid."

"Stop being mean to me."

"Or what?"

"That's for me to know and you to find out."

"Yeah, ok." Veda snorted, shaking her head.

Sabrina opened Daniel's message and typed out a reply. Just as she hit send, a message from Rose came through, wishing her good luck for her exam on Wednesday and Thursday.

"Aw," Sabrina smiled. "I really hope my brother and Rose get married soon. They're so precious together. It's sickening and makes me want to cry. I love it."

"They are pretty cute," Veda agreed. "Speaking of couples, have you spoken to Sabah?"

"Uh, no. She's being weird, not too sure why. She was here yesterday and Jake popped by as well, to pick her up. Apparently they were going on a date and she needed to pick up some fresh clothes."

"She's been staying with him for ages."

"I know. Do you know why?"

"Nope, she hasn't said anything to me." Veda's eyebrows furrowed. "I don't know. I feel like there's something up."

"She's being kinda off with me, to be honest. But I haven't done anything? Recently, anyway. Unless, maybe . . . do you think—"

"Possibly." Veda sighed. "It's been over a year and you two sorted that shit out. It was still a horrible, bitchy thing to do, but—I'm pretty sure she's over it now."

"I hope so," Sabrina murmured. Her phone buzzed with another text from Daniel.

Daniel at 23:57: *Baby, get some sleep. Now. You have an exam in a few hours. You need a good night's rest*

Sabrina at 23:58: *i'm not tired though, wont even be able 2 sleep*

Daniel at 00:00: *Count sheep*

Sabrina at 00:01: *u count sheep :)*

Daniel at 00:01: *I'm not the one who has an exam tomorrow...*

Sabrina at 00:02: *and?*

Daniel at 00:03: *Sleep. Have you eaten?*

Sabrina at 00:03: *nope*

Daniel at 00:04: *Why the fuck not, Sabrina?*

Sabrina at 00:05: *uh, im not hungry?*

Daniel at 00:05: *Go eat.*

Sabrina at 00:06: *no.*

Daniel at 00:06: *Sabrina*

Sabrina at 00:06: *Daniel*

Daniel at 00:07: *You're infuriating at times, u know that?*

Sabrina at 00:09: *sorry, daddy*

Daniel at 00:09: *You can say that after I spank you for not listening to me.*

Sabrina at 00:10: *ooh kinky, i like ;))*

Daniel at 00:11: *I'm aware of what you like loool*

Sabrina at 00:12: *don't u think it should be lllol so its laughing laughing laughing out loud instead of loool which is laughing out out out loud? it makes more sense*

Daniel at 00:12: *You're really weird*

Sabrina at 00:14: *but you love me anyway :)*

Daniel at 00:14: *Do I?*

Sabrina at 00:16: *yes.*

Sabrina found herself smiling and then frowned, realising. Veda was watching her, an amused look on her face. Whether or not Sabrina understood it, things had shifted and chances like this only came around once or twice in a lifetime. As she turned her attention from her phone to Veda, asking if she wanted to order McDonald's for dinner, the two of them went downstairs, into the living room. Lights from cars driving past their street shone through the window, a bright beam dancing on their ceiling and walls for just a few seconds before moving on.

CHAPTER NINE

BY THE TIME Sabrina got to the station, it had begun to drizzle, raindrops spraying down from the grey skies, concealing the sun. The world looked dreary and dull when she tapped her Oyster card to get through the barriers and jogged down the stairs, her phone vibrating with an incoming call. She looked at the caller ID, a picture of Sultana hugging a plush penguin toy with hints of glitter on its fur, a huge grin on her face, at Winter Wonderland the previous December.

"How did it go?" her sister asked the moment Sabrina answered.

"Pretty good," Sabrina said, tucking her hair behind her. The wind blew her hair forward, rain pounding against the platform. She sighed as a few drops landed on her head, rolling down the strands and slipping beneath her leather jacket. It went down her back like a cold teardrop. "I'm confident I'll get either a high two-one or a First."

"Your confidence is inspirational. Teach me."

Sabrina laughed. "Academia is the only thing I'm confident about these days. Which is actually kind of surprising, since I was so shit in school and college."

"I know," Sultana sniggered. "You had to retake Maths a million times."

"Well excuse me for not getting an A* on the first go."

"You couldn't get an A* even if you bribed the marker."

"Amar gu kha, ferothni."

"I'm telling mum."

"Go on then. See if I care."

"Don't be rude. It's Ramadan."

"Ok, hypocrite."

"Shut up."

"No, I won't."

"When do you ever?"

"Hey, that's mean."

"Boo fucking hoo," Sabrina rolled her eyes. "Be there by two, ok?"

"Chill, I will. Oh, by the way, I forgot to tell you," Sultana said, and then paused. Probably for dramatic flair, knowing her. Sabrina rolled her eyes again.

"Forgot to tell me . . ."

"I went to that art gallery in Shoreditch and saw your man's paintings. They're pretty good. He's talented. You should keep him."

"Ok, A) he's not my man and B) I'm well aware of his talent, thanks."

"Ew, I didn't need to know that." Sabrina smirked

at the disgust in her sister's voice. "So you're saying you wouldn't care if he fucked another girl?"

Something in Sabrina's gut twisted, a weird feeling creeping up inside her. She frowned a little, rubbing her chest. Her fingers pressed against the edge of her pink shirred top, showing just a hint of her cleavage. "No," she finally said.

"Mhm, really?"

"Yes," Sabrina said sharply. The sound of the Northern line train approaching reached her ears. "The train's coming. I'll see you soon. Don't be late."

"Acha, bye. Love you."

"Love you too, babe."

"Ew, don't call me babe."

"Ok. *Babe.*"

"You're annoying."

"Sorry, babe."

"*Sabrina—*"

There was a different kind of magic in *The Shack* during daytime. Everything was still the same, but there was a sense of wonder in the air as Sabrina sat across from Sultana in a booth, digging into their burgers. They were both quiet as they ate. Sabrina had ordered a chicken burger this time, a hint of spice kicking in as she'd eaten more than half of it. The bun sank a little beneath her fingertips, a drop of ketchup falling onto the plate, but she didn't notice. A tomato slice had fallen out from beneath the top bun, sesame seeds bouncing off the red painted nail on her index finger. Overhead, *Say You Won't Let Go* by James Arthur was playing, bringing Sabrina back to the winter of 2016, when she'd gone to Margate for the day with Sabah and they'd sat in a quaint little café just off the boardwalk, overlooking the beach. It was there that she'd first heard the song, as they ate fish and chips, laughing about something Sabrina couldn't remember now, talking about how boring everything was without having someone to crush on. They ordered dessert after, ice cream with strawberry sauce and a slice of cake with icing and sprinkles on it. It reminded them of the cakes from primary school during lunch time every Friday.

She looked at Sultana when she reached over and stole some of Sabrina's chips, dipping it into mayonnaise. "What's wrong with your chips?"

"You have more."

"So?"

"I wanted it."

"Oh my god."

"Leave me alone. I'm your little sister. Be nice to me."

"I'll slap you."

"Such violence," Sultana sniffed. "It's a bit worrying. Be careful you don't give the white men any ammunition to call us terrorists more than they already do."

Sabrina choked on her strawberry daiquiri. She coughed for a bit, her hand over her mouth, and then laughed. "Oh god. Remember when that fat man outside the chicken and chip shop called us terrorists?"

"Yeah," Sultana cackled, flicking the end of her hijab over her shoulder. "And then you told him to say it

louder but he kept walking. I legit thought you were going
to kick him."

"I wanted to," Sabrina said, venom coating her
words. "*Imagine* having the nerve to say that to little kids.
What a bastard." She shook her head, annoyance flickering
through her, like a lit flame.

"How many times did you get called a terrorist?"
Sultana asked, shoving three chips into her mouth.

"Um, twice, I think?" Sabrina frowned. "I got called
a Paki three times. The first time was, I think, when we
were at Naveda's house. Their old house, I mean."

"Was I there?"

"You were inside watching *Barbie*," Sabrina
laughed. "It was when Sabah and I were going to the corner
shop to get some milk and sweets. And a bouncy ball for
her. Two white guys, her neighbours, called us Paki when
we were going downstairs."

"I'm glad I never got called a Paki. I'd probably
have cried."

"Trust me, it fills you with so much rage, it's
unbelievable, especially given the history of the word. It's
despicable."

"I feel so sad," Sultana was saying, after she
finished off her burger. "Every time I remember Altab Ali
and how much our people suffered when they first migrated
here. I mean, god, he was *only* twenty five and then he got
killed just for being—" she broke off, sighing. "It's fucking
horrible. And to think, there are still people around now,
with those same bigoted ideologies and views."

"People like that will always be around," Sabrina
replied softly. "Altab Ali wasn't the first and he's not the

last."

"I fully wish those people could just, I don't know, fucking drop dead or something."

"Hmm, but if they did, then they won't learn, you know? Everything is a learning experience, and sometimes it takes one moment or an action to change the way you think. Sometimes you need to be filled with that kind of hatred to understand the true value of humanity and the kindness of people. Like, think about it. It took that veteran in America so long to accept that his hatred for Islam was unjustified. He wanted to kill niqabis in a shop just because they were Muslim. It was barbaric, monstrous, and the only way he came to realise that was because of the way his daughter looked at him. As if he was a monster, like he was crazy, because of the shit he was saying when she told him about her Muslim friend and his mum. And in the end, he went and studied the religion and converted."

"But why does it need to be on two extremes though? Either hate or love. Why not something in the middle, or just, I don't know, fucking respecting people?"

"Fuck knows, babe," Sabrina sighed. "People are people and we'll never truly understand the way their minds work. The only thing we can do is not respond to hate with hate. But that doesn't mean we sit back and accept the abuse. I mean, shit, I'll punch anyone who calls me a Paki."

"Let's hope your man's family don't call you that."

"Again, he's not my man."

"Whatever." Sultana rolled her eyes and took a sip of her virgin pina colada.

"Don't whatever me."

"*Whatever*," she said again, smiling.

"Dhurr, heti."

"You sound like mum."

Sabrina pulled a face. Just then, the waiter who had taken and delivered their order came by the table. Sabrina glanced up at him.

He smiled.

She smiled.

"Is everything ok?" his eyes were on Sabrina, gaze dipping to her cleavage before looking back at her face. She tilted her head slightly, shifting in her seat.

"Mhm, it is. Thanks." Her smile was a little flirty, lips a bright shade of red like a fairytale princess, voice soft.

"Do you need anything else?"

"Is there anything you're offering?"

He smirked a little. "How does my number sound?"

"Well, I don't know. I haven't heard it yet."

The waiter laughed and took out the notepad and pen tucked into the pocket of his apron, tied around his waist. He flipped it open and quickly wrote something on it, before ripping the page out. Carefully folding it up into a neat rectangle, he handed her the piece of paper.

Liam, it said, above his phone number.

"Text me sometime," Liam said, still smiling at her.

"Maybe I will."

Sabrina watched him walk away, a smirk tugging on her lips. She turned her attention back to her sister, who was staring at her, a sceptical look on her face at the scene that just transpired. She fluffed her hair up a little, running a hand through it and swept it over to her left shoulder, covering the thick strap and prettily tied bow of her top. Picking up her fork, she stabbed a few chips onto it and dipped them into the mayonnaise.

"What?" she said, mouth full, noticing Sultana still staring.

"Aren't you seeing Daniel?" Sultana asked, her finger tapping the stem of her glass.

"We're just fucking," Sabrina shrugged. "That's all it is." Sultana looked doubtful. "It is literally *just* sex, Tana."

"Hmm."

"Shut up."

"Didn't say anything," Sultana replied, sipping her drink, looking at Sabrina. "Remember when you said you'd never be with a white guy?"

A smirk flitted across Sabrina's face as she swallowed her chips, and lifted another forkful to her mouth. "I do. And I'm not with him, man."

"*Is* it? Then how come you're meeting his parents?"

Sabrina laughed. "I didn't know how to say no. Kill me, please."

"You're just dumb."

"Ok, Miss-Going-To-Study-Medicine."

"Shut up."

"Boro manusho logeh ola matoyn ni? Shorom nay ni?"

"Dekhray ni," Sultana sniggered. "Oto boro khota khoylay. Amar buzil shorom nai, zebla tumi shada betayn toh logeh sex khoray."

"Call me a hypocrite with your chest, fam."

"Don't tell me what to do, bruv."

"Shut up, blud."

"Nah, my g. I'm good."

Sabrina's laugh filled the air between them. They continued eating their chips (with Sultana stealing a few more from Sabrina's plate and Sabrina glaring at her and sighing, but then pushing her plate to the middle of the table), their conversation drifting onto other topics with moments of silence settling over them like a warm blanket. Take Me Home by Jess Glynn was now playing and Sabrina rolled her eyes when she heard the first few chords, thinking why the fuck would they play such a depressing song.

After they finished their food and drinks and walking out of the restaurant, arms linked, Sultana checked her phone to see a missed call from their mother. As they walked to the station, Sultana called her back. The rain had let up while they'd been eating, but the sky was still a dreary, gunmetal grey, off white clouds gathered together like an audience gazing at the unfolding play.

The Central line was packed and hot when Sabrina and Sultana stepped into the train, grimacing at all the sweaty bodies. The sleeves of her leather jacket felt uncomfortable against her bare arms as Sabrina stood, holding onto the pole, in front of her sister. They made eye contact as a few more people piled in, business men in suits and tall, pretty women with perfectly immaculate makeup, even after a long day at work. One of the men was on the phone, shouting into it as the train began to move. When the signal cut, he swore.

Then, noticing Sabrina's eyes on him, he glared. "What are you looking at?"

She simply lifted an eyebrow, saying nothing.

The rest of the journey to Mile End was uneventful and tortuously hot. As soon as they got off the train, Sultana exhaled loudly, saying "oh my god, I fucking hate the Central line." Sabrina laughed, agreeing, as they waited for the District or Hammersmith and City line to go home (for *home*, see: their parents' house.)

As soon as the train arrived, they took their seats on the first section, settling next to each other. Sabrina sighed, closing her eyes, and Sultana rested her head on Sabrina's shoulder. The train wasn't as jam-packed full of people as the Central line was, seeing as they'd already come into the East End, and slowly, at each station they were passing through, it was emptying out more than it was filling up with people. Someone's bag thwacking against her leg made Sabrina open her eyes, turning her head to look at the girl who had just taken a seat next to her.

An apologetic smile was on the girl's face, her afro resembling a pretty lilac candyfloss, a diamond stud glinting in her nose. Her skin was rich and dark; effortlessly smooth which Sabrina thought was a little unfair because it had taken years for her skin to clear up, with the help of a dermatologist and a steady rotation of creams, before finally settling on Neutrogena. The girl's lips were glossy, lids shimmery gold, false lashes long and wispy, her entire being exuding confidence. Sabrina smiled back at her, gaze flicking over her outfit: acid wash boyfriend jeans, a tight fitted white ribbed top, a white, pink and grey windbreaker jacket and black Balenciaga trainers.

"I love your lashes," Sabrina said, surprised at her

ability to form a coherent sentence in front of such a pretty person. She swallowed.

"Thanks," the girl beamed. "They're from the Insta brand. You know *New Fashion Trend Shop*? I'm wearing Nebula."

"Oh, awesome, thanks so much," Sabrina's smile was genuine and friendly. "I've been looking for a pair like that for ages."

"It's amazing, you should so get it. It feels really light on the eyes, too. And they have a bunch of other styles too. I've got their mermaid style brushes, which are fucking *everything*."

Sabrina let out a low laugh. "I'll check them out when I get home."

The girl smiled, saying *great, you should*, and then they lapsed into silence.

Later, when the train rolled up to their station and after the girl had gotten off at West Ham, Sabrina had quickly wrapped a scarf around her hair as she walked up the stairs to the barriers, Sultana laughing beside her. A few people had looked at her strangely as she covered her hair and adjust her jacket to cover the rest, since she didn't have a hair band with her. They walked out into the street, the rain just starting to fall again.

It started off slow, just a few, fat drops, as the two of them walked past familiar shops and a pharmacy: the William Hill, with a man in a hooded bomber walking inside, an off licence corner shop, a breakfast café that only white people went to, a chicken and chip shop with the best, hottest wings Sabrina ever had. (It even beat the naga wings from that popular place in Stepney Green). There were lines of cars driving past, buses bright and red coming to a stop at the traffic light, which had gone from amber to red, a group of boys in white thobes crossing the street, a rustling bag of chicken and chips in their hands. The smell of it wafted over to Sabrina as she walked, fixing the scarf on her head. The neat side parting she'd brushed it in was showing beneath the chiffon material, but she didn't really care.

One of the boys glanced over at her and Sultana as they walked behind them. He flashed a small smile, and then tugged one of the other boys over to the side, letting Sabrina and Sultana pass by.

"Thanks," Sultana said over her shoulder. The boy didn't reply.

Once they reached the long road their house was on, just across from another corner shop, the rain had increased, slashing down angrily. It hit the pavements in loud smacks, water droplets bouncing and glimmering on the surface. The world became distorted and wet in the rain. Sabrina swore and grabbed her sister's hand, beginning to run. They passed a woman in a niqab and a little boy, who looked to be about five years old, a brightly coloured umbrella popping out like a surprised butterfly. It was red, yellow, orange and pink, kind of like the one Sabrina and Sultana had when they were little.

Sultana rummaged around in her bag for her keys as they stood beneath the awning of their house, shielding them from the downpour. She found them, after what felt like forever, and inserted the key into the lock, turning it. As soon as the front door opened, they could hear yelling.

Sultana slowly closed the door. Sabrina kicked off

her shoes, and put them on the shoe rack.

". . . Tor manush oileh, tui kutta lakhan kham khorleh eneh. Beymanor beyman, zaneh sai gor taki sarya zaitam gi," their dad was saying. Or screaming, rather.

There was a beat of silence before Ruksana replied, her voice a little quieter.

"Aro ageh zudi khoytai, farlam eneh. Khayl keh beshi late, time nai. Ami ekh dinor bitreh oto torkhari randitam kilan?"

"Khobisor—" the rest of what their dad said was muffled by the sound of something being thrown.

Sabrina felt her sister look at her as she took a step toward the kitchen. Through the open door, she saw her father standing with his back to it, one hand curled around the back of a chair. She didn't know why or what it was about this moment, but he looked large. Bigger than he really was. Something about this tasted bitter in her mouth as she watched, listening to her father continuing to yell expletives at her mother. Her mother remained quiet as he talked, shouted, starting to a hand about, as if to punctuate his points.

The light touch of fingers against her hand drew Sabrina's attention away from the endless drama of her parents fighting. She looked at her sister questioningly.

"Let's just leave it," Sultana said gently. Her voice sounded defeated, as if she'd accepted that no matter what they did, their parents relationship would constantly be toxic and unhealthy, derived from years of their culture treating its men like gods and its women like slaves. Sabrina nodded in acknowledgment to her sister's words, sighing.

The sudden silence that befell the kitchen seemed loud. The gushing of running water from the kitchen broke it. The kitchen door opened a little wider and Sabrina turned her back to it, taking those few steps to the stairs a few feet away from the front door. She quickly walked up the stairs, Sultana right behind her. Their father went into the living room, muttering to himself about his wife and how he should leave. In the kitchen, their mother was doing the same and asking god why she had to marry that man.

It was always the same.

Upstairs, Sabrina went into the bathroom and sat on the toilet, sighing. She felt suddenly exhausted, drained of all her energy. She could barely lift the bodna. After, she got into the shower, scrubbing her face hard until it was red. The steam of the water rose up around her, safe and secure in those few moments away from everyone.

It had been like this every week when she'd lived at home, having to listen to the arguing, the fighting. It was a constant, when everything else was falling apart. Her parents kept up this normal. But it wasn't normal. It wasn't what a family was supposed to be.

But it was all she'd known, even as a child.

When Sabrina got out of the shower, she picked up the clothes she discarded in the hamper and shoved them into a carrier bag, knowing she couldn't let her mother see the clothes. She had a pale pink bathrobe on, tied at the waist, hair loose and dripping with water. She walked into her old room and put the carrier bag into another carrier bag, before slipping it into hers and shoving it into the corner of the room.

Her room still had all the furniture she'd picked out

years earlier, the wardrobe still had some of her kameezes, long dresses and abayas she'd never worn, gifted to her from various people after their trips to Saudi Arabia for Hajj. She looked around the familiarity of it all, imbedded in her mind, and swallowed at the memories pressing in the back of her eyelids. Downstairs, the house phone rang.

A door slammed.

Sabrina sighed and slipped into a black kameez and shalwar, with pink and yellow flowers embroidered on it, throwing the dupatta over her shoulders, covering her chest. Her phone buzzed with a text from Sultana asking if she wanted to watch *Someone Great* on Netflix. Grabbing the phone in her hand, Sabrina closed her bedroom door behind her, wincing as it creaked loudly. The carpet was soft beneath her feet as she padded across the hallway to her sister's room.

Not bothering to knock before opening the door, she slipped inside. "Yeah," she said aloud to her sister, in reply to the text. "Let's watch *Someone Great*."

CHAPTER TEN

AFTER HER FINAL exam was over, Sabrina met up with
Veda and Elle at *The Breakfast Crew* for brunch. The both
of them had one more exam left, each, and were using this
Thursday as a day off to relax and breathe a little easier,
despite the stress looming over their heads. When she
pushed open the glass door, the bell dinging with her
entrance, the sun peeking out behind fluffy white clouds,
she spotted both girls sitting over at their usual spot. They
each had mugs of coffee in front of them, and one in front
of where Sabrina would sit, having ordered for her once she
texted them she was a few minutes away. Elle saw her first
and smiled brightly, her lips tinted pink from her Glossier
lip balm.

"How was it?" Elle asked the moment Sabrina sat
down opposite her, throwing her bag down on the leather
booth. Sabrina sighed and picked up her mug with both
hands, blowing on the coffee a little, before taking a small

sip.

"Fine, I think," she replied. "I did well, until I got to the last two questions. I kinda ran out of time. I don't know."

"You'll be fine," Elle said. "You tried and that's what counts."

"I didn't, though," Sabrina said. "I didn't really revise until a few nights before. So whatever shit grade I end up with, it'll be my own fault."

"Your overall grade is going to either be a two-one or a First, though, no? You got an eighty-two percent last year." Veda's hands were coiled around her mug; fingers clasped together, her eyes on Sabrina, who shrugged.

"I'll probably just about scrape a First."

"Still a First," Elle laughed. "Chin up, buttercup."

Sabrina smiled, just a small one, not feeling quite as relieved as she'd anticipated earlier. The end of these three years brought about change, one she wasn't exactly prepared for or looking forward to because she just wasn't ready. She had become accustomed to barely trying for her essays and still ending up with one of the highest marks, gotten used to the distance from her house to uni, it was, still, a connection to the summer before she'd started, because she'd spoken about it in those three months of relaxation before, what *should* have been, stress, settled in her bones. But change, she'd come to learn, was inevitable and the only constant in life.

Even when you thought nothing had changed, you ended up looking back on how things had been or the events and moments that had taken place, only to realise that things, no matter how small, were different. These moments shaped the future, paving the way to a series of choices, even if, in the end, there was only one left to make, because there just was no other option. But Sabrina hadn't come to this moment just yet.

For now, she was sitting here, in *The Breakfast Crew*, as a waitress brought over two ceramic plates, one blue and one red, with two slices of toast, eggs, bacon, sausages, beans, a hash brown, three pancakes doused with syrup and a dollop of whipped cream on top, beside blue berries and strawberries, plus fresh slices of pineapple and kiwi. She put the plates down in front of Veda and Elle, smiling and then told Sabrina she'd be right back with her plate. Veda snapped a picture of her food, laughing when Elle joked about always feeding the phone first. A minute later, their waitress returned, with a red ceramic plate, heavy even without all the food piled on it. Sabrina grinned excitedly and then took a shot of the three plates, carefully arranging her mug of coffee so it was in the picture.

"If being a psychologist doesn't work out," she said. "I'm going to be a photographer."

"Good luck with that," Elle replied, daintily taking a bite of her bacon and a bit of her egg. She chewed, then swallowed. Carefully cutting her sausage into a thin slice, she picked up some beans with her fork too and lifted it to her mouth.

"Thank you," Sabrina smiled.

"You can kick-start your photography career with the pictures you take when travelling around Asia." Sabrina looked at Veda, swallowing the bite of egg and sausage before responding, pointing her fork.

"That," she said. "Is actually a pretty good idea."

"I was kidding," Veda deadpanned. "But ok."

"Don't rain on my parade, bitch."

Veda ignored this, scooping up her beans. The yolk of her egg split, running across the plate, and mixed in with the beans as she stabbed it with her fork and brought it to her mouth slowly. As she did so, two of the beans fell from the fork and landed on top of her hash brown.

They ate in silence for a while.

Last night, towards the end of *Someone Great*, when Jenny had been on the train and writing her letter or whatever it was addressed to Nate, Sabrina had broken down into tears. It had startled her sister, who had been a little teary eyed while watching, but not a sobbing, snotty mess like Sabrina was, as she wiped her tears with the sleeve of her kameez. It had been a moment that made her think of Musa, even though she'd been thinking of him, remembering every hour she'd spent with him, throughout the entire movie, during Jenny and Nate's fights, when they first saw each other in the party. She'd felt herself breaking, shattering, as the movie wore on, itching to send him a text, but stopping herself because she knew she would never get a reply.

"Do you think I can have one more kiss? I'll find closure on your lips and then I'll go. Maybe, also one more breakfast, one more lunch and one more dinner."

Tears glossed her eyes, slipping out as she stared at the laptop screen.

"I'll be full and happy and we can part. But in between meals, maybe we can lie in bed one more time. One more prolonged moment where time suspends indefinitely as I rest my head on your chest."

163

She took in a shaky breath, her hand squeezing her forearm painfully, nails digging into her skin.

"My hope is if we add up all the one mores, it will equal a lifetime and I never have to get to the part where I have to let you go."

God, she missed him. She missed him so much.

"But that's not real, is it? There are no more, one mores. I met you when everything was new and exciting and all the possibilities of the world seemed endless."

Her tears were coming faster, her breath in short, sharp gasps as she tried to control herself. Tried to stop crying.

"And they still are, for you, for me, but not for us. Somewhere between then and now, here and there, I guess we didn't just grow apart, we grew up."

A small sob escaped her mouth. She covered her mouth; feeling stupid, vision blurring as she cried. Sultana's hand was gentle, comforting, on her shoulder. "Sabrina." Her voice was a reminder that she was there. Still. Even when he wasn't.

"When something breaks, and the pieces are big enough, you can fix it. I guess sometimes things don't break, they shatter. But when you let the light in, shattered glass will glitter."

His name was a prayer on her lips.

"I miss him," she said, voice breaking with the sob unearthing itself from her broken, shattered heart.

"And in those moments, when the pieces catch the sun, I'll remember just how beautiful it was. Just how beautiful it will always be, because it was us, and we are magic, forever."

Her tears were sparkling diamonds in the darkened room with the curtains drawn and the only light from Sultana's laptop, as she sobbed, choking on his absence that felt like a gunshot to her soul. He'd left and he'd taken with him everything she'd ever wanted, *with him*, dreams dissipating into dust, ash in her mouth.

It still hurt, just as much as the night he'd ended everything over text, not wanting to listen to her crying when he said it wasn't working out. Even though she saw it coming, it was still enough to break her completely, unable to even breathe without wishing it was all just some kind of twisted dream. But it wasn't.

And now she was trying to survive each day, telling herself she was ok, because if she told herself she was *ok* for long enough, then maybe she would believe it and actually *be* ok.

". . . Graduation?" Sabrina heard Elle saying, a grin on her face, looking at Veda, who nodded, laughing.

"You're on. Loser pays for brunch 'til next summer." There was a glimmer of something in her eyes that Sabrina couldn't make out and she frowned, confused, blinking at the two girls sitting across from her.

"What are you guys talking about?"

"Told you she wasn't paying attention," Veda said to Elle.

"I think I gathered that from her lack of protests," Elle smiled wryly.

"*What* are you talking about?" Sabrina demanded again.

"You," Elle pointed at her. "And Daniel."

"What about us?"

"Oh nothing, *really*." Her laughter was melodious as she sung the words, exchanging looks with Veda, who was spluttering with laughter. "*Just* a little bet. You'll find out soon enough."

"He's not my boyfriend," Sabrina decided to point out.

"Oh, we know," Veda smirked.

"*Yet*," Elle added. They looked at each other again, laughing. Sabrina rolled her eyes.

Her phone vibrated with an incoming call from Daniel. She looked at it for a few seconds, before answering, glaring at Elle when she made kissy faces.

"Hey, baby. How did your exam go?"

She smiled. "It was ok, I think. Yesterday's one was better."

"I have no doubt you did amazing. You're intelligent," Daniel replied straight away, without missing a beat.

Sabrina sighed. "I could've revised more than I did, though. That's the thing. I could have done so much better."

"But you got a First in your essays from the first term, right? And for your dissertation draft?"

"Yes."

"Well, then. You have nothing to worry about. Coursework is weighted more than exams are. If you think you could've revised more, then you know what to do when you start your doctorate. It's a lesson learned."

"I hate it when you're right." She was smiling.

"I'm sure you do, baby."

"Stop sounding so smug." He laughed. "I'm

guessing you're on your lunch break now?"

"Yep."

"Have you eaten yet?" Sabrina shovelled the last bite of the sausage and bacon into her mouth, mopping up the beans.

"Yeah, I had a tuna and cucumber sandwich."

"Is that all?"

"And a white chocolate cookie."

"I want cookies."

"Go get some then."

"Maybe I will."

On his end of the line, she heard water running, gurgling down the drain. "What are you doing now?" he asked, the water shutting off.

"Um," Sabrina said. "I'm at brunch with Veda and Elle."

"Tell them I say hi."

"Ok." Sabrina smiled. To Veda and Elle, she said, "Daniel says hi."

"Hi, back," Veda said, taking a bite out of her kiwi slice and dropping the peel onto the empty plate.

"Hi, Daniel!" Elle practically shouted, gaining a few looks from the other customers. Two men, dressed in suits, glanced at her. Sabrina glared.

Daniel's laugh was warm in her ear. "They seem nice."

"By nice, you mean annoying, right?"

"No, not really."

"It's ok, I won't tell them," Sabrina promised, laughing. She poked at one of the blueberries, before embedding it onto her fork and biting it. "Ooh, this blueberry is really nice."

"Does it taste as good as you?"

She gasped. "Daniel. *Behave.*"

There was a beat of silence. And then, his laughter filled her ear, rich and warm, like starshine and honey. "My sincerest apologies, my love."

A smile danced on the edges of Sabrina's lips. "You're forgiven, babe."

Across from her, Veda made a kissy face and a heart with her hands. Elle cackled with laughter. Sabrina glared at them again. "Shut up," she said.

"I didn't say anything," Daniel interjected.

"Not you," Sabrina told him. "My idiotic friends."

Daniel was smiling as he responded, "I'll let you get back to your idiotic friends. I can't wait to see you tomorrow."

Sabrina felt a flutter in her chest, as if even her heart was swooning. She swallowed, fighting back a blush and a smile. "Me too," she said quickly. "Bye."

Across from her, Veda had her head cocked to the side, her hair dark and hanging down her back. Her skin was a warm brown tone, darkened a few shades by the few days of sun they'd had. Sabrina looked at her, lifting her coffee mug to her lips and taking a long sip, the coffee tasting lukewarm in her mouth now.

"You talk to him like you're together," Veda said.

Sabrina rolled her eyes, placing the mug down on the table. "You said the same thing about me and Musa." It felt like her heart twisted painfully at the mention of him.

"No, I didn't. With Musa, you *were* together and it was more like . . . you were married or something. The way you two just talked about your plan for the day or what you were doing, and," Veda smiled, almost pityingly. "When you ended the calling, it was like you'd done it a million times before, you know? The way you said I love you to him, it was like it was a part of you and you'd never get tired of saying it."

"I have no fucking clue what you're trying to say."

"You were in a comfort zone with Musa," Veda said, her eyes meeting Sabrina's, as if she was looking past all the *I'm ok*s, and staring right into her soul. "It was familiar and safe—"

"No. It wasn't." Sabrina cut her off, shaking her head. "Anyway, Daniel and I are not together and we won't be. We're, I guess, friends. Who enjoy having sex with each other. That's all it is. We talk like that because we're friends. And what Musa and I had, we were in a relationship, yeah, but there was no comfort zone that came with it. It was—fuck, ah, I don't know . . . the opposite of that. He pushed me to fucking be more—" she stopped and sighed. "Whatever. It doesn't matter. It's over anyway. There's no point rehashing the past or thinking about it or whatever." Even if it was all she did: think about what had been and what should've been.

"You really loved him, huh?" Elle asked. Sabrina looked at her and then nodded, dropping her attention to the pancakes left on her plate. She picked up her knife and fork, cutting into it and took a small bite.

After a while, she said, "yeah. I did. I do. I love him."

☼

It was nearing eight P.M., the sky a multitude of blues and greys, as Elle braked a little too violently at the traffic lights, glaring at the road ahead of her as Veda and Sabrina tried—and failed—to muffle their laughter. Mounted on her dashboard was her phone, showing that she'd been on the phone to her mother for the past seven minutes and twenty three seconds. In the back seat, Sabrina's shoulders were shaking, a hand over her mouth as she spluttered with laughter again, making eye contact with Veda in the mirror. Elle's mother was telling her how unladylike it was to swear, and she should be apologising profusely to Sabrina for calling her a quote "fucking cunt" unquote, and how dare she even use such a vulgar term to insult her sweet friend. Elle was still glaring as the light changed from amber to green, starting to drive again.

". . . So why do I still not hear an apology?"

"*God, Mum—*"

"Apologise, Eleanor Penelope Thompson!"

Elle sighed, glancing up at the mirror, meeting Sabrina's eyes. Sabrina's smirk was big enough to challenge the Cheshire Cat. "I'm sorry, Sabrina," Elle said, voice flat.

"You're forgiven, Eleanor," Sabrina laughed, amusement lighting up her dark eyes. The rain sheathed down, hitting the windows as Elle continued driving, turning onto Veda and Sabrina's street.

"Now, Sabrina, darling, I know your birthday is soon, so I want you all to come round to ours for dinner whenever you're able to, ok?" Elle's mum said. Sabrina opened her mouth to refuse, but Marion continued talking.

"I don't want to hear a no. You and Veda are like daughters to me. If you're not able to during this month, since I know it is Ramadan and all and I'm sure you'd like to spend this time with your family, then any time around Eid or after. Just let me know when, ok, darling?"

"Sure," Sabrina replied, knowing a no wouldn't be accepted. She smiled. "I'd love that, Marion."

"Good. Elle, call me tonight after you get home, ok, dear?"

"Will do, mum," Elle said. "I love you."

"I love you too, my precious. Stay safe."

A few minutes later, Elle parked outside Sabrina and Veda's house. They stepped out into the pouring rain, large drops landing on Sabrina's grey coat, leaving behind big, dark circles. Elle swore as she held her bag over her head, running to the front door. Keys were jingling in Veda's hand as she slid it into the keyhole, turning it, and the moment the door was unlocked, Elle rushed inside. Sabrina laughed, wiping her shoes on the welcome mat before taking them off and putting them onto the top shelf of the shoe rack.

"I swear," Elle was saying as she shrugged out of her coat and threw it over the armrest of the sofa. "It is constantly raining in this country."

"You don't say," Veda laughed, walking upstairs. Elle rolled her eyes.

Sabrina had her coat over her arm, her bag dangling over the crook of her elbow. "I'm gonna go up to have a quick shower. You wanna come up or . . ." she trailed off, leaving the blank space for Elle to finish with whatever she wanted to do.

"I'll get the popcorn and snacks ready, and find something for us to watch."

"Ok, cool. I won't be more than twenty minutes."

Elle smiled at her and walked through the dining room into the kitchen. Sabrina went upstairs, and saw the bathroom door shut, the shower running. She tucked her hair behind her ear and opened the door to the attic stairs, flipping the light switch on. The carpet silenced her footfalls as she ran up the steps into her room, turning the light on in the centre of her bedroom. She hung her coat on the coat rail, smoothing it in between the dusty pink one she'd purchased from *Missguided* a few months earlier and a long, black coat from Boohoo that she'd cut the hem of so it reached her calves, since it had been way, way too long on her (like no, seriously—it reached the bottom of Elle's feet, and Elle was 5'10.)

In the bathroom, Sabrina peeled off her clothes and chucked them into the empty laundry hamper. After a quick pee, she slid into the shower, letting the steam of the scalding hot water fog up the glass. She lathered her hair with the Vatika shampoo she'd ordered off Amazon a few weeks ago and used it alongside the black seed oil. It had made her hair thicker and shinier, after months of complaining and panicking about going bald.

Twenty five minutes later, she came downstairs, phone in hand, in Musa's Adidas t-shirt and a pair of her sweatpants, to see Veda and Elle singing along to Truth Hurts by Lizzo and busting out some pretty interesting dance moves. She stood in the doorway of the living room, unable to keep the grin off her face, watching as Veda belly danced and Elle showed off her skills from years of doing ballet.

"*You're 'posed to hold me down, but you're holding me back*," they were singing loudly, drowning out the music. "*And that's the sound of me not calling you back.*" Elle pointed a finger at Sabrina, holding her pinky and thumb out with her other hand, laughing.

"*Why men great 'til they gotta be great? Don't text me, tell it straight to my face*," Sabrina joined in, bounding over to the girls, shaking her ass as she danced. Veda whooped, laughing.

Elle picked up the bottle of Absolut lime and took a swig from it, pulling a face, before passing it onto Sabrina. She held it and twirled around, continuing to belt out the lyrics. The drink sloshed around in the clear bottle, the smell strong. She put the bottle to her mouth, guzzling it down, feeling it slide down her throat. Elle and Veda cheered her on, high-fiving, and then the volume of the song increased. Sabrina swallowed, wiping the back of her hand across her mouth, clearing her throat a little, and then passed the bottle to Veda.

"*I put the sing in single, ain't worried 'bout a ring on my finger*," Sabrina and Elle crowed along to Lizzo, as Veda drank. Sabrina lifted her arms, grinding her ass against Elle, who laughed, her hands on Sabrina's hips. Veda burst out laughing and took her phone out, recording the girls dancing together. Elle slapped Sabrina's bum, making her shriek and laugh, dropping down to the floor.

Veda continued laughing, placing the bottle on the floor, beside the sofa. Sabrina crawled towards it and hugged the bottle to her chest, blinking up at Veda and Elle as they continued singing and dancing. A smile made its way onto her face as she leaned back against the sofa, singing along quietly, and then pouring the drink down her throat. Elle grabbed it, spraying some of the drink onto her face, making her shriek, saying "fuck's sake, man," laughing. She stood up too fast and felt her head spin. Her fingers dug into the leather armrest, before she rolled her eyes at Veda blowing her a kiss.

There was a bowl of lightly buttered popcorn on the coffee table. She grabbed a handful as she walked to the kitchen, throwing them into her mouth. Walking around the island, she stopped in front of the sink and turned the tap on, watching the water flood out and into the drain. Sabrina cupped her hands beneath the running water and then splashed it onto her face, letting the cold water drip down.

From the living room, Elle and Veda were still passionately singing along, now to *Supercut* by Lorde. She laughed.

Lifting the bottom of Musa's—well, hers now—t-shirt, she tapped the water off her face. She slowly walked back to the living room, fingertips dancing along the wall as she went. In the living room, Elle was doing Michael Jackson's *Thriller* moves and Elle was doing a failed attempt at tap dancing. Sabrina rolled her eyes again.

"*'Cause in my head, in my head, I do everything right*," Sabrina sang along softly, grabbing onto Veda. They began doing the waltz, laughter in their voices. "*When you call, I'll forgive and not fight. All the moments I play in the dark, wild and fluorescent, come home to my heart.*"

Elle took a large mouthful of the vodka and then tapped the bottle against Sabrina's hip. Sabrina looked at her then down at the bottle, grasping it by the neck of it and held it to her mouth, drinking. She ended up finishing it off completely and tipped it back further, shaking out the last drop.

Sometime between finishing off the vodka and then Veda ordering Chinese food from one of the local takeaways, Sabrina wandered into the kitchen, threw the empty bottle into the bin and opened the bottom cabinet to the left of the washing machine. She moved the extra boxes of Bold 2-in-1 Lavender and Camomile, pulling out the Cabernet Sauvignon bottle Veda had tucked there, out of sight, just in case Sabrina's mother popped round and decided to open up the drawers.

She held it tightly in her hands as she walked back to the living room, where the girls were now sitting on the sofa, the two end seats reclining, which Elle and Veda had taken refuge on. She ran over to the sofa, settling in between the two girls and handed the wine to Elle to open, which she did, rolling her eyes. On the TV, the pilot episode of *The Vampire Diaries* was playing.

"Are we re-watching this?" Sabrina asked, feeling the hum of alcohol pulsing in her.

"Yep," Veda beamed. Sabrina shifted beside her, her movements feeling slower as the vodka rushed through her bloodstream. She had always been a little lightweight, compared to Veda, Elle and Sabah. "It brings back many memories."

"Are you guys Team Stefan or Team Damon?" Elle asked, looking at them.

Veda paused, thinking. Then she said, "Damon."

"Stefan," Sabrina replied. "He's the better guy."

"But Damon and Elena are perfect together—"

"They both deserved better than that selfish, conceited, pathetic bitch. All of her friends died for her, sacrificed everything for her. The town got destroyed because of her."

"Tell us how you *really* feel, Sabrina." Elle said, passing the wine bottle to her after taking a long sip from it.

Sabrina brought the bottle up to her lips, tipping it as she drank deeply, hints of coffee and dark chocolate buried in the wine. It tasted how she thought the devil's blood would be. She held it on her lap, as Elena bumped into Stefan outside the boys' bathroom in the school hallway.

"You gotta admit though," Veda was saying when Elena stuttered over her response to Stefan, finally saying that it was a long story. "Damon and Elena definitely had more chemistry."

"Stefan was the better person," Sabrina said.

"Yeah, but," Elle argued. "Damon did have a massive character development. He became good."

"He was still a bit of a selfish dick. Stefan was still the better brother and he didn't deserve the ending he got. Neither did Bonnie. They all deserved so much better than what they got."

"Are you forgetting Stefan tore Enzo's heart out?" Veda lifted an eyebrow, looking at Sabrina.

"His humanity was off. It wasn't his fault. And he did that to protect two little girls, right? I can't remember. It's been a while since I watched it," Sabrina shrugged, taking another long sip. Veda took the bottle from her and drank. "But either way, Damon did a whole lot worse with his humanity *on*. And *he* did for the hell of it."

"He changed though. Are you saying he wasn't a good person, even after everything?" Veda replied. Sabrina snatched the bottle back after Veda put it on the table in front of them.

"He did change, yeah. But that doesn't mean Stefan deserved to die for him. And people don't change like that, not in real life. Stefan was so much better."

Just as Elle opened her mouth to respond, the doorbell rang. Sabrina gasped a little loudly, and paused the episode right when Matt asked Tyler to tell him he wasn't hooking up with Vicki. She looked at Veda, eyes wide and grabbed the wine, knocking it back, swallowing.

After, when Veda stood up, she whispered, "Who's that?"

"Uh, the delivery guy?" Veda laughed, walking out of the living room.

The front door opened, Veda's voice a quiet murmur, saying *thank you*, with a deep voice responding, and then it shut again. Veda came back into the room, cradling the rustling white bag in her arms as if it was a baby she had to protect.

"*Food*," Elle cheered.

Veda laughed, putting the bag down on the coffee table. She took the containers out of the bag. Sabrina opened one and spying her hot sesame noodles, she grabbed it with both hands, the wine bottle supported by her knees. Veda handed her a fork and she smiled, muttering a quiet thanks as she opened the lid, placing it face up on the table. With the noodles container on her lap, she took up another large mouthful of the wine, and then handed the bottle to Elle.

After sorting through the food they ordered and laying out the appetizers on the table, Veda sat back down on the sofa, huddling in a little closer to Sabrina, who pressed play, making Tyler and Matt resume talking. They ate in silence, watching the show they'd all seen before. A car drove past outside, the music loud and the bass making the floor beneath Sabrina's feet jump. She sighed, twirling the noodles around her fork and brought it to her mouth, her head swimming with the alcohol pumping in her veins. After a while, the car moved on, the music fading quickly, as if it had never been there at all. She kept her focus on Vicki and Jeremy as he asked her what had changed since summer, thinking that she didn't want this moment with her friends to end.

CHAPTER ELEVEN

DANIEL ARRIVED AT exactly thirteen minutes past eight. Upstairs, Sabrina had just slipped on a pair of nude heels from Zara and ran her hands over the skirt of her dress, smoothing out non-existent creases. It was a gorgeous one shouldered, dusty blue wrap dress that reached few inches below her knee, accentuating her curves and bringing out the golden brown shade of her skin. On her ears, she wore diamond studs with gold plating, an eighteenth birthday present from her father, paired with a gold chain, a diamond heart dangling just below her collarbones. She'd gone for the no-makeup-makeup look, opting to use the last few drops of her Luminous Silk Foundation to cover up the fading blemish on the tip of her nose and light brown acne scar on her chin. She was just glad it actually blended in with her skin tone, so it wasn't really all that noticeable even without makeup.

Her hair was pin straight, just about elbow-length

with her arms hanging by her side, neatly parted in the middle. She breathed out slowly, staring at herself in the full-length mirror standing by the right corner of her bed, a white fluffy rug in front of it and an aloe vera plant in a ceramic white pot beside it, sunlight dancing over it from the slanted window. She took a step back, running a hand over her bare arms, just a silver *The Fifth* watch on her left wrist. I look good, she thought, taking one last look at herself, and turned to her bedside table where she grabbed her phone. She unplugged it from the charger and put it into her clutch bag. Meeting Daniel's parents tonight, even though they weren't together or anything, was a huge deal and she kind of, maybe, wanted to make a good impression.

Her leather jacket was thrown over her arm, bag held in her hand, as she walked down the attic stairs, fingers tapping on the banister. She pushed open the door a little more, rolling her eyes as it creaked. She could hear Veda's voice drifting up from the living room, and Daniel's deep voice replying. She swallowed, a flush unfurling in her chest and sweeping its way up to her face.

The middle step creaked a little as she came down, one hand on the banister and one hand clutching her bag against her stomach, filled with butterflies, heart pounding. She was suddenly nervous and she didn't like it. She sucked in a large breath that whistled through her nose, as she walked toward the living room, the stilettos clicking against the linoleum floor of the hallway. In the living room, Daniel was sitting on one end of the sofa and Veda was over by the dining table, leaning against it, smiling. They both looked at her as she walked in, anxiously running a hand over her silky straightened hair. Daniel's eyes marginally widened when he looked at her, rising to his feet. He audibly swallowed.

The grandfather clock on the wall above the sofa, given to them by Veda and Sabah's parents, was ticking away. It was now 8:26 P.M. Sabrina shifted, glancing away from Daniel to Veda, who had straightened up and was smiling wider. "You look good," she said.

"Thanks," Sabrina smiled, breathing out a little loudly. Her heart was still pounding faster in her chest, encased in a dusty blue and grey silk strapless bra.

"Yeah, um—" Daniel started to say, then shook his head. A pale pink flush covered his face. "You look, uh, really . . ." he paused, eyes trailing over Sabrina's body, stopping for a few seconds at the swell of her cleavage and her legs. "Um, you're—ah, god—uh. Wow."

Sabrina felt a breath whoosh out of her, before starting to laugh. His inability to form a coherent sentence at her appearance made her feel relieved. "You look pretty *wow* yourself." And he did, in a pale blue shirt (they really didn't coordinate their outfits beforehand), rolled up to his elbows, revealing his tanned forearms and a silver Rolex on his wrist, and black trousers and black shoes. "We match."

"We do." Daniel's smile was breathtaking as she looked at him. Sabrina blushed and inwardly cursed herself for doing so. Dammit.

"Ok, when you're done making googly eyes at each other," Veda began, voice teasing. Sabrina shot her a warning look, to which she smirked at. "I'd love to have a word with you, Bubbles."

Daniel looked confused. "Bubbles?" he asked.

"*Power Puff Girls,*" Sabrina told him. "I'm Bubbles, Veda's Blossom and Sabah is Buttercup."

He still looked confused. "Uh, ok."

"I'll meet you in the car, yeah?" she laughed, moving toward him, a hand on his arm, fingers stroking the soft, sun-kissed strands of hairs. He smiled at her and leaned down, giving her a quick, gentle kiss on the lips.

Sabrina smiled back at him, her dimples intensifying as he walked to the door. He paused in the doorway, one hand around the edge, looking back at Veda.

"It was lovely to meet you," he said.

Veda nodded. "Nice to meet you too. You live up to what I've heard about you."

He raised his eyebrows in response, opening his mouth to say something. Sabrina spoke before he could ask what she meant, laughing quickly.

"*Ok.* Babe, I'll see you in the car. Veda, what's up?"

Daniel rolled his eyes but left. Once they heard the front door open and then shut again, Veda cracked up laughing, a hand resting on her stomach. She was wearing a mint green kameez with white flowers on it.

"Are you nervous?" Veda asked. Sabrina thought for a moment, then shook her head.

"I was, a little earlier. And then I came downstairs and saw Daniel, and it was just, like, I don't know . . . I wasn't nervous anymore?"

"That's so cute, oh my god."

"Shut *up*," Sabrina said automatically. "No."

Veda opened her mouth to say something, but Sabrina interrupted, shaking her head. "Don't say it. *Do not* say it. *Fuck*. No."

There was a beat of silence. A few cars passed outside, music thumping, and soft chatter as a family walked by their house. Veda just looked at Sabrina, understanding etched across her features. Sabrina looked back at her, an almost pleading look flaring in her eyes. Another beat.

Then, "you should probably get going."

"I know." Sabrina nodded. Sighed. "I hope the food's nice, at least."

"White people hardly ever season their food, so doubtful."

"Thanks for dashing all my hope."

"You're welcome."

Sabrina rolled her eyes, as the two of them walked out into the hallway. "See you tonight?"

"I'll be the one waiting up to hear all about you meeting your boyfriend's parents."

At the front door, Sabrina rolled her eyes, one hand on the doorknob. She didn't bother replying to Veda as she opened it, the sun bright and glaring in the sky, dipping behind the row of houses across.

☼

Shades of pink and purple floated across the sky, turning the world into a dreamlike state. The clouds were feathery and light pink, the sky hovering somewhere in between icy blue and violet. Beyond that, above the towering buildings reaching up to the pink horizon, like a faraway world or perhaps Alice's Wonderland, the clouds creeping across the sky went from lilac to lavender to periwinkle to iris, accompanied by stretches of rose, rouge and strawberry, hints of light grey dancing on the edges, as if unsure. It felt like driving beneath some kind of paradise, the outside noise fading into nothing as the earth was coloured in pink.

Sabrina had leaned out of the window with her phone in her hands, snapping at least ten pictures of the sunset as the colours began to change, the light blue darkening as whispers of the night began to melt into the sky. The pale pink clouds deepened to shades of coral, rosewood glimmering around the borders, hints of orange, passion fruit pink and navy blue extending up slowly. Beside her, Daniel fiddled with the radio, switching from station to station, before sighing, and then, once they were at a red light, went onto Spotify on his phone, held securely in the holder attached to his dashboard. He scrolled through his playlists before settling on one titled *Old Throwbacks*.

The first song to play was *Cry Me A River* by Justin Timberlake.

Instantly, Sabrina and Daniel began singing along. Sabrina, deciding to forgo all the self-conscious thoughts flipping through her mind at record speed, began to dance in her seat in time to the music and sang louder. Daniel laughed, drumming his fingers against the steering wheel, keeping his gaze ahead of him. A message notification popped up across the top of his phone screen, which he ignored, continuing to sing.

The road they were driving down had completely detached houses (well, mansions would probably be the better suited word) lining it, lofty trees standing guard. Sabrina's singing trailed off as she caught sight of a gold gated, pale pink bricked house with three balconies overlooking the street, blinking at it. She turned in her seat to stare at it as Daniel drove past. He looked over at her.

"You ok?"

"Um, yeah," she said absently. "Just these houses . . . wow. I thought *your* place was impressive."

He laughed, almost nervously. A blush stained his cheeks. "*Yeah*, um, my parents are a bit . . ."

". . . wealthy," Sabrina finished for him, meeting his gaze. His blush deepened as he nodded in confirmation, rubbing the back of his neck.

Oops, I Did It Again began playing as Daniel turned left onto Upper Cromwell Street, making Sabrina gasp at the mansions they passed. He looked at her again, bemusement plastered on his face with a hint of nervousness creeping in. He cleared his throat and rested his hand on her knee. Without thinking, Sabrina put her hand over his, squeezing gently. Daniel flipped his over, interlacing their fingers together and squeezed back, his palm warm and comforting against hers.

Two minutes later, Daniel pulled up in front of a classic white stucco fronted house, six large steps leading up to the front door. He parked in the driveway, beside a flaming red Ferrari. Sabrina tried to not let her jaw drop open. She sat, frozen in her seat, staring up at the house towering over almost threateningly.

"Daniel," she whispered. "I don't think I can—"

He cut her off before she could finish her sentence. "*Yes. You can*, my love. My family will love you. You'll be ok."

It wasn't about that, she wanted to tell him. But

185

when she opened her mouth to do so, the words wouldn't come out. She swallowed. Taking her silence as agreement, Daniel opened his door and slid out of the car. Sabrina stayed seated, taking in deep breaths and counting. By the time Daniel had come around the car to her and opened the passenger door, she'd reached seven. She left her leather jacket on the seat she vacated, once stepping out of his car.

"Ready?" he asked, smiling. His hand was on the small of her back. She peered up at him. Even with her heels on, the top of Sabrina's head didn't quite reach Daniel's shoulders.

No, she thought. But instead of saying it, she smiled back at him and nodded.

They walked up the stairs together and Daniel unlocked the front door. The light from the foyer was bright as they walked inside and Sabrina felt her hands go clammy. She curled them into fists, their footfalls echoing in the large hallway. The chandelier was massive when she glanced up at it. The flooring was white marble, decorated with black diamond shapes in a horizontal line across it, and to the left of the foyer were four black pillars, attached to the archway ceiling and the floor. It looked as if it were on a stone coloured marble box from afar, but as they got closer; Sabrina saw it was the supporting foundation of the pillars and not a box at all. They walked through the archway and down the hallway, following the sound of voices talking, laughter floating through the air.

There was a staircase with a beige carpet running up the middle of the steps and when Sabrina looked up, she saw it led up to four floors and there were also steps leading downstairs. On the wall beside the pillar was a canvas of a dark volcano and a bright orange and red sunset, hints of pink threaded throughout. It looked like it was done in watercolours. Sabrina paused in front of it, transfixed. Daniel stood behind her, his arms sliding around her waist.

"You like it?" he murmured softly.

She nodded. "Yeah. I love it, it looks like the sunset is about to leap off the canvas." A laugh, then, "I've always wanted a sunset painting in my room to bring some colour in."

"Thank you. And I'll paint something for you, if you like."

Sabrina shifted, turning around in his arms. "You did that?" He nodded. "It's breathtaking."

Daniel picked her up and she laughed as he kissed her, quickly, once, twice and then again. Smiling. Her hands were on his shoulders when he put her back down on her feet. Footsteps coming towards them broke them apart as Daniel turned and Sabrina automatically slipped her hand into his, suddenly wishing she was anywhere but here.

"Daniel?" a woman's voice inquired. The voice belonged to a tall, blonde woman, her hair styled in a French chignon, lips a soft pink, pearls around her neck and on her ears.

"Hi, mum," Daniel grinned.

Sabrina took in a deep breath and slowly exhaled. The woman's eyes went from Daniel to Sabrina and then back again, a smile spreading across her face. She stepped forward, arms open wide. Behind her, a man with dark blonde, almost brown, hair and a clean-shaven face appeared. His gaze went to Sabrina straight away. She looked at him, as Daniel let go of Sabrina's hand, stepping into his mother's arms. He picked her up, spinning her around, making her laugh loudly. It echoed around the hallway, reaching up to the high ceilings, the sound dancing all around them like faerie dust.

After letting her go, Daniel pulled the man—his father, Sabrina presumed—into a hug, a smile on their faces. Sabrina tucked her hair behind her ear, feeling out of place. But all her thoughts and feelings drifted aside when Daniel's mother wrapped her arms around Sabrina. The scent of her perfume was floral and Sabrina breathed it in, hesitantly lifting her hands and tenderly placing them on her shoulder blades, awkwardly hugging her back.

"Uh, hi," she said, forcing a smile onto her face and hoping it didn't resemble a grimace.

"Hi honey," his mother said. "God, Daniel was right," she said, laughing. She looked over at her son, who was standing beside his father. They were both grinning, looking at her. Sabrina fought the urge to squirm uncomfortably under the heavy weight of their gazes. "You are incredibly beautiful."

"Thank you, Mrs Fitzgerald," Sabrina replied, blushing.

"Oh, don't call me that," she replied, waving a hand in dismissal. "I'd suggest you call me mum, but that might scare you—"

"*Mum*," Daniel cut in, a flush on his face. Sabrina stifled a sigh.

"I'm kidding, I'm *kidding*," his mother laughed. "Call me Steffani, sweetheart. Now come on, are you two hungry? Dinner will be ready in half an hour, but Dorota can provide us with some snacks."

Sabrina looked at Daniel in a panic and he smiled at her, reaching over to cup her face. He kissed her on the forehead and then lowered his hand, caressing her neck and then it drifted down her shoulder and arm and then he slid his fingers through hers.

"Dorota is the housekeeper," he told her.

"Oh," Sabrina said. She looked at Daniel's father, noticing his eyes were still on her. She looked away from him, into the drawing room that they had all walked into. Her breath caught in her throat as she glanced around, taking in the stunning bay windows that led into a garden that looked pretty massive. The flooring was dark wood, glistening beneath the light, and two beige sofas, decorated with bronze and silver cushions, on either end of a mirrored coffee table, all of it sitting on an off white rug. There were two armchairs, one bronze and one cream, on the other end of the table. Seated there were five other people, all insanely gorgeous and obviously rich.

In front of the French windows were two cream coloured chaise lounges, a cushion on each and another mirrored coffee table, on a fuzzy grey rug, between them. A few feet away from the windows, to the left, was a shining black grand piano that made Sabrina feel a little faint. Those things were *pricey*. To the right of the windows, were mahogany double doors, leading into the dining room, she noticed as she took another step further into the sight of the rest of Daniel's family.

She'd seen pictures of his siblings, Caleb and Elizabeth, and his brother-in-law, Edward. But she had no idea who the tall, ebony-haired, brown skinned beauty with blood red lips and impossibly high heels on was. The woman in question was eyeing Sabrina curiously, her gaze dipping down to where Daniel's hand was curled around Sabrina's.

The uncomfortable feeling unravelling inside of Sabrina was the same as the one she'd felt the night before, when Sabah had texted Veda, asking if, on Friday, Sabrina would be home. It had resulted in a moment of silence, the only sound being Damon and Stefan having a conversation in the Salvatore Manor. Veda and Sabrina exchanged looks, because it was the same as the year before when things had shifted in their friendship.

Veda replied to her sister saying no, Sabrina was going to Daniel's parents' house, why, and Elle was resting her head on Sabrina's shoulder. She kept her focus on the screen, not saying anything, even when Veda sighed loudly and picked up the wine bottle from the table and drank. Beside her, Sabrina bit her lip, feeling like she knew what was happening or what would happen, since the same thing had played out the previous April.

"Do you think," she began slowly, hesitantly, unsure of whether to ask or not. "That she's still hung up over it?"

"Wouldn't you be?" Veda simply replied. "If your best friend did that to you? *Oh wait*, Sabah *never* would have done what you did."

An awkward silence followed. Sabrina, of course, knew where Veda stood. The lines were drawn when it came to this, and Veda was on her sister's side. Anyone would be. But the two of them were still friends, and though Veda wasn't happy with what she did, she still stuck by her, something Sabrina didn't deserve. She picked up the popcorn bowl from the table, amidst the empty containers of their finished Chinese food, and grabbed a handful, making it dwindle down to the last few kernels.

A part of her wanted to go back to the April when she'd crossed a boundary, broken the heart of a friend who had been there with her through everything, except when Musa had left. That week, she had decided to walk out too. But she came back, Sabrina told herself. She came back. But. But. But. It wasn't an excuse. None of it was. And Sabrina had used it to test her loyalty in a way she never should have.

And she was still paying for it.

Forty minutes later, they were all in the dining room. The chef (because *of course* they had a chef) had made roast chicken, brown rice, sweet potatoes and steamed vegetables, which Sabrina was trying hard not to devour— she was starving, but obviously, eating the way she usually did at home (all messy and quickly) wouldn't be proper or make a good impression on these rich white people. Not that Caleb's fiancée, the stunning dark-haired woman, dressed to kill in a floor-length, off-the-shoulder black as night evening gown, was white (her name was Maya and she was Filipino.) But she *was* rich, which was evident from her seriously posh accent. Daniel's grandfather, Philip, hadn't said one word to Sabrina in the minutes that had passed, but had watched her as she talked to everyone else, feeling a little more at ease after a few sips of the *delicious* red wine. She was sitting in between Daniel, who was to her right, and Maya, and was talking to her about the upcoming trip with Elle in August.

Maya had studied at a boarding school in France, she told Sabrina, and then went onto Oxford University, where she studied History and then completed her GDL after graduating. She'd also travelled every holiday and had been to, basically, every country Sabrina wanted to visit. Now she was a human rights lawyer. Sabrina was impressed and possibly in love.

Across from her was Elizabeth, who was smiling at something her father, on her right and opposite Daniel, had said. She looked as if she was glowing, a happy flush to her face, blonde hair hanging down her back in loose waves, not a strand out of place. She picked up her glass of water and took a sip, nodding, and then glanced at her husband, on her left. He asked her if she wanted his carrots and she laughed, taking them off his plate.

Sabrina looked away from them to Daniel when he passed her the bowl of sweet potatoes, that his mother had passed to him, telling him to make sure Sabrina had some more. She smiled gratefully and loaded up her plate, carefully reaching over to give the bowl to Edward, when he asked for it. Their fingers briefly met as she handed it to him. She pulled her hand back quickly, almost as if he had sparks of fire shooting out of his fingertips. He lifted an eyebrow at her, amused.

"Thank you, Sabrina," he said.

She flushed, and said a quick "you're welcome," looking away, and sadly, met Philip's gaze.

He had been watching her the entire time and it

creeped her out. She held his eyes, not wanting to be the first to look away.

"I didn't know," he started to say, still keeping his eyes on her. Sabrina wasn't sure if he was addressing her or not. "That you were dating an Indian girl, Daniel." Guess he wasn't.

There was a beat as she processed his words. Fury, white-hot and burning, rolled through her, boiling in her stomach. It coursed through her veins like liquid fire, lighting her cheeks with a deep red flush. Her fingers tightened around the knife and fork in both hands, knuckles going white.

"I am not," she began, voice strangely calm. "Indian."

"No?" Philip asked, a hint of a smirk on his face. That entitled, self-absorbed, conceited, rich *bastard.*

"I'm Bangladeshi."

"Same thing, isn't it?"

Another beat. Steffani let out a heavy sigh, loud in the quiet room. Nobody was moving, daring to eat.

"I can see how you might think so," Sabrina replied. "Considering you invaded our land, malnourished my people, let four million of them starve to death and then split the country, thus causing fifteen million people to be displaced and another million to be killed."

He laughed in reply, as if she said something absurd. "You say that as if I'm directly responsible."

"Aren't you?" she shot back. "The people who are responsible were white. You're white. *Same thing, isn't it?*"

Next to Sabrina, Daniel shifted in his seat, the cream leather squeaking beneath his weight. From her peripheral vision, she could see the bright yellow of the sunflowers in a fiery red vase, arranged prettily on a mirrored table in front of the large bay windows. The white curtains were drawn, covering the garden from view. On the wall opposite the dining table, directly across from Sabrina's line of sight, were five more of Daniel's paintings. There were two on one section of the wall, painted a light grey, whereas the middle of the wall leaning out slightly, was white and had only one painting, and the next section was light grey, with two of his canvases. They were a collection of silhouettes against a twilight sky, mountains in winter and flowers blooming to life. It was incredible. Below the framed canvases, against the grey painted portions of the wall, were tables with square, lit, lamps, highlighting his talent.

In the brief silence that passed, Sabrina wondered what Daniel was thinking. She glanced at him quickly, seeing his eyes were on his grandfather, his jaw tense, a muscle ticking, his nostrils flaring slightly. His left hand was clenched around the stem of his wineglass. She slowly put her fork down and placed her hand over his, her thumb stroking the back of his hand. His hand relaxed under hers, letting go of the glass, his fingers splaying out over the mahogany table. She slipped her fingers through his and he glanced at her, his face softening. He smiled.

Philip looked as if he'd swallowed a lemon. Sabrina raised an eyebrow at him. He narrowed his eyes. "If that's how you feel, then why are you with my grandson?"

Daniel looked back at his grandfather, opening his mouth, his hand now palm-up against Sabrina's, anger darkening his azure coloured eyes.

"*Dad—*" Daniel's father, Blake, hissed.

Sabrina's voice was cool as she responded.

"Because I figured I'd let him colonise my heart the way his ancestors colonised my peoples land."

Silence.

It broke when Caleb, seated on Edward's left, burst out laughing. He smacked the table, the plates and cutlery jumping at the sudden sound and interruption. Slowly, tentatively, everyone else in the room, excluding Maya and Sabrina, joined in the laughter. She kept her eyes on Philip as he chuckled, shaking his head in amusement, the smile on his face not matching the hard look in his eyes.

Later, three hours after the crème brûlée was served, followed by tea and macaroons, Sabrina and Daniel were getting ready to leave. Out in the foyer, Steffani had her arms wrapped around Sabrina's petite body. This time, she didn't hesitate before hugging her back. She liked Steffani.

"I'm sorry about Philip," Steffani had whispered to her earlier, as she showed her around the house. They were on the roof terrace, looking up at the starlit sky. "He's . . . well, I'm afraid I have no excuse for him. I'm just sorry, sweetie."

"Don't be," Sabrina smiled. "You're not the obnoxious, bigoted racist." She didn't bother to mince her words.

She watched as they hit Steffani, keeping an eye on her . . . *friend's* mother's face, saw the eyes widening, mouth parting in surprise and then laughter.

"I like you, Sabrina," Steffani admitted, when they'd headed begun to head back into the warmth. "I'm glad my son found you."

Sabrina didn't say anything. There was a sudden lump in her throat, tears pricking her eyes, as she walked beside Steffani. By the time they got to the drawing room, the tea was ready, the macaroons were on the plates as they all sat around the centre coffee table. She sat next to Daniel, leaning against his body, feeling every solid part of him as she slowly sipped her tea. It had sugar in it, way too sweet. She didn't take sugar in her tea, but she didn't say anything.

Maya and Elizabeth had given her their numbers, promising to have a girls day out soon, to get to know each other better. She'd smiled, saying it sounded nice, the lights making Maya's hair look almost like a shade of deep blue, it was so dark. Lizzie pulled Sabrina into a tight hug before she left, lips curving into a soft smile.

"It was so amazing to meet you, hon. I know we didn't have a proper chance to talk, but we'll definitely do that soon, ok? Just text me whenever you're free and we'll do something."

Sabrina nodded, "sure. Of course. That sounds great."

Now, as Steffani let her go and hugged her son again, Sabrina let herself take another sweep over the house Daniel had grown up in. It was beautiful, painstakingly so, and it cost more than she would ever make in a lifetime. The front door was open, a chilly breeze making goosebumps rise on Sabrina's arms, making her look away from the decor and at Daniel. He pulled a face at her over his mum's head, before a happy smile danced on his lips, eyes crinkling at the corners.

Smiling back at him, Sabrina shivered a little.

Daniel noticed and gently untangled his mother's arms from around him.

He stepped closer to Sabrina, wrapping an arm across her waist. He kissed her on the temple, lips lingering. Sabrina's cheeks heated up when Steffani cooed at them, laughing. Just as she was about to say something, Blake tugged her into his arms, sighing.

"You'll see them both again, love," he said, a glimmer of a smile on his face. "Go on, you two. Daniel, let us know when you're home safe."

"Will do, dad," Daniel said.

"It was a pleasure to meet you, Sabrina," Blake smiled at her.

She smiled back at him, "you too."

They walked to the open door, stepping out onto the first step.

"Bye, love you," Daniel said to his parents as they descended the stairs.

"We love you too, baby," Steffani said on a sigh, leaning her head on her husband's shoulder.

Daniel got out his car keys, unlocking the Porsche. He opened Sabrina's door for her and she slid inside, shivering. She picked up her jacket and put it on as Daniel shut her door. He walked around to the driver's side and got in, the engine purring to life. Beeping the horn twice, he backed out of the driveway.

In the rear view mirror, Sabrina saw his parents still standing outside their house, hands lifted in a wave, watching him drive away. She kept her eyes there, as they got smaller and smaller, until she could no longer see them.

"I'm sorry," Daniel said suddenly, breaking the silence that had fallen over them. "For earlier. My grandfather. I just . . . I am *so* sorry."

Sabrina turned her attention away from the window, looking at him. "Don't be. It's okay. You don't need to apologise, babe."

"I do. It's awful. I'm sorry. I don't know—"

"Daniel, it's okay. Your grandfather is a prick, no offence. I get it. You don't need to say sorry."

This time, he looked at her. He sighed. "No offence taken, my love. Are you ok?"

"Of course," she said. Smiled. Looked away.

She was ok.

Ok.

Ok.

Ok.

Of course she was ok, she said.

Ok. Ok.

But was she really ok?

CHAPTER TWELVE

"I'LL SEE YOU next week," Sabrina said to her colleague, as she walked out of Sainsbury's the following Sunday, sliding her arms through her mint green trench coat. Alana waved at her, smiling, before turning back to stocking the shelves with crisps. Outside, the weather was a little chilly, the sun just about peeking out behind thin wisps of grey clouds. It had rained a little earlier, the pavements still a little glossy from the torrent of water, the car hoods still gleaming with water droplets, dripping down to the windows. Passerby's were wearing jackets or thin coats, because it was the kind of day where the morning was cold and damp with the looming rain, but by mid-afternoon, it was like a heat wave had hit.

Around two-thirty P.M., the rain had begun to pour again, mixing with the blistering hot weather, making the day horrible to step out in. Now it had gotten a little chilly again, as if whatever angel was in control of the weather couldn't make up their mind.

When she stepped out of the shop, tying the coat's belt around her waist, her bag thumping against her as she walked, Daniel looked up from his phone. Sabrina didn't see the smile lighting up his face or the way the blush flooded up from his neck to his cheeks or how he seemed to soften, melt, at the sight of her, his pulse jumping as he ambled towards her, excited, happy. *Excited.*

He stopped in front of her, causing her to blink and look up. She stared at him for a moment, eyes roving over him. A shadow of a smile flitted across her face when she took a slow, measured step, into his arms, inhaling that familiar scent, breathing it in deeply, tiptoeing. His hands were resting on her waist, holding her close to him.

"Hi, Daniel," Sabrina said, tilting her face up to look at him. He kissed her on the forehead and then on her nose and cheeks before kissing her on the lips, smiling.

"Hi, my love," he replied. "Did you miss me?"

She smirked. "No. I saw you on Friday."

"Ouch," he replied, holding a hand over his chest in mock hurt. "You sure know how to wound a guy."

"It's my speciality."

"Really? I thought that was sucking dic—"

"Oi," she laughed, smacking his arm. He grinned at her. She internally swooned. "That's a bit rude."

"True though, no?"

"You're going to have to tell me that, babe. I wouldn't know."

He laughed, throwing an arm around her shoulder as they walked down the street. She looked up at him, her hair blowing around her face with the wind. "I can promise you," he said, smirking wickedly. "You're *amazing*."

"Can't lie, babe, I already knew that. But it's always good hearing it again."

"Oh, so you were just fishing for compliments then, huh?"

"Sorry, not sorry," Sabrina shrugged, laughing.

"You're a heartbreaker, you know that." His question sounded more like a statement than a question and Sabrina felt herself pausing slightly before responding, imperceptibly shaking her head and taking in a deep breath. She forced a smile onto her face, ignoring the flicker of a memory rushing to the surface like driftwood and the broken pieces of a sailboat. Remnants of a time she tried to shove out of her head.

"Tell me something I don't know," she said instead, faking her laughter. It sounded, to her, too close to a sob. He glanced at her and then stopped, pulling her flush against his body, his other hand on her hip.

He dipped his head down, kissing her again. Almost instantly, Sabrina lifted her hand, pressing it against his arm and up around his shoulder. She had to tiptoe, her head tilted back to kiss him properly.

This kiss was soft and sweet all at once, conveying the message neither of them could say, the feelings Sabrina was trying to make herself not feel. Because why would she? She wasn't going to open herself up to getting hurt again.

Around them, the world faded into a blur, noiseless, as if they were the only two in the world. His mouth was velvet soft against hers, gentle in a way she hadn't expected, even though she'd kissed him before. A lot. But it felt like the first time all over again, as they stood in the middle of the pavement, the rush of cars and voices quietening into nothing.

All too soon, Daniel pulled away, just a few inches, their breaths mingling together. The tip of their noses touched, foreheads pressed together. Sabrina closed her eyes again, trying to commit this moment to memory, embedding into her brain so later, when everything went up in smoke, she could remember how good it felt to be in his arms.

They resumed walking to *Fairly Odd Pizzas*, Sabrina wanting to introduce him to the best pizza he'd ever have, and to the lovely family who owned it. As they walked, Sabrina tried to sort out her thoughts, untangling them the best she could in the fifteen minute journey to the best, charming pizza place on earth. When they entered the doors, the fresh scent of pizza and the dough Roberto was kneading hitting stronger, Sabrina breathed it in, taking everything in with all she had, knowing that feelings were fleeting and moments passed by too quickly.

It was weird, how suddenly kind of sad she felt. It sat on her chest like a boulder falling from the top of a hill until it flattened her at the bottom, stealing her breath. She waved a hello at Katherine when she glanced over at her, putting down three plates with individual slices of pizza in front of a family of three by the corner. In the usual spot close to the counter, Kira was sitting with only one of the boys who she said were her best friends.

Sabrina and Daniel sat opposite each other at one of the tables, away from the window. She fiddled with the cutlery placed on the tissue, making the knife and fork knock together as Daniel looked up at the menu on the board above the counter. They were quiet as he thought through what he wanted.

"What do you usually get?" he asked her. She'd moved on from playing with the knife, to pulling out two napkins from the dispenser in the middle of the table and had begun folding them into little squares.

"Um," she looked up at him, before looking back down at the napkin. Her fingers were pressing the folds in, trying to make it as small as possible. "Pepperoni and veggie supreme, usually, or sometimes Hawaiian or there's one with meatballs and pepperoni and peppers, which is really good. I've tried all of them, to be honest."

Daniel looked at her. "You have?"

"Mhm," she confirmed. "This place is, like, my home away from home away from home, you know? I swear, it literally saved me."

"High praise."

"All well deserved," she said seriously. "Get any toppings you want. Trust me. You will *love* it."

"Well, I can't exactly argue with that, can I?" Daniel smirked. "Especially since it's you." Sabrina rolled her eyes at the last comment, ignoring the pang in her chest and the onslaught of memories trying to bring her to her knees.

"Do you want to just try a slice first or get a whole pizza?"

"Um," Daniel looked back at the menu, then at the few slices behind the counter. Grayson appeared from one of the doors, pushing it open further as Ashton came out behind him. They went to the oven when it dinged, sliding out the pizza slices from the tray and transferring it onto crinkly white paper, behind the counter. "I'll try a slice first."

"Sure, babe," Sabrina smiled, looking at Kira when she jumped into Ashton's arms. He twirled around with her latching onto him, arms and legs wrapped around his body like a vice, both of them laughing. *Back to Black* had begun to play softly, filling the restaurant with Amy Winehouse's powerful voice. "What did you want?"

"Uh, I'll get pepperoni," he said, smiling at her.

Sabrina nodded, studying him for a few seconds, unable to stop herself from smiling back. Damn him and his contagious smile and pretty face and gloriously, knee-weakening voice and his—dammit.

She stood up, walking over to the counter where Katherine was now on the phone, a notepad and pen in her hands. "Uh huh," she was saying, the phone held between her ear and shoulder. Sabrina always wondered how people did that. "So one large pepperoni pizza, one large chicken tikka pizza, a box of onion rings twice and sixteen pieces of garlic bread?" Pause. "Mm, ok, that'll be thirty seven pounds."

Roberto looked at her when she approached, a wide grin on his face. "Hey, sweetheart, how are you?"

"I'm pretty good," Sabrina said. "You?"

"Not too bad, not too bad. It's quite busy here these days."

"I'm not surprised," she laughed. "It should be. This place is phenomenal."

His smile widened further. "You're an angel, you know that?"

"No," she laughed again, leaning against the counter. Her eyes went back to Kira and Ashton, who were sitting beside the other blonde guy. Every time she looked at him, something seemed so familiar, as if trying to spark up a forgotten memory or something. She frowned slightly, meeting his eyes. They were a brilliant shade of green, framed by thick golden lashes. Kira glanced over at her, waving. Sabrina waved back, her dimples flashing as she smiled. She looked back at Roberto. "So, uh," she said. "Can I get one pepperoni slice and one shrimp pesto slice, please?"

"Of course, sweetheart," Roberto said.

Kira glided over to Sabrina. "Hey, you!"

"Hi," Sabrina laughed. She felt surprise jolt through her when Kira pulled her into a tight hug. They were both the same height. Kira's hair smelt like strawberries.

"So," Kira said. "How are you? And who's that hottie you're with?"

"I'm good. And um, that's Daniel," Sabrina said slowly, cocking her head to the side as she looked at Kira, who had turned to glance over at Daniel. A feeling that was too close to jealousy was hissing inside her.

Kira looked back at her, arching an eyebrow. "Boyfriend?" she whispered, leaning in closer.

They both looked back at Daniel. He was on his phone, not paying attention to the two girls staring at him. One curious and one conflicted.

"Uh," Sabrina said. She swallowed, hard. "No."

"Why not?" Katherine asked her, making her jump. She hadn't given realised Katherine was listening.

Sabrina paused before answering. "Just. We're, um,

friends, I guess."

"You guess?" Kira laughed. "What does that even mean?"

"I have," Sabrina blew out a sigh. "No idea."

"Well," Katherine pitched in. "If you ask me, I think the two of you would make a lovely couple. Don't you think, Rob?" Her husband looked at her, then at Sabrina, before taking a long look at Daniel. He nodded, agreeing.

"Yep. Sabrina, you best snatch him up quick. He's a handsome young man. There'll *definitely* be long lines of girls wanting him." A laugh. "Why aren't you two together?" A quizzical look.

Sabrina shrugged, taking the two plastic plates, the corner of the wax paper brushing over her thumb. She ignored the stab of jealousy in her chest and smiled at Roberto. "Thanks."

"Let us know what he thinks."

"You can ask him yourself," Sabrina replied, laughing.

"Who's the guy?" Grayson asked her, coming over to stand beside his stepdad after adjusting the heat of the oven.

She bit her lip, tucking her hair behind her ear. "Uh, that's Daniel. He's my . . . uh, we're . . . *friends*." Grayson raised an eyebrow at her floundering, a smirk glossing his lips. She flashed a quick, fleeting smile at him, lifting the plates up a little higher. "I'll, uh, catch up with you in a bit. He's, uh, kinda hungry, so I'll just . . . um, go, ah, take these for us."

Grayson laughed, not saying anything. Kira

disguised her laugh as a cough and went to her table.

Sabrina slowly made her way back to Daniel, putting the plate in front of him, grinning. "Sorry about that. I know I took a while."

"Don't worry about it." He put his phone down. Smiled at her. "I'm now ready to be blown away."

"You weren't kidding," Daniel was saying, around a mouthful of his third slice. They'd ended up getting an entire pizza halfway through their first slice, after he'd exclaimed that it was the *best fucking pizza* he ever had and he *definitely* needed more than just the one slice. "Thish ish sho," he swallowed the bite. "*Good.* Fucking fantastic. Glorious. Amazing."

Sabrina allowed a small smile to inch up her face as she watched him dig in, taking a large bite of her slice. Half of it was pepperoni with extra cheese and the other half was mushrooms and spicy sausage, and boy, it was *good*.

"I'm glad you like it," she said.

"Like it? I fucking *love* it."

She laughed. "Good. I would've had to block you on everything if you didn't."

"Oh, really?" Daniel inquired, taking a swig from the coke bottle, looking at her. "I don't think you even have it in you to block me."

"You think too highly of yourself," Sabrina snorted.

Daniel rolled his eyes, smiling while he started on his fourth slice, taking a giant bite from it. There was tomato sauce on his chin now and Sabrina fought the urge to lick it off. Instead, she grabbed a napkin and leaned over the table, wiping it off. "See," he said now. "You love me."

"I do not."

"But you do. You're just in denial."

Now it was Sabrina who rolled her eyes. Her phone buzzed with a text from her brother and she looked at it, eyes widening. She ended up choking on her bite of pizza, a hand over her mouth. Daniel looked concerned. "Oh fuck," she croaked and quickly drank slurped down the ice cold water in her glass.

Bhaiya <3 at 17:26: *I told mum and dad about Rose. They want to meet her.*

Sabrina at 17:27: *holy fuuuuuuuuuuuuuuuuuuuuuck, what did they say? when r they meeting her? where? do tana & i need to be there too? bro. fucking.. wow wow wow!!*

"Is everything ok?" Daniel asked.

"Hmm? Oh, yeah," Sabrina looked up at him briefly. "Yeah. My brother's just told our parents about his girlfriend. They want to meet her."

Tana ♥∞ at 17:32: *Omg! Bhaiya what happened? What did they say??????*

Sabrina at 17:32: *BHAIYA WHERE TF R U?*

Bhaiya at 17:34: *Relax, I'm with Rose now. They were pretty calm about it tbh. Just said as long as she's Muslim and Miriam and Leanne like her, then its ok. I told them her mum and Daisy are Muslim too, so we're all going to have dinner together Friday night at mine. Yeah you two have to be there – its a family thing. I'm excited, man. I want to marry this woman.*

Sabrina at 17:35: *brb im gna go cry omg*

"Sorry," Sabrina said to Daniel, unable to stop smiling. "There's just . . . oh my god. So we're having a family dinner kind of thing on Friday night, apparently, with Rose and her mum and sister. Oh my god. I'm so fucking excited, Daniel. My brother, he's just—he really, uh, deserves this, you know? He's the most amazing person I know and god, it's just so wonderful. I'm kind of surprised that," she paused, taking in a deep breath and then another sip of water. "My parents were so accepting of it, considering she's not Asian or anything. But then again, I guess it's because he's a guy. And men in our culture can do whatever the hell they want or be with whoever they choose."

"What? So you can't be with someone that isn't from Bangladesh?"

"I can," Sabrina replied. "But my parents will probably have a heart attack or a stroke after finding out that I want to, uh, marry someone that's a different race. They'll probably end up kicking me out or some shit. I don't know." Daniel stared at her, surprised. "It's just, um . . . in the Desi culture, most of the time, girls have to sacrifice everything for the sake of their family, you know? Like, brown girls end up having to decide between leaving their families just to have some kind of freedom or compromising and sacrificing their happiness to conciliate their families instead and protect their honour and reputation."

She sighed, chewing on the last bite of her pizza, and then the crust. "It's always the same thing and it sucks."

As Daniel thought over her words, left in the space

between them, Sabrina looked around. In the time they'd been here, the family of three had left, there had been more orders placed, which Ashton had gone out to deliver, and a group of teens had come and gone, talking loudly and laughing, smelling of alcohol, a faded sticker on the back of their hands.

Grayson was now getting out two pepperoni pizzas and putting them into a large box. His mother shoved some jalapeño poppers into a paper bag, poured some salad into a plastic container and put them into the large black bag on top of a three legged wooden stool behind the counter. Roberto had popped out to the local supermarket to get some more green peppers and extra ingredients (and a packet of cigarettes.)

The atmosphere in *Fairly Odd Pizzas* was soothing to Sabrina as she picked up her last slice of pizza, delicately biting into it. Daniel was watching her, an unfathomable expression on his face. She met his eyes, staying silent. Letting him be the first to speak.

"I, um," he said, then sighed. He looked away from her, and then picked up his slice. He stared it for a bit then dropped it onto his plate, the checked wax paper half on the table. "That's really shitty," Daniel finally said.

A wry smile tugged on her lips. She shifted on her seat. "Yeah, it is."

"Isn't there any way you can . . ." he frowned, a dip forming on his forehead as his gauzy, golden eyebrows slashed down. "I don't know, um, maybe talk to your parents? Or just—"

"No," Sabrina interrupted. "They're set in their ways. They won't change. Sometimes no matter how hard you try to explain something to someone, try to get your point across or get them to understand things from your side, they will never understand. Or if they do, they won't care. Sometimes people just don't change, no matter how much you may want them to. And it's disappointing. It hurts, a lot. But it just . . . it is what it is."

Daniel's frown deepened. "But," he began. "That's not right, or fair to you."

"The world isn't fair."

An hour and a half later, Daniel had paid for their meal, telling Roberto, when asked how it was, that the pizza was beyond his expectations and tasted, honest to god, like how he imagined heaven would be, and now he'd always be coming here for pizza, because, Jesus Christ, it was the best he'd ever had. After he was done waxing lyrical about the pizza, handing over a ten pound note and some change, even though Sabrina told him to let her pay and he glared at her and said *no fucking way, you're not paying*, Roberto laughed and looked at Sabrina, raising an eyebrow. His look *clearly* said: *you need to marry this guy before someone else does*, and Sabrina flushed, her hands, that she'd washed after finishing her food in the cute little bathroom with cream tiling on the floors and turquoise and white tiled walls, flew up to her hair, braiding it.

When they went outside, hand-in-hand, Sabrina didn't dare to look back at Roberto or Katherine or Grayson or Kira, who she knew would all be smirking and giving her pointed looks. Her cheeks were blazing pink and the cold air felt welcome on her heated face, the darkening clouds rumbling overhead. Daniel was looking at his phone, frowning again, a look that could only be described as pissed off on his face.

"Everything ok, babe?" Sabrina asked.

"My, uh," Daniel swallowed. Sabrina's curiosity peaked. "My ex messaged me."

Sabrina tensed, her hand tightening around his. She felt his eyes boring into the side of her face and she unclenched her jaw, taking in a deep breath, because why the fuck was she suddenly feeling jealous? It's not as if she even *liked* him like that, for Christ's sake. "Oh?" she said, her voice high-pitched.

"I haven't spoken to her in months," he quickly assured her. "Really. I just, uh, well . . . it's just that, uh, we have a few mutual friends and it's Mason's wedding in July, so, um, we're all planning to throw a little dinner party with all of our mates and obviously she's going to be there." He took in a deep breath. Sabrina didn't say anything. "Um, but yeah, Gianna messaged me, I don't know—we're, um, in a group chat together but I don't have her number saved or anything. I promise."

"Ok," Sabrina said after a while. She loosened her grip around Daniel's hand, brushing her hair out of her eyes. "Um, who's Mason?"

"My best friend," Daniel told her. "We've known each other since we were little. Our parents studied together. I'm actually his best man."

"That's cute," she pushed away the green monster peeking out from buried rubble. The earlier grin had long since slipped off her face, replaced by confusion and an annoying sense of *what the fuck is going on.*

"Are you mad?"

She felt him look at her again as they walked to the

station, where they would part ways, since they both had work in the morning and she needed to prep for her interview with the Volunteer Recruiter at the Citizens Advice Bureau, which was during her lunch break. "No," she said softly. It was the truth: she wasn't mad. She was just a little annoyed. At herself, at him, at her parents, at the world. Because it seemed like, no matter how hard she tried, all her efforts to not *feel* things were futile, and here she was, *feeling things* for a man she had no intention of getting into an actual relationship with. It was a funny joke, but she wasn't laughing.

CHAPTER THIRTEEN

THE HOUSE PHONE was dangling in Sabrina's hand as she walked into the living room where her mother was praying taraweeh.

"Amma," Sabrina said, taking a step further into the living room. Her mother had lifted her index finger, palms just a few inches above her knees as she sat on the prayer mat, eyes focused on the image of the kaaba. "Um, amma namaazo ekhon," she said to Nasrin bhabi, her cousin's wife on her father's side. She leaned against the armrest of the sofa, listening to Nasrin ask her about how Ramadan was going now and how she was spending the last ten days of it and if she'd completed the Qurān yet. "No," Sabrina said. "Not yet."

Religion, to her, was questioning the existence of heaven and hell, and how could hell be damned when most of its inhabitants would apparently be women, because weren't women given the highest honour? Women were magical and beautiful and everything holy, when men were the opposite and dark and twisted and monstrous and cruel, viciously so. Just look at her father.

Almost hating him came easily to her, it was a bitter feeling that tasted like blood in her mouth, like she was choking on the memories of hands pummelling the soft, loving chest of her mother. It hurt her just as much, realising that her mum would never leave the man who brought his daughters up to fear him just as much as they loved him. The hate and love were something tangible, raw and cold, heavy like ancient archangel wings, beating her down when she tried to cut herself away.

But hating one's parent was a one way ticket to hell, travelling past the river of fire and lament, wishing something could be different. But it never was and never would be.

As her bhabi started talking again, Ruksana turned her face to her right shoulder and then her left and Sabrina interrupted Nasrin asking about whether she'd gotten her Eid clothes. "Amma ekhon salam disoyn," she said, practically flying over to her mum to hand her the phone, once she'd finished her prayer.

Her mum looked at her and laughed, shaking her head. "Khoyteh salam firaysoin. Disoyn na, there's nobody here to salam. Erdai khoyteh salam firaysoin."

"Oh." Sabrina shrugged and then walked out of the living room as her mother began talking to Nasrin, saying *wa'alaikum asalaam wa rahmatullahi wa'barakatuhu.*

She went upstairs to her old room, where she'd been watching *Gossip Girl* with Sultana, digging into their individual tubs of Häagen Dasz ice cream. It was Friday night, after the iftar dinner with Rose and her family, the nikkah date being set to the following August and the wedding party/reception/whatever it was supposed to be called on the twenty-sixth of October. Sabrina's parents had gifted Rose with a gorgeous princess-cut ruby and diamond triple halo ring and a gold bracelet, welcoming her into the family.

The engagement was celebrated with the cutting of a cake Sultana had ordered from *The Cake Shoppe*, a delicious red velvet and butter cream cake; because they all had known Adam and Rose would be getting married, regardless of what their parents said. This was how things happened in their culture: getting engaged first and then *maybe* a proposal would follow suit.

"What colour," Sultana was asking, as she dug further into the ice cream tub, watching Chuck tell Blair that being amicable wasn't in their blood and that they weren't friends, right before they had intense hate sex. "Do you think we should wear to the wedding?"

Thinking about the wedding meant thinking about the future which meant thinking about her *own* future after her brother's third or something Big Day, something that frightened her because it meant her parents deciding to find suitable suitors for her. It made her lie awake at night, fear electrifying every nerve in her body, the kind that she could write novels or poems about, immortalising it forever, in a way she would never be. It meant finally stepping out of her second life, away from the handsome men, reckless infused alcohol, dreaming freely about leaving and breathing and being. Alive. It meant giving it up. Because one day, she would have to give it all up.

It was a miracle that she even got out when she did, into another house, but still, always, trapped under the suffocating weight of their expectations and honour resting on her shoulders, taking hold of her fervour for a life out of *their* lives and yanking it bloody and airtight around her throat like a noose. Like she wasn't a person, but a daughter, meaning an object, meaning a pet, meaning a thing to control, meaning shouldering the burden of bearing the family's name, like a crown on her head. But the weight of the crown, infested with garnets for each drop of blood pumping through the body she was told to be ashamed of, threw her to the ground as a child, taught to make herself small, small, small.

So she was seen and not heard.

Because she wasn't supposed to be anything more than what she was told to be or expected to be. Because she was a girl and even if she became a doctor, even if she crossed the seas and travelled the earth twice over, she was expected to give it all up for the man who would claim her as his, marking her with mottled bruises the size of his hands, colouring the night sky into her body, blue-black marring the gold and brown of her soft flesh. A caged animal, born in captivity.

This was how the world worked, this was how her family worked: taking every hopeful thing and handing it to their girls, just a bit, just enough to make them think their prayers had been answered by a merciful god that damned them to an eternity in hellfire, doused in gasoline and the heated licks of an orange flame, charring their skin and bone until there was nothing left but ash. So this was why

Sabrina wistfully dreamed of going back to the days when she didn't have to worry or fear or stress about marrying some man she didn't know, because the man she did know had left her and it was his hand that she wanted to hold for the rest of her life, because his hands fit hers perfectly. Like they were made for each other.

He changed her and ruined her for all other men and even when she didn't want to, she thought about him and cried; he was the only one who could have saved her from the prison that was her home, with her father as judge, jury and executioner. But she should've known relying on a man to save her from a man was a wasted wish. He never would have excavated from her the melted-down broken mess of the girl she was.

And so she still was that girl. Burying herself in whatever she could find, because it was all she could do to not scream or crumble or quake or break under the load of everything resting on her shoulders, not just the world, but the entire galaxy, shooting stars and comets too, shattering apart and turning to ash around her and inside her mouth and cracking her chest wide open, clean down the middle, like cleaving the chest of a bleeding carcass.

On the day Sabrina decided to tell her parents that she was moving out and had found a place just twenty-odd minutes away by bus, she had just come back from a long day at university. There had been an in-class test that she was terrified she was going to fail, badly (she didn't—she got a ninety-seven percent), and so she was already in a sour mood, the sunlight bouncing off of her body as she walked, slowly, down the street to her dad's house. The sun lit her up like some kind of celestial hell-angel, shades of gold dancing across the brown of her skin, breathing life into her even when she felt like dying.

Unlocking the door felt like being asphyxiated by anxiety, paralysing and a car crash in her chest, sending blood and guts and body parts sliding across the roads, body sluiced with cold sweat, her dress sticking to her like second skin. Her throat was damp with beads of sweat beneath the wrap of her hijab, another noose around her neck.

Her parents were in the living room watching the five o'clock news and, for the first time in weeks, not arguing. The peaceful quiet between them was louder than the screaming and surprising.

Sultana was in the kitchen, doing her homework. She looked up when she saw Sabrina in the hallway, frozen and scared, trying to breathe past the lodge in her throat. It felt like drowning on land, with the water in her lungs and gasping for air.

"Are you ok?" Sultana asked, abandoning her Biology homework and coming to stand in front of Sabrina, who blinked at her. She lifted a hand to unwrap her hijab and then held the pin between her fingers.

"Um," she said. "Yeah. I think so. Uh, I'm gonna . . . tell them that I'm, uh, moving out." She swallowed. "Today. Now."

"Oh," Sultana said. She bit her lip. "Good luck."

"Thanks." Forcing a smile onto her face, Sabrina sighed and made her way into the living room. She stood in the doorway for a moment, watching her parents as they sat on the dark brown sofa, watching the news. The reporter was wearing a white sari with a red border, her hair jet black and pulled into a tight bun, eyes lined with dark eyeliner and lips a bright red. Sabrina's mum was wearing a cornflower blue meski, hair in a low bun, strands framing her bright, pale face, the kind of white glow that made the moon jealous, her lips full and pouty and the kind of pink shade that only fairytale princesses had, cheekbones sharp enough to cut a diamond, a terrible and heartbreaking sadness lingering in her eyes that Sabrina couldn't see from this angle. But she saw it, every day, after her dad gave her reasons to hate him more, but she hated herself for wanting to hate him, for daring to hate him even a little, for loving him, despite everything he put her mother through. He was sitting on the other end of the sofa. They never sat next to each other. He was wearing a white vest and a royal blue checked longi, what little hair he had was silver, beard white, kind of like Santa Claus, if Santa was a Bangladeshi man. Where Ruksana was fair and pale-skinned, Mohammed was dark as an oil slick, a face clear of any marks or scars or bruises or wrinkles, except for laugh lines. Because as angry as he was, her father was a man of the people and though he terrified everybody, he was the one they all came to when in need, whether it was advice or money or maybe someone who knew someone who knew someone that could maybe be a potential spouse for their son, for their daughter. Her father knew everything and her father knew everyone.

So that was what made this a little bit harder. Knowing that him knowing everyone meant it being brought up as an argument to silence her, to take away her freedom or her choices, like countless times before. *Manushe kita khoyba? What would people say?*

"Amma," Sabrina said, voice soft. "Abba."

She didn't know how they heard her but they did. They both turned to look at her, now a step further into the living room.

"Kita hoise tor?" her mother asked.

"Um," she took in a deep breath, her heart hammering in her chest. She felt gross with the sweat rolling down her spine. "I'm moving out," she said in English. At her father's raised eyebrow, she switched to Bangla. "Ami, uh, ghor ekhta faisi, bish minute away ontaki. Bhai dekhsoyn ghor, tanoro bala lagseh. Naveda ar Sabah logeh roymu, ar amra bed shobta loya harsi. Sayta room aseh, ar attic ekhta, ar garden."

"What?" her mother said. When Sabrina didn't respond, she stood up. "What?" she said again, louder this time. Her dad rose to his feet, suddenly seeming larger, bigger, towering over her, even though she was a safe distance away.

Fear pulsed through her, but she lifted her chin up slightly. "I'm moving out," she repeated. "We've already bought the furniture for our rooms and the living room. Everything in the kitchen is already provided."

"No," her father said. Just that one word. *No.* As if it was final. And to him, it was. What he said went. Always. No questions asked.

"Yes," Sabrina replied, squaring her shoulders, meeting her dad's eyes. "I am. Everything's done. Adam's helped me as well. I don't care what you say. It's done. *Khalas.*"

"Shuworor baicha," her dad suddenly shouted, making her jump. Movement behind her made her turn slightly, seeing Sultana come in to the living room. She smiled at her, grateful to have an ally. "Tui mono khoros—" he stopped, glaring. "You dare think you can move out? Without our permission? Without asking me? How dare you even—what makes you think we'll let you?"

"I'm not asking you, abba," Sabrina said gently. "I'm telling you. Regardless of what you say, I am moving out. I can't stay in the same house for another five or however many years it takes until I get married. I need my own independence and freedom—"

"You are a child," Ruksana hissed. "What do you know about independence?"

"That's my point. I need to learn. And I won't, if you keep me here. I need to be able to make mistakes and learn from them, and do things my way. I need to grow. I can't do that stuck here, in the same house, for the rest of my life."

"Khobisor suda, amra manush reh kita khoytam? Muk dekhaytam fartam nai!"

"That's not my problem. And you're acting as if it's the end of the world. It doesn't really—"

"—you never think," her mother said, pointing at her head. "With your brain. About how your decisions will affect other people. Allāh gave you a brain but you do not use it. Idiot. Besharam. Behaya ghoror behaya. Tor baafor naam noshto khorteh saas khali. Oto boro khanki oileh, khoy taki?"

"That's a bit rude," Sabrina muttered. "I'm not a whore."

"If you leave, that is exactly what you are." Sabrina rolled her eyes, stifling a sigh. "People will think—"

222

"*People* don't need to know anything, amma. They're not going into the graves with us when we die. You're acting like—" she was cut off by a loud, resonating slap. She stared at her father, a hand clutching her cheek, hurt but not surprised. Her face was burning, mortification flooding her red, anger curdling inside of her like rotting milk. To stop herself from saying anything else, she bit her tongue, hard enough to draw blood.

There was a beat of silence.

Sultana stood beside her, a hand on her back, a reminder that she was there. An ally, a friend, a sister.

Her father started shouting, spewing ugly, terrible words at her, face angry and twisted and horrible, spittle flying as he raged and seethed and yelled. He moved to hit her again, and when Sultana tried to stop him, he shoved her aside. His hand went flying across Sabrina's face, making her stumble and fall. She blinked up at him, anger giving way to wrath, hissing and swirling and swimming and roaring inside of her, wanting to explode and shatter and break and destroy.

In that moment, she felt like a half wild thing, a wolf trapped in sheep's clothing, bloody and hungry and aching for release, to take every hateful, angry thing inside of her and let it drag and drown her family's fucking izzat into boundless bodies of water. She slowly stood up, jaw clenched, fists clenched and ignored her parents raging after her as she stormed upstairs.

Her vision went red, the devil walking beside her now, laughing as she threw clothes and books into bags and boxes she'd collected over the past few months. It was always the same thing. They would never let her breathe for as long as she lived under their roof. Even when she moved to another house, they continued to watch her, continued to make sure she followed their rules, forcing her to shed her skin once she was out of their sight and step into the shadows of another life. Where the moon bore witness to her sins and her limited freedom, where she lied and smirked and drank to escape, just a little.

She was walking in a fleeting moment of liberty, one that would squander into nothing, as if it never existed, the moment she married a man her parents chose for her. So yeah, the future terrified her and she wasn't thinking about that now or ever.

"I'm thinking," Sultana said now, after finishing off the last of her Cookies and Cream flavoured tub. "We should go for, like, a bright colour, you know? Everyone's already done the nudes and greys."

Sabrina rushed back to present-day, where her parents had, somewhat, made peace with her leaving their house, not a home, a little over a year later, and looked at her little sister. "There's still time to decide, man. But yeah, those colours are way overdone now."

She put a large spoonful of Häagen Dasz's Strawberry Cheesecake into her mouth, giving herself brain freeze in the process. On screen, Colin was telling Serena he didn't care about being a teacher; he cared about being with her, while Dan creepily watched.

Sultana threw her empty tub into the bin and leaned down, opening the bottom drawer of Sabrina's old bedside table. She grabbed the box of brownies from *Tesco* they'd stashed there earlier that day, in anticipation of a *Gossip Girl* marathon.

"Want one?" she asked Sabrina.

Looking away from Sultana's laptop, Sabrina nodded and reached into the box. She bit into it, letting the taste of the gooey chocolate melting in her mouth take away the bitter, resentful thoughts running through her mind. Because when nothing else helped, chocolate brownies always did.

CHAPTER FOURTEEN

ON EID, Sabrina was upstairs in Amina khala's house, having just finished watching *Ek Ladki Ko Dekha Toh Aisa Lageh* on Netflix with her sister and her cousins' daughters. Some time after the credits had rolled and the sun had set, casting a gold glow over the earth, sending glittering rays splintering through the windows, Nafisa and Fahmida had wandered into Amanee's room and were now interrogating them about why they'd watch a movie featuring a gay female lead, because it was "disgusting, sinful and an embarrassment".

Sabrina fought the urge to roll her eyes, as she stretched across the bed to grab a keema samosa from the plate. "Why wouldn't we?" she asked around a mouthful of pastry, keema and aloo.

"Homosexuality is haram, Sabrina. You know that." Fahmida's voice was firm, a wary look on her face. Beside her, Nafisa sighed, shaking her head.

"You shouldn't watch things like that. It only promotes—"

"Ok, A," Sabrina interrupted, pointing her index finger at her cousins like an accusation. "Being gay *isn't* haram. Only acting on it is, which is a bit dumb because it's not like anybody can control their feelings or who they're attracted to. And B, what exactly is your point?"

"You need to watch the way you speak to people," Nafisa warned. There was a look on her face that Sabrina recognised, from having seen it on her mother every day for twenty one years. "And our point is that films like that glamorise gayness and we're supposed to stay away from things that support sin. It's haram for a reason. You shouldn't even be encouraging them to watch it at all."

Sabrina laughed, "Ok so I'm not *encouraging* them to do anything. I'm just telling them to watch a fucking movie, because it is good and raw and emotional. And since you're so passionate about them not watching a movie about a gay main character . . ." She paused. "Why don't you have that same attitude to shows and movies with premarital relationships and sex? Bit of a joke. Wagwun with the double standards?"

Sultana spluttered with laughter, her hand over her mouth. Amanee was smirking and watching her aunts for their reactions whilst Tasnia busied herself with scrolling through Instagram. Sabrina's words were met with an annoyed look from Fahmida, who, just as she opened her mouth to reply, was called by Rebecca, wanting to go to the toilet.

Every single Eid, for as long as she could remember, was spent at her aunt's house. Her older brother was lucky to be able to get out of it once he'd gotten married and had kids, so for the past few years and today, he had spent the morning across the road at his parents' house with his daughters in tow, and then taken them to Rose's place. Sabrina would've preferred that. But no. Tradition was tradition and she couldn't break it now.

She did, however, make plans for later with Daniel. He was coming over to hers for the pilau, tandoori, lamb chops curry and strawberry cheesecake she'd made the previous night, everything put in the fridge. Veda had gone to her parents' house for the next few days and she had no idea where Sabah was, whether she was at Jake's or her parents', because they weren't talking. The few texts Sabrina had sent went unanswered, making her grit her teeth annoyance and then altogether give up on trying to be the one to constantly patch things up. Because whatever. Fuck it.

It wasn't like she didn't miss having her best friend, because god, she really did. There were few things that only Sabah would get, things that only she would laugh at, and there was nobody to constantly send memes to on Twitter, so that royally pissed Sabrina off. But she would be mature about this and not give a shit. Because she didn't. Give a shit, that is.

She was twenty one now and would, hopefully, be acting like it. A few days ago, the day before her birthday, she'd gone to see *Aladdin the Musical* with Daniel, looking like a fucking goddess in her silk and gemstone white dress, a gorgeous beaded and pearled white blazer from the Instagram brand, *Khanum's*, the heels that made her legs look like they went on forever and subtle shimmery gold eye shadow across her lids paired with bright, blood red lipstick. Daniel's jaw had dropped open when he saw her, as he waited outside the black stretch limo he'd hired (like, who the fuck even does that anyway?), unable to keep his eyes off of her.

When, after they had dinner in this swanky, uber rich people restaurant where the portions were ridiculously small for the price (but oh so delicious, and god, the *wine*!), he took her to the boat he'd hired out on the Thames, as the sun was beginning to set and the sky was a rage of pinks and oranges and reds, as if it was on fire, Sabrina felt a little guilty for thinking he was being, like, a pretentious prick and throwing around his wealth. Her heart had been in her throat the entire time as they rode across the river, listening to the violinist, on the boat with them. The whole scene was straight out of a fairytale and brought tears to her eyes.

"Do you like it?" Daniel asked her, nervousness a flame in his crystalline eyes. Sabrina swallowed, blinking furiously so she didn't do something embarrassing like cry in front of him.

She nodded, unable to speak. This moment reminded her of *Tangled*, when Rapunzel and Flynn were rowing on the boat and the flying lanterns were glowing in the sky, lighting everything up with its gold, like a million wishes and dreams answered, falling around them like magic or fairy dust, was her favourite. She'd been watching it with Musa one day in the hotel he booked, after making love and fucking and kissing for a few hours and then ordering from *Burger Bros*, digging into their massive burgers and dipping their curly fries into mayonnaise and ketchup and chilli sauce. She couldn't watch it anymore without thinking about him and hating how everything had changed. A few tears cascaded down her cheeks, shining as the gold from the lights floated above her head. "I do," Sabrina whispered, tilting her head back to watch the sky, where a myriad of fireworks were exploding, as if they were phoenixes reborn from ashes, kissed to life by the pulp-free, velvet of twilight.

"Daniel, I love it so much."

"Yeah?" his entire face lit up.

"Yeah, babe. It's . . . you didn't have to go to all this trouble. At all. God, it must've cost a bloody fortune."

He shook his head. "No, don't worry about that. It's your twenty first. You have to enjoy that, you know? It's a milestone age."

Sabrina surreptitiously wiped away her tears, turning her face away from him. There were a few other boats out; people looking up at the gift Daniel had gotten her, videoing it all. She felt a blossoming of something in her chest, warm and glowy and scary all at once. The kind of feeling made it hard to look him in the eye and not blush and not realise it was *so much more*. Because it was starting to feel like *everything*. "I appreciate it," she said softly. "So much. You have no idea. God, this . . . it, everything, all this," Sabrina waved her hand out, encompassing the glorious white boat they were on, the champagne in a bucket of ice that they were drinking from, the bright glow from the lights strung around it, like magic and fire and faeries and fireflies and everything beautiful. "It's so much and means the world to me."

"You mean the world to me."

There was a lull between them as his words reached her, shimmering all around her like shards of glittering glass, and she inhaled sharply, eyes wide as she looked at him. Sabrina opened her mouth to respond, to say something, and then closed it. What could she say?

"I . . ." she breathed out, slowly. Her hair danced with her breath, golden strands flickering around her face. "You mean a lot to me, too, Daniel."

She'd learned a lot about him in the time they'd spent together, like he was the kind of person who couldn't hold anything back once he'd gotten comfortable with someone and that he cared a lot about his students. He was confident that Bailey, his favourite student, would get into Rhode Island School of Design, which was her number one choice. In the days between them going to *Fairly Odd Pizzas* and the eve of her birthday, Daniel had told her about Gianna and their kind of messy break up. It turned out they'd been together for three years and she was cheating on him for one of those, with some guy she met whilst holidaying in Greece.

Daniel told her the one thing he could never forgive or condone was cheating, the hurt it caused left a gaping hole that no amount of time could ease or fill or heal. He no longer had any feelings for Gianna, he'd sworn, but the hurt was always there, leaving him wondering where he went wrong. When Daniel loved, Sabrina realised, he loved with his entire being, it was all or nothing for him.

And it was why, Sabrina thought the next day, on her birthday, she would need to create a distance between them. She would need to take a few steps back and bring up the topic of their relationship or whatever this was, because it was starting to get a little bit too confusing. She was thinking about all this whilst cutting the giant, two tier floral birthday cake her brother brought over from *The Cake Shoppe*, edible glitter and flowers cascading down like a waterfall. Her parents were standing on either side of as Rose snapped picture after picture, memorialising the moment, as Adam had videoed her slicing the knife down the Victoria sponge cake with butter cream and raspberry filling.

For iftar that evening, her mum had made keema pilau, samosa chaat, roast chicken and issa bhuna because they were all her favourite foods. She'd been gifted a hundred quid from her parents, a Swarovski diamond tennis bracelet from Sultana, classic black Louboutins from Adam and the black Diorama calfskin clutch bag from Rose. Miriam and Leanne had made her an adorable birthday card decorated with sequins and glitter, and a pretty seashell bracelet, as well as buying her a giant Tatty Teddy bear clutching a pink heart shaped balloon with *Happy Birthday* stitched onto it in silver and pink writing.

She held her nieces tightly in her arms in response after reading their message in the card, closing her eyes, treasuring this moment, locking it away for safekeeping in what remained of her heart. "You girls are so special. Thank you so much, my loves," she'd murmured to the twins.

"You're welcome, fufu," Leanne said against her collarbone, her braided hair soft and silky and smelling like lavender oil. "It's your birthday. We wanted to make something pretty for you."

"Because I'm your favourite, right?" Sabrina

smirked.

"Uh, hey, no. *I'm* their favourite." Sultana glared.

"No, you're not. They made me a card *and* a bracelet."

"Yeah, well—"

Whatever Sultana was going to say was cut off by Adam, rolling his eyes, sighing, saying "both of you be quiet, you're giving me a headache". Sultana threw her glare at him, but from receiving a pointed look from their mum, remained quiet.

Later, after praying Maghrib, they'd played Monopoly, with the twins on opposing teams, when Adam and Mohammed had gone to the mosque. Sabrina's team ended up winning.

"You cheated," Leanne pouted.

"Did not," Miriam replied. "We just won because we're amazing and clever and you're not."

"No, we are. And anyway, let's pray Charades. We'll beat you in that and then you're going to be crying," Leanne glared.

So then they all played Charades until it was time for taraweeh, when they decided to put the game on pause. It was one of those nights that Sabrina would always think back to, feeling like everything was ok and she was happy, if only for a few hours. It was the kind of night that was full of love and laughter, where the people she was surrounded by made her feel like she was *home*.

She carried that feeling with her, all the way into the following day, when she was sitting around a table in *Mango Tree* with Veda and Elle. The three of them had caught a few stares as they walked in: Sabrina wore a black silk, knee-length dress with a plunging neckline and spaghetti straps, teardrop diamond earrings and the bracelet and heels her siblings had gifted her, paired with the clutch bag from Rose, makeup soft and glowy, statement red lips. Elle wore a chocolate brown satin blouse and cream, wide legged trousers, gold hoop earrings, Valentino heels and flawless makeup, with a cat eye and glossy lips. Veda was dressed in a slinky, khaki one-shouldered dress, white heels and silver bangles on her right wrist, a watch on her left, and subtle makeup with nude lipstick. They looked like femme fatales, witches sheathing their magic like a sword in their mouths.

While they waited for their food to arrive, Veda and Elle gave Sabrina her presents: from Elle, she received the Fenty Diamond Bomb highlighter and the Game of Thrones series, "because you have *got* to read the books, they're fucking amazing and have so much detail. They don't do the show justice. But then again, the show went to absolute fucking shit", and from Veda, she got the Anastasia Beverly Hills Sultry eye shadow palette and a Nivea lip balm, "since we can both afford it now". She'd hugged both of them tightly, blinking hard so she wouldn't cry, sniffing a little and laughed.

"God, Veda," she said after, giggling as she sipped the Pink Magician cocktail. "I can't believe you remembered."

"Duh, obviously," Veda rolled her eyes, laughing. "I can't believe it only took us more than a decade."

At that, they both cracked into loud giggles, leaving Elle with a perplexed smile on her face and raised eyebrows, looking at them as if they'd lost their minds.

"Uh, guys?" she said.

"Basically," Sabrina spluttered out, between laughs. "When Veda and I were, like, um, I think ten or something; we were at her house and about to start secondary school in a few months or something."

"Right," Veda nodded. She took a long sip of her Sex on the Beach drink before continuing. "So, we were just planning what to do when we got to year seven and everything. We talked about going out for runs every weekend—"

"*That never happened*," Sabrina cackled. Veda sniggered, nearly spilling her drink.

"None of it did, oh my god." They both dissolved into laughter all over again. After a moment, Veda cleared her throat, sitting up straighter. "Right. Ok. We were supposed to do that, and like for the pocket money we received or the lunch money our parents gave us, we were supposed to spend it for lunch only once a week and save the rest."

"I never got any lunch money though."

"Exactly. Because she got free school meals." Veda snorted and took another sip of her drink. She swallowed. "And with the money we saved, we planned on buying magazines like *Cosmopolitan*, *Sugar*, *Bliss*, shit like that, and *Teen Vogue*. And like, getting Nivea lip balms."

Sabrina giggled loudly and then took a large gulp of her drink. "We could never afford it." Her voice was a whisper, making Veda laugh.

Elle lifted her glass of Bloody Mary, twirling it around in her hand before raising it to her lips and sipping. She hummed in acknowledgement of what Sabrina had said, amusement plastered on her face. "You two are ridiculous."

"It's not our fault we were broke for the past ten years," Sabrina said crossly. Veda hooted with laughter, covering her mouth. Her shoulders shook as she laughed and soon, Sabrina and Elle joined in.

When the food came, Elle was telling them about her Foreign Affairs Analyst girlfriend, a Nigerian woman called Isioma and how they'd booked a weekend getaway in two weeks time to a remote, private cabin in Scotland. She was crazy smart and had a wicked sense of humour, and was the first in her family to go to university. All things Elle said with a huge smile on her face and a pink glow to her cheeks.

"So when can we meet her?" Sabrina asked, leaning forward. She was digging into the noodles stir-fried with lobster and a bunch of other things like peanuts and Chinese chives and bean sprouts, suddenly starving.

Elle took a bite of her rice and prawns, thinking. She chewed, then swallowed. "Um, maybe after our graduation or something? Is that cool?"

"It's up to you, babe," Veda said. "You decide."

"Ok. I'll talk to her, and we'll go from there."

"Ugh, I can't believe I'm the only single one out of the three of us right now."

"Hey," Sabrina interjected, frowning. "I'm single too."

"You're with Daniel . . ."

"No. We're not together. Shit."

Veda and Elle exchanged glances, rapidly communicating with their facial expressions. "If you say so," Elle said slowly, smirking. She sipped her drink, eyeing Sabrina over the rim of the glass.

"I hate you," Sabrina grumbled, annoyed.

"Mm, no you don't."

She shot Veda a withering stare, making her laugh.

A few days after, Sabrina met up with Layla at the cinemas and they went to watch the movie *Aladdin* that just came out, even though it looked totally low-budget and shit. It ended up being amazing, even though she still preferred the animated version and thought the 2015 *Cinderella* remake was so much better.

"I'm quite impressed with the movie," Sabrina said to Layla as they finished off their food. They were in *Burger Bros* in West End, the 1950's American diner theme evident in the red booths and the black and white checked linoleum flooring, and the black and white photographs of famous models and actors. Some were Victoria's Secret models. There was even a fake sheriff car outside.

"Right? I loved it," Layla said, after sending off a text to her husband. She'd left Alina, her daughter, at home with him. It was the first time, in months, Sabrina and Layla had hung out properly. She'd missed this.

"*Speechless* was my favourite song, to be honest. Especially since all us brown girls can relate to it on another level. *Prince Ali* was great, oh my god."

"Agreed. Oh, we should do watch a movie at one of our places. One of these days. Since we both graduate this summer. Before you go swanning off to Malaysia and Indonesia, anyway."

"You forgot Singapore, Philippines, Thailand,

Korea and Cambodia," Sabrina smirked, making Layla roll her eyes.

She pulled her hair up into a ponytail, running a hand to smooth out the flyaway baby hairs. "Right, right. I get it; you're jet-setting off around the world, while the rest of us stay miserable in this grey and rainy land."

Sniggering, Sabrina shoved the last of her curly fries into her mouth and chewed. She swallowed before replying. "God, do you blame me? It's so dull here in summer. It's always the same thing. And summer's a hard time for me anyway."

Layla looked sympathetic. "Still Musa?"

"Always Musa." A sigh. "I'm never going to move on."

"Don't say that. You don't know—"

"But I do. He was it for me, Layla. I'm never really going to be happy again. He's the love of my life and I thought we were endgame, you know? I thought we'd be together forever, which I guess, in hindsight, seems pretty dumb because we were only together for a summer. And in the end, he kind of turned out to be a completely different person. But god, I just love him and there's," she sighed. "Nobody else." Daniel's face flashed in her mind briefly as she said those words, but she pushed it away.

"You never thought you'd find someone like Musa though," Layla pointed out. "And you did. You have no idea what could happen. Maybe, yeah, you'll always love him. But you can't shut yourself off from love just because he hurt you."

"It's not just because he hurt me, though. It's because . . . I just don't want it with anyone else. That feeling, I mean. I don't want to feel that kind of love for someone ever again and give them the power to hurt me or destroy me or just . . . cheat on me. Like he did. I can't go through all of that again."

"It'll take some time. But one day, you'll see, it will get easier and not hurt as much."

Sabrina didn't reply, sucking up her salted caramel and chocolate milkshake through her metal straw. This place brought back memories for her. She saw him in every street, in every food place in the area. She couldn't help it. He was a part of her.

Now, in her aunt's house, in Amanee's room, Nafisa was telling her to be careful with the things she read or watched, because it could end up influencing her behaviour, et cetera, et cetera. She didn't say anything, just sighed, as her cousin finally left the room, leaving the door open a crack, so the smell of more samosas being fried wafted up the stairs and swirled around the bedroom. Sabrina's phone buzzed when she stood up, brushing crumbs off her kameez.

Glancing at the screen told her it was Daniel, letting her know he was thirty minutes away from her house. She cursed. It would take her five minutes to walk to the bus stop and another thirty to get home, and she wouldn't have time to change. She took a glance in the mirror. Her Eid outfit was a deep chocolate brown shalwar kameez with red jacquard patterns and gold sequins scattered throughout the dress, the neckline and hem were decorated with pink flowers and red and gold intricate embroidery, the dupatta matching the hem of the dress, one edge of the border lined with gold satin, while the other edge was red satin.

Sultana had worn a pale pink version of it, with white, gold and red work on it. They looked good, more like twins than anything.

"I'm going home," Sabrina said to Sultana.

"Daniel coming over?"

"Yep."

"Wait. Who's Daniel?" Tasnia asked.

"Her boyfriend," Sultana said.

"He's not my boyfriend," Sabrina sighed. "He's my . . . we're friends." Sultana snorted. To her, Sabrina said, "what? We *are*."

"Ok. Because we all have sex with our friends, right?"

"Shh," Sabrina hissed. "Lower your fucking voice. Do you want me to be killed?"

Her sister shook her head, a wide smirk on her face. Sabrina resisted the urge to slap that smug smile off and settled for another sigh. She looked back at herself in the mirror, phone clutched between her fingertips. It was fine; she looked beyond beautiful in traditional clothing.

The sun's light was bright and yellow when it pirouetted across Daniel's bare chest the next morning as he lay in Sabrina's bed, beneath the sloping ceiling and slanted windows. It traced a pattern across her walls, lace leaves dancing, black shadows gently floating along the pure white of her room, the sunshine of the early morning lighting up a golden rectangular line on the soft grey carpet. Her head was resting on the crook of his shoulder, inhaling his warm and comforting scent, calming the throbbing in her skull, one hand over his heart, feeling the steady beat going thump-thump-thump under her palm, a leg thrown across his thighs, holding him close to her bare body. Daniel's arm was around her, a hand curling around her rib cage, lightly brushing the underside of her chest, the other hand slowly dancing over her forearm, writing nonsensical words and figures, soothingly, with his fingertips.

It was intimacy in its purest form, a sort of quiet comfort as Sabrina awoke from the hazy, dreamless slumber she'd fallen into last night. Daniel had come over and then they'd continued where they left off in *Game of Thrones*, before Sabrina heated up the food after getting it out of the fridge. They'd eaten, and then sat and talked for what seemed like hours, about everything and nothing at all, things that were small in retrospect but at the time, had allowed them to learn more about each other, barely scratching the surface. Every moment with him felt like her future being written in a bright, hot flash of silver-white light, like it was all laid out before her, scaring and thrilling her all at once. Sabrina silenced the thoughts by tipping her head up to look at him as she sat on his lap, while watching the TV show, seeing him already looking at her and smiling.

She pressed her lips to his and that was all it took for them to turn the TV off and move upstairs, slowly. One step at a time, kissing as they went.

The next few hours were spent exploring each other's bodies all over again, taking in every dip and scar and beauty mark and every flaw that only added to the real humanness of it all.

After, when the moon had crept up into the sky, just a half circle shining its light, Sabrina had fallen asleep in his arms. Daniel listened to her soft breathing, her breaths tickling and warm against his neck. A little later, his eyes drifted shut, lashes fluttering like the feathers of an angel's wings against his skin.

She mewed a little as she woke up fully, blinking blearily. It took a few seconds for her to adjust, remember, realising that Daniel had spent the night and she felt like she was alive and home and safe in his arms. Sabrina breathed in through her nose, shifting so that her leg was off him and she'd rolled away onto her side of the bed. Her bed. She blinked up at the window, at the cerulean blue sky and the bright, blinding sun as it beamed down at her, welcoming her into the new day.

"Good morning," Daniel mumbled softly, the deep baritone of his morning voice making her inhale sharply. He curled his body toward her, throwing an arm over her stomach.

She turned her head to look at him. He had a sprinkle of freckles on his nose, as if someone had put them there by hand.

"Hi," Sabrina replied back, voice equally soft.

The sudden noise of her alarm made her jump and Daniel groaned, moving so that he was on his back.

"Turn it off."

"Sorry," she whispered. Her fingers fumbled as she grabbed her phone and silenced the alarm that always made her feel sick and want to dash her phone across the room. "I, uh, don't want to go to work."

"Me neither." Daniel sat up, making Sabrina stare at

him. He glanced at her, gaze drifting to her exposed breasts, the silk cover low on her abdomen. Her cheeks went pink. Daniel swallowed and looked back at her face. He reached across her, face a few inches from hers as he took his phone from the bedside table on her side.

"What are you doing?"

"Calling in sick." He held the phone up to his ear. As he did so, Sabrina sat up, yawning. She held a hand over her mouth and ran a hand over her hair. It looked more like a lion's mane. Daniel looked at her as he spoke on the phone, grinning. She looked back at him, unable to resist smiling back.

She stared at him for a few moments as he spoke, nodding and faked a cough. Her stomach rumbled when he paused, listening to the other person. His eyes went back to her, looking at her, as if to commit her face to memory. Sabrina swallowed and shifted on the bed.

Her phone buzzed with a text, smacking against the edge of her photo frame. It was a picture of Mount Fuji and a sunset, a reminder of the broken heart she'd tried to escape. Sabrina held her phone, blinking at the text, a frown marring her face. Instead of replying, she called the school just as Daniel hang up and dropped his phone onto the duvet.

"Hello, Nirvana Primary School. Lisa speaking."

"Hi, Lisa," Sabrina faked a sniffle and a croaky voice. "It's Sabrina Ahsan. I'm a volunteer counsellor at the school with the Place2Be organisation." She paused as a sneeze escaped her.

"Bless you, hon," Lisa said.

"Thanks. Uh, I just—I won't be able to come in

today, I have a really bad fever and a cold." She coughed twice, loudly. Thank god for taking GCSE Drama.

"Oh, your poor thing. Of course. I'll just let Kelly know, ok? I hope you get well soon."

"Thanks, Lisa. Bye."

"Bye, hon."

Sabrina ended the call and threw her phone down beside Daniel's, looking over at him. "So you want to sleep some more or . . ."

"Sleep. *Please.*"

Three hours and fifteen minutes later, after a lukewarm shower together, they were both downstairs in the kitchen. Daniel was wearing one of the t-shirts he'd left the last time he stayed and a jogging bottoms and Sabrina was dressed in a tank top and sweatpants, her hair air dried and loose around her face. She had just put in four slices of bread into the toaster and taken the butter and strawberry jam out of the fridge. Grabbing two plates and a knife, she put them on the island, while waiting for the toasts to be done and the water to boil in the whistling kettle.

"I'm sorry there's nothing else," she said apologetically. "Neither Veda nor I had the chance to do any grocery shopping recently, so there's literally just bread or cereal."

"Don't worry about it, baby. It's all good. I love toast. Honestly, bread is the best thing on earth. I could have toast all day, every day."

"Um, I'm not sure that's entirely healthy or anything."

"Who gives a shit?" Daniel laughed. "God, I love toast. Mm, especially buttered toast with strawberry jam."

"Me too! It's my favourite. And with Nutella, too. Oh, lemme get that out." She stretched up to take it out of the middle shelf in the top cabinet, the large jar bigger than her whole hand. She put it down beside the strawberry jam jar and turned to look at Daniel, grinning. He looked back at her, a twinkle in his eye, adoration in his smile.

"You look so pretty in the mornings," he said.

She lifted an eyebrow. "Calm down there, Romeo."

"Supposed to say thank you," he muttered, sounding offended. Sabrina laughed. The slices of bread jumped out of the toaster and she grabbed them, putting two on each plate, before buttering one and then spreading a layer of strawberry jam on top. On the next one, she spread Nutella neatly across it, and then did the same for the other plate.

"Here you are," she smirked at him. The water finished boiling and she turned to the kettle, pouring water into her mug. "Did you want tea or coffee, babe?"

"Coffee."

She nodded and dashed a spoonful of Nescafé into the other mug, with two spoons of sugar, and then poured in the boiling water. She carefully poured the milk into both mugs, slowly stirring. The delicious aroma of coffee spread throughout the kitchen, mixing with the sunlight stretching across, highlighting all the dust floating in the room. Sabrina handed Daniel his mug and they both headed into the dining room-slash-living-room, choosing to sit on the sofa instead, and watch TV.

She ended up going on Tiny POP, watching an episode of *Care Bears*, much to Daniel's amusement.

"Really?"

"What?" she shrugged. "I like cartoons."

He laughed, taking a bite of his jam and butter toast. "You said *Clifford the Big Red Dog* was your favourite, right?"

"Yeah," Sabrina nodded. "Oh shit, I forgot about *Trollz* and *Winx Club* and *W.I.T.C.H.* and *Max and Ruby*, holy shit. And *Bratz*, that was my number one favourite. It was a bad bitch cartoon, that was. But all of them were *the* best shows *ever*. My friends and I used to act them out all the time in primary school, during playtime and lunchtime."

"Ah, being a kid was so easy. You could just do anything and nobody would give you any shit for it."

"I know, right. I used to believe in Santa Claus too and get so excited around Christmas at school because of all the decorating we'd do in class."

"Oh yeah, you don't celebrate Christmas, do you?"

"No," Sabrina frowned. "I've always wanted to decorate a tree and the house and just . . . all of that stuff. It seems so fun. I mean, Eid is just—I think Eid would be great if it wasn't for my family. They don't do anything for it. Nobody bothers to make it special, which sucks." She looked at him, finishing off the first slice of toast. "I mean," she swallowed the bite in her mouth. "Eid is supposed to be special and beautiful, you know? But it's always the same every single year. God. When I have kids, I don't care. I'm gonna go all out for them, make them super excited for it that they wake up jumping around in the morning."

"That seems adorable." There was a look on his face that she couldn't decipher, but it was warm and enveloping and sent an electric rush of desire through her.

She leaned into him, pressing a kiss against the corner of his mouth. He turned his face a little and their lips met. It was the softest of kisses, making her feel as if she was floating on a canopy of clouds.

When they parted, the ads had come on and Sabrina picked up her coffee mug, the heat from it raising the temperature of her cold hands. She sipped it slowly, the sweet, hot liquid sliding down her throat and warming her insides.

"You know what I just realised?" Daniel said, breaking their silence.

"Hmm?"

"You have a lot of books."

Sabrina burst out laughing. "Really? You just realised that now, after being in my room how many times?"

He shrugged in reply, a faint pink on his cheeks. "I was occupied with other things."

Now it was Sabrina's turn to wear the blush. She forced it down with a roll of her eyes.

"But I mean, seriously," Daniel said. "You have a lot. An entire wall of shelves full."

"Yeah, um. The amount of money I spend on books is actually kind of obscene."

"I really couldn't tell."

"Shut up."

"Make me."

Sabrina looked at him, taking a giant bite out of her Nutella toast, a glimmer of a wicked smirk tilting her lips up. "I will later."

"Is that a promise?"

"Yes, daddy."

Daniel groaned, brushing crumbs off his hand and picking up his coffee mug. "I hate you."

"We both know," Sabrina folded up her toast and put the entire thing into her mouth. Chew. Swallow. "That you love me."

There was a brief pause. Daniel didn't say anything, but a flush had turned his face pink.

Sabrina felt a weird sensation sweeping through her as she looked at him avoid looking at her. She decided to change the subject. "When do you get off for summer anyway?"

"Uh," Daniel cleared his throat, running a hand over his beard. "Mid July, I think. Around the nineteenth."

"Good," Sabrina smiled.

"Your graduation is on the tenth, right?"

"Yep."

"Are you prepared?"

"To walk across a stage in front of hundreds of people?" Sabrina snorted. "God, no. But I am excited. I got a First for my dissertation and my essays. So I know for a fact I'm going to end up graduating with a First."

"That's amazing, Sabrina. Jesus. Really. How can one person be so cute *and* hot?" Daniel looked at her, his beard bristling against her cheek as he kissed her with a coffee tasting mouth. "You have no idea how much of a turn on you are. Your brain is so sexy."

"It's a squishy, slimy—"

Daniel cut her off with a kiss, laughing into her mouth. Sabrina smiled at this, tasting his happiness and his laugh. When they parted, she rested her head on his shoulder and he wrapped an arm around her as they continued watching cartoons, mugs and plates empty of their breakfast.

Silence held them in its warm embrace, a solace from the chaotic world around them. It wasn't awkward, filled with wanting to speak just for the sake of talking. They both accepted this quiet, enjoying each other's company, Daniel's fingers playing with the ends of Sabrina's hair, twirling it around his finger over and over, in a spiral and watching as it bounced back. She couldn't help thinking that he was different from Musa in this way. Musa had always wanted to pack their moments of quiet with words and sentences, hating when Sabrina fell silent. He never seemed to understand that not every instant needed to be brimming with conversation.

But thinking that she preferred this, enjoyed this, sent a small spark of fear flashing through her. Because she was ok. Right now, she was ok and she felt at ease and it terrified the shit out of her. Over the years, she'd come to learn that when something felt so good, when she feel like she was finally *fine*, it became a terrifying feeling because at any moment, the ground beneath her could split open and make her fall, endlessly down a rabbit hole.

And she didn't want to fall again.

CHAPTER FIFTEEN

A WATERCOLOUR OF blues painted the sky, the sun bright and hot in the few hours before it would begin a slow descent to the night, with no clouds in sight. The air was sticky and humid, barely any breeze to cool down the sweltering heat of the late Saturday afternoon. Cars beeped loudly as they were driven by annoyed and frustrated drivers down the busy roads, a few bright red buses bursting with life and throngs of people getting on and off at each stop.

The traffic lights changed from green to amber to red every so often, allowing pedestrians to safely cross the street to the other side, ducking into various other shops. A little way from *Zara*, stood a busker with an open guitar case at his feet. He strummed it with skilled fingers, crooning softly about a lost love and bitter regret. Once in a while, passerby's would drop spare change, and the odd five pound notes, into his case, pausing in front of him as they listened to his singing. Some of them held their phones out, recording him. A shadow of a smile flickered across the man's face when he caught sight of this, voice never wavering.

His confidence made Sabrina wish she had the guts to do something like that. But she couldn't sing to save her life. That, however, didn't stop her from doing so.

She threw down five quid in change into the case as she walked past him, flashing a quick smile. He nodded at her in acknowledgment, lips quirking up at the corner as he continued his song. Beside her, Sultana looked back at him as the two sisters headed toward *Bershka*. It was four hours after Sabrina had finished work, went home, gotten changed, met her sister at the station and came back to Oxford Street. They both needed to do some shopping for summer and she needed to get a few things for her trip around a few of the countries in Asia, plus hopefully find something for her graduation.

"He's pretty good," Sultana said as they walked into the brightly lit shop, manoeuvring past a couple and a group of girls coming out of it.

"You mean amazing, right?" Sabrina replied, eyeing a nude off-the-shoulder top on a mannequin. "The guy's voice was magical. I hope he gets scouted or something and gets a record label and makes millions."

"I'm sure he'll be happy that you're rooting for him."

"Mhm." She flipped through the same top hanging on the rack, searching for her size. Finding a size ten in the middle, she took it out and held it against her body and turned to her sister. "Thoughts?"

"It's nice."

"That it? Nothing else? Just *nice*."

Sultana shrugged. "It'll flatter your complexion for sure. What are you thinking of wearing it with?"

"Um," Sabrina looked down at the top she was holding against her. It was kind of like a half wrap top, an L-shape from her right shoulder to just below her other shoulder, showing the swell of her boobs and such a pretty shade of pinky nude. "I could wear it with a black skirt or culottes, or even white. Or grey. And heels."

"Hmm," Sultana hummed, pursing her lips. "That sounds good. Yeah, get it. What else do you need to buy today?"

Sabrina shrugged. "Whatever I can find, I guess."

In the next twenty minutes, Sultana picked up a burnt orange midi dress with a knot at the waist and a bow at the back, a ribbed ivory dress with a slit and a lace and chiffon white peasant dress, which Sabrina also got. After paying for their items, the bags swinging between their fingers, they went to *Zara* next. There, Sabrina found a pretty asymmetric dress, one half of it plain white and the other half black and white with pink floral patterns. It would be nice to wear in Bali. She already had three gorgeous floral dresses she'd bought from *Boohoo* a few months ago (see: a year ago) and never worn. Sabrina was a shopper. She saw something she liked and bought it. But recently, she'd managed to exert excellent self-control and saved her money, so she wouldn't be having to live pay check to pay check.

From a distance, she saw a bright red printed dress with light blue and yellow along the edge. Grabbing

Sultana's wrist, she rushed towards it, praying she found her size. There was only one left and she plucked it up, smiling. It had a high-low hem, perfect for a summer away and to get her legs gloriously bronzed under the sun.

"This," she said to her sister, holding it up. "Is perfect."

Sultana raised an eyebrow but didn't comment.

Sabrina ended up buying four more dresses, all varying shades from creamy beige to buttercup yellow and white to another red dress and a black ruffles one, as well as two tops: white flowing cape top and a red off-the-shoulder one. Her total was way more than one hundred pounds.

Outside, the sun burned only brighter, making her (*Musa's*) t-shirt cling to her body, sweat rolling down her spine. She'd paired it with no bra and ripped mom jeans, which she was now regretting. Jeans in this heat was never a good idea.

There was an ice cream van parked outside *H&M*, a queue of people lined up in front of the open window. The sight of the ice cream made Sabrina walk toward it, as if in a trance. Four people were ahead of her and Sultana, talking about what ice cream or slushy they would get and complaining about the weather. Sabrina wiped away the sweat beading at her temples, a thirst burning in her throat. Beside her, Sultana shifted on her feet, adjusting the light beige hijab she wore. While Sultana wasn't much of a pious Muslim, she did observe all the fardh commandments from god: wearing hijab and praying her five daily salahs and fasting in the month of Ramadan. Amongst other things.

Finally, it was their turn to order. Both of them got a slushy with all the flavours mixed together, totalling to five quid, which Sabrina handed over, pulling a face. It was only one pound in their area.

Her bags from *Zara* and *Bershka* were dangling on the bend of her left arm, the see-through plastic cup with red, blue, purple and orange slushy clutched in her right hand. The first sip of it felt like nectar of the gods and she stifled a loud groan of appreciation.

It was getting busier on the streets, more people filling up the few empty spaces around them on the pavements, loud chatter bustling around them, car horns beeping. It was like everyone was in a rush, walking rapidly, like they had somewhere to be. The pace Sabrina and Sultana were walking at was just as quick, annoyance bursting through her as they came up to two middle-aged women standing in the middle, just outside the *M&S Food Hall*. Sabrina bit back a growl of frustration, settling for throwing daggers at them with her eyes.

She slurped up the slushy loudly through the straw, lifting her hair away from the nape of her neck. She should've tied it up.

"I feel like I need to have another shower," Sultana sighed. She fixed the end of her hijab that was thrown over her shoulder, pulling at it a little. A flash of her neck gleamed brown and golden as the sunshine caught her. After a moment, she adjusted it again so that her neck was covered.

"Same, man. It's way too fucking hot. What is it, like thirty eight degrees?"

"Yep."

"Fuck's sake."

"I hate this weather."

"Prefer it to winter though. I love dressing like a whore."

"You dress like a whore anyway," Sultana pointed out, after a large mouthful of her slushy.

Sabrina laughed. "Hoes don't get cold."

"Well," Sultana said in an amused tone of voice. "At least you own it."

Laughter tumbled out of Sabrina's mouth again as they crossed the road, past a dark statue of a man on a horse. They walked along a familiar street, the crowd so much thinner here, just a few people milling around and one guy on a run. Sabrina wrinkled her nose. She hadn't gone running in a week.

The smell of freshly brewed coffee assaulted her nose when a quaint little coffee shop appeared on the corner of the pavement. She looked at it as she walked past, a slight frown on her face. It was new and crowded and smelt delicious inside. There were pastries and cakes on trays behind the window, making her come to a stop.

"Let's grab something from here," she said to Sultana. Her sister looked a bit confused but followed her in.

Once inside, a craving for a pain au chocolat kicked in aggressively at the sight of it. She ordered four of those at the counter, with two salted caramel brownies and six chunky looking chocolate chip cookies that she knew would just be soft and chewy in her mouth. Smiling at the cute cashier, she held her slushy cup in her left hand as she got her phone out. Once the card reader was ready, she tapped it on the screen. The food was put in three different brown paper bags, all of which were given to her in a yellow paper bag with the coffee shop slash bakery's logo and name on it.

She finished off her slushy and tossed it into the bin, and then rummaged around in the bakery's bag for her chocolate stuffed croissant. "Want one?" she asked with a full mouth. Sultana laughed then nodded, reaching in to grab one for herself.

Sabrina finished hers off in four large bites, her fingertips a little shiny with the butter from the pastry. She wiped it on her jeans, sighing in satisfaction. "That was good."

"Mfsgjh," Sultana said in agreement. Sabrina lifted an eyebrow at the gibberish that came out of her sister's mouth, a short laugh leaving her. It faded as she caught sight of the *Superdrug* that she'd been in more than a dozen times with Musa. That familiar ache in her chest came back, intensified.

Blinking back sudden tears that filled her eyes, she inhaled sharply, tucking her hair behind her ear. All her thoughts came to a shuddering stop, crash-landing as she fought back the hurt beginning to push to the front of everything all over again.

Continuing to walk past it felt like leaving it behind, the hurt, the memories, but then she came face-to-face with the cause of the broken heart still beating in her chest. He was walking towards her. Well, not towards her, just in the opposite direction she was going. But he was just a few steps away from her.

Seeing him made her freeze, barely noticing as her

sister glanced at her, bewildered, then followed her gaze. Sabrina felt her mouth going dry, her heart rate increasing to a tempo that was way too fast. It felt as if time came to a standstill, as she took him in, eyes wide open and hurt clouding her face. His obsidian black hair was different, messily tousled as if he'd been running his hands through it and flopping over one eye, jaw sharp and shadowed with his beard, thicker than the last time she saw him. When they'd tried being friends. When he'd cut her out of his life again a few months later, without an explanation or a goodbye. His face was heartbreakingly beautiful, the kind that turned heads and made people blush, with a smile to match.

Now, as she stared at him, his sea foam green eyes met hers. She'd always loved his eyes, sea foam shifting to emerald in certain lights, rimmed with flecks of gold and amber, like sunbursts. Once, when they'd been in bed, she'd been staring at him long enough for him to notice and a small smile to cross his face.

"What?" he'd asked, kissing her on the lips and then her forehead. She'd breathed him in, cuddling closer, her fingers splayed out over his chest.

"Your eyes are gorgeous," Sabrina replied, grinning. "Seriously. They're like a really light shade of green with hazel and gold around it."

He simply lifted an eyebrow in response. "You're weird."

"But you love me anyway."

Musa laughed in reply, tipping her chin up to kiss her again. "I do," he murmured softly against her mouth. "I do love you."

As they continued looking at each other now, him coming closer, Sabrina felt her stomach bottom out. She was frozen where she stood, lips parted. His surprise at her seeing her was less palpable, eyes widening only a fraction. Her stomach churned when he finally looked away from her and then he was close enough for her to reach out to him, tell him to *wait*. But he was already walking past. A sludge of memories rose to the surface as she watched him walk away, feeling her heart breaking all over again.

She didn't hear her sister calling her name as she remained right where she was, tears glossing her eyes and spilling down her bronze cheeks. She wasn't sobbing then, but she could feel it in her chest and in her throat. Missing him was a constant, even when it seemed like everything was falling into place. But it was all coming together without him and *seeing* him only made it clearer.

The first time Musa told her how he felt was on a Friday night, when the clock had struck one and Sabrina was beginning to fall asleep. It had just begun to take her into its clutches, when her phone rang loudly. It made her jolt awake, blinking, and disoriented, before realising someone was calling her. For a moment, she pondered over the thought of not answering.

But when she saw it was Musa, all logical thoughts flew out the window and she answered it, holding her phone up to her ear.

"Hello?" she said in a sleepy voice.

"Hi. Did I wake you?" His voice filled her ears and

she closed her eyes for a second, a small smile tugging on her lips.

"No," she lied. "I was just in bed."

"Oh, ok, good. Um, I was thinking about you today. At work."

"Yeah?"

"Yeah," Musa laughed. "I finished at eleven thirty and then went out for drinks with Shane and Abdul. Just got home now."

"How was it?"

"Uh, it was ok, you know? Just had a few beers, talked. Grabbed some munch. I'm still kind of tipsy right now, actually."

"Sounds nice," Sabrina murmured. "What did you eat?"

"Donner meat and chips. It was really good."

"I want some."

"I'll take you one day." He was smiling. She could hear it in his voice. It warmed her heart, a fuzzy glow lighting up her chest. She smiled.

"Good. Are we still on for Sunday?"

He confirmed with a soft yeah. "Listen. Sabrina. Um, there's something—uh, something I want to . . . tell you. But, uh, I don't know if I, you know, should."

"Tell me."

"I don't want you to . . . I don't want you to see me, I dunno, differently. Or just . . . freak out, you know? It's probably not a, um, good idea. But I'm tipsy as fuck right now, so—uh," he laughed. "You're cute, you know that?"

"Am I?" Sabrina was smiling wider now as she sat up in her bed, tucking her hair behind her ear. She shifted around beneath her duvet. Even in the height of summer, she needed her duvet.

"You are," Musa confirmed. "You're—god, you're really funny. You can make me laugh and I, um, r-really like that. I love talking to you. Especially these past few weeks. It's been nice. And," he laughed again. "You have the curliest hair I've ever seen on anyone and you're so fucking beautiful." He was talking quicker now, as if to get all the words out before he lost his nerve. "Do you know what I'm trying to say?"

Sabrina swallowed, her grin incandescent and bright in the dark of her room. "I think so," she mumbled. "But I don't want to be wrong. So tell me."

"I don't want this to ruin things between us."

"It won't," she promised. "Tell me."

"When I first saw you," Musa sighed. "It was like . . . god, she's so attractive. And I wanted to know you straight away. That's why I told Abdul that day to send you down with me to get the sweets. I wanted that time to talk to you and get to know you."

"Really?" Sabrina giggled. She felt happy, light. In a way she'd never felt before. It was refreshing. She moved her hair over her left shoulder, running a hand down her curls.

"Yep. I'm glad I did."

"Me too."

"Do you know what I'm saying?" he asked again.

"Spell it out for me."

There was a brief pause, in which Sabrina could just hear his quiet breathing. The headlights from a car passing outside lit a path on her walls, lighting up the corner of her wardrobe and a slash of her mirror, dancing across the ceiling.

"I like you. A lot." His voice was soft, almost a whisper as he said those five words. Sabrina's smiled kicked up a few inches.

"You do?"

"I do. Really. Does this, um, does this—you know, uh," he swallowed. "Make you uncomfortable or—"

She cut him off quickly. "No. No, I promise it doesn't. I'm glad you do. It, uh, it makes me happy."

"Good." She could hear the smile in his voice again. "Tell me the truth, when I called, did I wake you up?"

A laugh. "Um, ok. I might've been half asleep."

"Sorry."

"Don't be, Musa. I'm glad you called."

"So am I." He was smiling still. Sabrina was smiling. Happy. Giddy. *He liked her. He* liked *her.* "Get some sleep now, ok. We'll talk later, in the morning."

"Ok. Bye. Sweet dreams."

He kissed her on Sunday, when they were in a park, sitting on a bench. They'd been talking about their families, opening up about, well, *everything*. Sabrina could feel herself falling harder for him that day. And when he kissed her, it was like she finally felt whole instead of broken.

Now, after she'd parted ways with her sister and came home to an empty house, she climbed up the stairs to the landing. She felt numb and hurt at the same time, a sob scratching her throat as she opened the creaking door leading up to her bedroom. She walked up the stairs, her bags bumping against her leg. She chucked them in front of her bookcase the moment she got into her room.

The sun was beginning to fall, ribbons of pink stretching across the sky. Sabrina walked a few steps further, fingers grasping against the wall for support, tears slipping out faster now. A sob left her as she slid down the wall, legs out in front of her. It was like the night he left all over again. He blurred the line between hope and blindly waiting for something that, she knew, they would never have again. It was like she made him her home and he took that with him, his goodbye an explosion in the deafening silence. The lump in her throat made her choke on his name forming on her lips, crying as the memories swept through her mind, a broken sailboat in a storm.

There was no hope for survival, no matter how hard you tried to fight. Some things just didn't happen the way you wanted. And it was like a boulder of rocks sitting where her heart should have been, bloody and raw and painful, and filling up all the spaces in the museum of her chest with a heartbreak she didn't want to feel anymore.

He loved her and then he didn't. Or maybe he never did.

Tears blurred her vision, a river of salt cascading down her cheeks as she shakily took out her phone when it began ringing. It was a call from Daniel. She felt as if she couldn't breathe. And like so many times before, she cracked. Broken. Her soul spilled out of her in great, big, heaving sobs, and she realised just how utterly alone, and miserable, she really was in that moment.

She ignored Daniel's call.

She dialled Musa's number, putting it on speaker.

Cries left her and she put her hand over mouth to muffle the sounds. It went to voicemail. Sabrina closed her eyes, swallowing and taking in deep breaths.

His voice. She couldn't remember the sound of his
voice.

"I miss you," she said, tears choking her words.
They fell into the air, dancing around the quiet room, filled
with the sounds of her trying to breathe, trying to get
oxygen into her lungs, trying to calm the roaring in her
head, trying to soothe the absence that tore through her like
an arrow. "I miss you so much and I don't know what to
do. I feel so alone." She stopped, letting out a sob. She
gasped again, trying to stop crying. "I just . . ." she
swallowed. "I love you. And I miss you. I know you're in a
relationship. I'm kind of, I think, with someone, too. I don't
know what it is. But he's not you. He's not you and I wish
he was."

Sabrina wanted to tear apart the earth to turn back
time, go back to when he was still hers. He was her
soulmate, and no amount of time or people or distance
could ever begin to erase that or replace the feeling she had
with him. She wanted to carve their names in the sky,
because it was *supposed* to be them. It should have been.
But fate or destiny or reality or life or god or whoever
decided to fuck her over again, because it wasn't enough
for her to lose her childhood. She had to lose the love of her
life, too. She had to watch him walk away from her, give
up on them, using fruitless excuses as an attempt to make
the blow easier. And then weeks later, he was with
someone else and it felt like she was dying. But she wasn't.
She just wished she was.

"You were my home, Musa," her voice cracked.
She sucked in a deep, shuddering breath. Tears dripped

263

down her chin, sinking beneath the t-shirt. "I miss you and I will miss you for the rest of my life. I know you don't want me anymore. I just . . ." Sabrina dragged a hand through her hair, tears glossing her cheeks. She wiped them away even as more fell. "I love you and I'm sorry. God, I love you."

A pause.

It had started to rain and the drops pattered against the open windows on her sloping ceiling.

She continued. "I wish I had tried harder to fight for you. Or fought you when you said it was over. I wish I could've done something differently, to make you happier. I love you and I wish you were still mine."

CHAPTER SIXTEEN

THE SKY WAS a stunning shade of cobalt, rich and bright,
with only a few wisps of clouds. In the centre of it all, the
sun stared down at the country, beating with a golden
heartbeat, sending its searing heat pulsing through the
humid air. The weather was thirty eight degrees the
following Wednesday, as Sabrina came home from
working an extra day at the school.

A thin sheen of sweat layered her temples and upper
lip, glossing her neck as she inserted her key into the hole
and twirled it. She was wearing a flowy, pleated white midi
skirt and a white satin camisole, body heating up even in
the light layers and colours. Her hair was piled on top of
her head in a messy bun, a few loose strands hanging
around her face, having escaped. Inside, it felt a little better,
out of the sun's throbs and the blazing tarmac pavements.
Kicking off her white, heeled sandals, Sabrina quickly
rushed upstairs, ignoring the music coming from Sabah's

room. It barely registered in her head, as she pulled open the door to the attic's stairs, the metal cool against her palm.

The cold tiles of her bathroom floor were a welcomed relief, once she'd dropped her bag onto the floor of her room and stepped into her en-suite. She stripped out of her clothes, letting them pool at her feet. Filling up the bodna with cold water, Sabrina glanced at herself in the mirror, seeing the red flush to her cheeks, the light gleam of sweat on her body.

Turning the tap, she stopped the water from spilling out and then put it on the floor as she sat on the toilet, a sigh escaping her lips. She'd been dying for the loo since getting on the train.

After washing herself, flushing the toilet and then washing her hands again, Sabrina slipped into the shower, letting a rush of lukewarm water take away the sticky heat and lingering perspiration. It was the twelfth of June, flowers in full bloom around the city. Everywhere she went, bright colours popped up, bringing life to the streets and the bright greens of the tree leaves offered shade when the heat got to be too much. As she lathered her body with a marshmallow scented shower cream, Sabrina thought, again, about the call from Musa, the day after she'd left him a sobbing voicemail.

He'd called her at nine o'clock that evening, as shades of gold and butter and pale pink fluttered across the sky. She had been downstairs with Veda, who was celebrating the end of her final year and exams with a plate of spicy chicken curry and rice that Sabrina made, white wine and binge watching *Pretty Little Liars* all over again, since they'd decided not to watch the last two seasons of *The Vampire Diaries* because of how shit it got.

Sabrina swallowed the bite of chicken mixed with the rice, her fingers deftly breaking apart the last piece of it on her plate. She lifted it to her mouth as Spencer and Toby kissed, the fresh wound from yesterday still coating her heart. The missed call from Daniel was still red in her call log and she hadn't messaged or called him back, as if to prove to herself, and her friends, that they weren't in a relationship. But with that distance from him came a bout of loneliness and missing him. It surprised her when she caught herself aching to call him back or reply to his text, asking if she wanted to go with him to an art exhibit in two weeks time. The urge to say yes was strong, but her need to push him away overrode the small semblance of feeling she had for him. So she didn't reply.

As she finished off the curry and rice, wondering whether to get a second helping, Veda shifted on the sofa, leaning to the table to get her glass of wine. When she drank it deeply, Sabrina shovelled the last bit of the rice into her mouth and swallowed.

"God, I really needed this," she sighed. "Been craving some zaal khani for a while now."

"It's really good," Veda told her. "Seriously. You're an amazing cook."

"Thanks to my mum." Sabrina's smile was fleeting as it crossed her face. She picked up her glass and sipped it slowly, completely draining it.

The sound of her phone ringing, Musa's custom ringtone blaring as the next episode started, made her jump. She quickly put the glass on the coffee table, scrambling to pick up her phone. Her heart skipped as Musa's name appeared, taunting her. She stared at the ringing phone for a moment, an almost daunting feeling rising in the pit of her stomach.

"Hello?" she said softly, standing up and walking in the direction of the kitchen. She left Veda staring after her, a faint frown on her face.

"Hey, Sabrina." Musa's voice was distant, cautious, as he said her name. The sound of it on his tongue made her suck in a breath, tears pricking her eyes.

With the back of her right hand, she turned the tap on, rinsing her hand beneath the water. She squirted some hand wash onto it and then washed it off, letting the suds and the gushing water swirl down the drain.

"Uh," Sabrina said, shutting the water off. "What—"

Musa cut her off before she could finish asking him what he wanted. She went out of the living room (the TV on in the background and Veda clambering to her feet, ducking into the kitchen with the two plates stacked on top and the wineglasses balanced on them), into the hallway and sat on the steps.

"I listened to your voicemail."

"Oh."

"Sabrina . . ." he said her name quietly, a loud sigh following. She felt sick and closed her eyes. "I know this is hard for you. I know you're struggling. But it's going to be two years. You really—it's just, uh . . . it's been ages. That guy you're doing whatever you're doing with, give him a chance. I get he's not me but, Sabrina . . ." there was a pause. A silence filling her ears. She took in a slow breath through her nose, one slow tear trickling out.

Resting her head on the wall, Sabrina seemed to curl in on herself. Musa continued talking.

"What happened between us, it's completely over. We're never getting back together. You need to move on. I'm getting married this December, to this amazing—" Musa stopped himself from finishing the sentence. "I'm getting married, Sabrina."

She took in another deep breath, willing herself not to cry. "Congratulations," she muttered. She didn't know if she meant it or not. "I'm happy for you." This, she did mean. "I want you to be happy."

"And I want you to be happy." His voice was low. A thousand memories swept through her mind, each one making her heart clench painfully. "I need you to move on from me. I need you to be happy. Our breakup . . . it was for the best. I couldn't give you what you deserved and I only would've ended up hurting you further down the line. I hate that I hurt you, I'm sorry for the things I said after, but you need to move on."

"I know," she said quietly. Then again, as if agreeing with herself, an afterthought. "I know."

"I'll, uh, I'll send you a wedding invitation. I'm sending one to Layla, so I'll just pop yours into her address. If you want to come, come."

"Th-that, um, that sounds nice."

"Ok." They were quiet for a few beats. "I really hope you'll be ok. I'm sorry."

"Don't be. I, um, I'm glad you called."

She wiped away more tears that had begun to fall.

"Take care of yourself."

"You too. Take care, Musa. Goodbye." *I love you.* There was a click and he was gone.

Back in the present, Sabrina poured a dome of cherry scented shampoo into the palm of her hand and then rubbed it into her hair and scalp, massaging it in. She closed her eyes as the suds frothed around her hair, sweeping around her like freshly falling snow, sliding down her glistening arm. The shower smelt like a concoction of marshmallows and cherries as she continued massaging her scalp, running her fingers through the strands of her hair.

Four minutes later, she rinsed the shampoo out and let the water jutting out from the shower head cleanse her body, the thoughts of everything spinning down the drain with the dirt and grime and sweat of the day. What Musa said had whirled around her head endlessly, a tornado of words repeating over and over in her mind, and she knew he was right. She had to let go.

The realisation came with a sinking feeling, a stabbing hurt in the depths of her soul that rose up like a baby bird just learning to take flight. She felt as if everything was being drowned out by the thunder rumbling, it was loud enough to quieten the soft voice that kept telling her to *hold on, maybe all that's needed is time.* Because now she knew that no matter how long it was, whether it was another five years or ten years or thirty years, her story with Musa had ended. It sent her down a spiral of bitter hurt and regret, still wishing she could've done something differently, tears clouding her vision, but knowing that it was well and truly over. The weight of the world resided in her sigh, closing her eyes and tipping her head up to the water raining down on her face.

It turned out that love sometimes was never enough to save a sinking ship or a failing relationship, drowning beneath the relentless waves. Life had a funny way of tearing you apart, letting you watch as everything you ever wanted crumbled around you like an old cathedral, and then moving on as you tried to catch your breath and make sense of what had happened.

An email from Marcus, the volunteer coordinator at Camden Citizens Advice Bureau, sat waiting to be read in her inbox when Sabrina tugged on a pair of satin pyjama bottoms and matching lace trimmed camisole. She dragged a brush through her damp hair, knowing if she didn't get the knots out while it was still wet, her hair would be a nightmare to brush. She was sitting on the velvet chair in front of her dressing table, looking at herself as she eased out the tangles. Her hair was a mass of tight, wild curls, a trait she shared with her siblings—something they'd inherited from their father. In 2016 and 2017, Sabrina straightened her hair almost every week, hating her curls. It took the few months After Musa for her to realise how much she'd damaged her hair by doing so and then chopping it all off, to her jaw and then using a bunch of hair masques and oils to make her hair a little healthier.

Now, thankfully, her hair was a few inches shy of reaching her elbows when natural and a lot thicker, glossy and dyed blonde. Surprisingly dyeing her hair hadn't caused much damage. She'd been religiously taking care of it with a mix of coconut and sweet almond oil, as well as the *Vatika* black seed oil. She ran a hand over hair, twisting the few strands that came out around her index finger and put it on the tabletop. There were a few hairs caught between the bristles of her brush that she pulled out, grabbing them with the little ball she'd rolled the deadened strands to, and chucked it into the bin.

After putting her hairbrush in the top drawer, Sabrina leaned back and looked at herself. There was something almost different about her now that she'd made the choice to finally let go of the love of her life, although she would *always* love him—because after all, Musa was her *everything*, the first real serious relationship she'd been in and it hurt to admit it to herself, that it was over forever. *Or maybe not*, that same voice piped up. She shoved it away, that small flicker of hope still burning like a flame that would never die inside her.

Sighing loudly, Sabrina picked up her phone and unlocked it, seeing the bright red notification stating she had one unread email. She opened it up and a small smile curved her lips up. She'd gotten the role of Trainee Advisor.

Pumping her fist up in the air, she let out a little laugh. She would now be busy every single day, since the role required two days each week and she still had her work placement going on every Monday, Tuesday and Friday, plus her job at Sainsbury's on the weekends. She guessed this meant no more brunch on Thursdays, unless she met up with Veda and Elle somewhere local during her lunch break. The office was close to *The Breakfast Crew*, which was perfect. It all worked out.

With a small smile on her face, Sabrina's feet softly padded down the carpeted stairs into the hallway. The door creaked loudly as she opened it. Opposite it, Sabah's bedroom was visible. A small frown flickered across Sabrina's face as she saw the open door. She paused in the doorway, thinking something seemed different, but not being able to put her finger on it. Downstairs, she heard loud cursing.

The sound of it sent confusion rippling through her. Veda was out with her uni friends and Sabah was, well, she didn't know. The two of them still hadn't talked. Sabrina hadn't bothered to send another text after her last few were ignored. She ran her hand along the white banister, walking down the stairs. As she descended the steps, her eyebrows furrowing in a frown, she caught sight of two giant black wheeled suitcases and a pretty massive, crimson pink Nike travel bag, beside the shoe rack. She hurried down the stairs, looking at Sabah as she came out of the living room, a water bottle in her hand.

Neither girl said anything as Sabah shoved the bottle into her Nike bag, lifting it up to her shoulder. She opened the front door, tugging the suitcases behind her.

"Are you . . . going on holiday or something?" Sabrina asked.

Sabah looked at her. "No. I'm moving out."

"Wait. What? What do you mean you're moving out?" Sabrina took a few steps forward, confusion plastering her features. Her eyes flicked over Sabah's face, drinking in the black hair tied in a French plait, the oversized grey t-shirt that so obviously didn't belong to her, with a silver chain peeking out beneath her neckline.

"Where are you going to—"

"With Jake," Sabah interrupted. "I'm moving in with Jake."

"I don't understand. What?"

"God. Sabrina. Jesus. I'm moving out to go live with my boyfriend. I just . . . I don't want to live with you anymore. Lately, it's like, I can't stop thinking about how dirty you did me and continued to, even though you knew how I felt, even after I told you. You still kept talking to Jake for *weeks* after. You fucking sent him nudes. You sexted him. You had phone sex with him."

Each word was hurled at her like bullets, laced with anger and hurt. Sabrina swallowed hard. She opened her mouth to speak, ready to explain, to say that she was still sorry but nothing came out. She closed her mouth, sighing. It didn't matter anyway because Sabah wasn't done.

"I'm still having a hard time trusting you. I know we've been living together for the past year, but think about it. Most of that time, I was still at Jake's. I honestly don't think we can be friends and I do love you, Sabrina. I do and I've loved this past year of hanging out with you, but all I can think about, every time I see your face, is how much you hurt me. You knew how I felt about him and you still . . . you still did it anyway. I get that," she blew out a loud sigh, looking away. She threw up a hand, a sharp laugh tumbling out of her mouth. "You wanted to hurt me because I ditched you the same week Musa broke up with you. But I told you then that I just thought you were way too fucking selfish and toxic. And then I figured you'd changed so I decided to come back in your life. Then that whole shit with Jake happened."

"I told you I was sorry," Sabrina finally said.

"Sorry isn't enough. I mean, I was so angry with you. I was so furious with what you did with him and I thought you understood that when I sent you that email explaining how it made me feel. But then you still talked to him."

"I blocked him."

"*Yeah.* Three whole weeks later," Sabah shot back. "You kept talking to him, until he messaged me and then me and you met up to talk it out. So I decided to forgive you, because I missed you."

Sabrina bit her lip, feeling guilt churning in her stomach again, combined with diluted nausea. An uncomfortable feeling flooded through her as Sabah started talking again.

"And I just figured when we moved in together, it would be fine. Plus Veda's here. And it was. For a while, it was ok and I loved it. I love you. I'll always have mad love for you, man. But I don't like you at all. I think you're a selfish, conceited bitch and you don't care about how your actions affect other people. So I'm moving in with Jake because I just don't want to be around you anymore." She stared at Sabrina. "And what the fuck are you even *doing* with Daniel? Are you together or not?"

"What has that got to do with anything?"

Suddenly, a hum of anger took away the guilt, flushing away whatever remorse Sabrina had been feeling.

"He really likes you, Sabrina. Surely you've realised that. You can't just string him along and hurt him like you do everyone else."

"That's none of your business," Sabrina said flatly.

"I don't have the time or patience to babysit your insecurities. I've already apologised to you countless times. If you still want to stew over it, go ahead, but I just can't continue to say sorry anymore. You've forgiven Jake—"

"*You* were my best friend. It's completely different."

"—and still can't trust me, yet you're so sure he won't fuck you over? Ok. And in regards to Daniel, like I said, it's none of your business. So if you want to leave, go ahead and leave. I can't be bothered anymore." Her veins were on fire, lava burning through her as she narrowed her eyes at Sabah, who had walked out of the front door. The blistering heat poured into the hallway, wrapping her in its tight grip as resentment coiled around her. She knew that Sabah leaving now was the third time. And maybe the third time was the last time.

"Fuck you, Sabrina. Sooner or later, everyone's going to leave you. One by one. And you won't have anyone left."

"Hey, beautiful." Daniel's smooth voice did little to ease the anger smouldering inside Sabrina as she paced holes into the dining room floor. "How are you, babe?"

"I'm fine," she replied sharply. Swallowing back an apology, she filled her lungs through a slow breath in her nose. "I've just been going through some shit the past day. So uh, anyways. Yeah. I'd love to go to the art thing with you."

"Do you want to talk—"

"Nope. I don't. So, the exhibit?"

"Yeah, um." There was a hint of worry in his voice. Sabrina closed her eyes, pinching the bridge of her nose. "It's on the twenty-seventh, starts at eight o'clock. Dress code is black tie and classy. Have you got anything like that?"

"A black tie?"

He laughed. "No, that's for the men. I mean, have you got a dress that's not—"

"Slutty? Yeah, I do. You'll pick me up?"

There was a pause. "I will. Babe, are you ok?"

"I'm fine."

"You sure?"

"Yeah, Daniel. Really." She stifled a sigh.

"Can I see you tomorrow? I'll pick you up and we can go to *The Shack*? Around eight thirty?"

She stopped in front of the window, watching a pair of girls laughing as they walked past her house. She swallowed back the regret sneaking up inside her. "Yes," she said to Daniel. "That sounds great."

CHAPTER SEVENTEEN

"WE COULD POST something on Twitter?" Sabrina
suggested as she tore into her double cheeseburger the next
day. She took a giant bite from it, a dollop of mayonnaise
dropping onto the white plate. She was out for brunch with
Veda and Elle, with an intense craving for a big, juicy beef
burger and chips—so the girls had decided to go to the
KFC in Stepney Green. The scent of greasy fat filled the
air, the shop hot due to the three men, behind the tall red
counter, tossing chips in a vat of oil and flipping the
burgers. It was sizzling as the orders were prepared, loud
over the din of the men who owned the place and a few
customers talking.

　　　Outside the weather had taken a turn for the worst.
Sabrina knew the glorious sun and bright weather couldn't
have lasted, that it was too good to be true. The clouds were
grey and silver, rain coming down in sheets and
pummelling the ground, bouncing off the tarmac as people

hurried down the streets. There was, however, a lingering warmth in the air, combined with the falling rain that pissed Sabrina off. She would've preferred it to be cold and rainy, rather than humid and wet.

"That's a bit weird though, isn't it? And risky?" Veda frowned, swallowing the giant mouthful of her chicken burger. "We could end up getting a serial killer as a roommate or something. It's dangerous meeting someone online."

"Everyone meets everyone on social media these days," Sabrina said. "I met Soran on Twitter."

"And look how that turned out," Elle laughed. She took a swig of her strawberry Mirinda and then picked up her burger, the chicken piece poking out beneath the sesame bun.

"We're still friends. It just didn't work out as a relationship or whatever. I mean, it's not like we were even together."

"You had sex with him."

"Once," Sabrina said, biting into her burger. A sesame seed fell of her bun, bouncing off her index finger and landed on the plate with a few of the other fallen seeds and a strand of lettuce. "We had sex only once." She swallowed. "Well, actually quite a few times but just that one day."

"Yeah, but," Veda argued. "You two were exclusive. Or supposedly? Didn't he say you'll be his *girlfriend* and promise he wasn't talking to anyone else like that, but he actually *was*?"

Sabrina shrugged. "The past is the past. It hurt at the time, a little but I'm over it. We hardly talk now, but I do

SUMAIYA AHMED

consider him a friend. He's not a serial killer."

"Regardless, I don't want to have it being global news that we're in need of a roommate"

"Fair enough," Sabrina conceded. "We'll figure it out. It's not like we can't afford to pay two hundred and five pounds in rent each."

"Not the point."

"Yeah, I know. But it's fine. If anything, it'll probably just be June that we have to pay extra. I guarantee you, we'll find someone soon."

"Put out an ad in the papers or Craigslist," Elle said.

"Ew, god, no," Sabrina wrinkled her nose. "Craigslist is for freaks and who even reads the papers these days?"

"A lot of people," Veda deadpanned. "We can do something in the papers. We need to. Or even Gumtree."

Sabrina sighed. "God. Some fucking warning would've been nice."

Veda didn't respond.

They continued eating in silence, listening to the soft chatter of a group of men queued up in front of the counter, polishing off the calorie-induced, fat-filled burgers and chips. They'd also gotten six extra hot wings, which had been finished first. Veda came home last night a little after ten P.M., drunk on rum and vodka, when Sabrina had been crashing on the sofa, watching *Game of Thrones*.

"So Sabah's moved out," Veda huffed, tipping onto the sofa beside Sabrina. "It's just the two of us now."

"Mm," Sabrina hummed, not looking away from the TV. "I know."

"I hope she knows what she's doing."

"She practically lives with the guy anyway."

"It's silly. She's so young. Jesus. Sabah's only eighteen."

"Well, she has to make her own mistakes and learn from them. If she wants to live with a guy that's a bit of a fuck up, then that's her decision."

"And you're cool with it?"

Sabrina took in a breath, pulling a face as the scent of alcohol hit her. It was strong on Veda. "My feelings on the matter are irrelevant. We're not friends, even if we are family." She laughed. "I'm a selfish bitch, like she said."

"Yeah, you kind of are," Veda yawned. Her breath stank of vodka. Sabrina grimaced.

"Veda, you fucking stink."

She giggled in reply and stood up. "Oh shit," she laughed, grabbing onto Sabrina's shoulder when she stumbled. "Gonna go sleep."

"Good night," Sabrina said, smiling wryly. She watched as Veda walked out of the room and up the stairs.

Now, as she sat across from Veda, Elle beside her, Sabrina wondered how on earth they were going to find a roommate before their rent was due at the end of the month. She didn't want to have to fork out nearly an extra seventy quid or however much it would cost her to pay for what Sabah should've.

Instead of Sabah's words going over in her head, Sabrina was worried about who they'd end up with as a roommate, once they found her. She was close to Veda, having known each other their entire lives, and now they would have to fit someone else into their little group, living with this stranger. She sighed, dipping three chips into the puddle of ketchup and hot sauce. Once they were thoroughly coated in the condiments, Sabrina put them in her mouth, chewing slowly. A small sliver of anxiety was wiring through her system, flicking on and off like a light switch as the thoughts of a nonexistent roommate came and went.

". . . tomorrow night?" Elle looked at Sabrina.

"Huh? Sorry. I wasn't paying attention."

Elle rolled her eyes, an amused smile on her face. "Thinking about your man?"

"He's not my man," Sabrina said straight away. "What were you saying?"

"I was asking," Elle began slowly, tracing the rim of the can in her hand. "If you know what you're wearing tomorrow night."

"Uh," Sabrina picked up the last bit of her burger and plopped into her mouth. She chewed, thinking about the dinner at Elle's parents place. It was a late birthday shindig for her twenty first. Marion had been relentless in messaging both Elle and Sabrina about it, saying she wanted to do something to celebrate: *after all, you only turn twenty one once.* "I'm thinking about that light pink dress from *ZARA*? The satin one."

"You're obsessed with satin," Veda laughed.

Sabrina shrugged half-heartedly and tilted her head back as she finished her Mirinda drink.

"Sounds good. I can't wait to be back home. It's been a while," Elle sighed.

"One day," Sabrina said. "I think I might move to Meadowbrook. It's gorgeous there."

"Yeah?"

She nodded. "Yep. After getting my doctorate and maybe working for a year or two in a hospital here. I guess I'll see. But I definitely do want to get a place there. Meadowbrook is gorgeous and the houses are way bigger, compared to London."

"Cheaper, too."

"Everywhere is cheaper than London, Veda."

"Australia is a lot more expensive."

"Shut up."

"Make me."

Sabrina threw the empty packet of ketchup at Veda, who shrieked and chucked a rolled up wad of tissue. It bounced off Sabrina's empty drink can. Elle sighed.

At five o'clock, Sabrina was a little tipsy on the wine humming through her veins, coursing like liquid gold in her bloodstream. The whisper thin, grey clouds had let up, allowing a faint beam of the sun to weakly brighten up the evening as she sauntered into a bar in Shoreditch. It was dimly lit inside the bar, stools lining the counter and a few couches shoved together against a wall. There were a few black, chipping tables placed haphazardly in front of them, glasses of various drinks resting, with muted fingerprints smudged on the foggy glass. Hazy smoke danced through the air like a colourless snake, the hinges of the door creaking behind her as a man clad in a business suit entered.

The stench of alcohol and cigarettes hit Sabrina as

she walked deeper into the dark bar, squinting a little as she stumbled to a stool, where only one other man sat, nursing a short glass of pale gold, gleaming liquid. She grasped the splintering wood of the counter, her nails raking across it, clambering onto her seat, sighing loudly; the smell of everything mixing together was heavy, like black plumes rising from a burning block.

"What's your poison?" the bartender asked her, his gaze dipping to the low neckline of her sheer lace shirt.

She looked at him, pushing a hand through the blonde-brown hair she'd styled into loose waves, held back with a bejewelled clip. "Vodka orange," she said over the din of jazz music, conversation and laughter rippling through the air. The bartender nodded, glancing at her cleavage again before turning to get a wide glass and pouring pulp-free orange juice into it and a few splashes of Smirnoff vodka.

A few seconds later, the glass was placed in front of her and she stared down at the swirling drink, the fluorescent lights reflecting off it. She picked it up slowly and brought it to her lips, swallowing it all down. The smoke from someone's cigarette wafted over to her as the person, a woman with waist-length blonde hair, exited the bar, brushing past Sabrina. It curled in the air around her and she inhaled the bitter scent as she put the empty glass back on the scratched wood.

"The same, again," she said to the blue-eyed bartender. He mixed the drinks into her glass again in front of her, before moving on to a man in a white shirt, tie loosened around his neck. He asked for three bottles of beer, was sitting on one of the worn, brown sofas with two other men.

Sabrina took a large mouthful of her drink, knowing it wouldn't be long until the alcohol began to affect the way she walked and slowed down her movements. Even when she was drunk, Sabrina was completely aware of what she did, she never blacked out or forgot about it the next day, or got hangovers. She also knew when to cut herself off.

Two stools away from her, the man that was sitting there glanced over at her. The glass hovered in his hand, halfway to his mouth. Sabrina met his gaze, folding one leg over the other, dangling her Jimmy Choo heel, revealing more of her smooth, brown leg beneath her leather mini skirt. His mouth tipped up into a small smirk before he finished off his drink and put the glass down. He signalled the bartender to pour him another with a wave of his hand.

Paco Rabanne's Olympéa clung to Sabrina's wrists and the pulse beating in her neck, easing the stagnant reeking of body odour and spilled beer on the floor a few feet behind her as a man tripped over his own feet, laughing uproariously about something that probably wasn't all that funny in his drunken bubble. She breathed in the sweet scent from the inside of her wrist after finishing off her drink, feeling the buzz from the vodka simmering through her.

She looked at the barman when he came a little closer to her, traces of laughter on his face as a woman leaned over the counter, ordering a dirty martini. After he handed her the drink, he looked at Sabrina. She smiled a little, tucking a few strands of hair out of her eyes, pointing at her glass. He grinned and then quickly filled it up.

Movement to her right made her look over at the

man who had been sitting on the stool as he took a seat beside her. She cocked her head a little, watching him as he leaned an elbow on the wooden surface, facing her, one knee just barely touching hers.

"So," he said, eyes boring into Sabrina's. With the hand that was resting on the counter, he picked up the glass filled with the same drink he'd had earlier, sipping it slowly. Beneath the cuff of his sleeve, Sabrina saw the glint of a gold watch. "What's your story?"

"Excuse me?" Sabrina frowned, her voice a little louder than she'd intended. Alcohol always made her talk a little louder, more confident in herself.

"Why are you here? Everyone's got a story. I mean," he smiled a little, dimples denting his otherwise flawless, deep brown skin, his teeth perfectly straight and white. "I've had a pretty long, exhausting day at work. Dealing with numbers all day isn't all that fun."

"Dealing with numbers is never fun, full fucking stop," Sabrina snorted. "But uh, I've just had a few . . . shitty, um, days. Or a shitty year and a half, I guess." She shrugged.

"Ah," the man nodded gravely. "One of those. Guess we all have *some* shit in our lives to overcome." A frown, quickly erased with another charming smile, one that said he was always on top. "And you're right. Dealing with numbers isn't great, but it is satisfying."

"Mm. So what is it that you do?"

"I'm an accountant. Yourself?"

"A soon-to-be psychology graduate, working part time in a pretty shitty retail job."

He laughed into his glass, taking another sip. His

eyes never left Sabrina's. "Well, what's lined up after you graduate?"

"More studying," Sabrina smiled thinly. "I'll be doing my doctorate. It'll take another three years."

She received a low whistle in response and an impressed look. Sabrina's smile widened a little further as she swallowed a mouthful of her vodka orange.

"What's the end goal?"

"Becoming a counselling psychologist."

"That's amazing," he shook his head. "Wow. Props to you. Good luck. I'm sure you'll smash it all."

Sabrina tilted her head in thanks. "What's your name?"

"Micah. And yours?"

She sipped her drink again before responding. "Sabrina."

"Well, Sabrina," Micah said, tasting the sound of her name in his mouth. An excited shiver ran down her spine, recognising the glint of lust in his eyes as he looked at her. "What are you doing later?"

"Hopefully you," she smirked.

He grinned at her. "Yeah?"

"Unless you have something better to do?"

"Not at all."

"That's what I thought."

Micah laughed, running a hand over his long braids, the ends brushing against the tops of his shoulders. "You wanna get out of here?"

Sabrina shifted on the stool, ignoring as it squeaked beneath her. She uncrossed her legs, her skirt riding up a few inches. A hot flash of lust tore through her when

Micah's eyes momentarily dipped to her thighs. She finished her drink.

"I'd rather not wait," she said, standing up. He raised an eyebrow, a smirk glossing his lips. She stepped a little closer to him, one hand on his thigh, inching closer to the part of him she wanted in her mouth. "Come with me to the bathroom?"

Two hours after Micah fucked her senseless against the closed bathroom door in the dingy, stinking bar and then took her number down in his phone; he walked her to Whitechapel Station. He was bordering on tipsy; his gait not in an exact straight line as they glided through the barriers, laughing about the man caught urinating outside *William Hill*. He kissed her at the platform as she waited for the District line train, leaning down because he was a foot and four inches taller than her, his big hands cupping her face as if she was something delicate and fragile, easily breakable. She smiled at him drunkenly before whispering bye, watching as he walked down to the over-ground platform.

When the train came, she got on, her hair over one shoulder of her lacy white shirt. It wasn't as packed in the train as she thought it would have been and she nearly tripped on her way to the seat at the end of the carriage, which would end up being closest to the stairs she would need to walk up once she got to her station.

Opposite her was a girl that looked like she was the same age as Sabrina, scrolling on her phone. She had a

McDonald's bag on her lap and a backpack at her feet, and looked up at Sabrina, who had leaned her head against the window, eyes closed as she tried to get rid of the sudden sick feeling settling in the pit of her stomach. She breathed in deeply, a small frown pulling her eyebrows together as the scent of chicken nuggets and fries wafted over to her.

Her stomach rumbled loudly, making her open her eyes and blink. She put her hand over her stomach, sighing. The girl came over to sit beside her, plopping the backpack onto the floor between her feet.

"Here," she said to Sabrina, taking out a box with a mayo chicken burger in. She handed it over, and when Sabrina didn't take it, she put it on her lap. "Food always helps me when I'm drunk. Trust me, it'll make you feel better. Eat it." Sabrina stared at her incredulously and then glanced down at the white box on her lap.

"Um," she said. "I—I don't . . ." she trailed off, swallowing. Her tummy growled in hunger.

"You're hungry. Seriously. Eat. I've got another burger in here anyway," the blonde-haired girl smiled. "I always get two burgers and large everything else because I'm a fat shit."

Sabrina let out a little laugh, and then seeing the girl take out another burger box, smiled gratefully, saying a soft *thank you so much*. She opened up the one on her lap and carefully picked up the burger in her hands, savagely biting into it.

Ten minutes later, Sabrina finished her burger and was sharing the chicken nuggets with the kind stranger, telling her everything about Musa, Sabah and Jake, Daniel and now this Micah guy she'd slept with, her words running together a little as she stumbled over them, slurring a bit. She dipped a nugget into the small tub of barbeque sauce and then put the whole thing into her mouth.

By then, three other people had gotten onto the carriage and weren't trying to hide the fact they were totally eavesdropping.

"Ok, so it basically sounds like you've majorly fucked up," the girl, Courtney, said. "And you're obviously still in love with your ex, which is understandable. I mean, he was—or is, rather—your first real love and first serious boyfriend, so that's always gonna be there. But you know now that nothing will ever come of it. Still partially holding onto that hope is normal though, and time and distance will make it easier, even if you think otherwise. Trust me," Courtney smiled sadly. "I know what I'm talking about. I messed up with my ex and lost her. It took a long time to get over that. Anyways. It kinda sounds like you think maybe your friend is right about calling you selfish. I think—" here, she sighed and bit a chicken nugget in half. She chewed and swallowed before continuing.

"I think you're subconsciously trying to push everyone away, like a kind of self-destructive, defence mechanism, you know? That's why you did what you did with the Micah guy today. By the way, he sounds hot as fuck. So if shit ends up going south with Daniel," she smirked. "You can just keep fucking him."

"I'm not even in a relationship with Daniel though," Sabrina muttered. "Like we're not together. So I don't know why I'm starting to feel so guilty about it. We haven't even talked about anything, about us, I mean. We're not, like, a *thing*."

"Then it's fine," Courtney shrugged, taking another nugget. She pushed the box over to Sabrina, letting her have the last one. "There's nothing to freak out about. If you two never discussed being exclusive or being in a relationship, then he can't do shit. There's no label on your relationship or whatever it is, so you don't owe him anything."

Sabrina toppled out of the train, waving bye to Courtney, when she got to her station, her stomach full with alcohol, a burger, nuggets and water, the latter three thanks to Courtney. The walk up the stairs felt exhausting, her eyes heavy with a tiredness she knew sleep wouldn't be able to cure.

When she stepped outside, the air was thick with warmth, the clouds overhead pregnant with rain, about to pour any minute. The sun had hidden itself away as she walked the few minutes distance to her house. She wasn't able to walk in a straight line, getting a few looks from the people passing by, majority of them Asian and definitely Muslim. Sabrina heard the quiet murmur of a woman to her daughter, saying something about shorom and haya and haram and jahannam, making Sabrina roll her eyes and sigh loudly.

It felt like forever when she finally reached her front door, her fingers fumbling as she tried to unlock it. The keys fell from her hand and she swore, bending down to pick it up. A car going past beeped its horn, a guy yelling out some obscenities and telling her he'd like her to bend over like that for him as he fucked her. She stood up, the keys clutched in her hand now, half turning as the car sped away, laughter echoing in the street.

She swore again.

Once she was inside, Sabrina stepped out of her heels and slinked upstairs, gripping onto the banister tightly so she didn't accidentally fall to her death or something. The house was empty. Veda had gone to her grandparents' place for the evening, since it was her nephew's second birthday party.

Sabrina groaned loudly, seeing the mess she'd left her room in: clothes littered the floor and her dressing/vanity table was covered with her makeup products and brushes.

She slipped out of her clothes, walking in just her bra to the bathroom. Micah had ended up keeping her red silk and lace thong. It was one of her favourites and she'd forgotten to get it back from him once they'd left the bathroom and then the bar.

The heat from the water soothed her aching muscles as she tilted her head back, the water rinsing out the loose waves of her hair. She rubbed the Dove soap into her hands and scrubbed her makeup off with it. It slid down the drain, beige and black washed away with the scorching clear water gushing out of the shower head.

The alcohol clouding her mind was easing up; sopped up by the food she'd practically inhaled in the train. Whoever Courtney was, Sabrina hoped good went her way and she was happy as fuck, because she was an absolute angel.

Twenty minutes later, Sabrina pulled on a pair of

blue and white striped pyjama bottoms and one of Musa's t-shirts she still had, still wore, missing his smell on it. Her hair was still dripping water into her carpet, when the doorbell rang at eight thirty-three. She blinked, pausing at the top of the stairs, her phone clutched in her hand, confused.

Making her way downstairs slowly, Sabrina tucked her wet hair behind her ear, opening the door. In front of her stood Daniel, a smile on his face.

He raised his eyebrows at her appearance. "Still not ready?"

"Huh?" Sabrina asked, feeling lost.

Daniel stepped inside, his eyes flicking over her body. "Did you—" he stopped, eyes narrowing. He leaned in a little closer, a hand reaching out to the neck of her t-shirt. She moved back.

"What are you doing?"

"Is that a hickey?"

"What?"

"Sabrina." Daniel's voice was small as he looked at her, hurt and confusion etched on his face. "What . . . why do you—I don't . . ." he swallowed. "Why are there hickeys on your neck?"

She inhaled sharply, her hand lifting to the column of her throat. She unlocked her phone and flipped the camera so she saw her face. She moved it down a little and a small hiss escaped between her teeth as she caught sight of the love bites Micah had left on her.

"Sabrina," Daniel said again. "What the fuck? What the *actual fuck*—why the *hell* do you have fucking hickeys on your neck?"

"Relax," she muttered. "It's not like we're in a relationship. Are we?"

"Well, I don't know about you," he said, voice low. Angry. "But I thought we were dating. If that's not what we're doing, then what exactly is it?"

"I thought we were just fucking."

"So that's all this is to you? *All this time.* It was just . . ."

"Sex," she said simply, when he trailed off.

As if this word, this one word, explained everything. That was all it took. For things to change, a single word needed to be uttered. It was so simple, so easy, to just say it, but when it was spoken, when it reached the other person, it was too late to take it back. Words: they had the power to completely destroy a person, a relationship.

A small seed of regret planted itself in her heart, rushing through her veins after she said it. She swallowed back the bile that rose to her throat, pushing away the feeling of guilt, of hurt, of regret.

He stared at her for a few minutes, silent.

"Fine," Daniel replied. He didn't sound angry. He didn't sound upset either. His face was blank, an expressionless mask shielding whatever emotions he was feeling. "Fine. Whatever."

He turned around and walked out the door, slamming it shut behind him.

Sabrina didn't bother chasing after him.

CHAPTER EIGHTEEN

IT HAD RAINED a little earlier, the water droplets looking like falling stars as the sky had darkened to a rich, deeper shade of blue, hinting at the night that would envelop the country in its dusk. Rays of sunlight had burned bright over the past two weeks and it was the first time that afternoon they'd had rain, a respite from the blistering heat. Sabrina's skin had deepened to a darker, glorious shade of brown, much to her mother's annoyance. She always hated it when her daughters' complexions tanned into a more bronzed brown, as if they'd spent their entire lives living in the sun, kissed by its golden light.

Sabrina was upstairs in Adam's old room with him and Sultana, the three of them drinking lemonade, eating giant and soft, homemade cookies that Sultana had baked a few hours ago, and watching *Kill Bill: Volume 2*, whilst Miriam and Leanne slept in Sultana's room. Their parents were downstairs with Fulkumari khala and her husband,

discussing their son, Tawhid's upcoming nuptials to some
manager at a mental health facility that also dealt with
children who had special needs, as well as Adam and
Rose's wedding. When their parents had told everyone
Adam was getting married to a white woman, the reactions
were pretty much all the same from their aunts, uncle and
cousins: shock. Whether it was about him marrying a revert
or that their parents were totally ok with it, Sabrina didn't
know. But she loved seeing the looks her cousins
exchanged once they received the news, asking *but wait,
why*, and Ruksana saying *because my son wants to marry
her and she's a lovely woman* in a curt tone of voice.
Sabrina knew her mother definitely would not be so
accepting if *she* brought home a man that was a different
race.

In the past two weeks, Sabrina and her mum, sister
and Rose, Daisy and Irina had gone to Green Street
multiple times, searching for outfits for the nikkah, which
was coming up soon. There was less than two months 'til
the day and Rose had finally found a pretty silk, mermaid
tail white wedding dress that she planned to wear for her
nikkah, after eight visits to the East Mall. She would be
wearing it beneath a heavily embroidered white abaya,
decorated with diamonds and pearls, that she was getting
custom made from this cute little boutique Sabrina had
found on Instagram. Sabrina and Sultana planned to wear a
shimmery mint green shalwar kameez with silver beadwork
scattered throughout it, matching with the abaya their mum
would be wearing.

The day Rose found her dress, stars in her eyes,
they'd all been exhausted from the heat and wanting the

comfort of their home. Sabrina was gasping for a cup of coffee, despite the sweat pooled in the dip above her cupid's bow and gathered on her nose, temples and neck, beading between her breasts. She stood beside Irina as Rose stood on the little platform, twirling around in the white froth of silk, utter delight lighting her entire face up.

"This is the one," she'd laughed, turning to look at her mum and sister, joy radiating off of her. It was impossible to not smile back at her, to not feel just as excited, in that moment. As Daisy and Irina cooed over how gorgeous she looked, Sabrina's eyes trailed off her future sister-in-law's figure encased in the dress, highlighting her ample chest before skimming over her stomach and hips before it fell to the floor like a waterfall. She swallowed back the tears stabbing her eyes, the inescapable hurt shadowing her every breath, and looked away from Rose.

Her gaze wandered to the other dresses. A jolt of pain rushed through her heart, coursing through her veins like quicksilver. There had been a time when she thought she would be here, searching through all the dresses for the one, when she would be marrying Musa.

Distantly, she heard her mother tell Rose she looked like an absolute angel, stunning beyond words. Sabrina swallowed again, crossing her arms over her chest, gripping onto her elbow, nails digging into her skin, beneath the pale pink flute-sleeved top she wore, leaving behind crescent moon indents. Her head was pounding from the night before.

"Bhaiya is so going to cry when he sees you," Sultana cackled. She had tears in her eyes and a light smile on her lips.

Rose laughed. "I doubt that."

"Oh, he so will. Right, Bri?"

"Hmm?" Sabrina blinked when her sister addressed her. Noticing everyone's eyes on her, her cheeks flushed a bright pink. "Oh, um. *Yeah.*" After a beat, she added, "bhaiya is a big softie."

Sabrina had thrown herself into helping plan the wedding (and running every day) to keep her mind off of the events from two weeks ago, what with losing both Daniel and Sabah. It felt like things had come full circle and it made her laugh. She didn't let herself feel the guilt or the absence that was left from the door shutting behind them as they walked away. She had no one to blame but herself for it, anyway.

"This movie is a fucking masterpiece," Sultana said as the credits began to roll. "I love it so much. Beatrix is *amazing.*"

"I still can't believe she screwed such an old guy," Sabrina sniggered, breaking her cookie in half and plopping it into her mouth. The chocolate chunk in it melted in her mouth and she bit back a moan of pleasure as she chewed it.

"Like you wouldn't do the same thing. You have no morals."

"*Please,*" Adam said. "Don't talk about that shit when I'm here."

"Sorry, bhaiya," Sultana laughed. "Speaking of screwing—" Adam glared at her. She shrugged at him. "How's your boyfriend?"

"I don't have a boyfriend, so I wouldn't know."

"Daniel?"

"Who?" Sabrina shoved the rest of the cookie into her mouth, looking like a squirrel with nuts against her cheek. She held her hand over her mouth as she choked on a laugh, coughing a little as she finally swallowed the cookie down.

"Is there trouble in paradise?"

"He's, uh," Sabrina bit her lip, leaning over to the bedside table for her glass of lemonade, ice floating on the top. "Not in my life anymore."

She noticed her siblings exchange glances.

"What happened?" Adam asked. His dark eyebrows pulled down, creating the illusion of a monobrow as he looked at her.

"Um," Sabrina shrugged, taking another mouthful of her drink, and then said, "it just didn't work out, I guess. Not a big deal."

"But," Sultana frowned. "He was so perfect. And lovely. You two were—"

"You didn't even meet him, Tana."

"*Still*. From everything you said about him, he seemed like he was wonderful. God. What *happened*?"

"Nothing. I don't want to talk about it." I fucked it up, she silently said.

"Are you ok though?" Adam asked her, worry flickering in his brown eyes. He ran a hand over his beard as he chewed on a cookie. Sultana turned her laptop off.

"Mhm. Yeah. I'm fine."

"Sure ni? Tui zanos amrareh zesata khoyteh farbeh toh?"

"Yeah," Sabrina smiled. "I know, bhaiya. Thanks."

A week ago, when she'd come round after her first day volunteering at Citizens Advice on a Thursday, her mum had been the only one home. Sultana was out with a friend, rejoicing the end of her exams and the beginning of a nearly four month long summer holiday, and her dad was at one of his friend's house. With her parents, things were still kind of the same: they were constantly arguing over little things, on the verge of it becoming violent. But thankfully, Sultana had told her over text after one major fight, it didn't.

That Thursday evening, her mother was in the kitchen, stirring the dhayl in preparation for dinner. She'd also made chicken with hatkhora, as well as a mackerel chatni. The rice was on the stove, the heat on low, when Sabrina walked into the kitchen after putting her bag away in her old room and changing into a yellow kameez.

Her mum looked at her as she filled up a glass with cold water from the fridge. "Aizkeh foyla din asil ni volunteering o?"

"Ji oy," Sabrina nodded, leaning against the table in the centre of the kitchen. "It was pretty good, to be honest," she said, without her mum having to ask. "I enjoyed it. I mean, it was just a lesson obviously and getting to know all the laws in place regarding renting and debts and everything. But it was surprisingly interesting."

"Hmm. That's good, baby," Ruksana murmured, tasting the dhayl with a tablespoon. "Here, come see if it needs a bit more salt."

Sabrina took the spoon from her mother and rinsed it under cold water before shaking it off to dip it into the lentils, taking a bit of it onto the spoon. She held it over her left hand as she brought it to her mouth, swallowing it. "No, it's good. Nothing else needed, amma."

"Bhala," her mum sighed. "Tor abbay dhayl khayta saisla aizkeh."

"Ami kichu khortam ni? Ar khorar aseh ni?"

"You can hoover upstairs. Ami khali niseh khortam farslam, er badeh fon aiseh. It's in the living room."

"Alright," Sabrina smiled. She walked out of the kitchen and took the Henry hoover from the sitting room and switched it on, hoovering the steps as she went up them slowly.

Fifteen minutes later, after she'd finished, Sabrina let out a loud shriek. "Amma, amma, ufreh aybay ni?" she shouted, edging toward the stairs.

She heard the sound of footsteps hurrying up the stairs as she stared at the long-legged, big spider crawling on the wall opposite her old bedroom.

"Kita hoiseh?" Ruksana demanded, eyes worried, looking at her daughter. Sabrina pointed at the spider wordlessly. Her mum sighed loudly, taking the tissue from the pocket in her meski. "Dhurr funga, *dhurr* funga," she snapped. "Oto dhor dekhaysot, ferothor goror feroth. Fagolor lakhan seek dewa lageh ni?"

Sabrina found herself shaking with laughter as her mother continued grumbling about Sabrina's shriek scaring her, a hand over her mouth as her shoulders shook. Loud laughter ended up tumbling out of her mouth when her mum gave her a withering stare, nostrils flaring. She shook her head before going downstairs, taking the spider in the tissue with her.

The garden door opened for a moment and then

closed again.

Ever since Sabrina was little, she'd been terrified of all insects and bugs. Once, when she was nine, in Bangladesh, a red ant had bitten her on the ankle. It hadn't really hurt, just a bit of a sting but she still cried and clung to Adam as he carried her back to their house.

She'd had nightmares for days, of ants crawling all over her and in the bedroom, on the walls, on the floors, on the bed. Her father had to get a mesaab to come and give her a ta'wiz, which helped to end the nightmares.

Sabrina only wished it had helped to stop her childhood being taken from her. But life didn't work that way and god had already written how everyone's lives would turn out. Heartbreak was in every page of her story.

Back in Adam's bedroom, as the conversation drifted to remember-when's, Sabrina felt numbness eclipsing her, raw and icy, as it shrouded her in its darkness. It was similar to the feelings she'd had when she was in secondary school especially, even though she'd felt its clutches around her throat and her mind from the age nine and a half onwards. There was a diary she had, a bright blue Funky Friends one that she'd written in constantly, every single day when her brother had bought it for her. A few days before her tenth birthday, Sabrina wrote that the world would be a better place if she had never existed at all and how she knew her parents looked at her and were disappointed with what they saw. She was sad, she wrote, so sad and she didn't know why, but it was the only constant in her life for months, for years. It tangled itself in her mind, colouring everything in shades of black and grey, blinding her from seeing any colours for years.

Everything became worse once she started secondary school. In year eight, she started seeing a counsellor after a breakdown in front of her tutor, after telling the Child Protection Officer everything. Each week up until year eleven, Sabrina saw her counsellor and opened up about the blade she dragged across her flesh, leaving behind thin red lines mapping her depression. She hid it from her family and from the few friends she had, including Veda and Sabah. Nobody needed to know. It would just be a burden.

A few weeks after she was reprimanded for skipping psychology too much in year twelve, her tutor called her in for a meeting, saying her parents would have to be brought in. She'd broken the rules of her contract, which had stated she had to go to every single lesson and do every single piece of homework. Sabrina had broken down completely in front of her tutor, Jocelyn, unable to stop the tears once they started. Jocelyn took her into another, separate room, away from the other teachers in the office and the students waiting in front of the Financial Aids desk. Sabrina told Jocelyn that she wanted to kill herself. And then, a few days later, she started seeing the sixth form's counsellor.

Most of her nights were spent staring at the ceiling as headlights and taillights from cars traced patterns across it, tree leaves waving at her for a few seconds or minutes before fading into darkness, like the one that crept up in her soul. Tears glimmered on her red cheeks as she muffled her cries with a hand over her mouth, body wracked with sobs that didn't seem to have an end, no matter how many times she tried to stop, to breathe and control the hurt and pain tearing her up inside.

It wasn't like there was anything wrong, but it felt like she was in this bubble, like the walls of every room were caving in on her. She felt trapped inside of her mind for years, lost to a cocoon of darkness and this aching feeling of everything constantly shattering into a million pieces around her, debris and dust collecting at her feet. As if she was trying to dig her way through dirt, soil coating her nails, searching for a bit of light or fresh air or escape. Anything to get out of the prison in her head.

She'd crumbled, so many times, with a forced smile on her face and *I'm fines* leaving her mouth whenever someone asked her if she was ok because she looked so tired or so thin. But nobody really cared. They just pretended to, so they could feel like they did their one good deed for the day. Nobody cared. Nobody ever cared.

People always promised they would be there but they ended up leaving when she needed them the most. They forced themselves through the barriers she put up around herself, to protect her own heart, and then they made her lower her guard. Then they left.

It was the same old thing, over and over.

So this time, now, Sabrina pushed people away before they could leave her. And it *hurt*. God, it fucking hurt. Pushing him away, losing him because of *her own fucking stupidity* was hurting her so much. And it confused the shit out of her, because it wasn't as if Daniel *meant* anything to her, not like that. But she was listening to her siblings talking and staring at her hands, thinking she hated herself.

She had always hated herself.

For a few months, with Musa, she was ok. She was fucking happy.

And now she wasn't.

She hadn't been, for a long time. It was all just . . . falling apart and she was falling apart and she hated it. The cold hands of depression snaked around her throat, covering her mouth to stop her from screaming or crying out for someone to help her, because she was in this alone now.

It was her fault. Nobody could save her.

CHAPTER NINETEEN

WALKING INTO FAIRLY *Odd Pizzas* felt like stepping into a time warp, when everything was so much more different, yet somehow the same with the bitter taste of memories coating her tongue and running through her mind, like snapshots of a movie she didn't want to see. It was all of a time when she'd first stumbled into the place with the girl she betrayed a few months later and the one time when she realised her feelings for Daniel could *possibly* be something more, before she shook it away, telling herself she was just being stupid. But of course, now, the guilt and the hurt and the sudden emptiness that his absence left inside her was unquenchable, a gaping hole she couldn't fill, even with all the distractions and her busy schedule.

Sometimes it seemed like she was going to collapse, she was so tired of everything and herself. She wanted to just leave everything behind, walk out of her own life and become somebody else. But it wasn't easy to shed your own skin. Even if she, maybe, was a snake. *She was.* What she did to Sabah, it wasn't just a bitchy move—it was the kind of thing a snake did. Even after Sabah had forgiven her those few days after it had all happened, it constantly played on Sabrina's mind before she picked up all the memories and shoved it into a box, pushing it to the very back, into the furthest corners of her mind. She didn't want to remember.

With the act of remembering came the need to drown it in vodka, pouring it down her throat like a movie star desert survivor. She had six empty bottles lined up against the wall like tiny soldiers, ranging from Absolut to Ciroc to Smirnoff to Glen's and an empty carton of orange juice. She had finished six bottles in fifteen nights, still a little drunk the next morning, but not enough for anyone else to notice. It was all she could do to survive, to numb the pain roaring inside her like an undefeated monster that had been playing dead for a while.

On Sunday, she woke up at four thirty A.M. after sleeping for four hours in a drunken haze, nausea making her stumble out of her bed and into the adjoined bathroom. She'd knelt in front of the toilet, vomit spewing out and splashing into the water at the bottom, more liquid than chunks of food. The mix of her vomit and the alcohol made her heave again, fingers gripping onto the edge of the toilet seat as tears streamed down her hot cheeks, hair stuck to her skin with sweat and tears, a few strands getting in her mouth as she leaned over the bowl.

She'd gasped, sobbing, as she finally moved back from the toilet, her back against the bottom cabinet beneath the sink, wiping the back of her hand over her mouth. Everything was slowly spinning and it took effort for her to rise to her feet, hardly recognising the girl looking back at her from the mirror. Her eyes were rimmed with red and bloodshot, face flushed and pink with the summer heat and the alcohol in her bloodstream, poisoning her liver and her mind. There was a bit of vomit clinging to a few strands of her hair.

Seeing that, she'd broken down into cries again as she blindly flushed the toilet and then rinsed her hands beneath cold water. Cupping her palms beneath the water as it gushed out, she tipped her head down and rinsed out her mouth, knowing she needed to get into the shower. She stank. Of vomit, alcohol, sweat and she'd also just pissed herself.

In the two hours it took her to clean up the bathroom, mopping it top to bottom and then hand washing her clothes as she swayed on her feet, Sabrina had sobered up just a little bit. Enough to realise she started work in half an hour.

Her shower took an extra forty minutes as she scrubbed herself raw, skin blotchy and red as she rubbed the muslin cloth against her body, the water scalding as it rained out of the shower head. When she finished, she smelt like cherries and marshmallows.

She was an hour late to work. To make up for it, she stayed behind an hour and a half.

At work, she spent majority of the time in the office, the bright lights hurting her eyes and giving her a headache and making her empty stomach clench painfully. There were four new starters she had to show around, throwing them ropes to cling onto as they stumbled about on their first day, not knowing where everything went, stuttering as they served customers and messing up the cash register more than once. Sabrina had to bite back a growl of frustration after coming back to two of them for the fifth time, saying, "when you scan the items, do that shit quickly, but when it comes to counting the money they give you, you take your time. Even if they're in a rush, even if they're being impatient and having a go at you, no matter what, you take your time. If they say they're going to be late for something, that's their problem. You still do *your* job. Take your time to count the money and to make sure you put in the correct amount, ok?"

The rest of her nine and a half hours at *Sainsbury's* were spent barking orders at the other team members when the shop floor was a bit too messed up or when the stocks were running low on the shelves.

At four forty five, Sabrina stumbled out of the shop, squinting as the sun pierced her eyes. The fragrance of summer sealed itself on the light wind, gently blowing beneath a wispy, cloud speckled, lapis sky, making her breathe in deeply, inhaling the scent of flowers blooming along the streets. The bright colours of roses and tulips exploding on bushes and pots brought a subtle smile to her face as she made the journey to *Fairly Odd Pizzas*. She had an intense, crazy craving for saucy meatball pizza with extra cheese and the delicious strawberry gelato that only they had. She stashed away the emotions that had snuck up on her during her thirty minute lunch break, when she didn't have the distraction of faking smiles at her colleagues and customers, or telling the store manager they'd run out of plastic bags.

She buried the sadness inside of her, fastening it with a slam of the empty coffin in her chest, a haunted graveyard of sharp regret and astringent melancholy, wishing she could somehow turn off her humanity.

Fixing a skyward thing on her lips, Sabrina pushed open the glass doors of the pizza place, breathing in the doughy aroma of everything she was craving.

On the wall opposite the entrance was the huge gelato bar, various flavours in large, silver tubs with a stainless steel ice cream scoop resting on the granite counter just a little behind it, for Ashton or Grayson or Roberto or Katherine to use. A few feet in front of it was the table and chairs that Kira and two of her friends were, as usual, occupying, closest to both the gelato bar and the counter where Grayson was putting a freshly made pizza into the oven to bake, and taking out two other pizzas that Ashton took from him, cutting it into individual slices. On the wall above the gelato bar was a large board, magazine articles and Instagram pictures clipped to it, of reviews about *Fairly Odd Pizzas*, as well as a large black and white photograph of the family of four.

The moment she stepped in, she met Ashton's gaze when he glanced up, the warm breeze rushing inside with her entrance. He grinned at her, waving her over to the counter. Still smiling, Sabrina adjusted the bag on her shoulder and lifted hair up away from her neck, piling it up on top of her head into a messy bun. She'd taken off her white shirt and shoved it into her bag, along with the fleece she, along with every other member of staff (with the exception of the managers) had to wear. The inside of the shop wasn't roasting with heat, so it didn't make her feel like she was going to boil to death in it. The moment her shift ended, the fleece and the white shirt she wore beneath it went into her bag, letting the warm breeze cool her down. She was wearing a white tank top with a pair of high-waisted, slim fit trousers and brogues.

"Hey, you," she said, smiling at Ashton, when she came closer. She peered down at the steaming pizza slices, mouth watering at the eight meatball ones teasing her restraint on crinkly, crisp white paper. It was quickly greasing with a few oil stains and a bit of melted cheese clung to it from one of the slices. "How are you?"

"I'm good, I'm good," Ashton grinned. "Fucking hot, though."

"Mm, you look it."

His grin widened. "Are you saying that about my looks or—"

Sabrina laughed, cutting him off. "God, you're a terror."

Grayson's chuckle could be heard as the music quietened for a few, brief seconds. He met Sabrina's gaze, a huge smile on his face. "Yeah, he's a right dickhead."

"*Hey*," Ashton frowned, an offended tone in his voice. Grayson shrugged, smirking. Ashton rolled his eyes, turning his attention back to Sabrina. "Sabah's already here, by the way. With her boyfriend."

Feeling herself tense, Sabrina followed his gaze to where Sabah was sitting, at their usual spot, opposite Jake. The flat, black pan in the middle of the table had only two slices of pizza left on it. The hunger pangs in her stomach changed to queasiness as Sabrina looked at her ex best friend laughing at something. A few seconds passed as Speechless began playing overhead. Then, Sabah, feeling eyes on her, looked up, mid-laughter, meeting Sabrina's gaze. In that moment, Sabrina held her breath, waiting to see what she would do. It was as if this, whatever happened next, would shake everything, irrevocably setting it all in stone.

Sabah looked away.

She said something quietly to Jake. He looked over at Sabrina, scowling.

Sabrina looked away from him.

"Um," she said to Ashton. "Can I get a slice of the meatballs pizza, please? And uh, I'll get a bowl of strawberry gelato, too. But, maybe, um, later." She was stumbling over her words, feeling out of place. Lost. As if she was about to freefall into a hole that she didn't know how to dig herself out of.

"Sure," Ashton smiled. "I'll bring it over to you."

She nodded at him, swallowing, and then half-turned, eyes flicking over the restaurant. There were several other people sitting around tables, losing themselves in their own lives, immersed in the moment with their families, their friends, digging into the pizza and the garlic bread, jalapeño poppers and onion rings.

It felt like everyone was watching as she moved to sit at the table next to Kira, her hands clenched into fists to stop them from shaking. She needed the pizza to quell her craving and then she would be out of there like a shot. Taking in a deep breath, Sabrina's fingertips brushed against the edge of a chair, and just as she was about to pull it out, her name was called.

Startled, Sabrina jumped, whipping round to face Kira. The girl was biting her lip to keep from laughing, but it did nothing to stop the smile from stretching across her face.

"Oh my god," she grinned, pushing back her chair and standing up. She grasped Sabrina's wrist and tugged her over to the table. "Your reaction was fucking *hilarious*."

Looking at her warily, Sabrina sat down opposite the guy who'd winked at her the last time she was here with Sabah. "I, uh, didn't expect it. You scared the shit out of me."

"I know," Kira spluttered with laughter, eyes crinkling at the corners. She tucked strands of her coal black hair behind her ears, leaning forward, looking curious. "Why were you going to sit alone? You've always been with that girl every time I've seen you here."

"Except for the time you were here with that blonde chap," said the guy who'd winked at her. "I'm Wade, by the way. And that's Ezra," he added, pointing at the other dark haired guy. Ezra smiled at her, around a mouthful of mushroom and chicken pizza.

Sabrina smiled back a little, before swallowing. "Um, well," she said to Kira, meeting her dark brown eyes. "We're not really friends anymore. I don't think we have been for a while, even though it all kind of imploded a few weeks ago and she's moved out. So," she laughed. "Veda and I need another roommate because it's just way too fucking expensive for the both of us, you know? And I'm kind of just . . . spiralling. Everything's gone to shit. And I fucked it all up with Daniel, too. I don't know what the fuck I'm even fucking doing anymore." She stopped, her eyes going from Kira to her hands, folding them together, squeezing. "Sorry. I . . . that was so much, shit. Um, I'm sorry."

Just then, Ashton came over with her slice of steaming hot pizza and placed the plate down in front of her, smiling. She picked it up straight away, taking a large bite.

"No, god, don't be." Kira's voice was gentle as she put her hand over one of Sabrina's, smiling. Sabrina looked at her, as she swallowed the bite in her mouth. "Do you want to talk about what happened with your friend? Er, ex friend." Sabrina shook her head, not looking away. "Ok. You want to talk about Daniel?" She shook her head again. Kira smiled. "That's fine. We don't have to. So, you need a roommate?"

"Yep."

Wade took a swig of the tall, cold glass of Coke, his eyes carefully trained on Sabrina's face. Ezra was watching her too. The scent of all the food around them made her stomach rumble with hunger as she inhaled deeply and continued eating her slice, halfway through it.

"That's actually kind of perfect. God, you know I don't usually believe in fate or anything, but this is way too unreal to just be a coincidence. It's definitely fate that brought us together," Kira's eyes twinkled. Sabrina finished off her slice, washing it down with water, the ice clinking against her teeth. She was confused. And still hungry.

"Uh, at the risk of sounding incredibly rude, what the actual fuck are you talking about?" she asked Kira, before turning to look at the counter where Grayson had taken a few of the pepperoni and veggie slices to some of the customers that had just come in. Ashton was there, on the phone. He met Sabrina's gaze, lifting an eyebrow. She pointed at the counter, a pout on her lips, making him laugh. As he slid three more slices onto a bigger plate covered in red and white checked paper, Sabrina turned back to Kira, who had watched the exchange with an amused look on her face, waiting for the attention to be back on her.

"So, basically," Kira said, grabbing Ashton's hand and pulling him down onto the other chair after he'd put the mouth-wateringly delicious pizza slices in front of Sabrina. He rolled his eyes, but sat, leaning back in his chair as she continued talking. "My sister, Reina, just got back from travelling, like, a few weeks ago and she's looking for a place to rent. Even if it is a flat share. And so you said you need a roommate, right? Well, it all kinda works out, right?"

A small frown appeared on Sabrina's face as she processed the words. "I don't know," she said slowly. "I mean, I don't live anywhere near here. The house I rent is in East London, like in the really shitty, poor as fuck part of it and—"

"Doesn't matter," Kira interrupted. "Seriously, you don't think it's fate intervening right now, that brought you here to this very moment telling me that you need a roommate? And here I am, with a solution to that problem. It's *so* meant to be."

Ezra snorted. Ashton stifled a laugh. Wade guffawed. The three of them ignored the look Kira shot them. Sabrina slowly picked up her second slice and bit into it, chewing, thinking about it. "Look," she finally said. "Why don't we swap numbers and talk about this more? You can talk to your sister and I'll talk to Veda, and if Reina's interested, then we can arrange a meet up at the house and she can have a look at the two spare rooms. But," she added as an afterthought. "Neither rooms have beds or any kind of furniture. Sabah came back a few days after with some of her boyfriend's mates to take her bed, bedside table and dressing table."

"Bitch," Kira laughed. Sabrina smiled into the crust of her pizza slice. "What about the wardrobe?"

"It's a fitted wardrobe so she couldn't do shit about that."

"Alright, that's cool. No big deal. Here, give me your phone. I'll put my number in."

After handing Kira the phone, letting her save her details as a new contact, Sabrina gave her a missed call. As soon as Kira's ringtone blared out, she hung up.

"Fabulous," Kira beamed, tapping on her phone for a few seconds. Her smile was infectious and Sabrina found herself smiling back.

"So," Wade said. "Since things didn't work out with that guy you were seeing, I take it you're single?"

"*God*," Kira groaned, wrinkling her nose. "Could you *be* any more obvious?"

Sabrina smirked a little, tilting her head slightly as she started on her third slice. As she did so, Ashton stood up, heading over to the gelato bar. "I am single, yeah," she said to Wade.

"Cool," he smirked, eyeing her. "How old are you

again?"

"Twenty one, why? How old are you?"

"Also twenty one."

"Wonderful," Ezra said. "Now that we've established we're all twenty one here, can we talk about how the fuck I'm going to get out of going to the wedding?" To Sabrina, he said, "my father's wedding. The cuntfucking bastard cheated on my mum and has the audacity to invite me to his wedding."

"He's marrying the woman he cheated with?"

Ezra nodded.

"What a dick. No offence."

"Please," Ezra rolled his eyes. "No offence taken. He *is* a dick. I'm furious at him. He ruined our family."

"I'm still shocked," Wade said, sighing. "Never thought Ronan would do such a thing."

"How do you think my family feels?" Ezra asked drily, swallowing a mouthful of his iced coffee.

"Men ain't shit," Kira said. Ashton came back to the table, putting a bowl of strawberry gelato in front of Sabrina. She smiled at him gratefully.

"You can say that again," Sabrina said. "Although I'm one to talk. I'm not shit either."

"Don't talk about yourself like that," Ashton frowned. "You're my favourite customer."

"Excuse me?" Ezra gasped, mock hurt on his face. Ashton gave him the finger. "Rude. I'm telling Kathy."

"Suck my cock, Ezra."

"I bet you'll love that, wouldn't you?"

Wade burst out laughing, his shoulders shaking. "*I* know," he wheezed out between chuckles. "Someone who'd *love* to suck your dick, Ashton." He continued laughing and then winced, pain and amusement written across his face, shooting Kira a look.

"What? Who?" Ashton asked, bewildered. Wade sniggered.

"Can't say. That's classified information."

"Then why the fuck did you say it?"

"Because it's funny," he laughed again. "You're *so* blind," he whispered. Sabrina raised her eyebrows, curious to know who it was.

She glanced around at all of them, taking in Ezra's dark brown hair and hazel eyes, the dusting of freckles across his nose and cheeks, sun kissed complexion and stubble shadowing his jaw. He had the kind of look that was all boy-next-door and handsome, in a not-so-obvious way, as if he wasn't even aware of his good looks. Wade had closely cropped hair, a buzz cut, and dark brown eyes with thick, long lashes, blacker than fallen angel feathers and a strong, square jaw line covered with a five o'clock shadow. It was obvious he knew he was gorgeous and he prided himself on that, all heartbreaker eyes and a wickedly sinful mouth. Ashton was in between the two, jet black hair just about brushing his jaw, grey eyes and beautiful in a rugged sort of way, kind of like a rock star or a fallen angel, impossibly hard to look at without it hurting.

After a while, when they lapsed into silence, Sabrina broke it. "So what countries did Reina visit?"

"Oh, um, she went all over really," Kira said. "Literally. She was gone for two years and she went to practically every single country you can think of and more, including Antarctica. Lucky cow."

"That's amazing," Sabrina said. "Travelling is my biggest dream, honestly. I'm hitting up a few countries in Asia this summer, in August through to the first week of September, with my friend, and I'm super excited."

"If you say you're going to Japan," Ezra looked at her. "I will actually cry. I'm dying to go there."

She smiled demurely. "I've already been to Japan. My brother took me and our younger sister last summer."

"Fuck off," Ezra replied. "You for real?"

"Mhm," she said. "I have all the pictures on my Insta."

"Is that a hint for us to follow you?"

Sabrina let out a loud laugh, shaking her head. "It actually wasn't. But now that you mention it . . ." she trailed off, grinning.

"What's your Insta?" Wade asked, opening up the app and handing her his phone. "Shit, while you're at it, save your number into my phone, too."

"Subtle," Ashton breathed, laughing. Sabrina, smiling, saved her details into Wade's phone and gave it back.

"Subtlety won't get you anywhere," Wade replied breezily. "It'll just leave you silently suffering, wishing you had the balls to speak up about your feelings and then crying yourself to sleep when the person you want gets with someone else."

"Jheez," Ezra said. "Who the fuck broke *your* heart?"

Wade smirked. "Not talking about myself, young skywalker."

"You watch *Star Wars*?" Sabrina asked, eyes wide.

"I'm one with the Force. The Force is with me," he replied.

"He's chatting shit," Kira told her. "Like always."

"I find your lack of faith disturbing, Kira."

Sabrina laughed, holding a hand over her mouth as she swallowed the large bite of gelato, giving herself brain freeze in the process. She shuddered a little, shaking her head. "Leia is everything."

"Incestuous relationships are your thing?" Ezra raised an eyebrow. She pulled a face.

"Absolutely *disgusting* of you to assume such a thing, Ezra. Why, you stuck-up, half-witted, scruffy-looking *nerf herder*."

There was a beat of silence. And then simultaneously, they all burst into laughter.

Two hours later, after everyone else had left (see: Sabah), the four of them were still sitting around the table, lost in conversation as Ashton had gone out to deliver an order to a house ten minutes away. For the first time in days, Sabrina felt a little better; in company of people she didn't really know but had taken her in, almost instantly, no questions asked. It was like being transported into another world or another life, when the shit that happened, the mistakes she made, had all disappeared and she could just *be*, without fear of judgement or the burden of her past hanging over her head.

". . . Edinburgh? We could rent out a little cottage," Ezra was saying to his friends, after they'd decided to go away somewhere together for the week during his father's wedding.

"Ooh, yes, fuck yes, please, can we?" Kira asked,

looking excited. "Scotland is fucking gorgeous."

"Calm down there, love," Wade snorted. "You sound a bit too enthusiastic."

"Suck my dick."

"Go suck Ashton's." As soon as he said that, Kira punched him in the arm, making him yelp in pain. "Ow, what the fuck? That hurt."

"Shut up," she said.

"What? Ezra already knows you're in love with Ashton. Everyone knows you're in love with Ashton, *except* Ashton."

"I didn't know," Sabrina pointed out.

Wade rolled his eyes. "Well, duh. You've only just joined our group. You see, Sabrina, babe, Kira's been hopelessly in love with Ashton since year seven."

"Have not," she muttered, scrunching up a tissue in her hands.

"Yeah. You have," Ezra said.

"Why don't you say something?" Sabrina asked.

"No point—"

"You don't know that, though. If you love him, you shouldn't keep that to yourself in fear of it not working out, you know? What's the worst that could happen?" Sabrina's words were punctuated with silence as everyone contemplated over her words, then looked at Kira, who was frowning at the table. Sabrina understood the fear that came with loving someone, the inescapable what-ifs whirling around like a merry-go-round, constantly invading every thought, every breath, every heartbeat, every moment of every day.

"I lose my best friend?"

"That's not going to happen," Wade said. "Trust me."

Over the next few days, when Sabrina found herself back at *Fairly Odd Pizzas* each afternoon after work or lessons at Citizens Advice, she noticed why Wade said to trust him. It was clear that Ashton returned her feelings, to everyone except the two of them. This realisation came with a sense of duty to try to convince Kira to take the plunge, swoop over to Ashton and tell him how she felt. But no, Kira said again, she couldn't—she didn't want to lose her best friend over something as trivial as her feelings, it would tip the balance of their friendship and destroy everything. She couldn't risk that happening, no matter what anyone said.

"But it might not," Sabrina told her one day after she'd finished work at the school early and met up with Kira at *Mabel's Designs*. "When it comes to love, there's never one way of going about it. He's your best friend, yeah, and of course it's scary to tell him how you feel. It will be scary as shit to tell anyone. But sometimes, you just have to swallow your fear and take that leap of faith, because it's that faith that will carry you over to the other side, where they'll be waiting for you, to take your hand. And trust me, I'm pretty damn sure Ashton reciprocates your feelings. You don't see the way he looks at you, but I do. Wade does and Ezra does and Grayson does, too."

"It's just," Kira sighed. "Terrifying. I know you're right. I do. But we've known each other for such a long time. And say you're right and he does feel the same, and we get together. But what if we break up and it's so messy? What if—"

"You don't? What if it all works out and he's your soulmate and your happily ever after?"

"You believe in soulmates?"

Sabrina paused, then said, "yeah. I do."

The day after her graduation, Reina moved in with her and Veda, taking Sabah's old room with the gigantic fitted wardrobe taking up half of one wall. She'd bought a king size crushed velvet bed a few days before moving in, and signing the contract their landlady drafted up, from one of the local furniture stores, a few minutes' walk from Sabrina's parents house. At first, both she and Veda had been worried that it would be weird or awkward having someone who they didn't even really know live with them. But when Reina came round to check out the house and the two empty rooms upstairs, they found she was, well, to put it simply, *amazing*. Everything about her was a dream: black, glossy and waist-length hair fell straight down her back, dark brown eyes that Sabrina could only describe as bedroom eyes, cherry pink lips like she was some kind of faerie princess and a glowing face that rivalled the moon in its luminosity. She looked like Kira's twin, all elegant and gorgeous and alluring, with the kind of intelligence that made Sabrina feel like she needed to try harder, read more, be more. She was well versed in their culture, having stayed in Bangladesh for four months, in both Sylhet, which was where Sabrina and Veda were from, and Dhaka.

She could fluently speak both shuddho basha as well as the Sylheti dialect, picking up languages easily, impressing Sabrina's parents when she met them on the day of Sabrina's graduation.

"There was no point," she said, "going to a country

and staying there for a while without trying to learn their language and culture. It was ignorant, at best."

That Thursday night, the three girls were in the living room, watching *Pretty Little Liars*, eating the king prawn curry Sabrina's mum had made with rice and given to them earlier that day and drinking red wine. They would have invited Elle round too but she'd gone straight to Meadowbrook after Sabrina's graduation.

Somehow, it was almost as if they'd done this with Reina a thousand times before. There was no awkwardness. It was as if she belonged.

"They really should've ended it after we found out what a creepy stalker Ezra was," Reina said as Aria cried, scattering his manuscript pages.

"Mm," Veda hummed in agreement. "That's what we've been saying. It dragged on so much and the ending was a huge disappointment."

"Seven years of our lives," Sabrina added. "Wasted. Gone. On that *shit*."

"Ugh, and that disgusting British accent? It's beyond awful."

"Apparently we're all either cockney or speak like the Queen."

Veda laughed. "Cor blimey, mate."

"A cup of tea and crumpets would be absolutely delightful right about now," Sabrina said in a haughty voice. Reina spluttered with laughter, brown eyes dancing as she sipped her wine, looking for the entire world like a regal beauty.

"Would you care for some more wine, my dear?" Reina asked her in the same tone, making her grin and nod.

"Thank you, *dahhling*. An absolute angel, such a divine creature."

"Why, you flatter me."

"I speak the truth, and nothing but the truth."

"As you so swear on almighty god?" Veda smirked.

Laughter tumbled out of Sabrina's mouth as she leaned back on the sofa. Headlights from a car shone through the parting in their curtain, beaming in their dark room, a rectangle of light drawing a pattern on the ceiling and edging down to the opposite wall. It lit up the living room for a few, brief seconds as the girls sat, sipping on their wine and finishing off the spicy curry. Even when she felt like she was falling apart, there were moments, as fleeting as they were, when Sabrina felt like maybe, just maybe, it would be different this time and it would last.

This was one of those moments, with a girl she'd only met six days ago and a girl she'd known her entire life, when she chose to shake away the memories of the weeks and the months and the years before, to just live in the now. Everything that happened would always stay with her, that was a given. But it was how she would choose to deal with it that determined her future.

CHAPTER TWENTY

"ARE YOU SURE?"

Sabrina looked over at Sultana as they peeled an
entire bowl of garlic for their mum. It was exactly a month
since she'd screwed things up with Daniel and she missed
him in a way she couldn't explain. So maybe she *did* like
him. She knew there was a high chance he would never
want to speak to her again after what she did and said,
completely undermining their relationship because of her
fear of getting hurt again, but she had to at least try.
Messing things up and then leaving it without so much as
an apology was so much worse

"Yeah," she replied, using her nail to pick up the
white skin. Once the edge of it was slightly lifted, she
peeled it back. "I am. I need to talk to him."

"What are you even going to say?"

"I . . . I don't know, Tana. But I just know that I
can't leave things as they are. I need him to know I'm sorry

for hurting him. Because I am. And I miss him." There was a lump in her throat she tried to swallow away, an ache in her chest as she thought about the shadow of hurt in Daniel's eyes when he looked at her. "I've graduated now and I'm on my way to becoming everything I've wanted. I mean shit, for the first time in forever, mum and dad are proud of who I am. But I'm not."

Sabrina had ended up getting an eighty-nine percent in her final year, one of the top two students for her course and she wasn't second. Her parents' reactions brought tears to her eyes, their hugs making her feel warm and safe and alive after feeling like a disappointment in their eyes for so long. When she walked across that stage, hearing whooping and cheering from the crowd where her family and friends were sitting, Sabrina felt this aura of calm settling over her, a soft canopy of clouds beneath her feet, with the sun glowing down on her. She'd chosen not to wear a hijab that day, and though her parents were horrified with that choice, as well as the white maxi dress she wore (square neck, thick straps, figure hugging with a slit up one gloriously gleaming leg with sweet almond oil moisturised into the skin), they didn't say anything. Her makeup that day was a full face beat, heat-proof, with smoky liner flicked on her eyes, a pair of the Nebula lashes from *New Fashion Trend Shop* and a browny nude lip liner from Barry M colouring her lips. The sunrays made her highlight pop, her face glowing with a huge smile on her face as she shook hands with the presiding officer, laughing when he congratulated her and then continued walking across the stage to collect her certificate.

The celebratory dinner took place in a new

Lebanese restaurant that had just opened up in Forest Gate, a full three course meal where her parents gave her a gold ring decorated with an oval-cut pink sapphire, the date of her graduation inscribed in the band. She'd slipped it onto the middle finger of her right hand, tears glittering her eyes as she hugged them, breathing in their familiar, comforting smells, feeling grateful and for a moment, *happy.*

Her parents relationship was still the same though, it probably always would be. There were constant snipes at each other, the calm only lasting for a few hours before turning into arguments loud enough to be heard through the closed bedroom doors upstairs. Now though, both her mum and dad were out at a friend's house for a dinner invite while Sabrina and Sultana peeled garlic for the following day, when their cousin on their dad's side would be coming over with his wife and two kids. They were getting a head start on the peeling and chopping the ingredients, planning to make tandoori, pilau and a few other curries, giving their mum a break from the kitchen.

Sabrina was trying to be better for her mum, to mend the rift she'd caused between them with her decision to leave the house they'd move to when she was in her last year of secondary school. It was hard, especially when her mother still put the cultural values above everything, threw "what will people say" around way too often because it was the only way, for her, to get her daughters to think about their future, from the eyes of the older generation. Sometimes, most of the time, it made Sabrina want to scream. People would always, always talk. That would never stop. Her culture was vile and the way the entire reputation of the family resided on the girl was toxic and damaging and detrimental, letting their sons just dip their hands in blood and leave ruby red handprints on an all white wall, telling the world they could get away with murder and still nobody would care. That was how it worked, for centuries: daughters were born to live for their father, their brother, their husband, but never for themselves.

Trying to explain this to her mother was like walking across a thin blade, cutting the soles of her feet and blood dripping down, just to get to the other side where a better future was waiting. One that meant her mum would finally, after years, see her.

She didn't understand, but she was trying to. It was the first of many conversations that would follow, with both Sabrina and Sultana, and occasionally, Adam. It was a start of something new, a chapter turning, paving the way so she could be a little more herself around her family, without having to hide.

After her graduation dinner, Sabrina told her mum she wouldn't be wearing her hijab anymore. It wasn't her, and yes, she knew it was fardh, a compulsory thing for all women, but she just needed time and space to let herself breathe and learn more about it, without being forced and hating it, like she had for all these years. She'd received a lecture that lasted for an hour, but in the end, her mum had realised that no matter what she said, Sabrina had made her decision.

It was with begrudging acceptance her mother backed off, just a tiny bit. But not a whole lot.

After spending her afternoons at *Fairly Odd Pizzas* the last couple days, Sabrina often made an effort to come round to see her parents, at least four times a week. They were happier with this, talking to her about her trip around Asia with Elle, and the autumn, when she would begin the first of another three years of studying to be a doctor. Sultana would receive her A Level results in less than twenty-seven days, predicted all A*s, so she was taking the time before getting her results and her eighteenth birthday working full time and saving up some money.

She wanted to go to Switzerland and Belgium in the month long Christmas holiday; even though she obviously didn't have her timetables sorted out or know the dates. As soon as she found out, she planned on booking her flight with three of her friends. All four of them had applied to the same universities. Sultana and her friend, Estelle, both picked medicine, whilst the other two girls chose courses related to the field—Alessandra would be studying Biomedical Sciences and Bethany went for Biology. Sabrina was immensely proud of her baby sister, grateful that she was given more freedom than Sabrina had been at that age.

She was glad her parents were becoming more lenient, though that may have something to do with seeing how well each of their children were doing and how, on the surface, they all were. Because god knew Sabrina wasn't happy. The past few weeks, she'd been riddled with guilt and regret, trying to numb those feelings with alcohol.

For a while, it had worked but now, everything she'd been trying to run from was coming back full-force, hitting harder than ever as she finished peeling all the garlic cloves that had been in the bowl and Sultana moved on to grating the ginger. The chicken pieces, that they would need to marinade, were in the fridge. Sabrina pushed back the chair from the dining table, collecting all the garlic skin and cupping them in her hands, to throw it all in the bin. She carefully dropped everything in the new plastic bag Sultana had put in, sighing when a few floated to the floor. She picked up the stray pieces and threw them into the bin, before wiping the table clean.

In a silver bowl, after she washed her hands, Sabrina poured in two teaspoons of salt, cayenne, grounded coriander and extra hot mixed curry powder. Sultana had finished grating the ginger and she chucked it into the bowl, when Sabrina put in a teaspoon of turmeric, a sprinkling of fennel and two more teaspoons of cumin and paprika. After mixing it all together, she poured in a cup of yoghurt and three teaspoons of lemon juice to bring out more flavour, thickening it into a paste.

"When are you going?" Sultana asked, mixing the rice in with the onions, salt, a few green chillies, garlic, ginger, a bit of curry powder and turmeric in a big pan. Sabrina looked at her, putting the silver bowl with the tandoori paste into the fridge and sighed, shrugging. She closed the fridge door, the light disappearing as it shut.

"Um," she said, taking the spoon from her sister and stirring the rice and everything together. "I'm not entirely sure. Maybe around nine or something. I just . . . god, I don't even know what I'm supposed to say to him, you know?" Her voice cracked with emotion as she blinked back tears. "I just feel so awful and guilty for hurting him. I miss him."

Sultana's hand was soft on her arm, squeezing to show that she was there, like so many times before. "You can start with *I'm sorry.*"

The sky was a clear black mirror, not a single star visible as Sabrina walked out of the station. She felt sick, nerves and anger swirling inside of her, coiling tight around her throat. The warm breeze softly caressed her skin, blowing through her hair, as if to comfort her, give her the strength she needed to face Daniel after breaking his heart. Sabrina wanted to go back in time to stop herself from doing what she did, the feelings tumbling around inside her and tying itself in knots in the pit of her stomach. She hated herself for being so selfish, so immersed in her own story, her own tragedy, that she never bothered to see how her actions were hurting other people. Because it was and she hurt the one man who could've been the one to take her out of that dark place.

It wasn't just that he made her laugh when she felt like she was choking on her own sorrow, or the fact that when she was with him, she felt good. But she blew it all up in just a few, short minutes, because she'd wanted to tell herself she didn't need Daniel or that they weren't together, going through with it even when she knew it was wrong and the guilt was already smouldering through her like an inextinguishable flame.

The walk up to his house felt like it lasted forever and when she finally reached it. She stopped in front of the steps leading to the front door, swallowing. Nausea churned in her stomach, forcing her to take in a few deep breaths, tears pinpricking her eyes as she slowly, hesitantly, took those first few steps. Her hands were shaking as she went over her apology again, rehearsing it in her head. She swallowed again, hard. With one trembling finger, she pressed the doorbell, waiting, with a held breath, for the door to open.

Five seconds passed. Then another. Then another. She continued staring at the front door, waiting.

When it was clear it wouldn't open, that he wasn't home, Sabrina felt herself crumble a little, not knowing what to do. She ran a hand through her hair, the wind ruffling the sleeves of her flute-sleeved lilac top, frozen on the top of the steps in front of his door.

I'm sorry, she wanted to say. I'm sorry for everything, for hurting you and not trying hard enough to love you; I'm sorry for not allowing myself to open up to the possibility that you meant more to me than I wanted you to; I'm sorry for pushing you away when all you wanted was to be there for me; I'm sorry for messing with your head; I'm sorry for making you pay for the mistakes my ex made and still hurting you in the process; I'm sorry for still loving him even when I realised you were so much better, in so many ways; I'm sorry for fucking someone else knowing that it would hurt you; I'm sorry for ruining this; I'm sorry it took so long for me to realise how much I care about you; I'm sorry I didn't apologise before this; I'm sorry for not coming after you; I'm sorry.

But she couldn't say any of this because he wasn't there. He wasn't there and she didn't know what to do.

Tears slid down her cheeks as she took her phone out of her bag, dialling his number. It rang for a long time before going to voicemail. Sabrina closed her eyes, tears continuing to slip out, the breeze whipping them away. She was shrouded in darkness outside his house, wishing now, more than ever, that she could rewind time.

Without leaving a message, Sabrina hung up after his voice swept through to her, telling her he couldn't take the call right now, but to leave a message.

As she began to walk down the steps, her footsteps resonating with her cracked heart, headlights shone through as a car came into his driveway. The light almost blinded her as she squinted, staring at Daniel's sleek, black Porsche. He parked outside his garage as its door slid up.

The passenger door opened and a tall, curvy brunette stepped out, wearing jeans that made her legs look like they went on forever and a pair of Louboutin heels. Her hair was waist-length and shiny, falling around her like a curtain of chestnut silk, the porch light making her eyes look like a shade of amber. She looked at Sabrina as they stood a few feet apart.

The next few seconds passed slowly. Sabrina felt like she was dying inside, her heart pounding faster in her chest like a trapped bird in a cage, wanting to be set free. She hardly noticed as Daniel came out of the garage, the door now closed. Her eyes were focused on the gorgeous, dark haired woman as she turned to look at Daniel, who put something in her hand, murmuring something quickly and quietly. The woman met Sabrina's eyes, a small smile on her face before walking around her. Without a backward glance, she unlocked the front door and stepped into the house with the keys Daniel had just handed to her.

Light from the foyer lit up the driveway as Sabrina and Daniel stood there, opposite each other. Sabrina looked at him, gauging his reaction. His face was unreadable, arms crossed over his chest. She swallowed, lifting up a hand to brush away the tears from her cheeks.

"What do you want?"

His voice was flat, devoid of emotion.

"I . . ." Sabrina began, releasing a long, slow breath, not knowing what to say. Every word that had been running through her mind had disappeared, leaving her empty, grasping at air as she tried to form an apology, a coherent sentence. She wanted to tell herself that it was ok, she was ok, but it was pointless. Because she wasn't and nothing was. She fucked up and she was paying for it now. The way Daniel was looking at her made her want to cry, a sharp, painful ache rising from the middle of her chest, a bloody mess of a broken heart still thudding. She was all the bare bones of a clanging skeleton, hoping against hope that she could get back her second chance at love. "I'm sorry."

A beat.

Daniel continued looking at her, silently. Then he walked towards his house and paused, looking back at Sabrina. She looked at him pleadingly, taking a slow step in his direction. His name fell from her lips like a prayer, a plea, as he sighed and shook his head. The wind blew again, her hair flowing back as she looked at him, looking like some kind of broken, sad angel.

"Daniel," she said again. "I'm sorry. I am so sorry. I'm sorry for all of this." She swallowed, tears filling her eyes again. They ran down her cheeks, hot against her skin, salt on her tongue. "I know I hurt you and I'm sorry. I fucked up. I was scared and I know that's not an excuse—"

"It's not," Daniel said flatly.

She looked at him, taking another step. "I know. I know and I'm sorry. I am so sorry. I swear to god, I am. I hate that I hurt you, because you never deserved that. We just . . . we never talked about what we were, there were no labels, and I know I should've brought it up to you. I just . . . I'm sorry."

"That," he said. "Is the shittiest apology I have ever heard."

"I know," Sabrina whispered. "I don't know how to—I'm not good at, uh . . . I can't express myself with—with words or anything." She swallowed. "I'm sorry. I'm just really sorry. I need you to know that. You mean—"

Daniel laughed, cutting her off. He shook his head and walked up the steps to his house, swathed in light. Sabrina looked up at him, a silent plea on her face. She tried to push away the sadness lilting inside her.

"Sabrina, it's too late. I told you I don't forgive cheating."

"We weren't in a relationship," she said quietly. "If we were, if we had explicitly said that we were exclusive and together, then I never would have done what I did."

He narrowed his eyes at her. "Maybe so. But I just—"

"*Please*, Daniel. I don't want to lose you."

They were both quiet for a moment. Then, finally he said, "I need time."

"How . . . how much time?" she brushed away the tears falling down her face, hating herself. All the feelings were mounting up inside her and her lungs heaved, trying to get in air. She swallowed, taking in large gulps of air as he looked away from her, sighing.

"I don't know. I don't know, Sabrina. I just can't do this right now."

His voice was soft, his words hitting her like bullets. Without looking at her again, Daniel went into his house and shut the door behind him. Sabrina stood there, staring at the closed door, his words repeating in her mind. *I just can't do this right now. I just can't do this right now. I just can't do this right now.*

She knew what it meant: she'd lost him. He couldn't do this. Because she pushed him away. She messed up. She did this.

If you have been affected by any of the issues mentioned in The Art of Faking It, there are a number of organisations that offer advice and support:

☆ **ChildLine** is a free, 24-hour confidential helpline for children and young people who need to talk.
Phone: 0800 1111
childline.org.uk

☆ **The National Association for People Abused in Childhood** offers support, advice and guidance to adult survivors of any form of childhood abuse.
Phone: 0808 801 0331
napac.org.uk/

☆ **NSPCC** provides help, advice and support to adults worried about a child.
Phone: 0808 800 5000 (24/7)
nspcc.org.uk/

☆ **Karma Nirvana** supports victims and survivors of Forced Marriage and Honour Based Abuse.
Phone: 0800 5999 247
http://www.karmanirvana.org.uk/

☆ **Samaritans** is available for anyone struggling to cope and provide a safe place to talk 24 hours a day.
Phone: 116 123
Email: jo@samaritans.org
samaritans.org

ACKNOWLEDGMENTS

To Nahima and Shajeda Parvin, you two have kept me going even when I didn't think I could. You both have been my strength, my support, my day ones. I love and appreciate you, so much.

To Nila Mapplebeck, you have been the lifeboat that kept me afloat all throughout school. Your strength, your courage and your kindness are admirable and I can't thank you enough for being my best friend, even when we were in two different parts of the world. You're pretty freakin' cool, dude.

To Mr Hindes and Ms Dawson, you were the two teachers who made a difference to my life in school. Mr Hindes, you made me fall deeper in love with English, reading and writing, and Ms Dawson, you made the hardest moments a little easier to cope with. Thank you both,

To John Mcfadyen, you taught me how pure and beautiful love should really be. You helped me to believe again. You gave me the courage and the strength to put myself first, in the face of toxicity and every crappy thing. You're the best part of my life and proof that prayers get answered. You're my rock. Thank you for everything: your support, your patience, your understanding, your kindness. Thank you for your love, for being you, for being here. Thank you. I love you in ways I can never put into words.

<3

Sumaiya Ahmed is a freelance writer, aiming to break down the boundaries of cultural stigma and shame attached to mental health and sexuality within the South Asian culture and bring marginalised topics to light.

She specialises in sex and relationships, mental health, and PCOS, having previously written for Metro, The Sun, Lacuna Voices and Hello Giggles, and more. She has published two poetry collections, Lost and Found, and Reality. The Art of Faking It is her debut novel.

Sumaiya is a born and raised London gal, with a love of chocolate, Modern Family and romance novels.

You can find her on:
www.sumaiyaahmed.com
Twitter: @sumaiyawrites
Instagram: @maiyaahmedd
Email: sumaiyaahmedwrites@gmail.com

Printed in Great Britain
by Amazon